UNBREAKABLE

OHIO RUSTIES
BOOK 1

DANI GALLIARO

For those who tango with the darkness

And for the stay-at-home moms
Your work is real
Your work is hard
Your work is seen

AUTHOR'S NOTE

Dear Reader,

Thanks so much for taking a chance on me. If you're new here, I give a list of content warnings at the back of the book, but if I'm including something especially heavy, I put it up here too.

A number of my closest readers have asked for a story like this. So often, we see what happens when people first commit to each other, but we don't see the hard work that comes in the happily ever after: the day-in, day-out struggle to stay in love for the rest of your lives.

That's the real work.

And for many people who stay together for a long time, it's not necessarily one big thing, but a bunch of small things that add up over time and lead to hostility and ruptures. You can both love someone and love spending time with them, and also sometimes want to throttle them.

I hope you feel seen and heard through Jeannie and Dyl.

Their story felt like the right time to include pregnancy loss. It's a reality for many people and can have a huge bearing on a relationship. Though my husband and I went through pregnancy loss, this story is uniquely Dyl and J's.

Pregnancy loss and infertility can be incredibly triggering, so I want to fill you in on what to expect from this story, because that's the kind of thing I always want to know before I read.

It's alluded to in a few parts of the book in terms of "when we lost."

The miscarriage itself is told from Dylan's perspective, without any gore or graphic details. I wanted to capture how a partner feels when there's loss, and distance the pain a little for the reader. There's obvious grief in the loss, but I wanted to explore the impact on a relationship.

I did my best to treat it sensitively, but I also know there was a point in my own grieving process where I couldn't have fathomed reading a story like this without it ruining my week.

Jeanine, or Jeannie, also struggles with depression at various stages of their marriage. Even though Dylan and their friends provide valuable support when she needs it, those relationships alone do not cure her. Having a great support system is a part of managing depressive episodes, but I want to make clear that Jeanine also sees doctors and therapists.

In the United States, you can call or text the Suicide and Crisis Lifeline at 988, or call SAMHSA's national helpline, 1-800-662-HELP for free, confidential referral to treatment and care.

Please take care of yourself. You are so loved and I'm so glad you're here.

A full list of content warnings is at the back of the book.

All the best always,

Dani

THE OHIO RUSTIES

AN INCOMPLETE ROSTER

The Ohio Rusties logo represents the hardworking people of the Rust Belt. The hockey stick and nail are framed by Ohio's state flower, the carnation.

- Dylan Sorrento - forward, right wing #9
- Jacques "Jack" Leroy - forward, center #29
- Gavin Korowski - forward, left wing #41
- Yevgeny Dotsenko - forward, left wing #11
- Colton Jones - defenseman, captain #8
- Austin Garner - defenseman #81
- Sebastian Lindberg - defenseman #20
- Harlan Royce - goalie #30

PLAYLIST

You can find the playlist on Spotify under my name, Dani Galliaro and Unbreakable.

- Little Jeannie - Elton John
- Closer - Nine Inch Nails
- (I've Had) The Time of My Life - Bill Medley, Jennifer Warnes
- Bleeding Love - Leona Lewis
- It's All Coming Back To Me Now - Celine Dion
- Chasing Cars - Snow Patrol
- There Are Worse Things I Could Do - Stockard Channing
- The Space Between - Dave Matthews Band
- Don't Dream It's Over - Crowded House
- These Days - Foo Fighters
- Stick Season - Noah Kahan
- Jealous - Nick Jonas
- All the Things You Are - Ella Fitzgerald
- Still Into You - Paramore

- Curls - Bibio
- Snow - Bing Crosby, Danny Kaye, Peggy Lee, Trudy Stevens
- Suspicious Minds - Elvis Presley
- Strong Enough - Sheryl Crow
- I Belong To You - Lenny Kravitz
- You're Still The One - Shania Twain
- Anna Sun - WALK THE MOON
- Thank U - Alanis Morissette
- Once in a Lifetime - Talking Heads

PROLOGUE
DYLAN

"CAP, MY OFFICE, PLEASE."

It was media day, when we cleaned out all our personal stuff from our lockers after losing in the playoffs. It's a bittersweet day: another year with a playoff run, another year we didn't make it to the end. There were whispers on the internet about me being on the chopping block for a trade, but my contract had a no-move clause. I often joked that they'd have to haul me out of the locker room in a body bag.

A cold sweat broke out over my body when I rounded the corner to Coach's office and saw our general manager seated inside.

"Hey, Lou," I said, forcing a smile. He nodded and gestured to the chair next to him.

Sitting across from Coach, a red light glowed from his desk phone, indicating a caller on the other end. "Dev, he's in here now."

"Hey, Dylan," my agent chirped through a muffled speakerphone.

My mouth hung open. This didn't bode well. "Hey, Dev. What's the occasion?"

Coach looked like he was about to tell me my dog died. "Dylan, what do you have in mind for your future?"

He called me Dylan. My government name. Not Dyl Pickles or Dylly or Pickles or Picksy or Sorrento or any hockey permutation he typically employed.

I found my breath, blasting it out in a little puff. "I'm only sort of kidding when I say you'll have to get me out in a body bag."

"This is our fourth playoff run where you've been captain and we haven't made it past round two."

"I mean, the coaching staff turned over twice too," I said. Why the hell was I starting to fight for my life?

"We're afraid you've run your course with our organization, and someone else wants you," Coach said, looking miserable himself.

"What? Who? I can't leave L.A. My whole life is here. It's been here since I was twenty-two!"

"Dyl, you might like it," Dev tried on the other end of the phone. "It's Ohio."

My eyes grew wide and my stomach churned. "No. No way. I have a no-move clause!"

"Sorrento, you're getting up there in age—" Coach started.

"I'm thirty-three!" I croaked.

Coach cocked his head to silence me. He and I both knew I was past the average retirement age by five years. "Leroy was way older before you let him go!" I added.

"Leroy's not the captain," Coach said, licking his lips. "I don't like this either. You're the heart of this place and a forty-goal scorer. But Ohio needs some of that too."

"They're the worst in the league!" I hissed. "It's an embarrassment!"

"They need your kick in the ass," Dev chimed in, doing his best to put lipstick on this pig. "You could be the reason they turn around! You have until June 30 to think about it. Talk it over with Jeanine."

"She's going to hate this! Did everyone just forget? I have a no-move clause!"

"Which we could waive," Dev reminded me. "Aren't you from around there anyway?"

"Pennsylvania," I grumbled, shaking my head. "What happens if I don't accept?"

Coach gave me a sympathetic look that told me what I already knew: I'd be on the open market, begging for a contract that wouldn't likely last for more than a year. I'd have to start the negotiation cycle over again the following summer. "Cap, why don't you go home and think it through?"

"It's better traffic," Dev enticed me. "Cheaper. More private."

"We're in L.A. We're the very least important people here!" I nearly shouted. "No one gives a fuck about hockey players here!"

"Okay, okay," Coach put his hands out. "Just, please, take some time. Call me anytime to talk about it. And hey, I hear Leroy's been happy out there. Maybe call him."

"What is there to talk about? It sounds like I don't have a choice!"

"It's good money, Dylan," Dev said. "A chance to turn a new leaf in your career."

I stood and jostled my chair on the way out, half tempted to slam it into pieces.

Jeanine was going to hate this.

I WAS on my third stop after getting the news. First, I visited a liquor store, then a weed dispensary. Now I found myself in a grocery store parking lot, staring at the bottle and my dispensary purchases in the passenger seat.

If I drank, Jeannie would smell it on my breath.

If I was high, she'd be able to tell.

There was nothing to numb this pain or change the facts. I stared at my upturned palms in my lap, frantic breaths pressing against what felt like the narrowing walls of my lungs.

There was no easy way out of this. Everything had to change, no matter which option I took.

I started my NHL career here. Met Jeanine here. Fell in love with her here. Got married here. Had our kids here. Built a friend family. Went through dark, dark times and the sweetest of times. We were close to Jeannie's family, and the kids reveled in their grandparents' affection.

And the only way we could stay was if I retired from hockey. Financially, I probably could, though I'd have to pick up some kind of retirement gig.

But the problem was, I wasn't ready to be done. And being kicked out of the happiest stage of my life was terrifying.

How could I talk Jeanine into this? She'd have known I was lying if I said it was my idea. I knew she'd read the trade rumors. She wasn't oblivious. But I told her no one in management had said anything, and Dev said he hadn't heard anything. I thought I was in the clear.

I was crushed.

But if I let Jeanine know I didn't want to go, she'd campaign for us to stay. After all, she'd given up her passion so I could have my career and build a family with her. She'd conceded for my happiness. Was it time for me to concede for her?

And what about the kids? They'd probably be okay, but

they'd be looking to us for their cues. I had to hold it together and convince Jeanine to do the same.

Because if we didn't hold it together, it would all come undone.

ONE

JEANINE

NOW | OCTOBER

"SAY HALLOWEEN!"

Our kids were lined up in the wagon. Greyson, seven, was Spiderman, Alice, five, was Alice in Wonderland for the second year in a row, and our little ladybug Bella, three, was, who could guess it, a ladybug. I had on my usual cat costume: an all-black outfit with ears, a tail, and whiskers drawn on my face in eyeliner. Dylan wore a tight black long-sleeve that showed off his ridiculous physique, black pants, and a Scream mask that he kept tipped up most of the time because it terrified the kids.

It was our first Halloween in our new city.

Our kids blended into the neighborhood seamlessly, and overall, the parents were great too. We were fortunate to be in a community of houses where kids actually played outside and romped together.

But it wasn't L.A.

Was the traffic better? Yes. Was it quieter? Yes. But we were gearing up for a real winter, having to bundle the kids up in layers to go trick or treating.

Dylan and I had spent eight years together in Los Angeles,

where I pursued my acting career for three years prior. A decade in the city had made me accustomed to the year-round seventy-two-degree weather, the authentic Mexican food, and having the beach just a stone's throw away.

The most we had now was the banks of the Olentangy River. Columbus, Ohio bears very little resemblance to Los Angeles, California.

I'd grown up in the California mountains too. My parents ran a vineyard in Temecula, Mom running the tasting room and Dad running production. In L.A., I could drive to see my mom. My brother and sister had since scattered, with my brother in Oregon and my sister in Australia.

I missed pretty much everything about it. But most of all, I missed my friends. The group of WAGs was in its best position yet. Rachel Beatty was like a sister to me, and though we still texted about everything under the sun, it wasn't the same as being together. Plus, I had the Hollywood trio: Kitty Gatto, an actor and TV writer, Jessie Miknevicius, a costume designer and suit maker, and Annie Markham, who was technically a sports agent and not in Hollywood but she was Kitty's best friend from growing up so she counted. I loved them.

Our kids were headed out to trick or treat with one of Dylan's teammates' families. They'd introduced us to this neighborhood for being private while still having a strong community.

"Why don't you get in the picture, Mommy?" Dyl's hand slipped into the curve of my waist, the place where he'd always held me, his way of literally touching base with me.

But the thing is, he used to kiss my temple whenever he slid in like that. Now we were down to just the waist-holding. Affection had been chipping away slowly since we moved to Ohio in August. What used to be a waist hold and a temple kiss was now a waist hold. What used to be his arms around me at the stove, his nose buried in my neck, and a butt pat to finish it off was now him sitting at the kitchen island scrolling his phone. When we'd gone through stressful seasons before, casual touches were non-negotiable. Now they weren't even part of the table stakes, a distant memory.

"A selfie with all of us," I suggested, turning us and crouching so we could be on the same level as the kids.

"Say cheese!" I said.

"No, you have to say Halloween," Alice argued, scowling in the first shots.

"You're right, Al. Halloweeeeeen!"

"Let me take it!" came a friendly voice from the side. Dyl's teammate Seb Lindberg approached with his wife Christine and their son Clark in a wagon.

"Oh, great. Thanks!" I handed my phone to Christine and rushed back to get in the picture before the kids squirmed away. "Halloween!"

As we stood after and I got my phone back, I peeked down into our wagon. "Oh, shoot. Daddy, I forgot the water bottles."

Dylan, who I called Daddy in front of the kids to keep it easy, was distracted, lifting Bella to sniff her diaper. "Looks like we've got a diaper too." He held Bella out for me to take.

I hesitated. I would not make a stink in front of Dylan's new teammate, but I was pissed. Then again, I signed up for this life by marrying Dyl. I knew he'd be busy with hockey while our kids were at their smallest. My responsibility was to keep them, and our house, going.

Yes, I know I had little room to complain. We had plenty of money, though we did have to stretch it wisely. Dylan's career could end at any moment due to a serious injury, and I hoped it wouldn't be one that changed his personality. Multimillion-dollar contracts were only good for as long as he was hitting the ice. He'd made it past the average age of retirement, now well over thirty.

I loved my kids. I loved Dylan. But since we moved to Ohio, I kept catching myself fantasizing about a different life. Dylan and I had a major fork in the road early on. What if I'd chosen the other side? The fantasy was enough to make anyone depressed. I was no stranger to the darkness, and I feared another tango with it was right around the corner.

Pull it together, Jeanine.

I gave Bella a bright smile and shifted her to my hip. "Next time, just ask to go to the potty, Bells. Even if you're in your Halloween costume, we'll get you there."

Dylan and Seb's chatter rang out behind me as I clomped up the driveway, my mention of the water bottles already forgotten. Dylan probably couldn't wrap his brain around the fact that I got to do less socializing than he did, and maybe I really needed the adult conversation he was getting.

But he didn't pick up on that, staying immersed in talking to his teammate while I headed back into our house to change Bella's diaper. And get the kids' water bottles.

Then I thought better of it. "Dyl?"

He turned around with a grin. "J?"

"Can you come get the water bottles? I can't carry it all."

"Oh, yeah." He slapped his forehead to Christine and Seb's laughter. "Guess I could help out, huh? Can you guys watch the kids for a minute?"

THE CANDY WAS DUMPED on the floor and sorted into piles, pulling out anything with peanuts because of Alice's allergy. Then we sorted it again by who likes what. The kids were all strung out on sugar and irrational tears spilled from every direction.

But when we got them to make very calm trades of the things they liked, Dyl caught my eye. He made his hands into a heart shape, sticking out his bottom lip, something he did to capture those moments of parenting we wanted to remember forever. I held up one a hand heart to agree with him. We were crazy about our kids, and Dylan was a great dad.

I just wished I didn't have to be supermom all the time, all to no praise or thanks. My mom used to moan about the unseen labor when we were growing up, but I didn't get it until it was my turn. Do what you're supposed to do, your toddler kicks you in the face. Give in to their whims and you pay the consequences later.

But we're not supposed to have feelings. We're supposed to just weather it, suck it up and go. In that way, Dylan and I had a lot in common. He had to suck it up and go with hockey. We were comrades in the trenches, but I had less room to complain. And when I did, he was quick to write it off with, "Aw, sorry, babe," or "You'll figure it out."

Dylan leaned behind Alice's back, grinning to beg for a kiss. I met him there. "You look hot, Mommy Cat," he cooed, just so I could hear.

"You too, Ghost Daddy," I said, giving him another peck.

"After bedtime?" he asked, wiggling his eyebrows.

I smirked. "If you bring the mask."

He nodded. "Want me to be mean?"

My stomach swooped. "Please."

"Anything for you, J," he said with a wink. "Okay, kiddos, let's clean up our wrappers and go get on the bedtime train."

"Choo choo," I added as the kids protested, not wanting to go to bed.

TWO

DYLAN

NOW | OCTOBER

JEANNIE CLOSED Bella's bedroom door and tiptoed away. I was hiding as best I could in the shadows, then pulled my mask down and crept up behind her. I snaked my arms around Jeanine from behind, tugging her into my body. I swept her hair over one shoulder and put my face, or rather my mask, at her neck. My voice was muffled by the mask.

"The black bra and thong with the cat ears. You pick the heels, because you're going to be running. You have three minutes."

Jeannie gasped and melted into me, her eyes rolling back. "Dyl," she moaned, pressing her ass into my front.

"I'm not Dyl tonight, baby. I'm your worst nightmare."

"We haven't done this in a long time," she said, and a pang shot through me. We'd been pretty routine for a while. We had sex often, but it was standard issue. Good sex. Fine. Inoffensive. We got off and cleaned up. If it was before my pre-game nap and she could, she'd snuggle with me until I fell asleep. Same if it was bedtime.

Rinse and repeat, twice a week, or whenever it worked with my hockey schedule.

I loved Jeanine so fucking much. I was lucky we were still into each other after the beginning of our relationship was so rocky. Many couples don't get that privilege. And we're both physical people, getting our validation from checking in with sex. When you're parents of small kids and a hockey family, it adds up to not a lot of time for each other. We took what we could get.

But I knew Jeanine wanted more. She got hot when we played little games like this. "I'm starting my count now. You won't want to waste any time."

I let her go, folding my hands in front of me. She glanced over her shoulder as she entered our bedroom, biting her lip with a smile.

I needed to try more like this for her. She loved it. She deserved to feel cared for. I own that I wasn't very good at showing it.

We were deep in the worn-down stage of parenthood, and the move to Ohio hadn't done the romance any favors. It was harder on her than on me, but I was determined to convince her to love our new life. If that took me chasing her through our house in a mask, I'd do it.

And not like I wasn't going to enjoy it. I was getting hard already thinking of her running from me, our modified version of primal play that we pulled off every now and then. And since it was Halloween, why not add in a mask? I stripped off my shirt, put on a pair of black leather gloves, and slid my mask back on.

She appeared in our doorway, leaning against the frame with one arm up.

"Did I do it right, sir?"

Jeanine could wear a cardboard box and I'd think she was hot. Her body was different than before we had kids, but the changes made her more beautiful. She was a woman, proper. She had a dancer's body before, and while that's hot, I loved this Jeanine. This Jeanine was mine. Her hips got fleshier and her tits got even bigger, three rounds of breastfeeding doing its work on her. I know it's caveman and well, primal, but something about her body changing because she carried our babies did something so basic to me.

Slowly, I strode toward her, flexing my hands against my sides to make the leather squeak. I stopped in front of her, making a show of looking her over. I slid my hands into the notches of her waist, a part of her that had always seemed made just for me. My hands were a magnet to that spot, always.

"You did good, little kitty," I said, skating the chin of the mask along her jaw to her sigh. "You know what happens now."

Jeanine's shallow breaths hissed against my neck as I surveyed her. "I don't remember," she said, her voice trembling slightly and her chest heaving.

"Don't let me catch you," I warned. "You get ten seconds' head start."

My gloved hands followed the curve between her waist and her hips.

"A head start for what?" she tried.

"Stop playing games." I bent into her ear, coiling myself around her body. "Run."

Jeanine broke from my grasp, dashed past me, and flew down the stairs.

"One, two . . ."

The basement door creaked open, the path to our bigger

family room. Her feet pattered on the stairs in her ever-graceful way. Once a dancer, always a dancer. She could sneak up on me like no one I knew.

I started after her, knowing exactly where she was but wanting to build the suspense. With careful, even steps, I went down to the first floor, letting my footfalls be loud and slow. I walked through each room, fully knowing she wasn't there.

Opening the door to the basement, I said, "Here, kitty kitty."

I descended the stairs. She'd done good—I couldn't see her anywhere, even coming down the stairs where I had a higher vantage point.

"When I find you, little one, it's gonna be over for you."

As I looked behind curtains and furniture, my ears picked up heavy breathing.

"Oh, little one. It's almost like you want to get found. Like you want to find out what I'll do to you."

And there she was, crouching behind a chair. She gave out a tiny shriek, then sprinted out the side opposite me. I tore after her, catching her by the waist and lifting her off the ground. "Gotcha."

She put up a fight until I put my gloved hand over her mouth, her cat ears knocking askew. "Quiet now," I cooed. "Wouldn't want to wake the children."

I tossed her face down on the couch, then flipped her to her side so she could watch me. I stood over her, unbuckling my belt. Jeannie's eyes went big. I'd never spanked her with my belt before, though I'd threatened it.

In a fun way, of course. We knew each other's limits after so many years together, and she always spoke up if anything changed.

"What to do with you first?" I slid my belt out of my belt loops. "My belt or my hands?"

"Hands," she pleaded.

I pinned her hands together over her head, looping the belt around her wrists once, twice, until I could buckle her hands together. "Keep them up here for me."

"Are you going to be nice to me?" she asked, her voice all high and innocent.

"Pretty girl, I'm going to use your holes any way I want to." She whimpered as I ran my gloved thumb below her lips. "Starting with this one. But first, I need to spank your ass raw for running away from me."

I turned her to her stomach, her arms still bound overhead. My Jeannie, all stretched out for me. I smoothed my hands over her ass cheeks, giving them a playful squeeze. "What will you do if you've had enough?"

"Say 'banana.'"

"Or?"

"Or kick my leg."

I nodded. "Good girl."

Then I lifted my hand to give her the punishment we both knew was coming, something we've always loved together. I love dishing it out and she loves taking it.

I wound up and gave her a good spank, her ass bouncing from the impact. Again, and again, her head cocking back as she took it like a pro. Her ass was nice and red, my leather gloves adding to the experience.

"That feel better, baby?"

"Yes," she moaned.

I laughed, low and dark. "Too bad I'm not done with you yet."

Flipping her to her back, I gripped Jeannie's ankles, draping them over the back of the couch. She scooted so her upper body was on the seat, her head hanging upside down and her mouth open, tongue out.

"Look at this beautiful little slut, begging for my cock with her pretty mouth." I unzipped my pants where my aching hard-on throbbed, leaning over to position it in front of her lips. "You want me to use you like the little hole you are?"

"Yes, please."

"You want Ghost Daddy's cock all the way in the back of your throat?"

"Please," she moaned.

I traced her lips with my dick tip, wetting them with my precum. "Lick your lips, slut."

Looking up at me with those sparkling blue eyes, Jeanine ran her tongue around her lips and hummed. I used my hand to guide myself into her mouth, listening to her gag around my cock. "Taking it so fucking well, J. Now let me fuck this face."

She opened wider, her eyes watering as I thrust into her mouth. With her essentially upside down to me, I moved her panties to the side and lifted my mask to spit on her pussy. Her legs spread wider. "Such a fucking slut, spreading your legs like that for me. Did you want to come?"

Jeannie kicked her leg and I pulled out of her mouth. I lifted my mask and knelt by her face, cradling her head. "You okay, baby?"

She panted and stretched her jaw. "Yeah, I just needed a break." I kissed her forehead, a Spiderman kiss of sorts since we were upside down to each other.

"We can have a break." She sucked a deep breath through her nose, and I noticed the tears that had welled from me fucking her face weren't fading. "You sure you're okay?"

She sniffed and straightened her face. "Yeah. Yeah, I'm good."

"Do you want to stop?"

Her lips curved into a smirk. "Put your mask back on, Ghost Daddy."

"You mean you don't want me to eat this pussy?"

"You're in charge," she said.

"Damn right I am," I said, gathering her ankles and yanking her to the edge of the couch. "And it's time for me to use you some more."

I draped her face down and bent her over the arm of the couch so her ass was up and on display. I knelt, slipped between her open legs, and shimmied her thong off at her feet. Then I tugged her hips out so I could access her pussy. At first lick, she was dripping, her taste intoxicating. Spit aside, Jeannie got soaking wet from me fucking her face. When we first started playing around with rougher stuff, I was always afraid to hurt her. Then she told me how much she liked it, so when we got the chance, I gave her the full treatment.

Though it had been a while since the last time.

So I indulged in her taste, enjoying her squirms and moans. I ripped off my gloves and jammed my fingers in her pussy to go with my tongue's work.

"Fuck, Dylan," she moaned. "I might—"

I moved my face back as she squirted genuinely all over me, down my bare chest and onto my cock where it protruded from my pants. "That's my fuckin' girl," I growled.

I put my mask back on and stood, pulling her up by her hair to look. "See this fucking mess you made?"

Her satisfied smile told me everything I needed to know. "You look good like that," she hummed.

"Dirty girl," I said, shaking my head. I repositioned her hips over the arm of the couch and teased her entrance with the crown of my cock. "Is this what the dirty girl wants?"

"My hands, Dyl," she said. "Kinda hurts." I still had them locked together with my belt and over her head.

"Oh, shit, sorry, baby. I got you." I unbuckled the belt and lifted the mask to check her wrists for damage, pressing kisses on the red marks. "Are you alright?"

She didn't answer the question directly, but what she said worked just as well. "Mask down. Fuck me."

The edges of my lips curled up. Jeanine was insatiable sometimes, and a little bossy too. Truly my perfect partner. I moved back behind her where she was still splayed over the arm of the couch. I rammed into her, and she let out the sweetest scream, her cat ears giving up their fight and falling off her head.

"That's it, slut. Nobody's gonna hear you scream. This pussy is mine."

She peered at me over her shoulder, seeming overwhelmed. She wasn't even using words, just screaming and moaning so goddamn loud. Her pussy was so intensely wet, and I was all covered in her. We hadn't had it this hot in years maybe.

She reached back and laced her fingers with my gloved hands on her hips, and the sight brought on a sense of euphoria: her gorgeous skin and delicate hands with indentations from my belt, mingled with the harsh leather of my gloves. The mask was temperature hot, and my panting breaths made condensation against my face.

She was loud, and that was cranking me up, but I really didn't want to wake the kids. I reached forward and pinned her torso to my chest, putting a hand over her mouth as I pounded into her. She shivered and screamed against my hand, going limp against my chest and shoulder.

"That's fuckin' right," I hissed. Feeling her pulse around my cock almost had me there. "This hot, tight cunt is mine. You come for *me* and you're not done coming until I fucking say so."

She let out a wheezy gasp as I took my gloved hand off her mouth and slipped it through her wetness, splitting around my cock inside her. I kept it there, palming her with the heel of my hand.

"Shit, Dylan," she cried.

"Give it to me," I demanded.

Her abs pulled back from my forearm across her stomach, squeezing me tighter from the inside. She bucked against me as much as she could in my grip, keening and trembling.

"Come again, slut," I commanded.

With a piercing cry, she was pulsing around me again, and this time, I joined her.

She was so loose in my arms that I was afraid to let her go. "Push my mask up, baby."

She reached over her shoulder and tipped the chin of the mask to push it all the way off my head, falling to the floor behind me. Sweat dripped from my hair and down my neck, but I leaned to her shoulder, kissing her there.

"That was insane," she sighed.

"In the best way," I laughed, disbelieving. "Holy hell, Jeannie. We don't . . . we haven't ever like that, maybe?"

She leaned back against me more fully. "I loved it."

I'd lost my rude boy tone and was back to being the sweet husband I tried to be for her. "Let's see how much of a mess we made."

I slipped out of her, and handed her a glove to contain the mess. I dipped into the bathroom to grab a hand towel and sat next to her on the couch, helping her clean up. She wiped my face off. "Mask sweaty?" she asked.

I raised my brows and nodded. "Definitely. But it was worth it."

We made out as we came down until she sucked in a breath in a way that startled me.

I held her face in my hands, searching her rapidly welling eyes. "Jeannie, what's wrong?"

"That's the first time you've seen me, Dyl. In months. Maybe years."

My stomach sank, eyes widened. What did she mean? We were interrupted by a different tearful voice.

"Mommy?"

Alice.

"Just a minute, sweetie!" Jeanine called.

We scrambled to get some clothes on, gesturing to each other and trying to figure out who was more suitable to deal with Alice. Since J just had her underwear, I shoved my cock back in my pants and zipped them as carefully as I could, jogging to the staircase.

Alice frowned upon seeing me. "I want Mommy. You're all sweaty."

"Sorry, kiddo. You got me. What's up?"

"Is Mommy okay? She was screaming."

Jeanine stifled a snicker in the basement, covering her face with her hands. This was why we usually had quiet sex in our room, no screaming allowed.

"Yeah, honey. We were just dancing and Mommy was having fun. We'll try to be quieter."

"I like to dance," Alice said, getting upset again. "Why wasn't I invited?"

I rubbed my forehead. "Sometimes Mommy and Daddy like to dance alone. Sweetie, it's time for you to be in bed. You want me to take you back up there?"

"I want Mommy," she insisted, starting to fall apart.

Jeannie made a slicing motion across her throat, shaking her head as she was trying to clean our sweat off the leather couch. I had to stop myself from laughing, because Alice would not find that funny. I climbed the stairs and scooped Alice up.

"Mommy'll come give you a goodnight kiss when she's done exercising."

"I thought you were dancing," Alice protested.

"You're right. Dancing is a type of exercise. Let's go get you tucked in."

After I tucked Alice in and Jeannie gave the promised goodnight kiss—fully clothed, mind you—we had a good laugh about the almost-intrusion. The mood had shifted from where Jeanine was getting upset, so I didn't want to ruin it by asking what she meant about me seeing her.

I lay awake for a while, her head on my chest and my fingers in her hair. I mentally replayed our days together. The only time we got with just the two of us was in bed or when she dropped off the kids and came home for breakfast. It was usually something she'd meal prepped over the weekend if it was a weekday. In L.A., we'd gone out for breakfast when we could, taking Bella with us before she was in preschool. Bella had just started in the fall, and J and I hadn't picked up that brunch time for just the two of us since.

I thought I was attentive. I paid attention to her when I could.

Admittedly, I was just under a lot of stress too. Moving to Ohio and becoming a Rustie was not a smooth transition, but I tried to put a brave face on it. In one way, I wished Jeanine would see that in me. In another, I never wanted her to know. This was my choice, after all. My fault.

And I needed time to fix it before I got caught up in my own web of lies.

I needed my family to love this new life and if it took me faking it till we made it, I'd do it.

THREE
DYLAN
NOW | NOVEMBER

ANOTHER SHITTY GAME.

Another embarrassment.

Another day when I questioned the decision to haul my family out of our harmony and into this new hell.

The locker room had the air of a funeral parlor, except there were no sympathy simpers to convey that we all felt sorry for each other. There was just snorting, and spitting, and quiet grumbles as we all dissected the game with our respective allies.

That was the culture of the Ohio Rusties: blaming, bitching, and griping. My only ally was Jack Leroy, my veteran teammate from L.A. who'd gotten traded a few months ahead of me. Even though we weren't best friends out there, we had good chemistry on the ice, and I think we were a cheap enough package deal for Ohio to try to bring that chemistry here.

Let's be real, Jack's kind of a dick. A standup guy, and he'll fight tooth and nail for what and who he believes in, but a dick nonetheless.

"This place is fucked," I said to Jack under my breath.

He shrugged. "It's another day in the show. Couple of old shits like us gotta count our days."

"No, it's like every line is a different team. It's every man for himself."

"It'll be alright, guys. Florida's a tough team," Colton said, and the room quieted to give the captain room to talk.

I firmly disagreed with that sentiment. Having had three seasons of captaincy under my belt, it was hard for me not to pipe in. But Leroy made his distaste known with a scoff.

"We'll have to push harder next time, get on the forecheck," Colt went on.

I snapped. "That's not it. Every one of you is holding the puck too long."

"Oh, it's the expert again," Garner chimed in with a teasing tone.

"Yeah, Pickles. How'd they do it on your last team?" Yevgeny Dotsenko, or Dottie, made no secret of the fact that he wasn't fond of me. Here he propped his chin in his hand and his elbow on his knee like he was really listening to me. In other words, he was being a complete shithead. Fortunately, we weren't on the same line, but he took any opportunity to put me in my place.

But me staying in my place wasn't making the team win any games.

"No, let him finish," Colton said, waving Dottie off. "Go ahead, Picksy."

"If you're not moving it on to someone else in three

seconds, it's already dead. You're holding out for the perfect opportunity, and they're getting the chance to swarm you. Then on defense, we're hanging in the corners too much instead of staying tight on the net."

"Oh, fuck off," Dottie said.

"Alright, Coach," Garner said, adding to the efforts to mock me.

"Do you want to win or not?" I asked. "How many more games like tonight's do you want to have? Do you think Florida's that much better than us? Or does Florida just play like a unit instead of like twenty guys who only give a fuck about themselves?"

"The fuck," Dottie said, popping his jaw. "Colt, you're gonna let him talk over you like that? I don't know how the fuck you got to be captain—"

Coach stalked into the locker room at that moment. "Sorrento's right," he said. "And the sooner you can start acting like professionals, the sooner we'll start winning. No more bullshit excuses."

He launched into a review of our mistakes and the plan for our next practice. But after that, no one spoke to me or even looked my way.

FOUR

JEANINE

NOW | NOVEMBER

We're going to *have the time of our lives*

(pic)

RACHEL

OMG Dyl looks so sleazy

Please do the pose thing before you get drunk

"WAIT, what are you supposed to be?"

It was the weekend after Halloween, which was the first day the team could have a party around the holiday. We were at Dylan's teammate Gavin Korowski's house, who hosted with his wife Lacey.

Lacey held the role I did back in L.A. As the captain's wife, you're responsible for holding the WAG group together, welcoming new members, and hosting a lot of parties.

And technically, she wasn't the captain's wife. The Rusties' captain, Colton Jones, was notably single, and it was determined that Lacey, as alternate captain Gavin Korowski's wife, would head the WAG group.

Kinda like the Vice President's spouse being the First Lady or First Man.

Still, Lacey held the crown with grace, even though she tried to play it off like she was small potatoes. Her easygoing, friends-with-everybody personality suited her perfectly to the role. I wasn't sure "drama" was in her vocabulary, or at least from what I could tell.

That's how I had been before everything turned upside down. Now I felt like the walking representation of drama, except instead of stirring the pot with other people, the drama churned inside me.

So there I stood, making nice conversation on the Korowskis' brick patio, flanked by outdoor heaters. The nice conversation covered up how absurdly anxious I was. It felt like no one but the Korowskis and Lindbergs wanted to talk to us, and we carpooled with the Lindbergs. Dylan and I floated around the room, trying to butt into conversations that promptly broke up.

I wore a flouncy pink skirt and pink leotard with some character heels from my dancing days, my black hair curled to mimic a perm. Dylan accompanied me in an open black short-sleeved button-down and pants, unbuttoned about to his belly button.

I fixed my smile on bigger for Lacey, lining my back up to Dylan's front. "Dyl, we have to do the thing."

"Oh, right," he said, nuzzling the side of my face and putting one hand on my waist. We handed Lacey our punch cups so we could perfect the pose. Then, just as smoothly as Patrick Swayze himself, Dylan lifted my arm and hooked it around his neck, trailing his hand down my body.

Lacey stood with a wide but blank grin, clearly not getting

the reference. I guess Dylan and I were officially old. Two other wives were standing by, but the light in their eyes dimmed and they turned to join another conversation. Add that to the evidence for the social anxiety pile.

"We're Baby and Johnny from *Dirty Dancing*," I said, trying not to shrink. "You know, *nobody puts Baby in a corner.*"

"Oh, right! The movie where she jumps and he holds her up?" Lacey cocked her head to the side, her bright demeanor not matching her vicious-looking Harley Quinn costume. She handed back our drinks.

"Oh, hey. *Nobody puts Baby in a corner!*" Mara Leroy walked over, her cane perfectly incorporated into her sexy Mr. Peanut costume. She wore a yellow bodysuit with her assets well arranged, her red hair in a bouncy ponytail, black fishnets, white sneakers, and a monocle.

"Yes, you got it!" I said, excited at least someone knew what the hell our couple's costume was.

"Are you going to lift her up like in the big scene?" she went on, her dazzling smile and ice-blue eyes all lit up. She sang a few bars from "(I've Had) The Time Of My Life," and I joined in. We leaned toward each other, laughing together. Talking to Mara was like hitting the pressure cooker release valve on my keyed-up emotions. I really didn't know her well. Her husband, Jack, was Dylan's teammate in Los Angeles, but Mara had only come on the scene a few months before Jack got traded. But the few times I met her in California, we'd shown a mutual desire to have fun. And on a night like this where it felt like we were the outcasts, that camaraderie was needed.

Jack appeared at her side, handing her a can of seltzer water and rolling his eyes at our singing. I noticed how readily he touched her, with an arm around her back and a hand on her ass like it was second nature. Jack's shorter than a lot of the guys, but Mara was his pint-sized companion, sporting enviable curves to boot.

I was jealous of her in more than one way. Her body confidence when she wasn't perfectly petite was admirable. Who could question her when she was so comfortable in her own skin? And even with her physical struggles that sometimes required her to use a mobility aid, she boogied to the Halloween hits pumped across the heated patio. She had a contagiously positive spirit, an openness and curiosity about life that didn't veer into the obnoxious.

That used to be me as well, but it slipped through my fingers with each mile that stretched between us and California.

But what made my heart ache more about Mara was the ease between her and Jack. Without missing a beat, she turned her face up to Jack's for a quick kiss and leaned her head against his chest. He tucked her more tightly to his side, taking the place of her cane in holding her up.

"Jeanine made me try the famous lift exactly one time before I decided I didn't want to end up in the hospital," Dylan said with a smirk, then looked over to Jack. "What in the hell are you wearing, Jackie?"

Jack's costume looked like he'd sewn a bedsheet to be narrow at his shoulders and billowing at his knees, where his legs popped out. It looked like he had throw pillows next to his knees on the inside. Little black streaks dotted the tan fabric. He gestured between himself and Mara and with a face completely devoid of emotion, said, "We're nuts."

I snorted, a sip of punch burning the inside of my nose. I got a sea of nasty looks from the other partygoers. I regained my composure. "You would come dressed as a ball sack, Leroy."

Jack tucked one side of his mouth. "It's nuts. She's a peanut and I'm nuts. We're nuts."

Lacey smiled politely and excused herself. A man dressed as Chuckie walked by and scoffed at Jack's statement. Dylan's body tensed where I held his hand, so I gave it a tighter squeeze. Jack and Dylan launched into some hockey-related discussion, and Mara and I went to grab a seat on an iron bench on the party's perimeter. Mara propped the cane next to her and slumped back with an easy grin.

"Does it feel like everyone's avoiding talking to us?" I asked, looking across the party. Glances occasionally went our way but quickly returned to their own contented conversations.

Mara surveyed the space, closing one eye and squinting. "You know what? I really can't tell."

She launched into a series of giggles that had her folding over her legs, then jolting up when her back protested her flopping around. I laughed along with her while she clutched her stomach, pitching back against the bench and fanning her face. I gave her a look to get some sort of explanation for her over-the-top amusement.

"I'm sorry, I'm so sorry," she cooed, wiping tears from under her eyes. "I tried a new edible tonight and I think it's—" She set off again.

I sat back and marveled at her, taking a sip of my punch. "I think maybe I need whatever you're on."

"Ooh! Ooh! I've got more, hang on." She cupped her hands around her mouth, shouting, "Jackie! Jackie baby! C'mere! Jeanine needs drugs!"

"Oh my god," I said, burying my face in my hands. When I looked up again, Dylan had an eyebrow quirked at me. Smirking, he strutted our way with Jack on his tail. Dylan squished half his ass on the bench and I scooted closer to Mara. Jack's tattooed arm disappeared inside his costume until he extracted a plastic baggie.

"You're dealing drugs to my wife out of a plastic bag?" Dylan asked.

"Chill, bro, it came from a dispensary. I just didn't want them stinking up my nutsack."

"It really helps with my back pain," Mara said on a gasp, still struggling to stop laughing.

"I bet it does," Dylan said, amused. "You gettin' high, J?"

"Might not hurt," I said with a shrug. "Should I not?"

"No, do it! Have fun, babe. Lindberg's driving," he said with a kiss to my cheek. "It'd be good to see you laugh like that again."

His statement had hidden barbs in it. It was no secret that I hadn't been feeling fully myself since we moved, but this was the first time Dylan acknowledged the shift in any way.

Jack sighed. "You might want to take a smaller dose. I've still gotta get this nutjob home."

Mara leaned over to my ear, whispering at a volume that everyone in the surrounding counties could probably hear. "He already nutted in me earlier."

Jack's face was impassive. "Damn right, I did."

"I MEAN what the hell are they doing? Just sitting in a corner doing drugs?"

"She's being so annoying. They think they're better than everybody. You know, Austin said her husband's annoying as shit."

I'd just come out of the bathroom off the kitchen hallway, and the edible was starting to kick in. I felt loose and mellow, having just stared at my reflection while wondering when my lips got so pretty. I felt like I was in there for about twenty minutes, but a glance at my phone showed that it had been about five.

"Yeah, I guess he's really pissing everyone on the team off, acting like he's the coach. Dottie said he's the reason they're losing."

"Well, there's no way either of them will last more than a year here. They're both old and washed up."

I gripped the wall next to me, staring at a picturesque professional photo of Lacey and Gavin.

My brain was warm and soupy, but before I could pop into view, it hit me: the tea being spilled might have been about Jack or Dylan. I dropped into a crouched position like maybe they wouldn't know I heard them talking if I just army-crawled back out to the patio. I stifled a giggle as I pictured myself doing just that, but then the mood shifted.

Panic threatened to take me under. Was I the one being annoying? What was I doing wrong? *You're in your mid-thirties acting like a teenager, Jeanine. That's what you're doing wrong.* I needed to make a good impression, and me spacing out in a corner on drugs wasn't going to help my case.

Just then, the Korowski's golden retriever detected me as a friend, scrambled around the kitchen island, and barreled toward me. He knocked me on my ass and licked my face, and that launched me into the promised giggles.

My breaths came in big honking jags, causing Lacey to peer over the counter to see what was causing all the ruckus.

"Sawyer, down!" she shouted. "I'm so sorry, Jeanine! Are you hurt?"

I'd have told her "no," but I couldn't get coherent words out. Another of the wives appeared behind Lacey, narrowing her eyes at me. She disappeared and the back door creaked open. I heard an agitated shout of, "Sorrento, come get your wife!"

The next thing I knew, my personal Patrick Swayze was crouched in front of me. His warm brown eyes looked me over, tickled by my nonsense. "I think we need to take Baby home," he chuckled.

"But I wanted to do the lift," I protested, my abs hurting from the laughing fit.

With a grin, he hoisted me to my feet and let his hands slip to my hips. "Hold your body straight."

I gasped. "Really?"

Dylan nodded, getting into a low squat. "Jump."

On a wave of laughter, I put my arms out, bent my knees, and launched myself upward.

And like he promised, Dylan held me up in the famous *Dirty Dancing* lift.

Lacey and Christine let out a cheer, but other, less positive voices could be heard.

"Oh, wow, okay."

"They really did it."

And finally, a sarcastic, "Cute."

And those were the voices that haunted me as we went to bed that night.

FIVE

JEANINE

NOW | NOVEMBER

> Going on a targie run with another team wife. I want to state right now that it's not you and I hate that

RACHEL

> Well I'm always best but

> I'm sure you'll have fun

BELLA SAT in the Target cart in front of me, Lacey walking alongside me.

"I feel like I should apologize," I said. "I embarrassed myself at your house."

Lacey scrunched her brow. "What do you mean? You guys were so cute doing your little *Dirty Dancing* thing."

"I don't think everyone thought it was cute," I said, replaying my night sitting up worrying about what everyone thought of me at the Halloween party. Walking in on shit-talking when you're on an edible then doing some ridiculous attention-getting thing with your husband is not a great combination.

She waved a hand. "Pfft. They're fine. You guys are adorable. Dylan was so sweet with you."

I grimaced. "He shouldn't have to be sweet with me. I should have it together."

Lacey tipped her head to the side, dismissing my anxiety with an "eh" sound. "Well, hey. At least you didn't have to throw the Halloween party this time." She pointed at me with a manicured finger and her Starbucks cup. "I get pretty burned out on that stuff, captain to captain."

My stomach turned, and I didn't think it was just the coffee making that happen. A longing smile crossed my face. "I miss that. I was really close with a lot of the girls, and I . . . I had a purpose, you know? Beyond raising these kids and being Dylan's wife. A group of people who understand the good stuff and bad stuff that comes with this life."

She elbowed me gently. "Hey, our group is the same. Very few of us willingly chose this city, but we're all finding ways to enjoy it. And if you want purpose, I can give you plenty of things to do. I sometimes think I'm the worst candidate to be the captain's wife. I didn't know what I was signing up for when I started dating a hockey player."

That was an overwhelm I remembered all too well: the induction to a life you never thought would be yours. One day, you're a cocktail waitress and actor/dancer/singer, and the next, you're dating a guy who makes large amounts of money to push a piece of frozen rubber around on ice. "You're too hard on yourself. The Halloween party looked great!"

She rolled her eyes. "Please. I went to Party City, cleared the Halloween shelf, and hoped for the best. You're welcome to help me anytime. With the charity stuff too."

Lacey was too nice. My anxiety gremlin told me she was just saying things to make me feel better, but she actually thought I was a hot mess. Still, I had to acknowledge her kindness. She was at least making an effort, and beyond Mara, no one else was really reaching out to befriend me.

"Parties and events aside, you've made me feel welcome and," tears threatened to spill, "I really appreciate that. It's been hard and we weren't planning on this move."

Lacey patted my forearm. "We're lucky to have gotten you guys. We're glad you're here. It's no L.A., but we've made a good life here. Are you coming to the game tonight?"

I shook my head, stopping at the kids' clothes section. "I don't have a solid sitter figured out yet. We had one of Christine's nieces who was in town for the weekend watch the kids for the Halloween party. She's back at college now."

She leaned in. "Jeanine, why didn't you say something? Hang on, let me hit up the group chat. Somebody's bound to have an extra contact."

The truth was, I didn't even think to ask. It's the kind of thing I would have helped new wives with in California, so I should have asked. But I've been living in a fog since we moved. Not only was allergy season ridiculous in the Midwest, but I was so out of my element.

And Dylan kept sugarcoating it.

Ever since we got the notice that Ohio wanted him, he went into hype-man mode. I was devastated, and he didn't like it either. The Princes basically issued him an ultimatum: ship out or hit the open market. Ohio's offer was solid enough, so he took it.

But I struggled to adjust to our new life, feeling as out of place as a fish out of water.

The flash fantasies were tempting. If I happened to be driving west with all three kids in the car, I'd keep driving until I hit the Pacific Ocean. I'd go off the grid and just work at my family's vineyard. Throw my phone in the river. Hide out somewhere without hockey, or husbands who don't listen, or kids with constant needs who I felt like I was parenting on my own.

I wasn't, but it felt that way when Dylan was gone for long stretches, or busy with other stuff when he was home.

I loved Dylan. Dylan loved me. I didn't doubt that. But he got into a place where negative feelings were inconvenient, invalid, unacceptable.

"We have to set an example for the kids, J," he'd said. "They'll fall apart if we fall apart."

But the problem was, I was already coming apart at the seams, and I wasn't allowed to do that.

"Mama, are you sad?" Bella asked. I'd been standing in one spot, absently stroking a baby dress.

Lacey's warm hand met my shoulder, her voice quiet. "I know it's hard, Jeanine."

I pressed my lips together to stifle my tears. "We're lucky in so many ways." My voice wavered. "We got to stay in one place for so long when so many families move constantly. But I wanted to stay there forever."

My words broke, and without asking, Lacey hugged me. She scratched my back with her perfectly stylish talons of nails, and I noticed just how gone I was. The thought of having to keep up fake nails while juggling three kids in a new city made me so overwhelmed I wanted to sit in the floor of Target and just blend into it. "You've got this, mama. We're here for you."

But that was just the problem. What if I didn't have it?

SIX

DYLAN

THEN

"THAT'S the woman I'm going to marry."

Chapman Beatty and I walked into the dive bar with live music in Santa Monica, and I was spellbound. We were having one of our nights out to explore L.A. We'd decided to diversify our going-out locations, having seen all the scenery, AKA hot women, Manhattan Beach had to offer. I needed to stop shitting where I slept and see other parts of the Los Angeles world. Chappy was happily dating a very kind woman who I couldn't believe put up with his shit, but he was willing to be a wingman for me.

And upon walking into this bar, I got exactly what I was after.

A scantily-clad woman with legs for days sang some dramatic Celine Dion ballad on stage. She looked like a naughty version of Snow White: shiny dark hair pulled up in the back, cherry red lips, and when she flashed those peepers up, deep blue eyes that bordered on some version of turquoise. Her corset-style black top revealed a tantalizing strip of skin and a tiny blue jewel glittering in her belly button. Her waist nipped in just so, and it looked like a great resting place for my hands. Add that to her tiny black shorts, black boots, and trim hourglass figure, and she was easily the stuff of dreams.

I, at age twenty-five, was in love.

Instantly. Upon laying eyes on her.

Chappy and I settled in at a high-top table for two, which I noticed could have room for an extra stool. I planned my approach: I'd talk to her as soon as she got off the stage and tell her I loved the way she sang.

Because I did.

She sang with such conviction, both playing with the song's drama and somehow acknowledging that she *knew* it was dramatic and ridiculous with her tone. For a dive bar, this was some fancy karaoke, with a live band backing her up. I'd have thought it was her personal concert if it weren't for the sandwich board sign to the right of the stage indicating sign-ups and specifically saying "live band karaoke." She worked the stage, singing directly to the keyboard player and dancing around like it was her jukebox musical, and we were just living in it.

The way she belted out the line about nights of endless pleasure sent a chill zipping up my spine. Every hair on my arm raised and I had to fight a shiver, lest Chappy would give me infinite shit. What the fuck was going on that some woman singing a soft rock song was wrecking me?

Halfway through the song, she descended the steps from the stage and danced her way through the bar. My heart picked up, wondering if she'd stop at our table.

I had on a hat because I fell victim to the delusion that I was a celebrity and would thus get recognized in public. That was before I accepted that people in Los Angeles could give two shits about the hockey players. Not only did everyone feel important, but everyone cared far more about the actors on the screen, not the people who pushed a puck around.

But here was this woman, so close to me, circling our table and singing *to me*, with a voice so powerful that I could feel the air vibrating. She dropped the microphone from her lips, meeting my gaze.

Her speaking voice was buttery smooth. "Okay if I touch you?"

I nodded, probably a little too enthusiastically.

She slid herself across my lap and looped one arm behind my neck.

The puzzle pieces clicked into place. She fit. *We* fit. I knew you weren't supposed to touch strippers and that probably extended to women singing in bars too. But she asked if she could touch me, and there's some assumed touching back, right? We were already touching, and I had to keep her from falling off my lap. My left hand held her waist, and my right held her thigh.

It was perfect.

She smirked and kicked her leg up before crossing it over the other, making our embrace tighter.

She delivered the next slow lines, looking deep into my eyes. I vaguely wondered if she was a witch, hypnotizing me, but was too enchanted by her to worry about it. I breathed in her scent: something sharp and fruity with some kind of flowery edges. I was trying so hard to hold my face in some attractive formation that wasn't just my mouth gaping open.

She took off my hat while she sang, running her fingers through my hair like we were long-time lovers.

And just like that, she'd used me for all she needed. She put my ballcap back on, tapped the bill with a wink, turned it around backward, and headed back for the stage as the song built to another climax.

My god, she touched me.

I needed her.

As the song reached one final crescendo, she unclipped her hair and tossed her head, throwing the clip at me in the crowd. I caught it with a shocked laugh and Chappy shot me a look. "Somebody's got a crush."

Then, perfectly timed with the song, she dropped to her knees and crawled across the stage, thrashing in all the right places to accentuate the drama.

She finished her song and Chappy and I gave her a standing ovation—and we weren't the only ones. How could anyone resist an all-in performance like that? She called up the next singer and rather than coming back into the crowd, she disappeared out a door beside the stage.

I threw twenty bucks at Chap and grabbed her hair clip. "Get me a drink. I'm going to talk to her."

He chuckled at me and we parted ways. As I walked toward the door she left through, I unbuttoned my shirt one more and made sure my chain wasn't hanging weird.

I popped outside into an alleyway, a cluster of smokers gathered there.

She was one of them. I approached her, trying to come up with something hot to say. I went with a classic. "Hi."

"Hey, it's the prom king," she called, blowing a stream of smoke out her nose. "I'll be at your table soon, big guy. Mommy's gotta have a little smoke break."

A man I recognized from behind the bar snickered.

"Prom king?" I asked, drawing closer.

Her lips curled up in the prettiest smirk, her voice a low drawl. "Well, you were, weren't you? An upstanding gentleman like yourself?"

My brow wrinkled. Did I really look that clean-cut? I

thought I was rugged. I had a five o'clock shadow, dark and noticeable just like the rest of my hair. "No."

"My mistake," she said with a coy shrug.

"I was homecoming king," I said, meeting her eyes. "And you dropped this."

I held out her claw clip and she stepped forward to take it from me.

"Clumsy me," she drawled. Her gaze combed over my outfit, assessing me from my shoes and up. She lifted a brow. "You smoke, homecoming king?"

"If I can bum one," I said. The truth was, I'd chewed tobacco in the lower leagues for an energy buzz but only smoked a cigarette like once ever. But if smoking was an entry to talking to her, I'd do it. She popped the pack in her hand and I removed the proffered cigarette.

"I'll light you," she said, flicking her lighter on and shielding the flame with her hand. I leaned down and sucked, making sure the flame caught.

I sucked too hard, harsh smoke attacking my lungs.

I stifled a gag, which then made me hack out a louder cough. The bartender laughed, but my singing superstar just hooked one side of her lips up.

"If you don't smoke, don't start now," she said in that silky voice. "These things'll kill you."

"Then how can I talk to you?" I asked. Her gaze went dazed and amused.

"Careful, J," the bartender said. "Prom king likes you."

"It's homecoming king," she cooed, winking at me. "And I think I might like him a little bit too."

I extended my hand. "Dylan."

Switching her cigarette to her left hand, she straightened and met my hand in a very business-like handshake. "Jeanine."

"I love the way you sing, Jeanine."

"Thank you very much, Dylan. I like the way you talk."

I SAT on a stool at the balcony over the bar. All the other chairs were flipped on top of the tables, something I'd been helping with. Was it my job to help Jeanine close the bar? No. But I wanted to spend time with her, and that was an easy enough method. After teasing me about wanting to steal her cash tips, she dismissed me to flip the chairs upstairs.

"I'll close up, Jorge," she called out to her coworker before she appeared at the top of the steps. She turned to me with a smirk, slowly strutting my way. "Thanks for helping out, Dylan."

"It's no problem. Wanna go for an after-hours drink somewhere?" I offered.

She stepped between my legs, putting her hands on top of my thighs. Her face drew closer to mine. "Is that really what you want?" she hummed.

I swallowed hard, clamping my jaw. "No."

"Didn't think so," she said, and I could read the subtext. Her hands clasped around my neck and our lips connected. My hands reunited with the divots of her waist that tempted me since I laid eyes on her. She tasted like the Fireball shot she'd tossed back with the bartender at the end of their shift. I pulled her closer, and she tried to straddle me. The stool was sturdy but not sturdy enough for two people, wobbling as we toppled into the brick wall behind me. I caught her under the thighs just as the stool slid out from under us, her moans deepening as I held her up.

I leaned against the wall behind me and she locked her legs

around me, grinding away. She extended a hand beside my head, using the wall for leverage.

"Fuck, Jeanine," I whispered against her lips.

"Yes, let's do that," she laughed, a low, throaty sound. "Back to your place?"

I WOKE up in a very nice yet sparsely furnished apartment. My head rested on a decently hairy chest, but not just hairy. There was some serious lean muscle under there.

I looked up past his gold chain to his stubbled chin, putting the groggy pieces together. I didn't drink much, but I felt tired like I had. I sucked in my stomach and I was sore like I'd just done a hundred sit-ups. Speaking of abs, an extremely carved set of abs disappeared under the sheets, which were tented by his erection.

Homecoming king.

Shit, what was his real name? A memory of that chain swinging in my face, his lips hanging beside my ear.

"You like that, Jeanine?"

I did a quick kegel to assess the state of my pelvic floor, noting the beard burn between my thighs.

Dylan.

That's right. Dylan's face was lodged between my thighs for a good twenty minutes, not stopping until I came twice. The man was a machine.

And he seemed like a genuinely sweet guy. He played along with my dramatic performance like a champ. He held me so tenderly, and he had such a raw vulnerability in his eyes when I was singing to him. The song is meant to be somewhat funny—it was over the top on purpose and it was just karaoke, after all. But I think he both got the joke and took me seriously at the same time, which wasn't something I was used to. After all, being a dancer/actor/singer by day and a server by night was so much of a cliché in Los Angeles that I was basically a caricature.

But Dylan took me seriously.

So when he popped outside to bring back my hair clip and was willing to gag on a cigarette just to talk to me, the cynical part of me softened.

I sat up on my elbow, noting a sports bag that I recognized. My brother and his best friend Andy had played hockey for a while. Once I could drive, it was sometimes my responsibility to shuttle their stinky asses to practice. Ugh, I was in a hockey player's house.

Then I caught the logo stitched on the bag. *L.A. Princes.*

Holy shit, I fucked an NHLer. Not just fucked: I sat on his face, gobbled his dick, and judging by the ache in my low back took it pretty hard in doggy. I rolled off my side and onto my back, away from this hockey boy who railed me in every position imaginable. Tiny fingerprint bruises dotted my boobs, looking like when a kid draws a sun with rays poking out. In this case, my nipples were the sun.

I reached for my phone on the nightstand, which was plugged in. Nice work, busy-fucking-Jeanine. But in addition to my iPhone plug, there were two other types of plugs available.

This guy had girls sleep over often enough that he had an all-purpose charging station for their phones? Courteous and promiscuous! I lay back and googled "LA Princes roster," scrolling to look for a Dylan. And there he was, the man, the myth, the legend lying next to me. Dylan Sorrento, 6'2", 197 pounds, twenty-five years old. He looked all cute and serious in his photo, like he was trying to present himself as a big scary athlete man. I usually went for older guys, but—

"Are you looking up my stats?"

I startled, almost dropping my phone in my embarrassment at being caught in the act. "I should get going."

I shifted to sit up and an arm snaked around my middle. "Not so fast, gorgeous."

I shrieked as he hauled me over and on top of him, facing down. "What's the hurry?"

My breath snagged, the feeling of his stacked body under me and the whole situation throwing me off. "I just—I—"

He raised his eyebrows at me, waiting. His morning skin smelled like heaven and it was tempting to nestle my nose into his chest for a big whiff.

"I don't want you to get the wrong idea," is where I landed.

"You're not that kind of girl?" he teased.

"Well," I chuckled, "I am that kind. But I'm not a stay-for-brunch type."

"No?" he asked, brows pinching together. "Guess what type I am?"

I smirked and snorted, still on top of him with my naked-ness meeting his. "I don't think you're the brunch type either, judging by the abundance of charging cables on my side of the bed."

He ran his tongue along his teeth like I'd punched him in the mouth. "Not usually the brunch type, no. But for you, I'm the when-can-I-see-you-again type."

I laughed and my voice was a little hoarse. "Nice try. Last night was fun." I rolled off him and covered myself with the bedsheet.

"Shy now, huh? You weren't shy last night." His eyes were drowsy moving over me, like there was no reason for the bedsheet at all. "Can I convince you to stay for a cup of coffee?"

"I should . . ." I tried, but couldn't finish because he sat up and ran tiny kisses along the ridge of my shoulders.

"Your skin is delicious, Jeanine," he hummed as his lips moved to my neck. My eyes rolled back in my head.

"Dylan," I sighed as a surge of blood rushed between my legs.

"There you go," he rasped. "I bet you'd really like some coffee."

I giggled as he scrambled to my side of the bed and scooped me up. He was undoubtedly hot, but the thing that struck me was his hands. They were so big, with veins and more of that dusting of dark hair that covered him. I'd never been a big body hair girl, probably conditioned by California's oiled-up fitness culture. But Dylan was pulling it off without trying. His kitchen opened into a living room with floor-to-ceiling windows overlooking the ocean. He dropped me on the kitchen counter.

"I'm naked!" I squealed. "I'm going to traumatize someone on the beach."

He grinned as he folded my arms across my breasts and one leg over the other. "Hang tight."

He jogged back to his bedroom, seemingly unaffected by his jiggling junk along the way. Damn, that ass was tight. Like, bounce a quarter off it and get your money back tight.

He came back in holding his t-shirt from the night before and wearing boxer briefs himself. He gathered up the neck of the shirt and put it over my head. But before he pulled it over my breasts, he brushed gentle kisses over the bruises on them. "Sorry about this, baby."

Then he pulled the shirt all the way down. He rubbed his

lips together, his eyes drifting over my new appearance. "Better?"

"As long as this covers my ass."

He scrunched his nose and shook his head. "I'd rather it didn't."

As I was about to chastise him, he dropped to his knees and kissed the insides of mine. "Because now I can do this."

It was a long time before that coffee got brewed, and I could have cared less who I traumatized on the beach.

I gave him my number on the way out.

EIGHT

JEANINE

THEN

I STAYED at Dylan's place a lot more nights.

He came over to my place to prove to my roommate that he was real and I hadn't been kidnapped. The first time he had to go on the road for work after we met, I felt like I'd lost some vital piece of myself. I missed a guy I'd met a week before, something I never could have anticipated.

But it was Dylan. We were under each other's spell, completely wrapped up in us. I'd never felt like this for anyone.

By one week, he knew where to tickle me to make me unable to speak or breathe.

By two weeks, he bought me a toothbrush and called from the drugstore to ask which brand my facewash was.

So at the end of the second week, when he asked me if I'd spend my night off work at his game, I said yes.

I hadn't been shopping for a boyfriend, and certainly not for one who played pro hockey, but there I was, all decked out in the team colors and sitting next to the team captain's wife, Amber. She was gorgeous: blonde-haired, blue-eyed, and with a smile so white it could rival the ice in front of us.

Did I mention she was nice? Like so nice I wasn't sure I should act like what Dyl called my usual sassy cocktail waitress self. I should have gone to my first game by myself or with one of my friends.

"So how did you and Sorrento meet?"

It took a second for his last name to catch up to me. Obviously, I knew it, but not well. I called him Dylan or Dyl in most of the two weeks we'd been seeing each other. I'd never been in a relationship this fast and furious. I kept waiting for the other shoe to drop, for him to reveal his great flaw. Maybe how fast we were moving was the flaw.

I shoved that feeling down. I was twenty-seven and being jaded about dating was getting old. Dylan was allowed to just be a nice guy.

"He came into where I work," I said. "And the rest, as they say, is history."

"How fun! Where do you work?"

"Well, I'm an actor, but I wait tables at a dive in Santa Monica. He came in when I was singing karaoke with a live band."

"Santa Monica? No one really gets down that way much. Wonder what took him there."

"If I recall correctly from that night, he said he'd already seen what there was to see close to home," I said with a laugh. Her look of horror told me she wasn't overly comfortable with discussing my new boyfriend's promiscuity. "What about you and . . ."

Shit, I'd already forgotten her husband's name. He was the team captain. I should have had it down by now.

"Justin? It's much more boring than that. We went to high school together and just never broke up."

"That's a lot of dedication," I said, looking impressed.

She shrugged. "It's hard sometimes, him being gone so

much, but it's worth it. I don't really know any different at this point. It's better here than in the lower leagues."

"I bet," I said.

"You're the first Sorrento's brought around. He must like you."

I snorted. "What an honor."

At that moment, the puck clipped the plexiglass a few rows in front of us, making me jump. It was followed closely by one of Dylan's teammates getting checked into the glass. I gasped, and she laughed. "Not a hockey fan?"

"My brother and his best friend played," I said, "but not like this. These guys are annihilators."

"They certainly try," she said. "So acting, huh?"

"Yeah, I like to try and get into movie musicals. I've been chorus in a few shows, and higher in some stage productions."

"No shit," she said, now her turn to look impressed.

"Been at it for a long time now, though. Five years since I finished my arts school."

"Better watch yourself. Hockey players love to get families going quick. This is number three for me," she pointed to her perfectly round stomach. "And I doubt we're stopping after this. Last I checked, stage careers don't mix well with prenatal care."

She wasn't at all being rude, just matter of fact. She knew the life.

"But we've got a good bunch out here. We all support each other. A lot of faces come and go, but we try to make the best of what we've got."

I nodded absently, watching Dylan spill over the wall and onto the ice. Was that man the future father of my children?

THE NIGHT BEFORE, we were in his bed, facing each other on our sides. We both held up our top hands, his swallowing up mine. I slipped my fingers between his, and despite the size difference in our hands, they fit perfectly.

Dylan smirked, looking over my face.

"Jeannie, I feel like I've been here with you before."

I knew what he meant, but I wanted him to say more. "Like here here?" I pointed to the bed between us. "Or like . . . here." I gestured from his body to mine.

"Here. With you." He shook his head. "I know it's nuts."

I snorted. "Maybe, but I want to hear you talk about it."

He slid his palm up so my fingers drifted over it, his eyes intensely on mine. "I feel like I've known you in another lifetime. Like all this time, I was wandering around, just waiting for the moment our paths would cross. We were in the right place at the right time, and now we're . . . home."

I rubbed my lips together. "Have you heard of twin flames?"

He shook his head.

"It's some woo-woo concept," I explained, "where somewhere out there, the other half of your soul is split into someone else's body."

Dylan smiled. "That's how it feels, like half of me lives in you already. You say things, and I'm not surprised. I could finish your sentences because I just . . . know you. After a couple of weeks."

I nodded.

"I'd say I'm falling for you, but that sells it short. When I first saw you, it felt written in the stone, etched in me somewhere and I could finally read the words. Like I've been riding on a train without tracks for years and I finally rolled into the station. And even though it's a new town for me, I've been here before and it's my favorite place."

I grinned and covered my face as a fierce blush set in.

He gripped my wrists, playfully trying to pull them from my face. "No, let me see you, Jeannie."

"No! You're all cute and romantic and I don't know what to do with that!"

"You feel it too, don't you? Jeanine's got a crush on me," he sing-songed. "She thinks I'm cu-uuute!"

"Stop, no I don't!" I said, then opened my eyes to his adoring smile. I was fucking sunk. There was no way out of falling for Dylan. "Okay, I might like you a little bit."

He raised an eyebrow at me, lifting his fingers like he was going to tickle me.

"Fine! I like you a lot!" I laughed, then sobered and leaned in for a kiss. "It's not even like 'you complete me' or some fluff like that. You were always here."

Dylan shivered. "You gave me goosebumps."

I tipped my head. "The problem with twin flames is it's your mirror soul. And sometimes you don't like what you see when you look in the mirror. And that can get volatile."

He grimaced. "I don't want to find out what those things are."

I laughed. "That's probably exactly our problem."

"Eesh. I'm too busy thinking you're perfect, Jeanine."

I pointed at him. "Because if we're twin flames, I'm you, and you're me, you narcissist." I got one of Dylan's full belly laughs, the kind that made him throw his head back. He tugged us so we were chest to chest and kissed me. I pushed back enough to look up into his eyes.

"Why hockey?" I asked. "What put you here, in my warpath?"

Dylan got more serious, looking past me to the other side of the room. "You know, other than it being a great sport, and me being good at it," he paused, "I think the ice is the only place I don't have to worry about anyone but myself and the guys sitting on the bench. And the guys sitting on the bench are looking out for you, just like you're looking out for them. If you're on a good team, it all just gels. It's safe, even though it's inherently dangerous."

"So you like the community of it."

"Yeah," he nodded.

"Did people not have your back elsewhere?"

He winced and spoke to our hands, still sliding together and apart between us. "It's not that they didn't have my back. My parents would do anything for me. But that comes at a cost. I worried too much about making them happy because they invested so much in me."

I squeezed his hand. "Makes sense."

"But on your team, everything's equal. Everybody has a role to play and does it."

I flicked my eyebrows up. "I get it."

"Alright, if you're my twin flame and we have mirror problems and experiences, what put you here? Why theater?"

I rolled my lips, bobbing my head. "Probably the same reasons you like hockey, honestly. I love Temecula, and my parents were good to me growing up. But my mom was always overstressed and worked too hard on us kids and the winery, and my dad took a backseat to deal with the winery more. So when I'm there, it's safe, sure. My parents love me and each other so much. But for them I'm always trying to be good, to manage how they feel. It's more . . . a performance for them, whereas theater, I'm performing for me. I can be me on stage, even if I'm playing a character who's nothing like me. That's kind of the beauty of it. And you've got your supporting cast to back you up. You find and build chemistry, probably like your team."

"I think your twin flame theory might not be far off." He

sighed. "My mom gave up everything for me. She changed her job so she could more easily get me to practice. When she wasn't working, she was at home, making sure I had all my needs met. Don't get me wrong, my dad went to all my games. He was always my cheerleader. But Mom did a lot. And I felt like I owed it back to them. But I forget all that when I'm playing the game."

I shrugged. "Might be twin flames."

He grinned. "I can think of worse people to be a twin flame with."

"DYLAN, I NEED YOU NOW."

I straddled him in the driver's seat of his SUV, which hadn't yet left the arena parking lot. He had the seat shoved way back so we could both fit, and for the moment we were just making out and grinding. I was so turned on by seeing him work, by knowing that the guy on the ice was mine to fuck, to ride, to cuddle up to, to share silly midnight secrets with.

So yeah, we didn't even make it out of the parking lot.

"Fuck yeah, baby, sit on this cock," he said, unbuckling his belt.

I popped my hips up and unbuttoned my jeans, shoving them and my underwear down. Amber's words from the game, and her pregnant belly, rang in my head. "You got a condom?"

Dylan grimaced. "Let me check my wallet."

He shuffled around in the glove compartment and his wallet also came up dry. "Hand stuff?" he offered.

Looking at his cock there, begging for attention where it protruded from his lap, hand stuff didn't sound as fun as me getting split by it. "Pull and pray?"

He smirked. "You sure?"
"If it worked in high school, surely it'll work now."

NINE
JEANINE
THEN

"IT DIDN'T WORK."

My eyes met Dylan's where he sat across from me on the lip of the bathtub in his apartment.

He nodded. "It did not."

Pull and pray had become more of a motto than an in-a-pinch solution for me and Dylan. It felt too good for us to be raw together, and afforded us some spontaneity. I told him I didn't want to do birth control because it messed up my weight, which then could mess up my chances at auditions.

But you know what messes with your weight even more? Being pregnant. Growing a baby inside your body.

We'd both agreed we were cool with the risk, but I don't think either of us thought it would actually happen.

It happened. The two lines on the test in my hands were clear as day.

"I've got that audition Tuesday," I mumbled.

Dylan chewed his lip. "Whatever you want to do, Jeannie. I'm with you no matter what."

I shook my head. "We've been together, what, five minutes?"

"Four months, actually," he mumbled.

A beat of silence passed between us. It was a bombshell—one we knew was a possibility, but we were playing like it wasn't.

We did it everywhere. In the bathroom at my job. In his car after games. On every surface in his apartment. Over the phone when he was on the road, us talking dirty and him telling me what he wanted to do to me.

So, yeah. It wasn't all that surprising that my period went AWOL.

"Jeanine, I'll marry you."

"What?!"

He took my hand, his eyes completely earnest. "I love you, Jeannie."

We'd said it a couple of months in. We were lying in bed grinning at each other like fools, lacing and unlacing our fingers. Hormones were flowing and Dylan had the sweetest smile. Then he just said it. I'd had it said to me before, but then I was horrified, panicked even because that guy wasn't the right one.

This time, I felt it too, and it felt like my heart would splatter like a blueberry in a muffin. So I said it back.

But loving someone and loving someone enough to marry them are two separate metrics. And while I could see a long future with Dylan, I didn't want to jump into anything too fast.

"I know it's crazy, J, but I do want to spend my life with you."

My head got light. "You don't need to do this, Dylan."

"Jeanine," he shook my hand and made me look at him. "These last four months have been my happiest. I want whatever you want."

"They're your happiest because we fuck like bunnies."

"And I fuck you so much because I love you and can't get enough of you."

It was a valid point. Sometimes sex is just sex, and sometimes it's something more. With Dylan, it was usually more, and that's what made it so great. He'd been fucking me like he loved me since the first night I came home with him.

"But marriage, Dylan? It's not the 1800s. You don't have to marry me so we can have a baby. I don't want an *I'm the man doing the right thing* wedding. When I get married, I want it to be for love."

"Jeannie, I do love you. I want to marry you anyway."

"But this soon?" I asked.

He shrugged. "It's sooner than I was planning to ask, sure. A baby speeds things up."

I just shook my head, trying to quiet its spinning. "I don't even know . . ."

He pressed his lips together. "If you want this baby."

I stood up from the toilet lid and moved to the sink to wash my hands. "I need some time to think."

"J, that's not me judging you if you want an abortion."

"I know that, Dylan! My problem is if I have this baby, my acting career is basically over. But I don't even know if I want to keep going with that, or what comes after that, or if I keep waiting tables forever, or if I just give up and move home and take over the winery when my parents are too old to run it or—" I cut myself off with a jagged breath.

Dylan stood and spun me around, waiting for me to look into his eyes. "It's a lot to handle, Jeanine. No matter what you choose, I'm here with you. Okay? You want to have this baby and not get married? That's fine. You want to marry me? Great, I want to marry you too. You want an abortion? I'll be right there with you. Do what's best for you and what you want, and I'll back you up. I promise."

"Dammit, Dylan, what is wrong with you?"

He looked bewildered. "Huh?"

"Why do you always say and do the right thing? When am I going to find out something awful about you?"

He laughed. "I . . . don't know? I'm just a guy?"

I wrapped my arms around his neck and we fell into an embrace, where he kissed the top of my head. "We'll figure it out, J."

TEN

DYLAN

NOW | NOVEMBER

"NICE, NICE, NICE, THAT WAS A BEAUTY!" I called from the bench.

Dotsenko, or Dottie, huffed next to me and rolled his eyes. "He should be doing that anyway."

"Doesn't matter what he's already done. He's doing it right now," I pointed out. "No need to drag out old shit."

"Let me know what time we're having snack, teacher."

His dig at my encouragement was nothing new. Responding with animosity had gotten me nowhere, so I decided to try assuming he's joking. I shoved Dottie in the shoulder. "Lighten the fuck up."

He shook my hand off his shoulder. "Don't fuckin' touch me, washup."

"Hey!" Colton chimed in. "Pickles washed up on our shore, so he's our washup."

He shot me a wink behind Dottie's back.

"You playing, or just preaching?" Leroy said.

Even though Leroy and I both came from L.A., he was handling the transition much better than I was. In L.A., I had everything I wanted. Nothing was going right in Ohio. I didn't even have my number anymore, because Dottie wore my preferred number, 11. Being number 9 was a further reminder of how I didn't fit.

I was a respected leader with the Princes, the center of the team's morale. Leroy had always operated as something of a lone wolf. He had a best friend on the team, but he kept everyone else at arm's length. I couldn't even expect him to relate to what I was going through. Our personalities were too different. I couldn't stop thinking of myself as separate from the Rusties, like I was just a visitor and any minute, I'd be back in L.A. kicking it with Chappy and Stelle and hell, even hothead Mikey. I'd never admit it to Jeanine, but I missed my friends.

It was one of many things I couldn't admit to Jeanine.

I couldn't admit I was lonely and I didn't fit in. I couldn't acknowledge my fear that this was all a mistake. I couldn't let her know I saw her struggling, as it might cause her to fall apart. I needed her to stay strong so I could too. I was almost mad at her that she thought she could have the luxury of falling apart. I couldn't crumble. I'd carried her through our shared pain before.

But this time, I couldn't carry us both.

So I kept my head up, and I hoped that by seeing me do it, she could keep her head above water too.

When I got the news that we'd have to move, I was terrified of how she'd react. J and I had seen some dark times, and while her mental health had gotten to a good place, it wasn't always that way. Reflecting on those dark days was sometimes enough to turn my stomach, the thoughts of what could have happened haunting me. We were so rocky at the beginning, and though her mental health had been stable for several years, I feared this move would drop us right back onto that rocky path.

I knew she was going to hate moving. I was afraid she'd leave me in favor of keeping the life we'd built, even if it didn't have me in it. She had everything in California. Rachel Beatty was her best friend, attached at the hip to each other. Her parents were just a few hours away. The older kids were in a good school. She was happy holding the captain's wife role, thriving as the linchpin of that community. We'd finally gotten to a place where everything was good. The kids were good, J was good, and I was happy they were all happy.

And my job pulled the rug out from under us. But it was either go to Ohio or risk getting a worse offer on the open market. I couldn't stay in L.A. if I still wanted to play hockey. The only alternative was retirement, and I just wasn't ready for that yet.

So I didn't retire, and I took Ohio's offer, now adjusting to the new team. Every team is a family of sorts with varying levels of dysfunction. The chemistry was fundamentally different in Ohio. Blaming losses and "holding each other accountable" were commonplace, but the truth was, the vibes were off. The Princes had made Cup runs all three years I was captain. We gelled. I knew the tricks up everybody's sleeves. I was usually first or second line, but I could have jumped in anywhere to make it work. I could say the same for most of the guys.

By contrast, Ohio hadn't made a Cup run or even raced for a wild card spot in almost a decade. It felt like everyone was just looking out for number one, and not trying to back each other up.

But I was putting on a brave face, doing my best to stay optimistic and blend in.

Leroy was right and it was our turn to go in, him, Korowski, and I spilling over the wall. Immediately, I got caught in a battle for the puck at the wall, blocking my teammates out as best I could in this scrimmage.

"Fuck outta my way, Pickles," Garner teased as he jabbed at the puck between my skates. I laughed as I freed it, cutting it out toward the goal. Korowski had been waiting for just such an opportunity, shot, and netted it.

"Yes, that's what I'm talkin' about!" I shouted. From the bench, Dottie gave me a death stare. I can handle a lot of chirping and shit-talking, but when your own teammate seems to have it out for you, it's more daunting.

Practice wrapped up about ten minutes later, Dottie continuing to flick glances my way. I felt the reaming coming in my bones.

So it was zero surprise to me when I was mostly undressed and the bark of "Pickles" was heard.

I looked up with a bright smile, a part of my "kill him with kindness" plan. "Yeah?"

Dottie cocked his head to the hallway leading to the bath-rooms. I followed.

"What's up, Dot?"

His face arranged into a sneer. "You know this isn't Los Angeles, right?"

So it was gonna be like that. I rolled my lips and nodded. "Yup, pretty aware of that."

"I know you were top dog out there, but here you need to fall in line."

I laughed. "I don't think Colt has any issue with my perfor-mance, and he's the captain."

"He's not the only leader around here," he said. "You follow me."

I cocked my head to the side. "How many Cups has that gotten you? Playoff runs? Don't you think they brought me here for a reason? And Leroy? Why do you think they'd be trying to rebuild our line here?"

"Watch your tone," he gritted out, his face a red balloon that with one tiny pinprick could pop.

"Don't blow a vein, my guy." I winked and clapped him on the shoulder, sliding along the wall to get away from him and heading for the showers.

I WAS PULLING into our driveway when Ma started her antics during our call. I tried to call home whenever I could to catch up with Ma or Dad. Most of the time, I did it during drives so I could give J and the kids my full attention once I got home. We'd just finished settling the details of Thanksgiving weekend when she changed the subject.

"And how's your wife?"

Ah, yes. The very kind way that my mother referred to Jeanine. Jeanine, who'd had three of my children and had been married to me for eight years. Jeanine, who was not a fleeting girlfriend but in fact my partner in life. "Jeanine's okay."

"Just okay?" Mom probed.

I hesitated, pinching my lips together. It would be my first time admitting there was anything wrong to Ma. "I think we're both adjusting to Ohio."

"Why? What's she doing?"

"She's fine, Ma. Just hasn't found her groove yet I think." I opened the car door and got out my bag, hitting the garage button to close the door.

"Well, with all the free time she has, she should be able—"

I opened the door to the inside, and was greeted in my favorite possible way.

"Daddy!"

Three sets of feet thundered down the hall, Jeannie peeking out from the kitchen to watch the kids run at me. My phone was tucked into my shoulder as I carried my bag.

"Mom, I just got home, so I'll have to talk to you later. Love you!" I couldn't hear her response over the kids, so I just hung up.

"Mommy said to ask you if we could have ice cream when you got here," Greyson shouted before he even made it all the way to me.

"That's not what I said," Jeanine chimed in.

I crouched down, dropping my bag and holding each of my kids. I planted a kiss on each of their heads or cheeks, whatever I could reach.

"Daddy, I wanna show you the outfit I put on Charlie," Alice whined, dragging me by the hand as I stood. Charlie was her stuffed cat that had been her sidekick since she was an infant.

"And I want to play super freeze tag!" Greyson added.

"Me too, Daddy. Please?" Bella added.

"Hold your horses. I want to see your mama first." I made it to the kitchen, where Jeanine was cutting some potatoes for dinner. I slid my hands into her waist from behind and kissed her cheek. "Hey, J."

"Hi," she said, her cheeks going a little pink.

"I just got off the phone with Ma. We're hosting Thanksgiving for sure now. They're going to drive in from Pittsburgh and stay in a hotel."

"Oh. Great," Jeannie said, a chirp in her voice I knew she

didn't mean. "They could stay here, you know. We have the extra room."

I leveled her with a look. "I'm sure that's exactly what you want."

A small smirk tipped up the corner of her lips.

I swatted her butt. "Go easy. I'll make it worth your while."

I'm the first to admit that my parents, especially my mother, can be a handful. Whenever we have to see them, I make it a point to treat Jeanine to something special. Sometimes that's sex just the way she likes it, sometimes even extra naughty by sneaking off when we're with my parents. Sometimes it's an actual gift. Sometimes a date day together, just me and her.

But as I thought about it, it had been a while since I'd taken her on a nice date that didn't have to do with hockey.

"Daddy, will you come look now?" Alice wheedled me.

"No, play with me first!" Greyson whined. "Mom's been so busy!"

"Alice asked first!" I said. "Yes, sweetie, I'd love to see what Charlie's up to. Thank you for waiting."

ELEVEN

JEANINE

THEN

I finished the dance combo along with the other twenty people on the floor, my final pose a dramatic drop. I'd crushed it. My turns were 100% on the mark, my stage presence impeccable, and my kicks the highest they'd ever been, despite the churn in my stomach. I wasn't sure if that churn was from being pregnant or from nerves, but I leaned toward the former.

I even caught the casting director getting a soft smile watching me. This was good. I could even get called up for a bigger role.

Later, we stood on the line to hear who was getting to sing and who was getting sent home.

"Number sixty-seven!"

I jumped up as my number was called, stepping forward with a bow of my head to say thanks. I folded my hands on my tailbone and held my shoulders and head high with a smile. This could be a big one.

And when my number was called again to sing, I walked

out with no nerves. I handed the piano player my sheet music and stepped to the front of the stage.

"I'm Jeanine Wendlock. This is 'There Are Worse Things I Could Do.'"

The song choice was perfect for my situation. Much like Rizzo in Grease, I was pregnant and facing a big choice. Many could call me trashy, a flirt. I literally met the guy waiting for me outside while I was serving him drinks at a bar, then went home with him that night. I had no shame about that, but some people would take exception. So yeah, if I were any character in Grease, it certainly wouldn't be Sandra Dee.

I hit every note, had seamless vibrato, and belted the climax without a flaw.

It was my best audition ever. If I didn't land a part in the chorus, or maybe even the main cast, they'd have to be delusional. And not to mention, the little nugget growing in my uterus was making my rack look better than ever.

That damn nugget had me questioning everything.

Did I want to go through with the grueling hours of another production? Of working while rehearsing? I'd done it all. I'd been in the chorus. I'd had a few lead roles. I had an IMDB page from films where I occupied the background. Headshots, hair and makeup, endless dance classes, voice lessons, and rehearsals. I'd done it all.

And I could do it again.

Or did I want the life Dylan was offering me? Stability, love, and support. It's not singing and dancing for applause, but a quieter joy. Granted, the nature of his work made him gone a lot, but I'd have the support of other wives and girlfriends, most of whom I'd loved when I met them.

I got in Dylan's SUV when he picked me up from auditions. He greeted me with a broad smile. I was amazed at how understanding he was being, not pushing me once either way.

The only thing he'd asked of me was to stop smoking in case I chose the baby. I'd already quit so it wasn't a big ask.

"How'd you do, baby?"

I beamed with tears in my eyes. He raised his eyebrows, waiting to see what that meant.

"I killed it."

Dylan grinned just as wide as I was, slid his hand along my cheek, and leaned in to kiss me. "Congratulations, J. Do you think you got a part?"

"Probably," I said, drawing a shuddering breath. "But I don't think I'm going to take it."

His eyes rounded. "What? You're not?"

I searched the deep brown for some kind of opinion. "I think I might be more interested in a different offer," I placed my hand on my lower belly, "if that's cool with you."

His mouth flapped as he studied my face. "Jeannie, are you sure? You crushed that audition. You can take what they offer you and still have the baby. You wouldn't have the baby before the show."

I bit my lip. "That's true. I guess I'll see what they offer and the timeline and all that. But, um, yeah. Do you want to . . . have a baby with me?"

Dylan's hand came up to stroke my cheek as his eyes went glassy. "Jeanine," he whispered. "Really?"

"I want this. I want you. And them." I rubbed my hand over my stomach, still mostly flat with a little bloat.

Dylan's hand splayed across my stomach and he pressed his forehead to mine. I kissed the single tear flowing down his cheek. "So, it's yes?"

"Yes. Hell yes. Yes, I want you to have my baby. And for me to be the dad. And for us to, you know," he was beaming so hard his voice sounded weird, "do the whole thing together."

"Okay. Good. Let's . . . do the whole thing," I laughed, and he laughed along with me.

"I love you so much, Jeannie," he whimpered.

"I love you too."

"And I'm going to love this little one so much." He let out a mix of a laugh and a sob. "I'm going to be a dad. We're going to be parents."

I nodded, my heart pounding as I was about to deliver the next part. "And if you'll have me, I'll be your wife."

He clutched under my ear, pulling me to him for a kiss. A joyful, excited, terrified wet kiss. "I'll be the luckiest man to have you as my wife."

He kissed me harder, really going for it until I pulled away. "Okay, I need you to feed me greasy diner food before I throw up."

He laughed, putting the car in drive. "To the greasy diner we go."

"WHAT ARE YOUR FAMILY NAMES?" Dylan dipped his toast in some runny egg that I really couldn't look at. Normally, runny eggs were my jam, but apparently the nugget occupying my uterus did not care for such things. I stifled a gag, looking away and covering my mouth. "Are you sick, J?"

"I just . . . cannot look at that egg."

He chuckled, arranging a menu and a napkin dispenser from the side of the table to block my view of his plate. "Better?"

"Much, thank you."

He sat back and sipped his cup of coffee. "It's real, isn't it? You're getting sick and everything. This is really happening."

"Seems pretty real to me," I said, then cast my eyes to my plate. "You do want it, right?"

Dylan's fingers laced with mine on the table. "Yeah. I do. I honestly thought you were going to choose to end it. I'm just getting used to it is all."

"Did you want me to end it?"

He sighed and bent to get his eyes in my line of sight. "I know it's probably hard to believe, but I really want whatever you want. I'm really excited now. Having a baby with you sounds perfect."

I pointed at him with my toast. "And marrying me."

"Yes, definitely marrying you," he said, and his eyes went dewy. "Starting a family."

"With the girl you met crawling across a stage in Santa Monica."

Dylan laughed. "With exactly the girl who was crawling across a stage in Santa Monica, using those damn leather lungs to belt Celine Dion and sitting on my lap to introduce herself to me."

I framed my hands around my face. "Aren't I charming?"

"So fucking charming, baby. Now tell me your family names. Your dad is Joe," he baited me.

"Dad is Joe, mom is Maureen, sister is Andrea, brother is Joey—" I started.

"So our son will be Giuseppe," he said, like it was obvious.

"Who says it's a boy?"

"I feel like it's a boy."

"And why Joe to Joey to Giuseppe?" I asked.

"He's gotta have some Italian to match my last name."

I cocked my head to the side. "You're right. Dylan Peter is so Italian."

Dylan narrowed his eyes. "I'm reclaiming my heritage."

"And your parents are Carla and Phil."

"See? Carla. Very Italian."

"Maybe we go Charlotte so it's like Carlotta?" I offered. "Or Carl if it's a boy."

"Or Carlo," he countered. "Keep it Italian."

"Then where's my family? I thought the point was to combine the two." I gasped, realization dawning on me. "Dyl, we have more pressing business than this. When the hell are we getting married? And where?"

TWELVE
JEANINE
NOW | NOVEMBER

What are you guys doing today?

RACHEL

Going over to Obi's. Annie's excited to host

(frowny emoji)

I miss you guys so much

We miss you too. MIL still coming over?

Yes. Ugh. Thoughts and prayers appreciated.

Will mention your plight during the blessing at dinner

Perhaps I need more than a prayer

Just guzzle wine and light up a cig at the dinner table. That'll shut her up. Be everything she accuses you of being

Even better: weed. Get blazed while you carve the turkey. Let the ashes drop on the bird

(dead emoji)

"CARLA! PHIL!" I extended my arms to my parents-in-law as they waited on our doorstep. Carla's cloying Angel perfume drifted over me as I was wrapped in a hug with a cheek kiss. I'd told Dylan her perfume gives me migraines, but I was specifically instructed not to make a stink.

Ironic, since she's the one making it stink, but I digress.

"Hi, doll," Phil said, holding me close. "Ya look good, kid."

If only he knew how bad I felt, but I guess I was putting on the show as usual, so why would they know any different? Was there ever a time when my relationship with Dylan's mom wasn't strained?

"Oh, Jeannie, the place looks . . . well, are you finished decorating?" Carla took a spin in the foyer. *Let the passive-aggressive comments begin.* "Where should I put this casserole?"

I was in fact finished decorating. I just don't have her generation's taste for clutter.

Dylan appeared at the end of the entry hallway holding Bella, who he'd just been scrubbing cranberry sauce from her face. I had to admit, he'd done a good job. There was no trace of red or pink on her cheeks.

"Ma! You made it!" Dylan floated down the hall, kissing his mom on the cheek. He took the casserole in one hand and leaned to pass off Bella. "Trade ya."

"Hi, sweet girl!" Carla cooed. Bella stiffened, regarding Carla like she was an alien. The spitting image of me, and somehow always portraying my internal spirit as well, Bella was my girl. Greyson was pure Dylan, down to the occasional Pittsburghese phrase he learned off his dad: a "yinz" for you guys here, an "n'at" at the end of a phrase there. Alice was very much her own person, but even my parents laughed at how much Bella acted like me. My parents, who were out enjoying a nice wine country Thanksgiving with my brother in Temecula, while I was stuck in Columbus being the perfect, obedient hockey wife.

Get it together, Jeanine. Stop being so negative.

Phil and Dylan greeted each other and the casserole was passed to me. No problem, as I was ready to retreat into the kitchen anyway.

I took a steeling sip of my wine in the kitchen, leaning my hand on the counter and hanging my head.

You can do this, Jeanine. It's your in-laws. They made your husband, who you love. Phil loves you. Carla will be gone in a few hours. You'll get your post-gathering cigarette.

Yes, I know cigarettes are bad for you, but it's my one act of rebellion. I only smoked when Dylan's family pissed me off. And I guess that one time after Dylan was just so dismissive of my emotions. But that's it. And his family doesn't come around much and we don't fight that much either.

Who's to say whether that's healthy or unhealthy?

"Do you have anything to drink?" Carla interrupted my reverie.

"Oh, yeah," Dylan said. "J, can you get her some of that syrah from your family's place?"

"Of course," I said, reaching for one of the wine glasses I'd already set out. I'd been up since six working through the final details: triple-checking my oven schedule, setting out the placings, and leaving as little room for Carla to critique me as possible. Careful not to splash a single drop of red wine on my white blouse, I poured Carla the promised glass.

"ISN'T Greyson's hair getting a little too long? He'll get confused for a girl with hair like that," Carla said, peering into the living room where the kids, mercifully, were playing somewhat peacefully.

"Ma, it's just the hockey flow," Dylan said. "I've had long hair too."

"Yours was never like that. I bet you get it all the time, don't you, Jeanine?"

"I haven't had a problem with Greyson being misgendered," I said with as even a tone as I could muster, cutting into my perfectly moist and plump turkey. Who had I become that I prided myself on perfect turkeys and lovely white blouses? Twenty-seven-year-old me wouldn't recognize me now.

"He's going to get made fun of," Carla went on, and I gently tipped my neck to crack it. "You've got plenty of time, Jeanine. Can't you just take him after school someday?"

"I'll consider that. Thanks for the tip." I forced a smile and Dylan's hand landed on my knee under the table. Was he stifling me? Urging me to keep my mouth shut? My remark seemed innocent on the surface, but I was meeting Carla's passive-aggressive nature.

"What do you do all day, Jeanine?" Carla asked, sitting back and swirling her wine glass.

Dylan stopped chewing, his arm going stiff where he still held my knee. "Would anyone like more turkey?"

"Would love some," Phil cut in, lifting his plate. "Great gravy, kiddo. Dylan's got him a hell of a chef."

"Well, he should. He's busy all the time earning a living so she can sit back and relax. He's given her everything. Least she can do is keep up the house and keep him fed."

I was shaking, my jaw quivering from clamping it shut so hard. My tongue pressed into the back of my teeth. My mother-in-law was launching one of her classic arguments against me, though this time was more overt than usual.

"Mom," Dylan warned. "That's no way to talk about Jeanine."

"What, Dylan? I worked full-time and never missed a practice or game for you. Your hair was always cut. Your clothes were always clean. I just did it. All Jeanine has to do is drop the kids off at school and pick them up at three. She can afford all the help in the world, and she still can't manage to get her kids' hair cut."

Heat rushed to my neck, my eyes fixed on my plate. It wasn't just that she was trying to break me—it was that some of what she said was true. I was embarrassed. In theory, I should have been able to do it all. But every day felt like the tallest, steepest mountain to climb, even if I knew it was just a routine day. I couldn't handle things I could have easily handled in California. I was having more episodes of staring into space, of sitting in the floor and fixating on a crumb, but not being able to move to pick it up.

She was right. I should have been able to get Greyson's hair cut.

But that wasn't the point. This was my house, and she was being so critical of my every move without knowing just how much of a miracle it was that I got everyone where they needed to be on time and the clothes washed and folded and the house cleaned.

My fork dropped on the bone china with a clatter, my hands trembling.

"I am right. Here." I seethed, drawing a shaky breath. "Do not talk about me like I can't hear you."

"Kids, why don't you go turn on the movie?" Dylan said. "I got it all set up. Grey just has to hit play."

"Do we need to clean our plates?" Alice asked.

"No, sweetie, I've got it," I squeaked out. "Go enjoy the movie."

"Tell Mommy thank you for dinner," Phil said, keeping the peace. Hell, his own son didn't encourage the kids to do that. "We'll call you back for dessert."

With a few mutters of "thank you," the kids took off for the living room.

Dylan sucked in a breath. "Mom, I appreciated you being there for me, but we have three kids. It's a little different."

"Three kids *she* wanted, and now she can't handle them."

"Carla," Phil objected, drawing the line for once.

"I wanted all of our children," Dylan snapped. "*We* wanted them. All of them."

It was a simple statement, one that stood up for our little family. But it brought back a pain I hadn't felt in years.

"Excuse me," I whispered, wiping my lips on my napkin and backing away from the table.

I didn't even feel like going to the bathroom, or my bedroom. I wanted the garage. I could leave through the garage, putting this whole scene behind me.

But no matter where I went, nothing could shake the memories Carla had just unearthed, not only criticizing me but purposely provoking me.

Dylan's voice boomed on the other side of the door, cut by Carla's interjections.

I appreciated that he was actually standing up for us for once, but I just wanted him. I wanted Dylan to skip the arguments with her and just throw her out. I wanted him to stop making excuses for her, to stop rationalizing her behavior when it was anything but rational. I wanted her gone from our lives, never to return. I wanted to stop having to endure gatherings where she inevitably made at least a small remark to cut me down.

The voices calmed, and Dylan didn't come for me.

I was alone in this.

I reached for a bowl on top of our garage refrigerator, retrieving my precious little secret: a pack of cigarettes I kept for emergencies like these.

THIRTEEN
JEANINE
NOW | NOVEMBER

I STEELED myself before entering the house again. I'd had a smoke and a long sit on our side porch, sorting out my feelings about the fight.

Dylan still hadn't come out to check on me when he damn well knew where I was. I had to be the rational one even though I wanted to act like a bucking bronco in my kitchen. Smash all the china. Stomp our wine glasses into shards. Throw them at every adult Sorrento in sight, Dylan included.

"There she is," Dylan cooed when I came back in. I put on a weak excuse for a smile. "Get some fresh air?"

My lips fell open. Whose side was he on? I wasn't dignifying that with a response. I'd only feel better when Carla wasn't a constant thorn in my side.

"Should I get out the pies?" I offered.

"I'll get 'em, kiddo," Phil said, rising as he gestured for me to sit.

Dylan rested his arm across the back of my chair. "I took care of the dishes," he whispered before kissing my temple.

I flexed a weak smile. "Thanks."

"Ma has something she wants to say to you," Dylan said, tucking me closer to him so our chairs touched.

"Oh," I grimaced.

Carla simpered. "Dylan thinks I've been too hard on you, and I'd like to make it up to you—"

"That won't be necessary—" I started.

"So, I'm coming back next Wednesday to help you while Dylan's on his long road stand," Carla said. "I'll stay the whole week."

My lips popped open again, completely dumbfounded.

"Isn't that nice, J?" Dylan asked, all foreign and official. "You'll be able to get a break during the busy holiday season."

Phil walked in with four pies stacked carefully across his arms like a waiter. "Still got it, like I never left the old Campanello's Eatery! You know, Jeanine, you weren't the only one who used to wait tables."

Oh, Phil. God bless Phil. He was trying so hard not to make this day a complete disaster.

"You've mentioned!" I said, brightening. I couldn't help but humor Phil. He, like Dylan, just wanted everybody to get along.

"Dad, you've told her so many times," Dylan laughed.

Phil was non-plussed, setting the pies on the table. "Who wants pumpkin? Kids! I'm gonna eat all the whipped cream if you don't get in here!"

And with the thunder of feet from the living room, the topic of Carla's visit was settled. I was firmly steamrolled by my mother-in-law.

"WELL, there was a little bump in the road, but I think it was a hit overall," Dylan said, sweeping me into a hug after we closed the door behind his parents. "I'm really sorry about Ma."

Not sorry enough.

"She knows how to bring up the trauma," I said.

"Well, she is still a bitch. That didn't change," he said, kissing my forehead. "But at least when she comes back, she's going to help."

"Dyl." I cocked my head, trying to get him to see reason. Historically, when had I ever gotten along with his mother? And under no fault of my own. She was hell-bent on attacking me, and for what? Would she have rather married her son?

"Babe, she needs to make it up to you. I think some of the problem is she's never taken the time to get to know you. And I know if she knows you, she'll love you. There's a lot to love about you." He tilted my chin up, planting a soft kiss on my lips. I barely kissed him back.

Oh my god, it was worse than I thought. It wasn't even Carla's idea to come visit; Dylan had concocted this messed-up version of a parent trap to force us to get along.

"And you could use the help, right? You said December was going to be hectic with a lot of events at the school."

This is one of those moments when I questioned whether I was just losing it. Yes, I had told Dylan things would be hectic, and to his credit, he listened. But the takeaway was so far off the mark that I wondered how I could have led him to believe that this was a good idea.

I rolled my lips, leaning a hip against the doorframe. "Dylan, I don't know if I can spend a week with your mother. *Alone.*"

Dylan put out a hand. "J, come on. It's my mom. She'll love you once she knows you."

"She's had eight years to get to know me, Dylan! This isn't someone I have to pass a puck to. This is a woman who has been outwardly hostile to me since we started dating. A leopard doesn't change its spots."

He leaned into the wall too, brushing my hair behind my ear. "She wants to see her grandkids around Christmas."

"*My* parents won't be here," I tried.

Dylan sighed. "Jeannie, they got the last seven Christmases. Ma has the time to come help you. You won't let her?"

"She won't be help, Dylan."

"Will she not be help, or will you not let her help?"

I ground my teeth, my eyes shooting daggers. "What is that supposed to mean?" I spat.

He pinched the bridge of his nose. "It's no secret that you like to run the show, J. You know that."

Oh, this was fresh.

"I *like* to run the show? I *have* to run the show, Dylan. I don't see anyone else around here volunteering to hold these three kids together. I don't see anyone else folding laundry, or making breakfasts, or sticking to nap schedules, or packing lunches."

Dylan threw a frustrated hand out. "Babe, we're not hurting for money. Hire help if you need help!"

"Oh, good, another task for Jeanine to do," I said, pushing off the wall and strutting toward the kitchen. "I need help, so I have to take the time to research help, vet the people, make sure they're not going to steal from us or touch our kids—"

He followed behind me. "Then let my mom come, Jeannie! I am trying to help you here! This is what I can give you."

I whirled on my heel, speaking directly to his face. "You certainly don't care to give anything else. All you do is take, Dylan."

He pressed a hand to the side of his face, massaging his temple. "Let's take a beat." He snorted a breath and put his hands on my shoulders, his thumbs rubbing over my blouse. "I know I've asked a lot of you, baby. We have to give this move time."

My lower lip trembled and I sucked in a choppy breath. "It's hard."

He nodded, pressing his lips together. "I know, baby. I'm sorry." He pulled me close, palming my head against his chest. "But you have to stick it out, Jeanine. I know you can."

My jaw tensed again. "This, Dylan. You always do this."

"Do what?" he asked, affronted.

I backed out of his embrace. "You dismiss the things I say. 'Just keep your head up, Jeannie.' 'Just wait, you'll make friends.' Just just just."

"Well, it does take time! We've only been here a few months! And in that time, you've had someone from L.A., but that Halloween party was the first time you met up with her!"

"Oh, so it's my fault that I'm miserable. Here we go again. Jeanine's the crazy one."

"Jeannie, stop," Dylan said, going stern. He took a deep breath and rubbed the back of his neck. "I have never once said you're the crazy one, or that you're crazy. We've been through a lot. Okay? We just have to give this move time. I'm having Mom come help you because it's what I can do. I wish I could do more to fix it, baby. I do."

My eyes burned as I stiffened in his grip. There he was

again, dismissing me and offering solutions when all I wanted was for him to truly hear and see me.

Of course, I wanted help, but I wanted it from him. He was the person who I decided to take this journey with. The person I said yes to and accepted this life. But I knew doing so much of it on my own was a condition of choosing this life.

It's so complicated. I loved Dylan and couldn't see my life with anyone else. But loving Dylan meant being a hockey wife. It meant raising our kids somewhat alone during very challenging years. And when we were in L.A., it was bearable. I had a community. I had more than people gossiping about me at parties.

Would my life be better if I'd chosen a different path? Easier? What if I'd kept dating scummy bartenders and musicians I met while waiting tables? Scummy was fun for a while, but Dylan, and the baby we chose to keep, brought a sense of stability I needed at that point in my life.

Now that stability tasted pretty sour. I was the picture of stability, and all I wanted was to be that wild girl who used to hide among the vines and dream of making it big.

I'd been silent for a while.

"You're always wanting some alone time, J. Mom could give you that."

At a price.

Soft kisses met the side of my face. He was trying.

"You wanna . . . meet up in the kitchen?" he asked, waggling his eyebrows.

I sighed and gave him my tired smile. "I think I might need a minute. I'm exhausted."

I walked into the kitchen and observed everything around me. I say 'everything' because there were still piles of dishes and food not put away. What, exactly, had Dylan done to clean up?

Like he read my mind, Dylan walked up behind me, wrapping his arms around my waist. "I started the dishwasher," he said, pinching my earlobe between his teeth.

Wow. Get this guy a trophy. He can load a dishwasher.

I stretched my face into a smile and nodded. "Yeah. Thanks for that. Your mom couldn't help?"

"She was a guest," Dyl shrugged.

I stepped away from him and got out containers to put food away. "Is she going to be a guest when she comes next week, or is she actually going to help?"

He chuckled. "She'd help."

"She'd help on her own terms. She'd do the jobs *she* likes to do. And she'd do it her way."

Dylan shrugged. "Well, maybe her way would help." I glared at him, and he laughed again. "Heard, got it."

I got to work shoving stuffing into a container, satisfied with the way it compacted under my spoon. Since Dylan just stood there watching me, I fantasized about squishing his hopeful little face under the spoon.

"Can't that wait?" he asked. "I owe you a little bit of pampering after all that."

I rubbed my fingertips on my temples. "I can't exactly enjoy getting pampered if this kitchen, that you were supposed to clean, is still filthy."

"I did clean it," he said.

If I did half the job every time, our home would be a pigsty, but what did I know?

"You're right. Go sit. You have a game tomorrow."

"No, wait," Dylan said, acting like he was doing me some huge favor. "I guess it is a bigger job than I expected. You go sit. Get ready for the week."

Yes, checking the calendar each night was part of my post-kitchen-cleanup routine, but I was really not looking forward to it here. I was staring down the barrel of December. The most wonderful time of the year!

Or at least, that's how they tell you you're supposed to feel.

But this was my first Christmas out of California—the first without my parents and my friends.

And not like a California Christmas was perfect. I still had Dylan gone most of December when I was out there, putting together all the Christmas fun for the kids on my own.

This December in Ohio would be no different. The calendar was packed with pancakes with Santa, silly sock days, food drives, volunteering at school, wives' charity day, and, on top of that, shopping for presents—all while trying to find a sliver of sanity in the chaos.

Maybe Dylan was right. Maybe getting a little help during a busy time would lift my fog, even if it came from a less-than-savory source.

JEANNIE

Hey I ended up being able to pick up your dry cleaning

Thanks babe

(blowing kiss emoji)

WE DESPERATELY NEEDED to win this game. Since my arrival in Ohio, we were now the second worst team in the league. It was an improvement over worst, I guess.

We should have been a good team, since we had a lot of talented guys. The problem was that our talented guys had their individual ideas of what winning looked like.

Most of our wingers seemed to think winning was them individually succeeding. My definition is actually scoring goals and recording wins. All their attempts to show off for personal gain were futile anyway. Hence, we were in the second-to-last spot in the league.

Not to mention our main goalie, Royce, was apparently a sieve.

If I sound critical, it's because I was beyond frustrated. The culture shock was much worse than I anticipated. It had been a really long time since I played with a team that wasn't cohesive.

Then I had to remind myself that sitting back and accepting the status quo wouldn't get us anywhere. I had to be a part of the change. I couldn't just expect everyone to get better.

But just one problem: Dottie was leading the "let's all hate Sorrento" charge, reducing my chances of swaying everyone to embrace a more positive culture.

This game, we were at least playing someone evenly matched. Montreal was the lowest-ranked team. But that also meant they had a decent chance with us.

Not on my watch.

When Dottie went in for a shift, I pulled in Leroy and Korowski. "Remember what we did Sunday?"

They both nodded.

"We're doing that as soon as we get the puck. Got it?"

Dottie's line was headed back after doing (surprise) jackshit again, so we went over the wall. I moved in quick, trying to swipe the puck before Montreal crossed the blue line. Unfortunately, I was unsuccessful and our d-men were fighting to keep Montreal out of our goal.

After a glove save, we had a faceoff in front of our goal. This was our shot. Leroy won the puck and passed it to me. I pushed it Korowski as he entered the neutral zone. I caught up to him as we crossed the blue line, and it was time to hit our play.

We passed it around like we were a clock, three, twelve, nine, twelve. Leroy clapped it from the line and we netted a goal.

Fucking finally.

As it turns out, cellies feel better when you're up against a lot.

IT WAS A HARD-FOUGHT GAME, and even though we won, it left me physically and emotionally drained. All I wanted was Jeanine—my person. I craved her touch, her scent, and the way her soft hair fell against my neck when she hugged me. She seemed to be pulling away, and all I wanted was to connect with her.

I found her in the middle of the living room floor when I got home, taking the vacuum apart. She looked upset already, so it wasn't the time to ask for the comfort I needed.

I crouched to give her a kiss. "Hi, baby. What's this?"

"Girl hair," she sighed. "These are the moments I debate shaving their cute little heads."

I settled next to her, taking the knife from her hands and kissing her temple.

"You don't have to," she said.

"No, let me do it, babe. This falls under my umbrella. Knife stuff."

"I'm used to doing it," she mumbled. "You need to eat. Your snack is on the counter."

"If you insist." I grinned. "You're the best."

She gave me a small smile, but it didn't seem genuine. That's how it had been lately with Jeannie. She was physically there just as much as always, but it was like she was under-water and I was on land. I could see her, but couldn't quite reach her, her image distorted by the moving water.

All I wanted was to pull her out. Well, I really wanted it to not be happening at all. The longer it went on, the more I was afraid to bring up the growing space between us.

And I was even more afraid that she might be falling into one of her depressive episodes again. Everything was so tentative that I was scared to bring it up.

"So we actually won this one," I said as I dug into the bento box she'd set out for me. All healthy stuff: nuts, fruit, beef jerky bits, and my favorite chocolate-covered banana chips.

"I saw," she said, pausing to look up at me. "Nice assist."

Then she cursed under her breath and hissed. She rushed past me for the kitchen sink.

"You cut yourself, babe?"

She nodded, grabbing a paper towel and holding it to the cut. Red poked through the fabric quickly.

"You should have let me take over," I said, my chair scraping as I got up to look at her hand.

"I can do it myself," she huffed.

"Clearly not," I said, now at her side and gently lifting her hand across my palm. "Let me see."

"I said I can do it myself, Dylan," she bit out. "Do you have a problem with the way I do things?"

I put my hands up. "Baby, I'm just trying to help." I shook my head, frustration building in me. "You know how much you make things harder on yourself? You could have help, but you won't let anyone else take the wheel. We could hire help. I'm not even fucking captain anymore, J. You should have less to do than you did in L.A."

I knew it was stupid the second it slipped from my mouth.

She bobbed her head, grinding her teeth. "You're right. There are no responsibilities as your wife unless you're the captain."

"I just meant you probably have less here than you did in California. We're not there anymore, so it should be easier."

"I'm fucking aware of that!" she snapped. Her eyes

slammed shut, her jaw tensing. "I should be able to do it, Dylan. I just can't."

I softened my tone, tipping my head to look at her. "Jeanine, I'm okay if you need to hire help."

Her mouth popped back open, as did her eyes. "But there's no excuse. You know what sucked the most about your mom criticizing me? She was right. I'm weak! You take me out of my perfect little terrarium of a life and I wither up in the sun."

"Baby, I'm trying to fix it," I pleaded, running my hands through my hair and clawing my fingers down my face. "Can you just take what I'm giving you?"

Her face fell. "What you're *giving* me?" Her breathing picked up, and heat pulsed off her body. "What exactly do you think you're giving me, Dylan?"

Jeanine never got like this. I was taken aback. Was she losing too much blood? "Will you just let me see your hand?"

"No. Answer my question."

I pinched the bridge of my nose. "I'm giving you a chance to lighten the load, J."

"It's not lightening the load. Your mother helping would make things worse. You know why? Because all she ever does is pick and pick and tell me how good I have it and how much better my life would be if I just raised my kids the way she raised you."

I shrugged. "She means well. I think some time together could be good for you."

Jeanine shook her head and stomped into the first-floor powder room. When I followed she had her right hand over her head as she tried to use her left to get the first aid kit from under the sink.

"Baby, let me help." I bent and pulled the kit out while she jerked back. She was really furious. "Will you—just say whatever it is."

"You don't want to know," she mumbled.

"I'm pretty fucking sure I do," I shot back.

"I should have known better," she said.

"What is that supposed to mean, Jeanine?"

She snapped to look at me directly. "You want to know? Fine. Your mom raised you to be helpless. To let her do everything for you so you could thrive. Have you ever cleaned a bathroom a day in your life, Dylan? Would it kill you to completely clean the kitchen when you say you're cleaning the kitchen? Do you know how clean the house is when you're gone? You're like a grown baby sometimes. And then I'm always the bad guy with the kids while you get to be the hero fun guy. You've always had someone else make it so *you* could shine, Dylan. First, it was your mom, and now it's me. You've always had someone else build a life for you."

It felt like a slap to the face. Hearing her defend my mom was shocking enough, but it made me realize that, with those two main women in my life, I was always trying to make them happy. I weighed every choice I made against whether my mom would be proud and Jeannie would be happy.

"What the fuck, Jeanine. You . . . you chose me over your career. I've given you everything. All I do is try to make you happy."

Her whole body went rigid, closing her eyes again and sucking in a shaky breath. "You're right. You've given me a big house to take care of, and mandatory friends who don't actually help with anything much less *like* me, and a life of isolation with very little end in sight."

I shook my head. "Jeanine, I can't make Ohio become California. You need to find a way to be happy here. We have to make this work."

"Or what?" she said. "I have to make it work or what? What's the alternative to this move not working out?"

My breath stuttered. "Jeannie, are you saying what I think you're saying?"

Her eyes flooded and her lower lip trembled.

I didn't mean to, but I raised my voice. "You mean that after all I've done for you, after continually trying to do anything and everything to make you happy, you're just going to bail on me when shit gets hard? You'd leave me over this? You want a fucking divorce because of *this*?"

Her eyes narrowed into slits, and her jaw clamped before her voice went low. "You sound just like her."

Her. My mother.

Jeanine watched me for some sort of rebuttal, but she knew she had me. Holding one hand over her head, she grabbed the first aid kit and went back to the kitchen.

I paused for a moment, sitting on the toilet lid and staring at my toes. From the kitchen, I heard her suck in a weepy breath, and I couldn't leave her alone like that.

I found her at the sink with her hand upturned, watching the cut bleed and dabbing at it with the paper towel. Her head hung as her tears accelerated.

I stepped to her side and put my arm around her. "I don't want to split up, baby. We're just going through a rough patch."

She sobbed harder, lifting her hand to cover her mouth. I bent to look at her hand.

"Baby. Let me. Please?"

A tear dripped onto the countertop as she nodded. There was no way she was actually mad at me. She was mad at the situation. We got along. We were united against every obstacle. Me and J against the world.

But now it felt like J against me, and that felt pretty lonely.

We'd come through it, though. We'd certainly been through worse.

Her cut was pretty deep. "Baby, I think I'm gonna have to glue it. Unless you want to go to the E.R. by yourself."

She finally cracked a little, snorting a laugh. "Glue me up, hockey boy."

I kissed the tip of her nose before I wrapped her hand back up. "See? I am good for some things. You would never have glued your hand if I hadn't come along."

I held her shoulders, and her blue doll eyes met mine. "It's going to be okay, J. I've always got you. Yeah?"

"Yeah," she managed through her tears.

I left to get the skin glue from my hockey bag, rattling around in there since I had a split at my eyebrow a month back. I came back and flicked on the lights under the counter so I could see better. "Let's get you fixed up, baby."

"You're being sweet now," she said, chancing a glance at me.

"I don't like fighting with you."

"Me either," she said, watching me finish up with her hand. I worked quietly, just the sound of our breath and her occasional giggle at my sloppy work.

"You ready for bed, baby? I feel like we both need some rest."

"Yeah." She went to stand but I threw her over my shoulder.

"No way you can walk with a hand like that," I teased as she giggled and swatted at my ass behind my back.

FIFTEEN

DYLAN

THEN

I MARRIED my scrappy cocktail waitress over All-Star weekend at her family's winery in Temecula. We gathered as many friends and family members as could come on short notice. My parents were not thrilled with the quick wedding, Ma encouraging me to give it a year before rushing into things. But even if Jeanine hadn't been pregnant, I'd have married her that fast. I didn't care. I was in love.

Our little secret remained just that during the wedding weekend, even though Jeannie had a tiny bump on our big day. Only I could really tell, but by then, I knew her body as well as my own.

She was the love of my life, the one I'd been waiting for. Yes, everything moved fast, but they say when you know, you know.

I remember the lace of her dress under my fingers as we had our first dance, the glow in her turquoise eyes, and her smile that gave me no doubt about forever.

I remember how invincible I felt, having my perfect partner

and our perfect little nugget under my hands, a heart we made out of our two.

I remember thinking how easy this was, and how lucky I got.

I remember the perfection of the day, and how nothing could get us down. The way she smiled when we sealed our commitment with a kiss. Tiny white flowers in her hair. A smear of chocolate cake on the waist of her dress where I grabbed her after I delicately fed her a piece of our wedding cake. Sitting with my arm around her while Chappy toasted us, reminiscing on the night we met.

I remember stroking her tiny belly as we lay awake in the little guest house her parents put us up in, admiring how her body was changing from the life we created.

I remember everything.

NOTHING CAN PREPARE you for it. You know it's a possibility, but you hope it won't happen to you.

We flew to Cabo the morning after the wedding, staying at a resort for a couple of days before I had to be back at work. That first night, she complained about her stomach hurting, but she thought it was just the juice she had at dinner. We kept it easy the next day, taking a short walk in the jungle and mostly lounging by the pool or in our room.

We had dinner that night at one of the resort's restaurants. As we sat, she got a strange expression and excused herself to the bathroom. My phone rang in my pocket, and I almost ignored it since we were on vacation. But it was her name on the screen, and her panicked voice on the other end.

I burst into the women's room and found her shaking on the

toilet, holding a piece of stained toilet paper. "I'm sure it's okay, baby," I tried. "Let's just go back to the room."

"I don't think it's okay, Dyl."

The next twenty-four hours were a nightmare. She saw a doctor in Cabo, who couldn't do an ultrasound, but said it was probably nothing. She didn't have any more bleeding, but she was still having pain.

The horror, the cruel juxtaposition of being in paradise when a worst-case scenario is happening to you. We couldn't get a flight out until late the next morning.

I held her hand in the cold doctor's office where we got the bad news. Our baby had no heartbeat, and at some point over the next few days or weeks, her womb would empty.

"It's no one's fault. These things happen. Many couples go on to have healthy children."

I remember watching a single tear flow into her ear as she lay back on the exam table, trying to hold it together while the ultrasound screen gave us the answer we did not want.

I remember the way Jeanine wailed, how it struck me as otherworldly and animalistic.

I remember thinking there couldn't be a grief deeper than this, and it's one you mostly have to endure alone.

I remember how foolish I felt for thinking we were invincible, because no one is.

I remember how my back ached from holding her so tight across the console of the car.

"I don't want another baby," she sobbed in the car. "I wanted this one."

She blamed herself, the wedding, flying, the honeymoon, her auditioning while she was pregnant. She said we shouldn't have had sex. She came up with all sorts of terrible theories as to why everything was her fault.

I listened to every single way she blamed herself and tried to talk her out of it. It wasn't her fault. It was no one's fault.

Coach gave me the next week off, and I became my new wife's nurse. By the middle of the week, she still hadn't passed the pregnancy, so she decided to have a procedure to remove the remnants. She couldn't endure any more torture than she already had.

She was heartbroken.

I was heartbroken.

We had so much hope and joy tied up in that little beating heart, and it had been taken from us, a light snuffed out.

I took to giving her washcloth baths because I couldn't get her out of bed. I fed her anything she would eat. I spent a fortune on delivery service just to be able to stay by her side.

I was afraid to leave her alone. She hadn't said anything like she'd hurt herself, but I was afraid she was thinking it. I'd never traveled a road as dark as the one we were on. My bright, scrappy Jeanine had faded into a withering flower.

In the middle of one of those hellish nights, I woke to her crying so hard it shook the bed. I kissed her forehead and snuggled her close to me. "What if it never stops hurting?" she asked.

"I know this pain feels permanent right now, Jeannie. It won't be, and I don't know when it'll stop hurting. But I'll sit with you in it as long as you need to."

"I'm afraid to move on. I'm afraid if I'm not sad, it didn't mean anything. We changed everything for this. We're married now."

"I wanted to marry you, Jeanine. No matter what. And now that we're married, I hope you know that I'm in this with you. I'm not going anywhere. I will always have your back, Jeanine. It's you and me against the world."

There came a point where I had to leave her side. I couldn't stay out of play any longer, having already been off three weeks when you counted the All-Star break. I was terrified, afraid I'd come home to no wife. I called Chappy because his girlfriend Rachel was a nurse. I wondered if she'd have any advice to get Jeanine through this awful time.

Her determined voice piped in from the background. "What time does he leave for the airport tomorrow?"

Rachel showed up at our door the next morning with a stuffed-full bag and open arms. She stayed with her all four days we were gone. She got Jeanine up and made her take walks by the ocean. She let her cry. She found her a grief support group. She got her to eat more than I ever could—she cited nurse magic on that one. She even slept in my spot so Jeannie was never alone.

She hardly knew Jeannie, but she stepped right in. Whether it was trauma bonding or simply meant to be, they became best friends from that moment on.

When I came home, Jeanine was different. Her skin was no longer sallow, her hair was clean, and she'd changed our sheets. Our apartment smelled like fresh air. For the first time since her stomach started hurting at the resort, Jeanine smiled.

I hugged her close, peppering her neck with kisses. She held my cheeks and gave me a big smooch. "I'm still sad, but I think I'm going to make it."

"We're going to make it." I pulled her tight again and whispered in her ear, "You and me against the world, baby."

"You and me."

> Do you ever want to stab Chappy

> FBI agent, there's no way I could kill my giant husband

RACHEL

> Of course, all the time

> Also FBI agent, see above. Same for me.

DYLAN WOKE me with a soft touch to my arm, dragging his fingertips over my skin. My eyes blinked open to find him lying on his side, watching me.

"Morning, beautiful."

"Morning."

"How's the hand?"

I held it up. "Throbbing, but not bleeding."

He flexed his biceps. "I used all my big strength to glue you back together."

I gave a hoarse laugh. "Watch out, ladies. He's good with glue."

Dylan put a sloppy kiss on the side of my neck. "I'm good at some other things too."

He braced himself on top of me, putting more kisses down my chest. "Is this your way of saying sorry?" I asked.

"Hmm?" He was using his teeth to peel up my satin nightgown. Teasing licks and nibbles covered my belly. I arched up, his mouth inching closer to where I wanted him. He tugged at the sides of my underwear until I lifted my bottom to help him remove them. "That's my girl."

A series of torturous kisses went all around my pussy, blood rushing to the area. "Please, Dyl."

He chuckled, then his hands hooked on the tops of my thighs and his tongue sank into me. I rolled my hips, taking in the pleasure of his intricate work. I moaned as he drew a long suck, followed by flicking with his tongue.

"Quiet now," Dylan hummed, climbing out of the sheets with a face covered in me. He kissed me deeply, my taste coating his tongue and lips. I moaned again as I reached into his pajama pants, finding him rock hard and pulsing. I pulled on him, once, twice, swiping my thumb over the precum on the head. I drew my thumb up to my lips and sucked it into my mouth with a salacious smile.

"Dirty girl," Dylan whispered, lowering himself to kiss me.

Then, there was a blood-curdling scream.

"GREY HAS A KNIFE!"

Dylan leapt off me and yanked up his pants. I was already halfway to the door while he was trying to tuck his erection away.

"I'll go!" he yelled after me.

"You have a fucking boner!" I hissed back at him as I tugged my nightgown down and hit the top of the stairs. I thundered down them, jumping the last three stairs and almost eating shit at the bottom.

I turned the corner and made it to the living room, taking in the scene.

Bella was covered in vacuum dust, while Greyson stood amidst couch fluff, knife in hand.

"Drop it," Dylan barked, skidding up behind me.

"Don't yell at him," I said.

"Don't fight," Bella cried, launching into actual tears.

"You left the knife out!" Dylan argued.

"*We* left the knife out," I said. "I cut my hand and we didn't clean up what I was working on."

"Mommy, don't fight with Daddy!" Bella went on. For how little Dylan and I fought, and almost never in front of the kids, I was surprised by Bella's absolute meltdown over this. How Alice slept through all this, I'm not sure.

Dylan turned to Greyson. "Why did you cut the couch, Grey?"

Greyson's eyes misted. "I don't know."

I got on my knees and held out my hand. "It's okay, buddy. Can I take the knife?"

Greyson placed it in my palm. I handed it back to Dylan and wrapped my little boy up. "It's alright, Grey. I'm glad you and Bella are okay. It's our fault for leaving a knife out, but next time, either leave it alone or put it in the kitchen, okay?"

Dylan rubbed his hands through his hair looking at the sea of couch fluff. "Buddy, come on," he whined.

"Enough, Dylan," I said quietly.

"He needs to know what he did was wrong!" Dylan argued.

"He knows," I stated.

"Bella, how'd you even get out of bed?" Dylan asked.

"Climbed."

"You fucking kidding me?" Dylan breathed.

"Daddy, this is not the hockey rink," I gritted out. "Please go upstairs and let me talk to our kids. Come back when you're calm."

"Don't do that," he said darkly.

All my muscles tensed. "Excuse me?"

"Don't treat me like I'm one of the kids. I'm their father."

"Then be a father, and treat them with respect," I bit.

He shook his head and headed for the back door. "Then you treat me with respect, dammit!"

My jaw tightened and I swallowed hard.

"I'm going outside." He didn't quite slam the door, but he didn't not slam the door, either. Bella's tears turned into full-on wails.

"Come here, baby," I said, fully sitting on the floor and pulling both kids into my lap. "Daddy's okay. He doesn't always know what to do with his feelings."

"You know what to do with your feelings, Mommy," Bella said.

"Not always," I said. "Not always."

The door to the back deck flung open again, cold air pouring inside. "Jeanine, can I speak to you outside?"

My stomach sank and my heart pounded. Dylan never acted like this with me. For the first time ever in our marriage, I was scared.

"Now, Jeanine. I've got practice soon."

I kissed Bella's head and pulled Greyson close to me. "Go get yourself some cereal, okay? I'll be right back."

My guts turned to liquid as I stepped out into the cold November morning. I wrapped my arms around myself, shivering as my skin prickled, the cold composite deck material chilling the soles of my feet. Dylan seemed unaffected by the frigid temperature, his eyes full of rage.

"You almost got our kids hurt," he bit out, low.

"I'm sorry. You were there too, though. It was an accid—"

"It would have been picked up if you hadn't picked a fight with me. You're telling me I'm not acting right, and you're the one not taking responsibility for what you did."

"It was an accident, Dylan," I insisted.

"An accident that wouldn't have happened if you'd just try a little." He shook his head, looking out into the yard. "Do you know how fucking hard I'm working, J? Huh? I get shit at work, then I come home and get more shit from you. You treat me like I'm one of the kids, and I'm supposed to be your fucking partner."

My mouth flapped. "I'm sorry work's not going well. Do you . . . want to talk about it?"

"Oh, now you ask about me," he said, shaking his head. "All you care about is yourself, and your little problems. You're probably only asking so you can point out how right you are, that we just need to go back to California and magically, it'll all be better. Meanwhile, I'm out here busting my ass and all you can do is complain about how I ruined your life."

My shivers became trembling, adrenaline igniting my insides and the cold chilling my outside. "Dylan, I never said—"

He turned to me, gritting his teeth and curling his lips, like he was trying to hold something especially vicious back. "You said I built this life for me, but what you won't see is that I built it for *you*, Jeanine."

"You built it for *you*," I protested. "We wouldn't be here if it wasn't for you—"

He breathed hard, little clouds emanating from his lips and nose as he got closer to my face. "Enough!" He cut me off. "I'm only going to tell you this one time, Jeanine. Stop fucking whining and step up. Get it the fuck together. Be my fucking wife, or you might be getting that trip back to California you've been wanting so bad."

My lip wobbled. He'd never spoken to me like this. It was

the meanest he'd ever been, a side I'd never seen except when he'd bark at his teammates on the ice. What happened to my sweet, compassionate Dylan? Was that a thinly veiled threat to throw me out?

He walked past me back into the house, and before the door shut, I heard him speaking in soft, apologetic tones to Greyson.

At least he was nice to the kids. But what the hell had happened between the two of us?

THINGS WERE tense with Dylan when he left for practice. I crammed as much stuffing as I could back into the couch cushion and duct-taped it in place. Then I flipped the cushion over to hide the damaged side.

"See?" I told Greyson. "Good as new."

"I'm sorry, Mom," he said, his head down. "I made you and Dad fight."

"No, you didn't, honey. And all mommies and daddies fight sometimes. It's okay."

In my head, I knew the *how* and *why* Dylan and I fought was more of the problem.

All I did all day was try to climb out of my hole, and I thought I was mostly successful.

I was giving it my best.

But my best wasn't good enough for Dylan.

It didn't matter that I was the default parent. I was the one who looked up child psychologist-approved methods of discipline. I was the one who worked to break the cycles our parents instilled in us. I was the one who demonstrated as much healthy coping as I could.

Meanwhile, I was not really coping.

Dylan didn't even like me anymore. He implied I should leave, that I was the one on thin ice.

How much longer could I live like this? The December to-dos piled up. The family calendar in the kitchen had something listed every single day. Zero of those things were for me. Everything was either for Dylan, the kids, or the team. And on Wednesday, Dylan's mom would be coming to stay for a week.

Could I tolerate a week of Dylan's worst traits on steroids? Should I? I was cracking. Crumbling. Holding it together just enough to fool the kids.

But when I started to cry at a traffic light on the way to take the kids to their Saturday morning skate and hockey practice, I knew something had to change.

Maybe Dylan was right. Maybe I just needed to push through it and get back in the game. Stop whining. Stop making excuses.

Step up to my life.

But the thought alone overwhelmed me.

The walls were closing in. I was miserable in my own life.

> You ever just stare at the wall after you get the kids in bed

RACHEL

> Sure, all the time

WHENEVER I'M CONFRONTED with a bout of depression, I sometimes go through this brief high where I think I'll just muscle through it. With sheer willpower, I could fix my life.

So after the kids went to bed on Saturday, I put on a full face of makeup, a bra that did ridiculous things to my breasts, and my sexiest panties. I slipped a silky nightgown over top in case one of the kids woke up and saw me, but the effect was still there. I cleaned up everything from the day, packed up Dylan's after-game snacks, and poured myself a glass of wine.

I put Dylan's game on and watched, trying to fall back in love with my husband after he'd been a complete shit that morning. Not only was he a shit, but I was bracing myself for his evil mother's arrival.

The Rusties were actually up 2-1, and it was the third period. They might actually take home a win again. And there was Dyl, sending the puck across the blue line, where his d-man sank it in the back of the net.

As they celebrated, I realized it had been a long time since I'd sent Dyl a sexy picture during a game. Maybe getting that part of our relationship in gear again would help lift my fog. Dylan and I are both physical people, so sex isn't just sex for us. It's how we stay close to each other. Aside from postpartum times and when I was recovering from the miscarriage, we had sex pretty regularly.

But quantity doesn't always mean quality.

It's safe to say our sex was pretty run-of-the-mill. Half the time, it was part of his pre-game routine. We kissed, sure, and he went down on me to get me wet enough to take him. I'm sure if I'd asked him to eat me out until I came, he'd have done it. But he wouldn't think about me needing that most of the time.

And I can't say we'd never used sex to Band-Aid a bigger problem. Take that very morning for example. He knew I was right and he was wrong and that he'd fucked up arguing with me the night before. So you know what a good Band-Aid is? Waking your wife up and going down on her.

Is good, try-hard sex once a month enough? I couldn't remember the last time before Halloween. We'd been in a collective funk since Dyl found out we had to move to Ohio.

Was I not trying enough? Did I need to surprise Dyl more? Here I was waiting for him to serve me, but when was the last time I blew him, off the cuff?

Dylan was right. I needed to be less selfish and think of *his* needs. I could do that.

A nagging voice in my head told me he wasn't attracted to me anymore, because he usually drilled me from the back or spooned me. He said missionary wore him out before games, and I just chose to believe him. What if he really didn't want to look at me?

But that couldn't be true. Even in my scummiest sweats, he told me I was pretty. And not to be full of myself, but I'm a fucking hottie and I know it. I wouldn't have been cast so much in L.A. if I weren't.

Time to put those good looks to use.

With my tits almost under my chin, I sent Dylan a selfie, making sure my blue eyes glowed and I looked like I was ready for fun.

If he could use sex as a Band-Aid, so could I.

Nice assist

I could assist you with something

As the wine hit my system, I decided to take it a bit farther. I went upstairs into our closet, getting out my box of toys. I pulled out the big purple dildo and took it back downstairs into the good lighting. I put it in my mouth, the silicone taste hitting my tongue. I got it good and slippery wet, making sure the dildo had a nice, sloppy sheen to it. Again, with a look all doe-eyed and innocent, I snapped another picture like his vantage point if I was on my knees for him.

Getting it wet

I hit send with a self-satisfied smile, thinking how crazy it would make him to think I was using the dildo without him. Maybe he'd text me back and egg me on. There was one really hot time where he directed me and just watched me play with my toys. I didn't let him touch himself until I came, and he was a human fountain by the time I did.

Ah, the good ol' days. Time to bring them back. That would cheer me up.

The game ended with a win, and after the goalie hugs, the Rusties filed into the locker room.

I waited five, ten, then twenty minutes. At first, it was sexy, knowing maybe he opened it and had to hide it quickly. Maybe he'd have to relieve himself in the bathroom at work. Maybe he didn't respond because he was racing home to me.

But twenty minutes became an hour. Was he okay? I was starting to get sleepy. And anxious.

I idly scrolled Instagram, clicking on a friends-only story from Lindberg. The time stamp was from a few minutes before, with Dylan laughing at a bar, a pretty brunette watching him laugh in the picture.

Oh, hell no.

I held my thumb over the picture for maybe three straight minutes without moving, analyzing every detail.

It's not that I thought Dylan would cheat, because I didn't. But the idea of him even having a wandering eye while I was begging for attention was sickening.

Here I was, sitting all dolled up and waiting to be some kind of sex kitten goddess for my husband, and he was out shooting the shit with the boys. And some brunette who was just his type.

Not responding to my texts. He couldn't have stepped into the bathroom to text me back? I felt like a complete fool.

I knew I was being ridiculous. I was only begging for attention because I needed reassurance that Dyl and I were okay.

The impulsive side of me wanted to drive down there just like I was and hit him with my stupid dildo. Another demon on the same side wanted me to message Lindberg and tell him to send Dylan home right fucking now.

Maybe Dylan wasn't attracted to me. Maybe all those little voices were right.

Deciding not to let my insecurities show by messaging his teammate, I gave up at the hour-and-a-half mark. I dumped the rest of my wine glass in the sink, not even bothering to wash it down so it wouldn't stain.

I tried not to look in the mirror as I took my makeup off, too ashamed to face myself.

I tried, and for what? I wasn't Dylan's top priority. The guys were. Hockey was. After all, hockey was why I was even sitting alone in cold-ass Columbus when I could have been in temperate California.

The tears that hit me when I was driving the kids to the rink came back.

Dylan had chosen hockey over my happiness. Why was I trying to impress him? I wasn't a stick, a puck, and some ice.

I finally looked in the mirror, my dark eye makeup smeared, giving me the look of a sad drag queen.

I scrubbed my face until the rest of my makeup was gone, perhaps scrubbing a little too hard. I tossed off my bra and underwear as I went to get in bed, leaving on the nightie.

What had I become? I went from being a triple-threat performer to being a mom of three in a Midwestern town in the blink of an eye. With a husband who chose the boys over me.

I don't think I fell asleep, just lying there in a stupor until I heard the garage door. I didn't move. Dylan's footsteps stopped in the kitchen, probably scarfing down the snack I left out for him. Maybe ten minutes later, our bedroom door creaked open.

"Where's my naughty girl?"

He crawled on the bed over me, caging me in from above.

"Hey," was the best I could give him.

"I got some really hot texts from this slutty girl I know," he cooed, planting a kiss under my jaw.

"I'm tired, Dyl," I lied. Well, maybe not a full lie. I was tired, but it was tired of his shit.

He chuckled. "Too much wine? Or did you dick yourself too hard with that dildo?"

I gave up the most pathetic excuse for a sympathy laugh. "Neither."

Dylan's breath caught. "Ohhhh-kay?"

I clamped my teeth together so hard my jaw almost cramped.

"You going to tell me what's going on, Jeannie?"

I drew a breath through my nose. "You didn't text me back."

He scoffed, like he was begging me to see reason. "J, I was with the guys. I had to slap my hand over my phone to keep them from seeing you looking so hot."

"Oh, well, at least you think I'm hot," I said, "but not hot enough to come home to."

"Jeannie, I'm here right now," he said, acting like I was being irrational. "The guys asked if I'd go out and I went."

"And you couldn't tell me that? And then you come home expecting me to still be waiting for you?"

He crawled off me, sitting on the edge of the bed and facing away from me. He rubbed his forehead with his fingertips. "Should I have asked your permission to go out tonight? You already did bedtime and everything. It's not like you needed help."

"Maybe, Dylan, I just wanted you to want me enough that you couldn't wait to get with me. That you'd step away from your friends for a fucking minute to play a sexy game with me. We've fought twice in the last few days. Maybe I wanted to know things were okay."

He threw out an exasperated hand. "We're fine, Jeannie. You don't need to show me your tits for us to be okay."

My eyes brimmed with tears and I turned to face away from him. This was so embarrassing. Instead of appreciating my efforts, he flipped them back in my face. "Come on, J. Are you crying?"

"I just want to go to sleep."

Dylan heaved a sigh. "Jeanine, you looked hot. I was excited to see you, but I also need to fit in better with the team."

"It's fine. I get it." My voice was a little too bright.

He put his hand on my upturned hip. "I love you, J." He paused like he was going to say more, but didn't, giving my hip a playful wiggle. "I'm going to get ready for bed."

Dylan wriggled into bed behind me a bit later, skating his hand under my nightie. "You took the bra off," he hummed.

Well, when you ignore me, the lingerie goes away.

Kisses pressed into my neck and shoulders, and he lowered the strap of my nightie, dipping his hand to move around my breast.

You need to leave.

The thought came out of nowhere, but I knew it was true. Dylan wasn't getting it. I was trying to show him what I needed, but until I was gone, the message wouldn't be received.

The thought of leaving turned me on. Dylan groveling after me. Dylan cleaning up his act. Dylan *hearing* me. Dylan begging for me back.

I rolled my hips to put my ass against his erection to his delighted groan. Tonight, I would give him my body. I'd make it so good, going all in. Blow him. Ride him reverse cowgirl so he could stare at my ass. Make my ass and tits bounce. Cup his balls when he came.

Tonight, I'd give him something to miss. Something to make him feel sorry. Something to show him that I'm not selfish. Something that wouldn't let him take me for granted again.

And tomorrow, I'd make my plans to go.

EIGHTEEN
DYLAN
THEN

JEANINE WASN'T WAITING for me after my game. I thought for sure she'd come to it, though I never was able to spot her in the crowd. I shot her a text, making sure she wasn't in the bathroom or something.

> U here or u go 2 bed?

JEANNIE
> I'm home

> U ok?

She didn't respond. Something was off. I got scared. I said a quick bye to Chappy and speedwalked to the parking garage.

I called Jeannie from the car and she didn't answer. Shit shit shit shit.

It was a few weeks after the miscarriage. Jeannie was seeing friends and getting out. She went back to her dance class, one of which she came home from crying. Like, bawling hysterically. I couldn't do anything but hold her. She said she couldn't talk about it.

I got it out of her a little later. She wouldn't say it directly, probably trying to spare my feelings. But what she said made sense: she didn't just lose the baby. She gave up a great theater role for the baby and me. And she didn't feel the same going back as she did before we got married.

My worst fears were coming true. Was she done with me? Or my very worst fear: had she hurt herself? I had these flash panics where I'd be the one to find her, and it'd be too late.

The night before this game, I'd broken the news about the miscarriage to my parents. Dad responded in an appropriate way, with a *gosh, I'm sorry, kiddo. How's little Jeannie?* Ma, however, thought this was excellent news and meant I could leave my, and this is a direct quote, "slutty Hooters waitress girlfriend and get the marriage annulled." She also added that the loss must be something from Jeanine's side of the family because she had a healthy pregnancy with me.

Needless to say, I was horrified, appalled, and absolutely heartbroken that she'd talk about Jeannie like that.

Luckily, Jeannie was in our bedroom asleep, saying she didn't really feel like telling anyone else. The thought that she could have overheard what Ma said was nauseating.

It rattled me. How could my mom say that about Jeanine? About the child we wanted so badly but lost?

And what if Jeannie heard her?

Mom went on. Now the wedding made sense, because it was just a shotgun wedding. That was part of the reason we didn't tell anyone she was pregnant. I really did want to marry her that soon, regardless of whether we were having a baby. I didn't want people making assumptions about the nature of our relationship.

Jeannie's mom had quoted some famous movie and said, "When you realize you want to spend the rest of your life with somebody, you want the rest of your life to start as soon as possible."

That phrase perfectly captured how I felt. Jeannie was the end game. Why not start right away?

All those thoughts swam through my mind as I raced home to J. When I got home, I called out for her, throwing my suit jacket over the back of the couch and checking every room until I found her with an open suitcase on our bed. Her back was to me, meticulously folding a t-shirt and putting it in the bag.

"Jeannie?"

She peeked over her shoulder and gave me a weak smile.

"Where are you going?"

"Home. To my parents."

I bobbed my head, stepping to her side to run a hand down her back. She stiffened under my touch. "Yeah. Okay. It'll probably be good to get some support from them. Would you rather go when I'm away for the next road stand, though?"

She pursed her lips and stared at her hands working to fold another shirt. "I need to go now."

"Sure, yeah. I get it. Do what you need to do, babe." I put my arm around her shoulders and kissed her cheek.

She closed her eyes and drew a shaky breath. "I might not come back, Dylan."

I couldn't breathe. This was all a bad dream, right? "You're . . . leaving?"

She didn't say anything, staring into the suitcase and running her fingers under her lower lashes.

"It's just not working out, Dylan."

My mouth gaped and I had to consciously shut it so I could swallow. "Jeannie, we said forever. Till death do us part. All that stuff—I meant every word." I paused, watching her. Her face didn't change. "I know you're grieving, and I am too—"

"She wanted you to leave me and you didn't argue with her."

Fuck. How much had she heard? Did she hear the awful insults too?

"Jeannie, what she said was so out of line—"

"Then why didn't you defend me?" she seethed, finally turning to face me with wild eyes. "Defend us?"

I squeezed my eyes shut, my nose stinging.

"You'll fight a man in pads and skates for saying something stupid about one of your teammates, but you won't argue with your mother when she says you should dump," she broke into sobs, "the woman you married, the mother of your child that we *lost*—"

She trembled and I pulled her into me. Her tears and some saliva from crying so hard soaked the chest of my dress shirt. "Jeanine. Baby. Please."

"Why didn't you?" she wailed, shoving me back.

"It shocked me. It hurt me too, hearing her talk about you like that. It crushed me. She was a monster."

"And yet you talked to her. You didn't defend me. You didn't hang up on her. You didn't cut her out of your life."

She wasn't wrong. I could have done more. "She's my mom, J. I . . . I don't know how to talk back like that. If it had been my dad, I could have done it. But my mom's just—I don't know how to describe it."

She nodded, seemingly sobering. "Well, while you figure it out, I'm going to Temecula."

"Jeannie, no, please stay. I love you so fucking much. I don't know what the hell is wrong with my mother, but you are number one. Okay? You are my top priority."

"Am I? Then why didn't you do something?"

I rubbed my forehead. "I should have. I'm sorry, Jeanine. You're everything." I gripped her upper arms in my hands.

"We're going through so much right now. I'll never be able to feel exactly what you're feeling, but I've been trying to put myself in your shoes. But a lot of the time, Jeannie, I feel hopeless. I can't take your pain away. I can't kiss it better. All I can do is be here and keep loving you."

Her eyes were on the floor between us. "I don't want you to do anything you don't want to do."

"Jeannie, look at me." I cradled her chin in my hand. Her red-rimmed blue eyes met mine. "This is the hardest thing I've ever been through, and there's still no place I'd rather be. We will get through this. I don't know if it will ever stop hurting, but we're going to figure out how to live. Our baby will always be part of us, Jeanine. They will always be our first."

I stopped talking as she sobbed into my hand. I pulled her to me as tightly as I could, hoping that if I held her a little closer, I could squeeze her pain out of her. When her crying slowed, I kissed her forehead.

"Your mom's still a bitch," she said with a wet laugh.

I laughed too. "Yeah. She is."

"Who the hell does that?"

I held her back by the shoulders and shrugged. "This bitch I know."

Jeannie laughed, like belly laughed, for the first time since our wedding day. It was beautiful to see, and a relief.

"I know I don't deserve it, but will you give me a chance to love you? We're just getting started, Jeannie. We've got a good long life ahead of us if we give it a shot."

She rolled her lips between her teeth and nodded.

"So you'll stay?"

She smiled softly. "I'll stay."

Hey can u check the calendar to see if I can golf tomorrow morning after training? Weather's supposed to be nice

"HEY, GUYS!"

Guy Stelle was on the other end of the FaceTime call, while our captain Colton Jones and I leaned in. It was a couple of hours before our Tuesday game.

"You're still handsome, you son of a bitch," Colt said, shaking his head. "How's Kitty?"

"Ah, she's good. It's so fun that both of you are there together! Two of my friends combin—"

"PICKLES!" came a shout from the background. Ben Miknevicius, or Mikey, popped his head into the frame. "We miss ya, Picksy. How are ya?"

I laughed. "Believe it or not, I miss you dumbasses."

I'd played with Mikey and Stelle in L.A., and Colton had been on their team in college. The hockey world was forever small.

"Colt, my boy," Mikey added. "Please give Pickles so much shit. Fight with him a lot so he doesn't miss me too bad."

I rolled my eyes. "You want me to replace you?"

Mikey tucked his hands up like he was going to swoon. "Dylan, how could you? I'm irreplaceable."

"I figured as much," I said.

"Mikey, how's Maddie?"

"She's the most beautiful girl in the world," he cooed.

"Don't tell Jessie," Stelle cracked.

"Jessie's the most beautiful *woman*. Maddie's the most beautiful girl. Stop infantilizing my wife, Stelle," Mikey objected.

"That's a big word, Mike. Jessie must be getting through to you," came another voice, followed by a hyena laugh.

"I went to an Ivy League!" Mikey protested. "I'm smart!"

Guy tipped the camera up so I could see the source of the hyena laugh: L.A.'s goalie Nick Oberbeck. My best friend, Chapman Beatty, leaned into view too.

"Hey, Obi. Hey, Chappy," I said. "This is Colton. He's okay."

"Aww," Colton said, laying a kiss on my cheek and hugging my neck.

"Had a change of heart?" Jack Leroy crept up behind me, putting his face between mine and Colt's. "What's Jeanine think of that?"

"The more the merrier," Colton chuckled.

"You're still such a pill," Stelle laughed.

"Hey, Jackie baby," Mikey chimed in. "I miss you big, brother."

"Aw, we miss you too," Leroy said. "But hey, we'll see you soon, right? Next week?"

"Yep! You'd better not beat my ass on the ice or I'll give it right back," Mikey warned.

"Can't wait," Leroy said with a grin.

"Hey, figure out a way to bring Jeanine," Guy said, swinging the camera closer to himself as the chatter picked up in the background. "The girls miss her."

"Women," Mikey corrected.

I gave a wry smile, knowing how rough things were with Jeanine at the moment. "Maybe. She sure misses them."

The boys suddenly went silent and the camera was a closeup of Guy's chest hair. Then his mouth got close to the camera. "We're in trouble, gotta go, bye."

I didn't realize how badly I missed Los Angeles until I saw all my old friends at the same time. They were still living, laughing, and loving, and I was out here trying to make a new start. By force, not by choice.

But I had to keep my chin up. I zoned out so hard during the national anthem at the game that I didn't realize I was singing it super loud. Lindberg was stifling giggles before he jabbed me in the ribs.

"You gonna do the same for 'O, Canada?'" he asked.

My face reddened but I tried to recover. "Guess you'll have to find out."

Toronto was a middle-of-the-pack team. Good, not great. Might get a playoff spot in the spring, might not.

In short, we could beat them if we got our shit together enough.

When I came in from my first shift, I chatted with my line on the bench. They were trying Garner with Korowski instead of Leroy. "Why aren't you trying the thing? It worked in the last game."

Garner hardly regarded me.

"I'm speaking to you," I stated.

"Yeah, I hear you, old man."

I glared at him. "You want to win this game? Do the things

that actually score goals. What do I need to do to get you to run the play?"

"We get paid whether or not we win," he muttered.

My head was about to explode. This team was infuriating. "Is that seriously the fucking attitude around here? Are you hearing this shit, Coach?"

"Snitch," Dottie grumbled.

"You fucking kidding me?" I rose and threw off my gloves.

"Sorrento, Dottie, enough."

"No, this is bullshit. If you want to keep your job in this league, stop playing selfish and start getting us wins. You need help with something, you ask. You don't phone it in every game. That's a recipe for us to get worse, get injured, or get fired."

The fourth line came back in, so it was time for us to go out. And lo and behold, look who's running the play. And also, look who's scoring a goal. I got the assist, but hopefully this was enough to stop the shit attitude that plagued this team.

After the game, Coach called me into his office.

"How would you feel about adding an A to your jersey?"

"Sir? For real?" I asked. "Dottie will kill me. I'm honored, but you're putting a target on my back."

"They're pushing back on you, but they're hearing you. Keep it up and we'll have you taking the C from Jones. You might need to take him under your wing a bit, captain to captain. This place is falling apart, but if we keep pushing, we might actually get somewhere this year."

I hesitated. Of course, I'd love to take a leadership position again. It had always come naturally to me, but it could have a lot of consequences for a team already walking on eggshells.

"I'll think about it."

TWENTY
DYLAN
NOW | NOVEMBER

I GOT HOME from the game late, heading into the kitchen where I knew Jeannie would have left me out some snacks.

But what I found when I walked into the kitchen was an empty countertop and Jeannie sitting at the island.

"Oh," I said, assessing the no-snack situation. "Tired tonight, babe?"

Jeannie rolled her lips, her eyes going glassy.

"You don't have to get my snacks. I've got it. Were the kids good tonight?"

"Yeah, they were fine," she said quietly. I poked around in the fridge, unearthing a half-eaten container of grocery store sushi.

"Nice," I said, popping the top and turning to face her at the island. "So, Coach said they might give me an A soon."

"Oh," she said, her lips forming the weakest smile to even count as a smile.

A wave of panic came over me. Weak smiles never boded

well. I worked to chew and get the piece of sushi roll in my mouth to a manageable size so I could talk. "What's wrong, J?"

She sucked in a deep breath, pushing it out evenly. "Dylan," she said, her chest flushing, "I don't think I can do this anymore."

My chewing slowed as I realized I'd completely misread the room coming in. I swallowed quickly and gulped my electrolyte drink. "Jeannie. What?"

"I'm going to go spend some time with my family," she said, her eyes devoid of feeling, her voice robotic like she'd rehearsed this.

"J, I'm your family. The kids. We love you so much."

"Your mom will be here to watch the kids, so you shouldn't need to hire any help—"

"You're leaving?"

We'd been here before, but not for a long, long time. I called it "the old bag trick." She'd really only done it when I didn't defend her to my mom after she miscarried. Jeanine packed a bag and acted like she was leaving. I begged for her back and she stayed. I crawled in bed with her and made sure she knew how much I loved her. It was miserable, but we worked through it. We got back to me and J against the world and had been mostly harmonious since.

And I guess there was the time she dropped her depression medication dosage too quickly, and her brain decided to tell her that I hated her and thought she was "ugly and frivolous" (her words). It was much easier that time to talk her into staying. It was a simple matter of her brain's chemistry being off, not an issue we were having.

"Not . . . leaving, per se," she said, casting her eyes down. "Just taking a little break."

I planted my hands on the counter and hung my head. "How can I help? I know I haven't been as supportive as I could be lately. Do you need me to find you a new therapist? I know that's hard for you."

"Dylan, this isn't about therapy." She took a shaky inhale. "It's you."

My brow wrinkled and the space behind my nose stung like I'd just gotten popped in the face. "It's me? Just me? You're telling me you haven't been depressed since we moved here."

Her jaw feathered. "I might be depressed, but you can't deny your role in all this. And if you knew I was depressed, why didn't you say anything? Why did you steamroll me and pretend everything was fine? Do you even see me?"

I spread my thumb and forefinger across my brows. "Jeannie, baby, I see you. You work so hard with the kids and you always take such good care of me." I crossed to stand next to her barstool, almost tripping over her bag. I reached for her wrists. "Jeannie, you are so loved."

She set her jaw and grabbed her keys, putting her finger through the keyring and bunching the keys in her fist. Her eyes rose to mine slowly. "Then maybe you should show it."

"Baby, I do. I know what I've said to you lately has been bad, but I've been trying to make it up to you," I argued. "I ate your pussy the other day. Because I wanted to." I searched through my memories to find more examples showing I cared. "On Halloween, I did the Ghost Daddy thing."

Her brows knit. "Sex doesn't fix everything, Dylan. You can't just treat me like an afterthought and yell at me for accidents, then expect a few encounters fix patterns of behavior."

"Patterns? What patterns?"

She scoffed, crossing her arms. "How are you any different from your mom? When you yelled at me the other day, you said I was whiny. Or sorry, I believe it was *stop fucking whining*."

I rubbed the heel of my hand into my eye socket. "I never should have said that, Jeanine—"

"You believed it to be true, though. Doesn't really matter if you said it, does it? You think I'm just whining about life not being good right now. I'm doing my fucking best, Dylan, and it's not good enough for you."

"Jeanine—"

She held up a hand, rolling on, "You mentioned things were bad for you on the team, something you'd truly never brought up until that moment. When I showed interest in your problem, you flipped it back on me, saying I only whine about myself."

"I fucked up," I pleaded.

She flicked a look at her watch. "Dylan, I should get going to the airport. My flight leaves in three hours."

My eyes flooded, my lungs searching for air. Jeanine was actually going to leave me this time. "No. No. Jeannie. Please don't go. You . . . you can't."

"Why not? You wouldn't have anyone to take care of every little thing?" She stifled a cry. "You wouldn't have anyone to cook your mother Thanksgiving dinner, and host her, and entertain her, and keep my smile on when I'd really rather be with my family or with our friends? But no, I have to be here to put on the perfect daughter-in-law show for my husband's family," she said it with shocking vitriol, "when he doesn't even think of me as anything but the ass he taps and folds his laundry and makes his snacks. When he sees me struggling and ignores it until it goes away. Good news, I'm going away. My feelings won't be inconvenient for you anymore."

My mouth dropped open, heartbroken. "Jeannie, that's not how I feel at all. Do you even want to hear my side?"

"I just can't do it, Dylan," her voice wobbled, tears starting to drip down her cheeks. "I can't keep putting on the show and doing everything when I wish you'd just fucking see me for once. Carrying on like I don't wish you'd acknowledge how this move has been the worst thing that's ever happened to us."

"J, I know it's been hard—"

"Wow. Now you admit it," she threw out a hand. "Too little too late."

I grasped for another reason for her to stay and give me a chance to make it right. "The kids' Christmas stuff at school, Jeannie. You're just going to let them down?"

Rage bloomed in her eyes, her voice lowering to a snarl. "You don't get to do that. I am the one who does *everything*. Every skinned knee. Every bully problem. Every parent-teacher conference. Every practice. With no breaks. No days off."

"J, my mom's coming to help. You'll get time to yourself."

"You know how I feel about that, Dylan," she snapped. "And if you don't, then things are a lot worse than I thought."

I put my hands on her shoulders. "J, look at me."

Her upper lip curled, nostrils flaring. "You've lost the right to tell me what to do. I'm not going to be your perfect little pristine hockey wife, the receptacle for your babies, the one who vacuums and dresses everyone and runs around just doing the things to put on this life you built for *you*. You tried to flip it back on me, Dylan, but you have to know that you started this fire, and only you can put it out."

My breath caught. I lowered to my knees, putting my hands on top of her thighs where she sat back on the stool. "Jeannie. J. I'll do anything. I-I don't think you understand. I never wanted this. I'll do whatever you want. Whatever. You're everything, Jeanine. Just please, please don't go."

"No," she said, turning her chin up and raising her eyebrows. "Hockey is everything. You couldn't just retire like any sensible person would have so we could stay in L.A."

"Jeannie, you agreed that was the best choice!"

"The best choice *if* you had to keep playing hockey! You chose what was best for you, not what was best for our family."

"The kids are fine," I said. "You mean I just didn't do what you wanted. You wanted to stay in L.A. because it's what you liked."

She flapped her hands to the side. "Maybe. Maybe being essentially a single parent to three kids is harder than I thought it would be. Maybe living without the friends I've spent the better part of a decade cultivating is harder than I anticipated. And you miss your friends too. You just won't admit it. Because negative feelings are inconvenient. Because I'm not allowed to have a bad feeling about anything. Just gotta pull myself up by the old bootstraps!"

She made a yanking motion from her waist with a sarcastic smile.

"I need to go."

"Jeannie. Please. I love you."

"And I love you too. But I can't do another day of this. I deserve better than being ignored, and then being yelled at to 'get it together' when I call you out on your bullshit."

The panic swelled inside me, my breath shuddering as my wife stood to go. "Jeannie, I know I fucked up, baby. Please give me a chance to make it better."

She sucked in another breath, setting her shoulders. "Goodbye, Dylan."

She took her bag from her feet and walked to the garage. She was really leaving.

When the garage door opened, I walked out there. I stood in Jeanine's headlights until she backed out and closed the door behind her. I sat with the smell of the garage floor and tires and the feeling that I couldn't stop fucking up.

TWENTY-ONE
JEANINE
NOW | DECEMBER

I snapped

(picture of boarding pass)

RACHEL
Are you coming to see me?!

Not exactly

Temecula

Are you alright honey?

TBD

BIRDS CHIRPING, the dense mountain air. The quilt on my childhood bed.

I was home.

The journey had been neither short nor easy. I threw up in the airplane bathroom, guilt, shame, and rock-bottom sadness surging through me.

I didn't know how else to show Dylan I was serious. He

wouldn't listen unless I showed him what life was like without me.

And it's not like I totally left him in the lurch. His mom was arriving the next day to help with the kids. She was just going to be helping more than anyone anticipated.

I didn't allow myself to think what Carla thought of my sudden departure.

Mom and Dad knew I was coming. All I sent them was my flight information. If I'd been planning a trip for the whole family, they know I'd have called them a bunch of times to coordinate. Surely, they could read between the lines on my solo ticket.

And they had. Dad was waiting at the airport with a little sign with my name on it. They had my room made up with fresh sheets and my favorite copy of The Secret Garden on the nightstand. Knowing they had my back no matter what and would always be looking out for me meant everything.

In my sloppiest pajama pants from high school and my messiest hair, I padded out to the kitchen for some coffee.

"You get some sleep, sweetie?" Dad asked as I came into the kitchen. I stood next to his chair and he hugged me to him. I reached for a coffee mug, then noticed he'd already put my favorite one on the counter.

"Yeah, Dad. You working today?"

"Barrel day," he said.

"Got anything I can do in the tasting room?"

"Oh, we can put you to work, Jeannie. I think your mom's packing the Christmas shipments. She could always use a hand."

"What can Mom do?" Mom breezed into the kitchen, already dressed and primped with what I consider her winery uniform: a black long-sleeve, a zip-up vest with Wendlock

Wineries on it, and nice jeans with her hair in a French twist. Preppy, chic, and practical.

"Jeannie was just asking how she can help around here," Dad said.

I slumped into a chair at the table, pulling a section of the newspaper toward me. Mom slid into the seat across from me.

"We'll take you however we can get you, J, but you know what we're going to ask," Mom said, tilting her head down at me.

Once a child, always a child. I figure I probably gave my kids that look all the time. "Why am I here?"

"Bingo," Dad said.

I sucked in some air as my eyes watered. "Dyl and I are . . . I'm mad at Dyl. I just needed to come home."

Mom nodded, patting my hand on the table. "Sorry, honey."

She was waiting for me to say more. "He just—this move has been harder than we thought it was going to be. I really would have rather stayed in L.A. Moving took away my whole world. And then, he expects me to just adapt. But I can't. I don't have anyone in Ohio."

"We miss you out here," Dad mumbled.

"Joe!" Mom chided him.

"What? We do. I do, at least," he argued.

"Well, I do too, but we don't need her feeling worse than she already does," Mom said, turning to me. "You're always welcome here, Jeanine."

I sniffed and lifted my gaze. "I get it now, Mom. All the stuff about unseen labor."

Dad flattened his lips and Mom spoke up. "It's true that women pick up the slack a lot. But I have to give your dad credit. The years with young kids are just hard. You can both be working at it nonstop from sun up to sun down and still feel like the other person didn't do as much as you did. And some days that's true, but it's not a race, Jeannie. You and Dylan are in it together."

"He's gone all the time, Mom. He doesn't know what it's like and he just tells me to keep my chin up. I just want him to see how hard it is. He doesn't know and I'm not sure he cares. I have my role to fill and he has his."

Mom took a sip of her coffee and twisted her lips. "It wasn't all sunshine and roses when you kids were little. Right, Dad?"

Dad gave me a morose smile. "Nope. It's just hard, kiddo. Hoping a little time in the country will fix you up and get you back in there."

"I hope so too."

I WAS COVERED in cardboard shavings and kept sneezing from the little particles getting into my nose. Mom and I had been packing holiday shipments for the wine club since the morning, making paninis in the office for a quick lunch.

"Andy'll be by soon to pick these up," Mom said, referring to my little brother's best friend who worked for the winery.

Who was also my ex.

I nodded, a pit developing in my stomach. "Oh, yeah. Haven't seen him since the summer. How's his mom?"

"Not great," Mom sighed. "He's good to her, though. It's worked out well that he could stay here."

"Definitely. I get it." I had to clamp my jaw together to keep from crying. I wished I could stay. My mom didn't have a long-term illness like Andy's did, but I still wished I could be in Temecula, or at least Los Angeles, long-term.

Mom, who misses nothing, eyed me sidelong. "We're fine,

Jeannie. You don't need to be here with us. Your kids need you."

I sniffled and turned my back, spending a little too long picking up the next set of bottles. I'd only been gone a day and some change, but I kept seeing Alice, Grey, and Bella in my head. Was I right to leave them alone with Carla and Dylan? Even if they were physically and emotionally fine in their care, I had set a terrible example by leaving when things got tough. My babies needed me, and I walked away.

Maybe Dylan was right. Maybe I was selfish.

The door to the office creaked open.

"There she is." Andy's bright voice filled the space. I flipped my head up to find him already halfway across the room to me. He opened his arms. "How are ya, G9?"

I laughed off the name he and my brother called me, a play on how my name is spelled, and I reached up to hug him. "Hey, Andy."

"You didn't get any taller," he said, stooping to wrap his arms under mine.

"And you didn't get any shorter," I teased, ruffling his hair.

"How long do we have ya for? You gonna stick around this time? Dyl keep the kids?"

My mom made a very obvious slicing motion across her throat and he held up his hands.

"Well, it's good to see you either way."

"How's your mom?" I asked, changing the subject.

His smile was wry. "Hangin' in there. I'm sure she'd love to see you."

I nodded, not really sure how much longer I'd be hiding from my life at the winery. I was also unsure how much time I wanted to spend with Andy. I'd seen him the summer before when the whole family came up for a week at Gammy and Gampa's, but that was with Dyl and the kids. There was something unsettling about potentially spending time alone with him. "Tell her I said hey, at least."

He looked over the stack of boxes Mom and I had piled up. "These ready to go?"

"Yep," Mom said. "Oh, Andy, why don't you and your mom come for dinner tonight? Then we can all have a chance to catch up."

Maybe it's because Andy was my little brother's best friend, but to me, he still had this boyish smile. A permanent haze of sandy hair covered his cheeks and neck, making his deep blue eyes pop out of his tan face. He was long and lean, but not quite as lanky as he was when we were kids.

In short, he could easily be cast as the humble hometown hero in any given Hallmark movie.

He flashed that wholesome Hallmark grin at my mom, his whole face brightening. "Yeah, that'd be great. I'll let her know."

They droned on about something pertaining to the tasting room that most certainly didn't involve me, so I zoned out. Eventually, Andy loaded the shipments onto a dolly and was gone.

When the door closed behind him, I turned to Mom. "What are you doing?"

"What?" she asked, bringing a hand to her chest to indicate her obvious innocence.

"Don't think I don't see you," I said. "I'm still with Dylan and I'm hoping to stay that way."

"I know, sweetheart," she said as she put down a tape gun. "Sometimes you just need to see what the other choice was so you can know how good you have it." She got a little smirk. "Besides, never hurts to have an old flame make you feel pretty when you're going through something."

Andy and I had the most minimal of history. He always

carried a torch for me, and for one summer in college, I gave in. I was a junior and he was a freshman. We kissed one very late night at a party of kids home for the summer.

I woke up in his arms in the twin bed at his mom's house. Clearly, she knew what we'd gotten up to, because she placed a tray with two plates of pancakes with coffee outside his room.

Mortifying. She was already trying to fill the role of meddling mother-in-law. I slammed the cup of coffee and left out their side door.

But then I couldn't get away from him. We were both seasonal workers at my family's winery, and he just . . . kept being his charming self. He convinced me to give him a real chance. So, we dated. We had a sweet month or so where we stole kisses among the vines and went through a lot of boxes of condoms.

He told me he loved me in the middle of the night in the bed of his shitty truck. I didn't reciprocate, and I think it killed him.

Right when I was about to end things, he showed up at my door in tears. "Mom's sick."

Well, I couldn't dump him then. I loved his mom, and everyone in town would have known how cruel I was if I dumped him right when he found out his mom would be disabled for the rest of her life, needing frequent attention and care.

So I was there for Andy. I boosted him up. I listened to him while he vented and grappled with how his future might now hinge on caring for his mom.

It was a future I'd decided wasn't for me long before we found out his mom was sick. I had to do what was best for me, and not what was best for my little brother's best friend who was obsessed with me.

When I went back to school in the fall, I told him we

weren't meant for the long haul. I always felt guilty about it, but at the time, I was still trying to become an actor. You can't do that while you're tethered to the boy back home.

He begged, told me he'd wait for me. I told him not to. He pleaded, told me I was cruel if I left him when he was going through such a hard time. I did feel a pang of guilt about it, mostly because that life could have potentially been a happy one.

But I was holding out for something more than accepting someone's love. I wanted to engage in love with someone, to feel that push and pull of care and desire.

I held out for something bigger, and I found it in Dylan.

Still, the "what if" hung over me in dark times.

These were dark times.

I would have had a mother-in-law who liked me. My kids would grow up running in the vineyard like I did, with their grandparents a few farms down. It would have been a nice quiet life.

But it wasn't the life I chose. My kids were Dyl's kids, not Andy's.

"Mom, there's a name for that and I think it's 'emotional affair,'" I moaned. "Andy doesn't need to be caught up in my family drama. Dylan and I are going to work it out."

I just didn't know how yet.

I know you probably don't want to hear from me, but I miss you and I'm sorry

"SHE LEFT?" Even Jack Leroy knew to keep his voice down, having been to the end of the road with marital trouble.

Except his ended in divorce, and I was absolutely not letting that happen. But then again, he remarried in a short period of time, so what did I know?

I loaded up my squat bar. "Yep. Went to stay with her parents in Temecula."

He narrowed his eyes. "Weren't you the one who talked about her pulling 'the old bag trick,' like she packs a bag when she's mad at you?"

I winced. "Yep."

"And you didn't convince her to stay?"

"Not this time."

"Must be serious," Lindberg said. "How often does she pack a bag?"

"Not very often," I groaned, putting a clip on the end of my weights. I peeked at the clock on the wall. "I better hurry up. I'm going to have to get Bella from school soon."

"You aren't going to run after her?" Leroy asked.

"I want to. I'd already be there if my mom was here and we didn't have games."

"What's this?" Coach cut in.

"Mrs. Pickles ran off to California. She wants Dylly to run after her," Lindberg said so very casually, like it wasn't the most excruciating detail of my life. I made such a point to not talk shit about Jeanine to the guys, because it didn't seem fair to her. I knew she probably vented about me to Rachel, but I just felt like I'd be betraying her if I said something bad about her. It's not like she acted irrationally all the time. Jeanine was an excellent partner and she deserved the benefit of the doubt from me.

But I was struggling with all of it. Did Jeanine know how much of a rock she was for me? I needed her so badly, but I didn't have the balls to ask for her. What do you do when both partners are going through a tough time and neither of you has the capacity to be there for the other?

Coach's brow scrunched. "This is the first I'm hearing of this? Why aren't you out there going after her?"

I sighed. "I didn't think I could just skip out on the team? And besides, I don't have anyone to help with childcare until my mom gets here tonight."

Coach shrugged. "We're going to California. Just get a car when we get there and go get her."

"Seriously?"

He nodded. "Be back by the L.A. game?"

"Uh, yeah. Sure."

Coach patted my shoulder. "Wives aren't a guarantee. You gotta keep that shit locked up."

Lindberg eyed me as Coach walked away. "You still look like you're about to yak."

I flipped a weak smile. "I have no clue how to win her back."

Jack stood by, stretching his hip flexor and looking pensive. "Let her peg you."

"What?" Three voices chimed in at once.

"Yeah, it gives her the power," Jack shrugged. "She can fuck out all that rage."

"This is simple," our goalie, Harlan Royce, called from across the room. How the hell did he even hear us? The music wasn't exactly quiet and I wasn't broadcasting my situation. He sauntered over from where he'd been running a sled. "You cook?"

"No, no, back to the pegging thing—" Lindberg said, eyeing Jack.

"Wait," Colton put his hands out. "Who's Peggy?"

I shrugged, rolling my eyes and responding to Royce. "I mean, I can cook."

He popped his gum. "Cook for her. What's she like?"

My eyes searched the floor, like it somehow knew what foods my wife liked to eat better than I did.

Jack did that super awkward stretch of putting your foot on a bench and thrusting your hips forward. A little too close to my face. "Where did you take her on dates?"

That sparked a memory. "Oh! She loved this one fish taco truck."

"Perfect. Send me their menu and I'll make you a grocery list for how to make it," Royce said, sifting his sweaty hair through his fingers. "I'm thinking a citrus salsa with a tomato vinegar reduction for a sauce."

I shook my head to clear it, fighting the headache building between my brows. "I—yeah, I'm not that good. I can do the basics. Pancakes. Eggs. Stuff with instructions on it. Jeannie spoils me."

"There's your problem right there," Jack grumbled. I glared at him.

"Fine, I'll send you a list of premade stuff you can put together," Royce offered. "But I'll give you a step-by-step on how to level it up."

"*Easy* step-by-step, please. And one meal is not going to fix our problems, anyway," I groaned. "It needs to be more than that."

"You ever use Pinterest? The one where you can arrange links all pretty," Colton chimed in. "Chicks love that shit. I used to have a girlfriend who kept all these mood boards with aesthetics. But they have good date ideas."

"Or you can just . . . search the internet?" Lindberg said.

"No, but the app gives you the keys to women's brains. They put on there what they like. I bet Jeanine even has one of her own you could creep on," Colt said. "Trust me. It's curated to a woman's taste."

"Curated," Leroy teased. "Look at the single guy giving advice."

"Says the guy who said to let her peg him," Royce cut in.

"Yeah, I give advice because I have to work ten times harder to get people to stick around," Colton shot back, throwing out a hand. "You guys think once you have wives, you've got it in the bag. You've got to *date* your wife."

"Tell us more, oh wise one," Korowski cut in. Colton flipped him the middle finger.

"No, really. I think he's right. I stopped romancing J a long time ago. I've just been going through the motions," I sighed. "So you're saying dinner and all these dates too?"

"Figure out what makes her feel good and give that to her," Colton said. "Don't make it harder than it is."

"Probably oral. They all like oral," Leroy said.

"Or a citrus slaw—" Royce cut in.

"No citrus slaw!" I barked. "And not just sex." I rubbed the back of my neck.

"She's your wife. You know her best, right?" Colton said. "You'll work it out."

"Look, I really gotta go get my daughter," I said, reracking my weights and checking the weight room clock. A hand met my shoulder.

"So, hey." Jack coughed into his fist and looked beyond me somewhere. "I know we weren't best friends in L.A. or anything, but . . . if you need somebody. . ."

I smirked. Jack Leroy was the opposite of in touch with his emotions, or at least that's how it seemed. He'd been slowly shifting since his divorce.

"Yeah. Thanks, man."

"And maybe Mara and Jeanine could meet up or something, I don't know. Or Mara could see if Jeanine's okay. I don't know what women do," he said.

"I think she'd like that."

Jack nodded and sniffed before strutting off to the other side of the weight room. "'Kay."

"DADDY, the cart's really full. Did you look at Mommy's list?"

Bella pronounced "list" like "nist," having trouble with L sounds. She made them either a "y" or a "n". Yellow, for example, was "yeyyow." I briefly closed my eyes and sucked in a breath.

And no, I did not have a "nist" for the Target trip. I was doing exactly what Jeanine would do on a Wednesday: pick Bella up, go to Target, then go home to make shape mac and cheese for lunch. "What list?"

"She puts a list for the store at her desk."

"Fuck," I whispered.

"Daddy, this isn't the hockey rink," Bella said with a devious look that looked exactly like her mom's. And that phrase is exactly what Jeannie says when I cuss in front of the kids.

I sighed. "You're right, Bells. It's not. Do you remember what she gets?"

Bella got a little smirk. "I think sometimes she gets treats."

I stifled a laugh. "Treats, huh?"

"And toys."

This kid was good. I guess youngest siblings have to get creative, quick. "Hmmm. You're sure Mommy does that?"

"Yeah."

"Are you sure that's not just what a little tootie stinker wants?" I tickled Bella's tummy and she squealed, kicking her feet. Unfortunately, since she was sitting in the cart with her legs flailing, she was perfectly positioned to kick me right in the balls.

And she did, the toe of her cute little Mary Jane shoes slamming directly into my testicles.

Well, that backfired. A heartwarming moment with my daughter turned into me doubled over trying not to throw up in Target.

"Does your tummy hurt, Daddy? Do you need to go poop?" Bella asked, expressing the utmost concern for me, her folded-in-half father. A woman passed by and bugged out her eyes to try not to laugh.

Another voice chimed in from behind me. "Hey, aren't you Dylan Sorrento?"

Could the timing have been any worse? I nodded and waved a hand from my hunched-over position.

"Daddy?"

"Yeah?" I wheezed.

"It's okay if you have to go poop. We just go to the potty and go."

Dammit, she is her mother.

Her mother managed the potty training for all three of our kids. I hadn't even been involved in that aspect. My discomfort stabbed a little deeper at that thought.

I rested my forehead on the cart's handle, working my way back up to standing. "Thanks, Bella. I'll keep that in mind."

TWENTY-THREE
DYLAN
NOW | NOVEMBER

Hey. I don't know how else to say this.
Jeanine left me.

You might want to have Rach check on her

CHAPPY

I'm calling you on my way home

"WHAT DO YOU MEAN, SHE LEFT?" Ma's hand was pressed to her chest. "I'm supposed to take care of these three alone?"

My mom was not handling the news of Jeanine's departure well. Frankly, neither was I, having sat up most of the night trying to figure out why I didn't see the signs that it was worse than I thought. Even though I was furious, and most of all, hurt, I felt the need to defend J to my mom.

Mom arrived while I was cooking dinner. It was a lemon chicken and rice skillet that Jeannie leaned on when time was tight. How did she get the rice done, though? I'd been cooking the shit for over thirty minutes and it still seemed like the rice was fresh out of the bag.

Bella was also attached to me during this whole process. She was being extra clingy since we got home from Target and she realized Mommy really wasn't going to be home for a while. She complained that her tummy hurt.

So did mine, but you can't take tummy-hurt breaks when you're holding together a house of four.

"Gangee has death breath," Bella whispered in my ear after Ma entered the house. "She's scary."

I had to press my lips together to keep from laughing. I strummed my fingers over her belly. "It's probably your toots, sis."

That made Bella giggle. She had entered the stage in which farts became the peak of humor. Given a good percentage of locker room humor had to do with bodily functions, I'm not sure I ever left that stage.

"I think she just needed some time away. She's been under a lot of pressure," I said to Ma.

"Pressure?" Ma blustered. "She's a housewife with all the money in the world!"

Clearly, my mother learned nothing from our discussion at Thanksgiving. Maybe Jeanine was right about her being difficult.

Ah, fuck. And I'd done the exact same thing to her.

"What's a housewife?" Alice chimed in from her seat at the island, where she and Grey watched all this go down.

"That's not what Mommy is," I said sternly, glaring at Mom. "Mommy does a lot of things."

"Are we rich?" Greyson asked.

I hitched Bella higher up my hip. "We have more money than a lot of people, yes."

"Are we richer than Jeff Beeswax? Tyler said he's the richest man in the world."

I scanned through my brain to figure out who the hell Grey was talking about. *Bezos.* "No, we are not richer than Jeff Beeswax. Now mind yours and go set the table with your sister, please."

"You can't make children set the table, Dylan," Ma said. I got a pang in my stomach. Maybe Jeanine was right about Mom's incessant picking, and teaching me to be helpless. I'd never been on the receiving end of the picking, but now in place as the default parent, it was hitting hard and fast.

"They're perfectly capable of it," I said through an almost-clamped jaw. Bella's tiny little kitten nails dug into the side of my neck. "Bella, honey, that hurts. Can I put you down?"

"No!" Bella whined, tightening her legs around me and winding up to break into a full-on wail.

Meanwhile, Mom just sat at the kitchen island like she had nothing better to do. "Can you do something? I'm struggling over here."

"What, Dylan? I've been waiting on you to tell me what to do. You said you wanted my help before Christmas."

I had my suspicions that Mom visiting was the straw that broke Jeanine's camel back or whatever. She'd always been tense around my mom, but it only got worse after we had Greyson. Hell, even before that. When we lost the first pregnancy, Mom said it must be a problem from her side of the family, because she had an easy, healthy pregnancy with me. At the time, I was grieving and just focused on Jeanine. But that was just the tip of the picking iceberg.

And here, I invited Mom to come help Jeanine. I could see the folly of my ways now.

I couldn't let my mother ruin my marriage. "Would you make the salad, please?" I barked.

Mom's mouth gaped. "Dylan, that's no way to speak to your

mother. And in front of your children, no less. Is that how you talk to Jeanine?"

"Are you here to help or not?" I asked. She may be my mother, but I was a grown man, and she was treating me like a teenager.

"I'm just saying, she might have left because you're not treating her with respect. I raised you better than that, Dylan Peter."

Mom had a point. Had I really been treating Jeanine as well as I thought I was, or was my frustration from work seeping into life at home? When did I start seeing Jeanine as my adversary rather than my partner?

She peered around in the refrigerator. "Shelves could use a clean," she grumbled.

Was it really this bad, and I just never noticed?

"Sounds like you'll have something to do when I'm gone then," I griped back.

Mom screwed up her face. "Your wife shouldn't have messy shelves."

I turned from the pan on the stove to face my mom fully. "Did you really come here to help us out, or did you come to find new evidence of everything we've done wrong?"

Mom glared everywhere but at me. "*You* haven't done anything wrong. That's why I came to help. You asked me to come here, and you know I'll always support you, Dylan."

Bella tightened her grip on me, and I set my jaw. She was trying to cover up her critique of Jeanine by pointing out her own superiority. Did she not even realize how harsh she was? "Who is it you're implying has done something wrong, then?"

Mom sniffed.

"If it's Jeanine, you need to make a choice. Jeanine is not going anywhere if I can help it. If I can get her to take me back after all the ways I've let her down, then I plan to keep her in my life forever. If you can't respect my wife, we need to have a different discussion about your position in my life."

"Dylan Peter—" she raged.

"It's simple, Ma," I cut her off. "Respect my wife, or—"

"Or what?" she dared me. "What are you going to do? Cut out your mother, who gave you everything? Cut me out when I'm the reason Jeanine even went after you?"

I screwed my face up, shifting Bella again. "What?"

"You think she'd be interested in you if you didn't have the money and the career? You think you'd be where you are without me?"

This was a fresh one. Consider my temper lost. "Are you fucking kidding me, Ma? Do you even hear yourself?"

As if on cue, a plate broke in the dining room, followed by an "uh-oh." I closed my eyes and sucked in a calming breath, but did not feel any calmer.

Well, I'd done it now. She was stunned to silence.

"I want Mommy," Bella whimpered.

I want Mommy too.

I'd parented without Jeanine plenty. When she went on girls' trips or visited her parents in California, it was a cinch. The kids were decently behaved, and other than that time the girls got sick and I had to call in reinforcements, I was perfectly capable of parenting solo.

But there was a difference this time. Conflict was in the air. I didn't know when Jeannie was coming back. I wanted Jeannie too. I needed her. Even when she wasn't feeling her best, we were there to prop each other up. A team. But I didn't know when I'd have my teammate again. I was cracking under the pressure.

I totally fucked up when I yelled at her. I should have been there for her instead of going after her. I should have opened up to her sooner. I never even gave her the chance to be there for me.

With Bella still clinging to me, I got the broom and dustpan out of the closet and headed for the dining room.

"I told you those kids couldn't set the table," was all Mom said.

RACHEL

You doing ok?

It's good to be here. But I feel sick

Can I come see you Saturday? Chappy's off, so he can watch the kids. We can have a girls' night

"SAY HI TO MAMA," Dylan said, pulling Bella in his lap. We were on FaceTime. Dylan looked like he'd been punched in the face multiple times, but I knew it wasn't a product of hockey. He looked about how he looked the last time we fell apart.

"Hi Bells!" I chirped. "Did you show Daddy around Target today?"

Bella and I had a tradition of going on our Target run after she finished her half-day preschool program on Wednesdays. I'd left Dyl a note of what he'd need. I really did take care that he wouldn't have an awful time without me. I didn't want to be cruel—I just wanted to be seen.

"Yeah. He filled up the cart, Mommy."

I laughed. "Is that true, Daddy?"

His smile indicated he wasn't all that pleased with it. "I did okay."

"Mommy, will you be back for my art show?"

Dylan's face went slack, a shell of a human looking back at me. "I'm going to do my best, sweetheart. Are you being good for Daddy?"

Dylan kissed her cheek and her fat, squishy cheek pressed in. I missed those squishy cheeks so deeply in that moment. "She's still a stinker," he joked, sending her into giggles.

Alice and Grey both got on, showing me what they made at school, and then it was time for all of them to go to bed.

"I miss you guys," I said, my heart aching looking at the four of them. "So much."

"We miss you, Mommy," Dylan said, his eyes looking so earnest. "I miss you. Can we talk later?"

I winced. "Andy and Kathy are coming over for dinner later. I don't know how late they'll stay."

"You're having dinner with Andy?" He coughed it out like it was on the end of a breath, his face reddening.

"And Kathy. And my parents. Kathy's been having one of her flare-ups. Think she needs a distraction."

Dylan bobbed his head, blinking fast and deflating from his jolt of anger. "Right. Right. It's good you're seeing her then. Give her my best." He took a breath, glanced away for a moment, then looked directly at what must have been my face on the screen. "I love you, Jeanine. So much. I miss you, baby."

"I love you too."

Can you send a pic? The kids want to see the
winery in December

JEANNIE

(pic)

Give them kisses for me

AFTER A DINNER of burnt chicken breast, both over and undercooked rice, and a perfectly fine salad, I sent Mom to the store while I put the kids to bed. I needed her out of my hair.

"Dad?"

I had just flipped the light switch to leave Greyson's room. "Yeah, bud?"

"Why did Mom leave?"

My back was to him, and I squeezed my eyes shut. Why *did* she leave?

And it was a wake-up call. I'd been so worried about how Jeanine's leaving impacted me that I hadn't given enough thought to how much the kids were probably struggling.

"Mommy just needed a little break. A vacation."

"I like vacation," Greyson argued. "Why didn't she bring me?"

I sat on the edge of his bed with a smirk. "You're still in school, bud."

His next question wiped any amusement I had right off my face. "Is Mommy okay?"

Was she?

"She will be, buddy. She sent me a picture today. You wanna see?"

He nodded, sitting up in his sheets. I pulled my phone out of my sweatpants pocket. "See? There she is with Gammy and Gampa."

"I want to be at the wine house," Greyson said.

"We'll go there again soon, buddy."

He blinked, seemingly taking all that in. He and the girls thrived when we went to Temecula, playing hide and seek in the vineyards and getting spoiled rotten by Jeanine's parents.

"I miss California," he said quietly.

I nodded, patting over his hair as he settled back into his sheets. "What do you miss about it?"

"I miss my friends. And Uncle Obi too." He paused. "We were happy there."

If this day had been a series of knives inserted into my gut, this was all of them getting turned at once. Maybe Jeanine was right. Maybe I had been selfish to want to move here.

Her words about making the right choice for me instead of the right choice for our family rang in my head. The kids had made friends on our street, but that didn't mean they didn't miss California or feel upended by the move.

I leaned to kiss Greyson's forehead. "I miss them too. We'll have to go see them soon."

"And Mom."

"Mom will come home, Grey. Sometimes moms need a

break. I'm going out of town tomorrow, but Gangee will be here to take care of you. Can you promise to be good for her? Listen to what she says?"

"Okay."

"And be nice to your sisters."

"Okay."

"And don't worry about the broken plate, buddy. There are plenty of plates. There's only one you." I punctuated that with a boop on his nose. He smiled, even though I knew he was getting too old for stuff like that to be fun.

I got a little choked up. Jeanine was the one who had taught me to stay calm when the kids had accidents, whether it was breaking a plate or spilling a glass of water, or a potty accident. I always got chewed out growing up if I made a mistake like that, but Jeannie pointed out that you have to let kids try stuff and screw up, then support them when stuff goes wrong.

And yet, I'd gotten mad at her when she accidentally left that knife out, then Greyson got to it and cut the couch. She was treating the kids the way she wanted to be treated, with compassion and understanding. I was treating her the way my parents, and my mom in particular, treated me.

Jeanine was so smart. So kind. I was a better dad because she was their mom.

I had to get her back and close the space between us.

MOM WATCHED some garbage network show while I got things ready for the next day. I needed to leave her some specific instructions for how everything worked. Jeannie had carefully penned everything into the family calendar hanging in the kitchen. She used erasable pens so it was dark enough to read, but not so permanent that dates couldn't be changed.

The previous owners built a little desk space into the kitchen. All the bills and papers were organized. Alice's EpiPen was there so it was easily accessible in an emergency. And Jeanine had even left my mom a detailed guide to all the kids' comings and goings, their schedule, what they'd eat, and what was already in the fridge or pantry.

Looking over the calendar, I saw where all my practices, games, and events were figured in. The kids' school recitals and plays. Bella's preschool art exhibit. Pancakes with Santa. And next Thursday, after I was back from the road trip, she'd written *ask D about date, get sitter?*

Of course. A date. A time for the two of us to be alone before Christmas.

But also, I got why she was stressed. The calendar was jam-packed, and a lot of the stuff was fundraiser stuff with the WAGs group. Maybe I wasn't specifically part of the problem, but the lifestyle that I led put stress on her. Being a hockey player obligated her to be part of the wives' group, on top of everything else. And she hadn't quite found her girls in Ohio yet.

I thought back to what she said before she left. She didn't want to live the life I built for me.

All this time, I thought I was building a life for her and the kids, but that disregarded everything they'd built for themselves.

Jeanine chose me in the strongest way she could, leaving her work and signing up for a life with me. Bit by bit, she made friends in my social circle and created a supportive community among L.A.'s wives and girlfriends.

Then, after eight years of her creating this solid life for our whole family, I took it away from them.

My heart ached. Why would she come back to that? She could just as easily spend her time away, then decide she was taking the kids and going back to California. She'd be within her right to want a divorce. I was ruining everything, from our family's life to my team. How could I blame her for leaving?

I needed to give something back if I wanted her to come back.

I needed to come up with a plan, and hope to hell it would work.

"SHE TALKING TO YOU?" Jack Leroy asked as I settled in my seat on the team jet.

"Yeah, but nothing serious. I really don't know how this is going to go."

"Well, worst case, she serves you papers."

I chuckled. "Wow, Jack. Thanks for that."

"What? Sometimes it's for the best," he said.

I rubbed my lips together and stared out the airplane window. "How did you know things were over with Sydney?"

Jack blew a sloppy breath out of his lips. "It was a lot of things. In the beginning, she always convinced me to hate people along with her. I started realizing how those people weren't actually bad people, and were kinda cool. And if I pushed back on her about someone being fine and, you know, worthy of basic respect, she got so mad at me. I don't know, man. She was just mean."

I chortled, surprised by his statement. "You're mean, Jack."

He put a hand to his chest. "Excuse me! I've come a long way. Now I'm just mean on the ice."

"I'll have to ask Mara whether that's true," I said.

"No, really. Sydney wasn't just mean. So many things she did were selfish. That's not how Jeanine is, though, right?"

I picked at my nails. "I think she's the opposite. She gave up too much of herself and it's just now hitting. But it's my fault for taking so much."

"How come?"

I rubbed my forehead. "I don't know, man. I've known she hasn't been doing well since we moved. I guess I thought if we didn't talk about it, she'd get over it somehow."

Jack scoffed. "Well, that's one thing Sydney and I were good at: fighting. God, she could dish out some nasty ones. If she had a feeling, I knew it right away."

"And I'm sure you were shy too," I said, smirking at him.

He screwed up his face into a sneer. "Ha ha, you're so edgy, Pickles. Look in the mirror. You'll fight with me about something stupid, but you won't fight with your wife who needs you."

"I don't like fighting," I said. "I like us to be peaceful."

"Yeah, well, sometimes you need to fight. If you sit on everything, neither of you will get what you want."

I laughed, impressed. "Since when did you become a marriage expert?"

"I've had two now. I'm a pro."

"I . . . don't think that's how that works," I said.

"Look: Sydney taught me to fight her. Mara's teaching me *how* to fight without being an irrational dickwad."

"Wonder what the next one will teach you," I tease.

"You wanna go?" he snapped, turning to me and going to stand, but his airplane seatbelt held him in place. "We could fucking go. Right here in the aisle."

Colton's head poked over the seat in front of us. "You make him mad, Pickles?"

"He said Mara wouldn't be my last wife," Leroy shouted. "Take it back, fucker!"

"It was a joke, Jack," I said, putting my hands out.

"Don't think I won't deck your ass—" Leroy started.

"No friendly fire!" Colt shouted over us.

"I think maybe you're still an irrational dickwad," I muttered.

"Say it again, punk!" Leroy yelled.

"You're just proving my point," I said.

A hand slapped me upside the head, to which I yelped. "Say anything else about my wife, and today might be your last day on this planet."

"You need to be like Leroy, Pickles," Colton said.

"He just smacked me!" I objected.

"He smacked you because he was standing up for his wife," Colt explained. "You need to stand up for Jeanine. Back her up. Let her know that nobody can do anything to her because you've got her."

"But she's mad at me, not the world."

"Well, is she right?"

"I mean, probably partially," I mumbled.

"Then go win her back," Colton said.

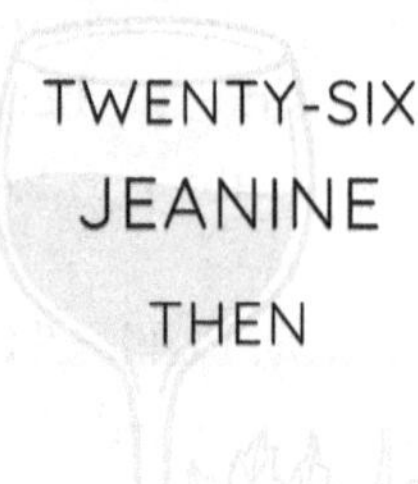

TWENTY-SIX
JEANINE
THEN

"CAN I COME IN?" Andy's face peered around my bedroom door, his knuckle still raised to knock.

I sat up, shook a small colony of graham cracker crumbs from my shirt, and ran my hands through my hair. I was in my childhood bedroom, marinating in my parents' house while Dylan was away on a road stand. This was the first time he was gone and I would be unsupervised after the miscarriage. While I knew I could manage on my own, I craved my parents' comfort. I was sure Mom would feed me and keep me from falling too deep into the grief rabbit hole.

It was starting to get dark outside, and I'd wasted most of the day staring at the wall or scrolling my phone. I intended to watch a movie but it never happened.

Andy stood with folded arms and leaned into the door frame. "Your mom told me what happened. I'm so sorry, J."

I twisted my lips and nodded. "Yeah. Thanks. How's your mom?"

I already knew how his mom was from my own mom, but I needed something to talk about other than my misfortune.

He forced a smile. "She's alright. Been better, of course."

"She's lucky to have you," I said.

"Yeah, I guess," he said, staring at the ground. A few beats of silence passed between us. "Jeanine, did . . . fuck. Never mind."

"What?"

He sniffed in a breath. "Did you marry him because you were pregnant?"

I tented my fingers at my temple. "Andy . . ."

"You just met him."

I heaved a sigh. "I'm not going to justify my marriage to you. I've done it enough in the last few weeks."

"Oh, so I'm not the only one who thinks this whole thing seems fast?"

I shook my head. "Why did you come up here to talk to me?"

He rubbed his forehead. "I'm sorry. I'm being rude." He chewed on his lip. "Can I sit?"

I gestured for him to sit at the foot of the bed. My mind's gears started turning and for perhaps the fiftieth time that day, tears blinded me. Andy's gaze sealed on me. "Jeanine."

He scooted closer to me on the bed, wrapping his arms around me. I was so out of it that I didn't resist, caving to his familiar scent and feel.

"It just hurts so bad, Andy."

He held me tighter, rocking me from side to side. "I'm so sorry. It must feel awful."

"I wanted that baby."

"I bet," he said. "I can't imagine."

We sat for a while, me with my grief and him with me. I guess enough time passed to where I thought I could trust Andy with the most hurtful part of all.

"His mom was glad I lost the baby," I hiccuped. "Because now we could get an annulment."

He gasped, which I felt was an appropriate reaction, confirming I wasn't just being dramatic. "That's so fucked up."

"Right? And I just wanted him to stick up for me, you know? But he didn't. He just let her say all that."

"Oh, J. You deserve better."

That really sent me into hysterics, the tears pouring out. "Do I leave him over that?"

When I met Andy's eyes again, he just gave me a sad look. "I can't say."

"You think I should, don't you?"

He shrugged and twisted his lips. "You could be loved so much more than that."

I gasped and a thousand thoughts ripped through my cloudy head. I had a choice. I could leave L.A. I could come home, work for my parents, and prepare to take over the winery when they retired.

The man sitting on my bed would be more than happy to love me.

I could leave all the drama behind me. Maybe this was a dalliance with a life that was never meant to be mine. Maybe how hard and fast my relationship with Dylan burned flamed it right out. Maybe losing the baby was meant to be the end of my story with Dylan.

Maybe the hometown hero sitting in front of me, the kind man who didn't take the easy road, was meant to be mine. Maybe my future was sitting on my bed in my parents' house, offering me a quiet, gentle life. It would be a life without the clack of pucks against the wall, and the scrape of skate blades, and the smell of refrigerant and stinky hockey equipment. It would be a life without fancy dresses and glamorous parties, but it could be a happy life.

I could choose to leave Dylan and move home. I could choose to return to the comfortable, the path of least resistance.

I could choose Andy.

He seemed to think I was choosing that. Andy's eyes flitted to my lips and slowly, gently, he leaned in to kiss me.

And for a moment, I thought I was making that choice too.

Then his breath on my lips snapped me out of it. At the last second, I turned my face and his lips crashed into my cheek.

"You need to leave," I said. "Get out!"

Andy jumped away from me, putting his hands up. "Fuck. Jeannie, I'm sorry!"

"Go!"

His scent trailed in his wake and I sat, hardly breathing. What had I just done? I almost cheated on my husband. I was so desperate for a reprieve from everything that I almost blew up my new life. I pressed my fingertips to my temples, willing my muddy brain to work.

Instead, I returned to my previous activity of staring into space, trying to figure out if I'd ever break the surface of this gloom.

"WHERE'S MY GIRL?" Dylan's bright voice echoed through our apartment. I was right where I'd been for the prior twenty minutes, staring at the knobs on the washing machine. Something about deciding whether the clothes needed to go on hot or cold made me freeze. I'd been doing that since I got back from Temecula.

But as I went out there, everything that had happened since I met Dylan smacked me in the face. Meeting him. Loving him. Getting pregnant with him. Getting married to him. Losing. Him not arguing with his mom. Us making up.

But my mind kept going back to him not defending me. The hurt was so raw after everything we'd endured.

But it didn't merit what I did.

"In here," I called.

Dylan's expression turned concerned. "What happened?"

"Dylan, I screwed up." Tears spilled out of me that I knew I didn't deserve. I was the one who screwed up, and boohooing about it wasn't fair to Dylan. But I couldn't find my breath, continually sucking it in between gut-wrenching sobs.

"Slow down, baby." Dylan held my upper arms, trying to get me to meet his eyes. "It's okay. I'm sure whatever it is, it's fine."

"It was so weird, Dylan. I was so confused." I gasped for air between crying jags. "I was just hurting so bad and he asked if we got married because of the baby."

"J, who is he? Your dad?"

I shook my head. "Andy. My brother's friend. My ex," more gasps, "Hang on. I think I'm going to get sick."

I ran for the bathroom, crying so hard I'd worked myself into a dry-heaving spell. My eyes were so puffy they were almost shut of their own accord.

Dylan leaned in the bathroom doorway with a furrowed brow. His voice was low and stern. "Jeanine, did you cheat on me?"

I looked up at him from the bathroom floor. "I don't know. I-I told him we lost the baby and that your mom said we should break up and you didn't disagree with her, and he said we should too. He was just so sure about it, like it was so logical and I thought maybe I was the stupid one. I've just been so confused, Dyl, and I'm so sad, and I'm still mad at you, and—"

His jaw flexed, then clenched. "You cheated on me."

"No, I didn't. I mean, he almost kissed me before I turned

away." I breathed out a silent sob, squeezing my burning, swollen eyes shut.

"That motherfucker," Dylan bit out. "He was at our wedding, right? The skinny dude?"

"Yeah, he was there. That's him."

Dylan shook his head, getting increasingly agitated. "He took advantage of you, Jeanine!"

That wasn't the direction I was expecting. "W-what?"

"You were upset, and he used the opportunity to pounce." He ripped his keys out of his pocket, turning like he was going for the front door.

"I told him to leave. But I shouldn't have let it get that far. And the worst part is, I'm still so confused."

That stopped Dylan in his tracks. He pushed a shaky breath through a small O in his lips. "How are you confused?" His voice was flat, dead inside.

I sighed, sitting against the wall next to the toilet. "This has all been so fast, Dyl."

His eyes fixed on mine, lifeless. "You don't know whether you want me."

"Dylan, I'm so sorry."

He nodded, licking his lips. "Is this why you go to Temecula? Him?"

"No. Not at all. I went for my parents, and I ran into him and we started talking. I'm still just so lost, Dylan. I want to go back to normal, but my whole life got upended by . . . by us. There is no normal now."

"You know what sucks the most about this, Jeanine?" Dylan's hands went wide, then he put them on his hips, pitching forward like he was out of breath. "When my mom questioned us staying together, I didn't have any doubt that I wanted you. That's why I didn't argue with her. It was ludicrous. Unthinkable. I thought we were on the same page.

Because it doesn't matter to me what anyone outside of you and me thinks. So what if we met six months ago? I love you, Jeanine. I fucking love you and you aren't sure about me. And that's—" he put a hand to his forehead, "fine. It's fine. You don't have to love me."

"I love you, Dylan. I do."

"You're just not sure you want to be with me."

I sniffed, holding back a fresh round of tears. "Every day is so hard, Dylan. I don't even have anything big to do, and it's like lifting a five-hundred-pound weight off me to get out of bed. It's hard for me to want to do anything because I just feel like . . . a burden. Like everyone thinks we're crazy and it's all my fault. I want to want this, Dylan. I want to be in this, but I'm barely hanging on. I'm just weighing you down and everyone knows it. You'd be better without me."

Dylan's lips popped open and his eyes softened. He approached, lowering to the floor with me. He crossed his ankles in his lap and pulled me sideways across him. His arms enveloped me and his head tucked to my shoulder. His hand brushed over my hair and he kissed the side of my face. "You are not a burden, Jeanine."

"Then why won't you fight for me?" I blinked hard. "I mean, I get it. I've got issues. My brain goes haywire when I get sad. So you'd be better without me dragging you down."

Dylan's amber eyes met mine. "I should have stuck up for you, Jeanine. But I think what I want . . . I want to be loved despite my issues too. And maybe my issue is trying to make everybody happy, including my mom. Nobody's ever stuck up for me. I'm always so worried about everybody else."

I laced our hands together. "I'll stick up for you. And I'm sorry for not seeing that." I gnawed on my lip. "So, are you leaving me?"

He kissed my temple. "I don't want to. Unless you want that other guy."

I shook my head and laughed. "No. Not at all."

Dylan's eyes glowed. "Can I kill him?"

I laughed until I snorted. "He's not worth jail time. Then you really wouldn't get to see me."

"I mean, maybe I could just take my skate blade—"

I clapped my hand over his mouth. "No, Dylan—"

"Just a fingertip! I'd just take the skin off!" he whined.

"Forget about him. He's not important."

"He's such a jagoff*," he scoffed.

"You're so mad, you're speaking Yinzer?"

"He tried to hork† my wife!" Dylan grinned. "Can't just get away with that stuff."

"What the hell is 'hork'? You've never said that to me once!" I laughed.

"He tried to steal you. And he has to pay."

"I promise, Dyl, I really don't think about him."

"Fine," he conceded. "Can you stick it out with me until we figure all this stuff out?"

I nodded, grabbing his cheek and kissing him. "Let's stick it out."

---

*   Pittsburgh speak/Yinzer for dickhead/jackoff
†   Pittsburgh speak/Yinzer for steal

TWENTY-SEVEN
JEANINE
NOW | DECEMBER

RACHEL

AFTER DINNER, Dad lit a fire in the fire pit, and we all gathered outside with a glass of wine. Andy helped his mom into her seat, and I was relieved to see her spirits weren't too dampened by her illness. Kathy had always been the cool mom among our friends' parents—single, with a classic and effortless style. Andy's dad had been out of the picture since I knew them, but Kathy always seemed unaffected. I admired her independence.

Andy and my mom stepped inside to put the dishes away while I sat with Kathy.

"Kathy, can I ask you something?"

"Sure."

I pinched my lips together. "Was it hard being Andy's mom alone?"

She rolled her eyes like she was long-exhausted. "God, yes. I mean, he was a good kid, but there were times I cursed his father for leaving me to deal with everything."

I nodded, swallowing a lump in my throat and she studied me. "This is going to sound insensitive. I'm not parenting alone, but sometimes it feels like it. He's gone so much, and he just doesn't get what it all takes."

"I don't think they ever do," she said. "But your Dylan's a good one. Or at least that's how it looks. Hell, if he's not, drop his ass and go get yourself a hot young boyfriend and enjoy the hell out of it. Life's too short for bad sex, dear."

I chuckled. "Well, that part's not bad. It's all the other stuff that adds up."

"I can't speak to that," she said. "I never had someone willing to stick it out for me and Andy. You know, I had one guy I thought might work out, but he treated Andy like he was inconsequential. The minute you have a kid, they come first."

I found it interesting that my mom had once told me the opposite. Her advice was more, *you have to get your marriage right before you can get your kids right.* "He's still good enough to keep, I think," I said, sipping my wine. "It's just going to take work."

"Well, nothing in life worth anything is ever easy."

Andy and my mom came out of the house, toting another bottle of wine and a plate of truffles. We sat around the fire, catching up for a while. I kept catching Andy watching me, his gaze flicking over me. The more wine we had, the more his eyes lingered, adding a soft smile when our eyes met.

Mom may have had a little something right when she said it's nice to have someone make you feel pretty.

But what I really wanted to feel was loved. Understood. Seen. And those weren't things I wanted from Andy.

"I think it's about time for me to turn in," Kathy announced after we sat for a good hour.

"I'll take you home," Andy said, standing.

"No, no, I'll take her," my mom said.

"Aw, thanks, Maureen," Kathy said. "Andy's always taking care of my sorry ass."

Mom winked at me. "Feels like I could give him the night off."

"Mom, it's really nothing. I have to be up early tomorrow," Andy argued.

"Oh, stop. We've got things to gossip about anyway," Mom said, shoving his shoulder to make him sit again. She brought the bottle over and put it on the patio table between me and Andy. "You kids have fun. Don't get into any trouble. Andy, you don't have to come in early tomorrow, but walk home if you drink anymore, okay?"

"Yes, Mrs. W," he said with the insolent tone of a high schooler.

For a while, Andy and I just stared into the fire, not saying anything. The way we'd gotten to be alone like this was innocuous, but I still felt uncomfortable. Andy had made passes at me in the past, even while Dylan and I were married. Hopefully, Andy and Dylan spending time together last summer while we visited my parents was enough to shy him away. Or better yet, with the number of years it had been since we were actually involved, maybe he got over me.

Yes, it felt nice to have someone always think you were the one who created the sun, especially when my life was in shambles. But I shouldn't have been enjoying that. What would Dylan think if he saw us now? I might have been helping him bury a body instead of shivering against the chilly air. I wrapped my sweater tighter around myself.

"Alice still a spitfire?" he asked. She'd hung on "Uncle

Andy" like a spider monkey when we came to the winery last summer.

I shook my head with a laugh. "That child, I swear."

"She's got a lot of you in her," he said, taking a sip of wine.

"Nah, she's very much her own child. Bella's more like me," I said. "You were good with them. You always did like kids."

I said it, then immediately regretted it. He was probably thirty-three or so, and I had a whole brood of kids. He had none, and seemingly no prospects on the horizon. He'd given so much of his life to his mom, to my parents even. Temecula was his life.

"Yeah," he said softly. We had another silent stretch of staring into the fire. "What are you really doing out here, Jeanine?"

I did everything with my lips: rolling them between my teeth, chewing them, twisting them to the side. "Figuring that out myself."

Andy drew a few breaths like he was going to speak, but didn't. False starts, like he was gearing up to say something.

"You don't have to stay with him." His voice was quiet and low. "You can take the kids and still have a happy life. You're young, Jeanine. If he cheated on you, you don't have to take it."

My eyes narrowed and met his as I sat up straighter. "What the hell are you saying?"

"Jeanine, you deserve happiness. He's taking that from you. I hate to see you like this. You're not who you used to be."

"Yeah, I'm not. I grew up," I said, draining my wine glass and setting it on the table between us. Andy topped it up with a half-pour and looked at me with a certain sadness.

"So did I. And I still want you, J."

I sat up bolt in my seat. "Are you seriously doing this again, Andy? You don't even know me anymore."

"Well, I want to," he panted, his eyes going glassy. "The door's still open. With me. For us."

I was aghast. What the hell? I was married with three children, and Andy was telling me he'd sweep me away into his life? He went on.

"I don't know what he did, but it must be bad if you're home without your kids and you don't know when you're going back. There has to be a reason you always run back here when you're mad at him. We've been here before, Jeanine. I was patient. I gave you space to heal, to figure out what you wanted. We are inevitable, J."

I could barely breathe, the wind knocked out of me. "You think *you're* the reason I'm here?"

Andy blew right over that detail. "If he cheated on you, Jeannie—"

"He didn't cheat on me."

"Then what did he do?"

"He didn't do anything!" I barked. "That's the problem. He's let his mom bully me for years. He knew I was drowning and instead of throwing me a lifeline, he just told me I'd get through it. He uprooted our family and told me to put up and shut up. I tried to be there for him and he yelled at me that it wasn't soon enough. I do everything for him, the very best I can, and it's never enough for him."

I said it, then couldn't believe I had, both out loud and to Andy. I panted, my eyes burning. He leaned forward and put his hand on my knee. "I'm sorry, J."

I buried my face in my hands, my tears coming in hot. I cried in the way I needed to, in the way I'd been holding back from. Because if I cried like this, that made it more real. Andy stood, tugging on my upper arm. "Come here."

I stood and fell into his embrace. He patted my hair and swayed me. He'd just hit on me, but I thought I gave him enough resistance to make him stop. I thought he understood that I needed a friend right then.

Apparently not.

It got weird. "You deserve better, Jeanine." His lips pressed into the top of my head. I wrenched free from him.

"What is that supposed to mean?" I snapped.

Andy snorted in a breath. "It means you could have had it different. You still could. You and the kids, you could be here." He pointed at the ground, going full drama.

I curled my upper lip. "You don't know what it takes, Andy. You don't know what longevity looks like."

"Maybe I don't," he shouted. "But you never let me."

I shook my head, backing away from him. "No, you don't get to do this."

"I've waited, Jeanine."

"I never told you to do that. I said I was done. It was over a decade ago, Andy! You were at my wedding. You said you were happy for me."

"And a month after your wedding, you were back here, mad at him." His stare was fierce, his eyes flitting between mine. "I was happy for you, Jeanine. All I wanted was for you to be happy. And I hate that you're not happy now."

Rage coursed through me so hard it shook me. I threw my arms wide. "Life isn't all sunshine and rainbows, Andy! Sometimes you have to work for it."

He shook his head. "If you were with me, I'd never let you feel unloved. Unseen. Unhappy."

I looked to the black sky overhead. "You're all the same," I said, exasperated. "Everyone's allergic to someone being unhappy. You can't have a negative feeling or go through a real human emotion! What if shit's just hard sometimes and all you want is someone to sit in the shit with you?"

Andy stalked up to me, staring down into my eyes. "I would sit in it with you. I wouldn't leave you alone like this."

I rolled my eyes and turned to go in the house. "Easy for you to say."

TWENTY-EIGHT
JEANINE
NOW | DECEMBER

"WHAT DO you think of that pinot?"

Andy took the day after our fight off work, so I covered the tap room Thursday. It was now Friday, and though he was allegedly back at it, I hadn't seen him yet.

That was fine. I didn't really care to see him after he launched his incel pitch to me. Just because he'd been "waiting for me" didn't mean I had to do anything about it, and frankly, it was kinda creepy. It was entirely his problem if he'd been holding out for me since he was what, eighteen? Nineteen?

So there I was, behind the bar at Wendlock Winery, waiting on a couple who was taking some time away from the city before the hustle and bustle of the holidays. They were so cute together: their bar stools almost on top of each other, feet on the rungs of each other's stools, hands across each other's laps.

It made me wish Dylan and I'd gotten more time to just be a young couple in love, before kids and life got in the way. Maybe I wouldn't have been standing there right then if we had.

"Oh, it's great," the woman gushed.

"Another round, or something different?"

They looked between each other and without words, they decided. "Anything sparkling?" the man asked. "She loves some bubbles."

I smiled. "Dry okay?" They nodded. "I have just the thing. Let me get you the right glasses. I'll be right back."

I pulled out flutes, but I'd forgotten to restock the cooler the night before with sparkling bottles. The doors at the opposite end of the room blew open, ushering Andy in on a gust of wind. His arms were full of packages, and he gave me a friendly nod. I returned it, hoping his good mood meant he'd gotten over the bullshit he threw at me two nights before.

I headed for the office behind the bar, where we had a less cute secondary refrigerator. Andy followed me in there.

"Hey," he said as he set the boxes down.

"Hey. Doing better today?"

He didn't respond right away, so I turned to look at him. He leaned against one of the worktables, where Mom and I had been staging shipments two days before.

"I, uh, I feel like I should apologize, Jeanine. What I said was really out of line." He had one hand in his pocket, and the other toying with the back of his shaggy hair. "Things have just been kinda hard for me lately. But I want what's best for you. Genuinely. Even if that doesn't involve me."

I tipped my head to the side, nodding slowly. "Just focus on what's best for you, Andy. I'm fine."

I prayed he'd get the subtext that I was not what's best for him, because I was still holding out hope that Dylan would get together some sort of apology beyond a texted "I'm sorry."

Because even though I wanted to pummel his face, I still loved Dylan to the core of my being. It was just hurting me to love him when he made a habit of disregarding my needs.

Andy and I stood in a stare-off until I gave him a placid smile. "I should get back out there."

"Oh, oh, yeah. Didn't mean to get in your way."

I grabbed the cold bottle of Blanc de Blanc and returned to the bar. I got a certain satisfaction from working the bar again, serving people who didn't yell at me for arranging Cheerios in the wrong order. Or who didn't just eat the food I made without a word.

I pushed those dark and resentful thoughts down, centering myself on the task at hand.

"Want me to do the whole sword thing?" I asked with a grin.

"Ooh! I've always wanted to watch that!" the woman answered.

Popping up on the step stool behind the bar, I jumped up to get the sword from its decorative hanging spot. Except the sword was higher than it used to be. Or else I'd shrunk about a foot. While I tried to problem-solve whether I could climb all the way up on the bar, I distracted the couple with conversation.

"See that basketball hoop over there?" I asked, gesturing to the hoop adjacent to the bar. A bucket hung under it to catch corks. This was a game my brother and I came up with in high school. We opened sparkling bottles with a sword and aimed the corks through the hoop and into the bucket. It ended up becoming a phenomenon, with Food and Wine coming out to interview us.

"No way," the man said.

"We'll see if I still can. I'm way out of practice," I said.

I hiked my knee up on the bar, not wanting to put my dirty shoe up there. I wobbled and almost fell, until large, warm hands captured my hips.

"Got you," Andy said, low.

I was startled by his closeness, his grip. "Oh, thanks." His steadying me actually did help and I was able to snag the sword. As I descended, Andy's hands slid to my waist, facing our fronts together.

Sunshine burst into the room as the tall oak doors opened. A lone figure was silhouetted in the blinding light, a voice booming from it. "Get your hands off my wife."

Andy didn't let me go as my eyes widened and I turned toward the voice, a voice I knew like my own. My heart thudded, my stomach tightening.

"Dylan?" I still held the sheathed sword as I tore out of Andy's grasp.

"You okay?" Andy asked under his breath. I ignored him, walking toward the bar and getting hemmed in by it.

Dylan rushed toward me, concern knitting his brow. "Jeannie."

"I, uh, Andy, can you do the honors?" I asked, handing him the sword with shaking hands. The couple sat with gaping mouths and raised eyebrows. Dylan kept his eyes on me as he came around the counter, slamming his hip into it because he wasn't watching where he was going.

"You're here," I whispered when he got to me.

Dylan held both my hands, panting as he looked down at me. "I'm here."

"Um, J, I'm technically not working right now," Andy interrupted with a tap to my waist.

Dylan shot him a glare that, were his eyes laser beams,

could have withered Andy down to dust. Sweat broke out on his palms where he still held my hands. "I'm sure you could clock in, big guy," Dylan grumbled. "And if you're her boss, I'm certain you shouldn't be touching my wife the way you were."

While some patriarchally brainwashed part of me was folding at Dylan's 'my wife' routine, I could fight my own battles.

"Well, Dylan, maybe Jeanine wouldn't be here in the first place if you treated her with the respect a wife deserves—"

"If you two are done with your dick-measuring contest," I shouted, silencing them, "I'll open this bottle."

The couple at the bar looked like they were about to explode at this soap opera scene going down, and frankly, I would have been too. What had my life become? My husband, the father of my children, was fighting with my brother's best friend and my ex-boyfriend to defend my honor or prove their ownership of me, or something equally ridiculous.

Still, it's not like there wasn't anything to it. Dylan was well aware of my history with Andy, and one wrong move could land my husband with an assault charge.

Neither Andy nor Dylan moved, their stares locked. I was sandwiched between the two of them, heat pulsing off their bodies. I shimmied out from between them, reaching back in to get the sword from Andy. I put on a bright smile, plucked the bottle off the bar, peeled off the foil, and untied the cage.

I unsheathed the sword and positioned it at the bottle's neck. "Ready?"

"Wait, wait, let me get my phone," the woman said, snapping out of her amazed daze and reaching for her back pocket. She got her phone out and gave me a thumbs-up.

Dylan stood behind me and leaned a hip on the bar, boxing Andy out. Neither of them had left, hovering over me. They both had their arms crossed like they'd assumed their roles as my bodyguard from the other.

With a clean slice, I sent the blade up the bottle. The cork flew off with a satisfying pop, followed by two thuds as it hit the backboard and went into the bucket.

"Still got it!" I laughed.

The couple cheered and Dylan bent over my shoulder to kiss my cheek before I filled the two champagne flutes.

"You did good, baby," he cooed in my ear. Dylan couldn't have been claiming me more if he took his dick out and peed on me. I blushed as I poured, then dropped the couple's bottle into an ice bucket. I didn't realize how much I missed Dyl, his scent, the way his warmth radiated into my back, his lips on me.

"It's a family affair here," Dylan assured the couple as his hands slotted into my waist. "Jeannie's parents own the place, so she grew up here. And I'm her husband."

"I caught that," the woman grinned, clearly taking her side on Team Dyl.

"How nice," the man tittered, still looking like he was anticipating a brawl breaking out.

"You guys need anything else?" I asked.

"All set," the woman said, widening her eyes at me for a *blink twice if you need help* look.

"I'll be right back. Andy, can you cover for a few?"

Andy's jaw flexed as he stared, then turned to the hand-washing sink. He cast his eyes downward. "Sure."

One of Dyl's hands slid down to my ass, gently cupping it and urging me forward. Andy was forever on thin ice with Dylan, always afraid he was just waiting to pounce on me at any opportunity. They'd made nice the summer before when our kids were so enamored with Andy, but Dylan kept one eye on him at all times. Based on Andy's confession the other night, he wasn't wrong to feel protective.

And yet, Dylan was making one million percent certain he marked me as his. I reached back to take Dylan's hand, pulling him toward the office behind the bar.

I closed the door behind us and Dylan bent to lock the handle. Then, without a word, he spun me around and put my back against it, stepping between my feet and pressing his weight into me.

He crooked his finger to tip my face up to his, eyes flicking over every part of my face. He panted, then held his breath, brow furrowing.

It was no longer the Dylan vs. Andy show. He'd wholly shifted his focus to me.

"Jeannie." So much hung in the way he said my name. Apology. Pain. Longing. Hope. Fear.

Tears flooded my eyes as all the feelings bubbled like peroxide on a wound. The person I wanted was right in front of me. But there was a distance that we had to resolve or the future for us was muddy.

"Tell me," he whispered, drawing his thumb across my cheek.

I just kept saying "I—" and stopping. Starting and stopping. Not being able to go on.

"I want to know, J. Everything. I want to fix it."

I squeezed my eyes shut, sealing out his image so I could focus on myself, what I needed.

"I want you to crawl for me. To kiss my feet because you're so sorry you abandoned me and ignored my cries for help. To beg and plead for me to take you back. To say you're going to stop avoiding my feelings and that you're going to listen and that you actually want to see *me*, Dylan." I opened my eyes and he nodded, eyes rounded. "The real me, Dylan. Not just happy Jeanine or obedient Jeanine or Jeanine who does everything."

Breath puffed out of his nostrils as he leaned to kiss my

forehead. Then slowly, he lowered himself onto his knees in front of me. He put his hands on my hips, looking up at me. He kissed right above where my jeans buttoned, then sat back on his heels. He tapped my right foot and I lifted it. He placed it on top of his thigh, unzipping my heeled boot. He wiggled it, struggling to get it off. I held my leg up higher, trying to give him a chance. We laughed together.

"Just pull it," I said, smiling as I ran my fingers through his hair. He tugged the boot off, then went serious again, peeling my sock down. Closing his eyes, he placed a lingering kiss on the top of my foot.

"Jeannie, I'm so sorry."

I nodded, starting to cry in earnest. "I'm sorry I left, Dyl. I didn't know what else to do."

He shook his head, sliding up my body to stand. His eyes were watery. I'd seen him cry pretty much when our kids were born, when we got married. When we lost. But that was about it. "I left you a long time ago. And I'm so sorry. But I'm here now, Jeannie. You've got me. I don't blame you for leaving. But I don't ever want to let you go again." His hand framed my face, brushing some hair behind my ear. "Please come home, Jeanine. You're my home. My twin flame. And I'm lost without you."

"Those are all things about what I do for you, Dylan. What are you going to do for me?"

"I'll be better. I see now."

"It can't be the same," I sniffed.

"It won't. I promise it won't, baby. I'll spend my life making it up to you."

"I can't wait forever, Dylan. I was drowning out there. I want our old life back."

He nodded, holding both sides of my face. "I know, baby. I want you to have it back. I'd give you that back if I could, but I can't. Okay? Know that I miss it too. And I'm sorry I left you feeling like I didn't. I miss it."

Shame flared through me, remembering the morning when things came to a head. "You yelled at me for a simple mistake, Dylan."

He sniffed, his eyes going even sadder. "I know, baby. I fucked that up, bad. There's no excuse. I'm stressed, but I shouldn't take that out on you. I'm so sorry."

"You need to stop lying to me when things aren't going well for you," I said. "How was I supposed to know you were struggling? All you did was tell me how much we had to love Ohio and that I was whining."

He squeezed his eyes shut. "That was unfair to you, Jeannie. I'm so sorry."

"Thank you."

"But I have a plan."

My laugh was watery and I swiped under my nose. "A plan, huh?"

"A plan."

I quirked an eyebrow. "What does this plan entail?"

"I'm going to put us back together again." I eyed him skeptically. "I know it's probably hard to believe it'll be different, and it's not going to be easy," he said. "We've both got to be in. Are you in? Will you let me try to make it up to you?"

His face went serious, warm brown eyes searching mine. I slumped down onto my bare foot, even shorter than him then.

"J," he whispered. "Please. I know this is my fault. I saw you struggling and I just tried to carry us through it. But when I couldn't . . . it took me right back to when we lost."

"I didn't want you to carry me, Dylan. I just wanted *you*. All I ever want is you, and you left me."

Dylan's eyes went glassy, his breath stilted. "I needed you

too, J. I didn't know how to say it, but I needed you. You're all I want too. Please work on this with me."

I ran my thumb over his cheek and cracked a smile. "What's the first step of the plan?"

He pinched his lips together, grabbing my ass to lift me against the door to my squeak. "Wouldn't you like to know?"

"I think you don't have a plan," I teased. "Or the plan involves a lot of orgasms."

He laughed. "I mean, there will be sex, but it's not *all* sex."

"Good. Because even though that's good, it doesn't fix everything."

"I know. But it feels pretty good, right?" I giggled and he leaned into me, tugging my earlobe into his mouth. I let out a deep sigh before he snarled in my ear. "You like this, don't you? This little cat-and-mouse game? You wanted me to chase you across the country and fall at your damn feet. I bet you didn't think I'd do it. But I'm here, Jeannie. I'd chase you fucking anywhere, and crawl through whatever mud you want, because I don't have a life without you in it."

"I missed you so much, Dylan," I whimpered, a chill zipping down my arms. "I need you."

And then his lips were on mine. Desperate, ferocious kisses. Firm and gripping, then loose and sloppy. Taking every part of him and giving him every part of me. My legs curled around his waist as I writhed against him. He rocked back into me, the door creaking with every thrust against me.

"Dyl," I admonished him against his lips. "They'll hear."

"Oh, he's gonna hear it," Dylan growled, pulling out of our kiss. "I can't let you stay here and have your little Hallmark movie moment where the single mom comes to her small-town farm and falls in love with her brother's best friend because her big-city boyfriend is mean."

I raised an eyebrow. "Oh, you're not?"

"No way. The villain's getting the girl this time."

I made a shocked expression, bringing my hands to my cheeks. "Oh no, the villain's going to get me! Whatever shall I do?"

"Run," Dylan hissed in my ear to my giggle. "Just kidding, we can't do that here."

I smirked. "The villain's gonna have to work for it. Andy would make a pretty nice brother's best friend hero—eep!" I squeaked when he spanked me with a grin.

"Shut your sassy cocktail waitress mouth and let me show you how the bad guy does it." He plopped my feet to the ground and lowered to his knees.

I had to hide my laugh as he fumbled to get my boot off and unbuttoned my pants, working them and my underwear over my ass. While he was working, I gave him shit.

"Don't think I missed that little 'my wife' moment out there. You in a pissing contest with my brother's best friend? Gonna slam him against the boards?"

Dylan narrowed his eyes up at me. "If he thinks he's going to lay even a finger on this pussy, then yes, I will fight him."

"You'll fight for pus—oh shit," I sighed as he nibbled my inner thigh. His fingers laced with mine and he waited for me to look into his eyes.

"I'll fight for you until I'm blue in the face, Jeanine. Because you are *mine*. And there's no way I'm letting you go without putting my whole self on the line."

Then his hands groped my ass as he buried his face in my pussy, eating like his life depended on it. In a way, you could argue that his life with me did depend on it. As he was sucking extra hard, I pushed his face away.

"This does not fix everything, Dylan. You're not off the hook because you do this."

"I know, baby. This is just the beginning of the plan. Can you trust me?"

"I trust you."

The corner of his lips hitched up, slick with my arousal. "Then sit on my face on the floor of this office."

With a grin, I shoved his shoulder to send him backward, double-checking the door was locked. He looked oh-so-pleased with himself as he wiped around his mouth. "Let me clear off your seat for you."

I cackled. "That joke is never going to die, is it?"

"Not if I have anything to do with it." He slapped his cheeks. "Sit."

I yanked my jeans and underwear off my feet, then lowered myself over his face. We're all jokes leading up to sex, but when we get into the nitty-gritty, we're hot, filthy, and immersed. We loved this position because we got to look into each other's eyes. I got to have the power, receiving pleasure just for the sake of it. And it turned him on to no end. My favorite moment was the inevitable time when his upper arm started to shake where he was touching himself too.

And when things got really serious, I leaned forward and genuinely fucked his face, grinding my hips over his mouth while he drank me up. It was wet, and uninhibited, and feral, and everything I needed in that moment. We had to be quiet because the office shared an open ceiling with the tasting room. Surely Dylan's sucking and slurping sounds were audible, but there was nothing to be done for that. I needed him, right then, no matter who was around. And just as I started to come, he backed down, detaching his mouth from me.

"Ride my cock," he whispered, pushing his pants and briefs a little further down to give me room. "Right now, Jeannie."

I shifted back, spreading my legs as my orgasm continued pulsing through me. My years of dance paid off, able to hold a wide straddle and push myself back until I was fully seated on him.

Him. My Dyl.

He held one hand on my hip and the other between my shoulder blades, still wearing my sweater. My head hung low over his, my hair making a curtain around our faces.

"Jeannie, I'll follow you anywhere," he said. It's a sweet thing to say, but a voice pinged in the back of my mind. *Then why didn't we stay in L.A.?* I shoved the thoughts away for the moment, rolling my hips to try for another climax for me. "Stay with me, J. I'm right here, loving you so hard I can't breathe."

He didn't just mean stay his wife. He meant *stay with me* like *don't go off in your head.* His hand slid under my shirt to palm my breast, his thumb dipping into my bra to flick my nipple. I moaned, then shifted my weight to my left hand so I could touch myself.

"Let me," he said, replacing my hand with his own. "This is about you. You're so beautiful like this."

I ground down on him so hard his ass made a squeaking noise against the hardwood floor. Emotions swirled in me: anger, fear, sadness, hurt. I held the side of his face.

"Never again, Dylan. You don't get to leave me like this again."

He nodded, panic in his eyes. "Never, J. I'm in. I'm here."

"Then fuck me like you are," I gritted out.

I slipped my thumb inside his cheek, a dominant move that opened him to me. Normally, he's the dominant one, but this time, I needed the control. He closed his lips around my thumb, sucking hard in a way that drew more pleasure out of my body.

His fingertips dug into my hips, the points feeling like they'd bruise as he rutted up into me. I jolted on top of him from the force. "More," I growled in his ear. "Harder."

He whimpered, where our pelvises slapped together almost painful. "Everything, baby. You get it all."

My edge approached, my eyes pinching shut as I teetered on the brink. To this point, I'd been in control, but when Dylan grunted, "Eyes open," I obeyed.

I lost all sense of where we were, just me and him and everything we'd shared in the last eight years passing through me. I was obscenely loud when I came, Dylan raising up to pull me into a kiss to shut me up.

"Fuck, Jeannie," he whispered against my lips until he emptied himself inside me. He stroked my hair behind my ear. "I love you so much."

"I love you too."

Got her back

LEROY

K

That's it? That's all I get?

Good job?

Better

JEANNIE WAS SPRAWLED out on my chest, having a cat nap after our latest round of sex. She texted Andy that she needed the rest of the day off, like they hadn't been doing just fine before she came home. I drifted in and out of sleep, enjoying the feeling of having J in my arms without the kids bugging us.

Since her parents were both out of the house, we showered together, which turned into more sex. Two more times, which I was damn proud of. I hadn't seen that kind of performance since I turned thirty.

A knock at the door stiffened my whole body. "Um," I started.

My cock and balls were just out to the air, spread eagle with an equally naked Jeanine splayed out on top of me.

"Jeannie, Andy said you were si—oh my god!" Jeanine's mom had just peeked around the door, jostling a cup of tea in her hand. I jolted to try and cover my junk, waking Jeanine in the process. "Hello, Dylan," she said from the other side of the door.

"Hi, Maureen."

"It's, ah, good to see you here? Um, we'll grill out for dinner tonight, just come down whenever you're . . . dressed?" Maureen was clearly snickering behind the door.

"Mom, get out!" Jeanine cried, sounding like a rebellious teenager.

"I made you a cup of tea since you're sick," she chuckled from the hallway. "I'll just set it out here."

"My god," Jeanine groaned, sitting up and laughing. "Well, welcome home."

"CAN YOU PASS THE SALAD, DYLAN?" Maureen asked.

I handed it her way, still struggling to make eye contact after she caught J and me in the nude.

"Are you missing a game today, Dyl?" her dad, Joe, asked.

"I am. Coach gave me a healthy scratch for today."

Jeanine put her fork down. "Did you tell everyone what was going on?"

"Um, a few of the guys, yeah. They wanted to know why I had to leave early to get Bella," I said, shrugging it off.

She looked worried, and I squeezed her knee under the table. "Leroy asked if I wanted Mara to reach out and check on you. I don't think anyone was judging. I think they were more judging me."

"Great, now all the Ohio wives will know I'm a head case too," she grumbled.

Maureen made an "aww" face. "Jeannie, you know you'll find your fit in Columbus."

Jeanine's eyes were fixed on her plate, pushing a piece of lettuce around. "I just don't want them to gang up on me before they even know me. But it's my fault anyway."

"Show them you, sweetheart," Joe said. "They'll like what they see. And if they don't, you don't need 'em anyway."

I scooted my chair closer to her, put my arm around her shoulders, and kissed her cheek.

"Are you still taking meds?" Maureen asked quietly.

Jeanine shook her head and I squeezed her shoulder a little tighter. She was asking the questions I was too afraid to ask, fearing she'd lash out at me. I knew she wasn't on meds anymore, but I knew suggesting them was a sensitive subject.

"You're going through a lot right now," Maureen pressed on.

"I know, Mom," Jeannie said with a watery smile. "I appreciate the concern. I do."

"Kiddo, you ran from home," Joe added.

"I know what I did, Dad," Jeanine said, an edge coming into her voice.

"We're just trying to help, sweetheart. There's nothing wrong with needing help."

"So what, I'm the crazy one because I don't like being ignored by my husband?" Jeanine scooted her chair back and threw her napkin on the table, preparing to stand. "Can't anyone accept that this guy might be in the wrong?"

"I did screw up, Jeanine," I said, backing her up and slowing her roll just a little. "I think I ignored the signs because

I thought I had time to fix it. But ignoring you just made every-thing worse."

Her lips pressed together and she stared into her lap. I took her hand with my free one. "It's all so much."

"I know, baby," I said, wrapping her up in a hug.

"I'll have to find a new doctor, a therapist," she said.

"I'll help you."

"You don't have time," she argued.

"I'll make time," I said firmly. "There are people on the team to help with this stuff too. We're not alone."

"I don't know if I want to start with the meds again. The side effects . . ." she started.

I held her by the shoulders and looked directly into her eyes. "We don't have to decide that today, and I'm not making you do anything you don't want to do."

Joe and Maureen's heads bobbed on the other side of the table, so I kept going.

"This move was hard on both of us. And I feel like I failed you because I saw you but I just thought . . . it would get better with time. I should have seen the signs. I should have known it was worse."

Jeanine sniffled. "You could have said something."

It was a little embarrassing that her parents were sitting there witnessing this big moment in our relationship, but I wanted her to feel like she had support too.

"I was afraid if I said something, we'd fall apart, Jeanine."

"Well, we kinda did," she said, swiping under her nose.

"Well . . ." I started, taking a moment to think. "Now we get to glue us back together. I've got a plan."

She laughed again. "Glue me up, hockey boy."

I GOT UP EARLY the next morning because there was something on my mind I needed to address. I wanted to catch Andy without Jeanine around. So, I didn't mean to be lurking in the dark of the wine cellar, waiting for him to come to work, but it helped set the tone.

"Jesus," Andy jumped, putting a hand to his heart. "You scared me, man."

I ground my teeth. I would not apologize for scaring him because that was the whole point. His brow wrinkled and he quickly took stock of me. I had my hands in my front pockets, my lips pursed, and drew myself to my full height. I cocked my head to the side.

"Can I . . . help you?" He was trying to act annoyed, but his voice trembled slightly.

I chuckled. "What you can do is stay the fuck away from my wife."

He recoiled. "She's not your property."

"She's not yours, either. I don't own Jeanine, but she is mine. This is the second time you've had your nose where it shouldn't be."

"Second time?" he echoed.

"Don't think I don't know what you've tried. Don't think she hasn't cried to me about it. Not only did you try to meddle in my marriage, but you made my wife uncomfortable." I put my tongue in my cheek and made my hand into a fist, glancing at my nails. "You ever watch hockey, Andrew?"

He scoffed and shrugged. "Sure."

"Then you must know how easy it is for me to break someone's face. Wouldn't even split a knuckle. And if someone's nose is where it shouldn't be, it's truly my pleasure."

"You threatening me?" he asked. "You must really think Jeanine's going to leave you."

I popped my lips. "What happens between my wife and

me is not your concern. But know this." I stepped close to him, my voice low and even. "It would be so easy for me to put your ass in the ground and make it look like a fucking accident."

Andy stiffened. "Jeanine would hate you."

I smirked. "Jeanine wouldn't even think of you."

He narrowed his eyes. "Why do you think she always runs back to me? You treat her like shit, and she runs here."

I scoffed. "She runs back to her *parents*, Andrew. And then you're here, waiting to pounce on her with your pathetic knight in shining armor routine. Then you get mouthy with me and act like you have any fucking role in this. "

Andy's jaw ticked and I stepped back. "Don't let me catch you with your hands in the cookie jar a third time, Andrew. I hate getting dirt under my nails."

I ambled toward the door to the stairs. "Now if you'll excuse me, I'm going to go take my wife some breakfast in bed, help her pack her bags, and who knows? Maybe make love to her. Give it to her just the way she likes it. Really take my time with her, worship her sweet, beautiful body. And then I'll take her home, where she belongs."

RACHEL

Can't wait to see you tomorrow!

I KNOW

Are you already here?

Yes but Dyl's taking me on a date

Ugh FINE

"HOW'S IT feel to be back?"

Dylan and I decided rather than going out to some fancy dinner in L.A., we just wanted to go to where we met: the little dive bar in Santa Monica. And wouldn't you know it, we hit it on a live band karaoke night. We hit our favorite taco truck on the way in, then bellied up to the bar. I wore a flouncy little dress with a leather jacket and boots, and he wore a sage-colored cuffed button-down and dark jeans with the jacket I always called his "cool jacket." His outfit was topped off with a backward ballcap and a watch that accentuated one thick, hairy wrist.

"I feel like you planned this," I said, narrowing my eyes as I hooked my jacket on the back of my barstool. "How'd you know it was karaoke night? Is this part of The Plan?"

Whenever we talked about the plan, I pronounced it with special emphasis, like it was a trademarked term: The Plan™.

"I promise it's not. The Plan starts when we get back home."

I puffed out my lip as a little pang went through me. "It's weird to think this isn't home, you know? But then, home is where our kids are, our house."

He shrugged. "Wherever you four are, it's home."

My eyes were hot, but I was so over crying that I wasn't giving in. "I'd normally give you shit for being cheesy, but you're too cute. How's it feel for you to be back at the scene of the crime?"

Dylan gave me a drowsy blink, his five o'clock shadow just the same as it had been back then. "Like it was just yesterday."

I hummed a laugh. "A lot's happened since yesterday, then."

"Three little lifetimes, to be specific," he agreed.

"God, I miss them. It's hard not to go home today."

"Jeanine?"

I turned to face the gray-mustachioed man who'd backed me up on piano during countless karaoke nights. "Rick! Hi!"

I jumped off my barstool and hugged him, the smell of Curve cologne filling my nose. "You look great! How are you?"

"Oh, same old. Good to see you two here again," he said, reaching to shake Dylan's hand. "Happy to see you again, Mr. Sorrento."

Dylan had certainly done his time visiting me at work, so

the guys in the band all knew him too. "Good to see you, Rick. You guys sound amazing."

"You going to come up and sing one, J? We miss that angelic voice of yours."

Dylan watched me with hopeful eyes.

I tossed my hand. "Oh, I think I hung up my microphone a long time ago."

Dylan booed and Rick joined in. "You two, stop."

Someone else called out to Rick, Dylan headed for the bathroom, and I was left to my drink. When he got back, Dylan popped his hands into my waist and kissed my temple. I leaned into the touch, a sentimental whimper escaping me.

"I've missed that," I said.

Dylan looked confused as he settled on his barstool. We were knee-to-knee, one elbow on the bar and our other hands playing together. "What do you mean?"

"You stopped kissing my temple. A while ago. Not really sure when, but you've just kinda . . . gotten less affectionate."

Dylan's eyes rounded. "What?"

"Do you not believe me?" I asked, starting to get annoyed.

"No, no, I do. I just—" Dylan looked heartbroken. "Jeannie. I don't know what to say."

I shrugged. "Sorry?"

He shook his head. "I've always loved you. All this time. No matter how much or little I've touched you . . . fuck. I can't believe . . . I'm really sorry. I didn't even notice."

I pursed my lips, staring at our hands. "I've always loved how you touch me, how physically having you close is such a big part of us. And when it faded . . ."

"Oh, Jeannie." He looked out into the bar, then met my eyes with his watery ones. "Please never doubt that I love you. I always do."

I nodded. "But I need you to show it. Or else it's the temple kisses going away, and then it's the snuggles, and then it's—" I paused, trying not to get emotional in a place where people knew me, "It's you not responding to my sexy texts. And it's you not wanting to look at me during sex."

"Oh my god," he breathed. "Jeanine, you are so beautiful. Like, nobody else compares. I always want to see you. To think you ever doubted I loved you—"

"Oh I know I'm hot. I knew you loved me. I doubted that you were still into me."

He put a hand on my knee, giving it a squeeze. "I'm so fucking into you, Jeanine." His chocolate eyes bounced between mine, his brows scrunched. "I hate that I failed you like that."

Dylan cupped my neck, gaze flicking from my eyes to my lips. "You're my wife. You've been here through all kinds of hell. You've been here when *I* put you through hell. You've given me three beautiful children and you raise them to be such amazing people. You, all the things you are, you're *mine*. My wife."

My brows drew together, my chest flushing. Dylan was a sweet man, but not typically so poetic.

"I'm into you, J. So fucking into you." With a little smirk, he pulled us together, our lips meeting in a slow, tender kiss. He leaned more into me, partially standing to clutch my lower back as he took the kiss deeper.

We pulled apart at cheers and a familiar piano chord. Then the melody kicked in, and Dylan laughed. "I think they're summoning you, babe."

"No, no way," I said, my face reddening. The band's lead guitarist appeared at my side with a microphone.

Dylan couldn't stop grinning. "They're waiting for you, Jeannie."

"You put my name on the list," I scolded him.

"Maybe. Go."

With a shake of my head, I took the proffered microphone, dragging my ass to the stage with Dylan starting the crowd into raucous whoops.

"Folks, tonight, we have a Harvey's alum in the house. Give it up for our very own Jeanine Wendlock!"

I turned and pointed at each band member, mouthing, "I hate you."

I put the microphone to my lips and pointed to Dylan at the bar. "And I really hate you."

"SING!" Dylan shouted.

So, I did. I sang the song that brought me and Dylan together, the one that put us in each other's paths, the one that told me to sit on that cute wholesome-looking guy's lap and mess with him.

At first, I was hesitant, hitting the notes and cues just fine but without the emotion I used to bring. Gradually, I let my energy build, allowing myself to get lost in reliving a wonderful memory. By the time I hit the first "baby, baby," I was giving it my all like I was Celine in her Vegas residency.

By the second verse, I took the stairs into the crowd, working the room like I would have when I was in my twenties. And at the point when I sat on Dylan that first night we met, I slid into his lap. That man had the biggest shit-eating grin I've ever seen, groping me exactly how he would if we were at home, then ripping the microphone out of my hand.

"This is my favorite part!" he said, taking my hand and escorting me back to the stage. He scream-sang in his very offkey hockey locker room way until it got to a part far out of his vocal range, letting me take over while he hyped the very modestly sized crowd. My cheesy-ass husband stood in front of the stage, clapping non-stop and cheering like the most earnest asshole on the planet as I finished the exceedingly long power ballad.

"That's my wife!" he shouted, pointing to me on stage.

I hated it. I loved it. I was both surprised and unsurprised by it.

This was the guy I married. The guy who did everything he could to make me happy. The guy who loved me—the real me. Power ballad me who would always have a soft spot for performing. The guy who had told me time and again that he'd back me up, and whenever he could, he did.

Maybe that was the crux of our problem: he'd met his limit because he was knee-deep in shit too. He was out of capacity, and it added to his pile.

We needed each other, but we were both out of reach—twin flames in the most fiery of ways.

I hugged Rick and gave him my microphone before letting Dylan lift me down from the stage and squeeze me tight.

"You were perfect," he beamed. "I love seeing you sing."

"Even though I didn't crawl on the stage?" I asked, quirking a brow.

"Even so. Plus, that would have shown everyone your tits, and those are mine."

I peered down my dress. "That's so funny because I'm pretty sure they're attached to my body."

Dylan's jaw dropped. "Oh, I see we've got the scrappy cocktail waitress back."

I nodded. "You better watch yourself, mister. I'll take you in that back alley and fuck you up."

"I've got a better idea," he said, turning on his heel and heading for the bathrooms. I stood bewildered for a moment, but when he looked back and cocked his head at me, I realized I was supposed to follow.

When I got to the hallway, I couldn't see where he'd gone,

until a hand clapped over my mouth and I was lifted off my feet, my back against Dylan's chest. I squeaked, genuinely surprised and not trying to make a scene.

"Quiet," he growled in my ear.

Within an instant, we were in the graffiti-littered, wood-paneled bathroom, and Dylan locked the door behind us. He spun us until we both faced the mirror, slipping his hand off my mouth and down to my throat, pinning me to the front of his body. He lowered his lips to my ear again, hissing in a deep voice with his eyes meeting mine in the mirror.

"Here's what's going to happen, little one. You're going to watch yourself take me. You're going to watch me watching you, and you're going to see how much I want you and this sweet little body because somewhere our wires got crossed and you think I don't want to see my wife taking what's hers. I want to see you stuffed full of me, to see how well your body fits with mine, to see how I own you and you own me. Got it?"

I nodded, my breath heaving my chest as the music to "Highway to Hell" kicked on. I had a fleeting thought as to whether that was my old regular who always sang "Highway to Hell" on karaoke night, but was quickly brought back into the present.

Dylan's hand left my stomach and wandered under my dress, smoothing up the back of my thigh to palm my ass that was left bare by my thong. I let out an irrepressible sigh as I held his hips behind my back. "Say 'Yes, sir.'"

"Yes, sir."

"Good," he cooed. His fingers slipped between my legs from behind, petting over the thin lace before moving it aside and exploring my wetness. I tightened, and he hummed, putting a sucking kiss under my ear. "So, did you get wet when you were singing for me, or just now when I told you how good you're gonna take me?"

Our hips rocked, teasing his thick cock with my ass. "When you pulled me in this bathroom."

"That's my girl." With the hand that had been on my throat, he tipped me to meet him in a kiss over my shoulder. Our tongues clashed while his hand worked until he pulled away and dropped to his knees. "Legs wide, ass out."

Dylan pulled my panties to my knees, kissing the backs of my thighs. His hands met the juncture of my ass and my legs before his mouth landed at the apex of my thighs, greedily sucking and stroking. I kicked one foot up as I leaned into the bathroom sink, my head rolling back at the pleasure. One of his hands left me and metal clanked on metal, his belt coming undone and his zipper lowering. He stood, and I looked at him over my shoulder.

"This thing rip easy?" he asked, tugging at the shoulder of my dress.

"No, it's stretchy."

"Good." He pushed the top part of my dress to my waist, quickly unhooking my bra. Before he could let it fall to the floor, I caught it.

"Dirty floor," I laughed. Dylan grinned and hung it over his shoulder.

"That work?"

"Uh huh."

Then he lifted the bottom of my dress, leaving me bare except for my middle. He flicked his chin forward, his hard length pressing into my ass. "Look at yourself, Jeanine."

Holding my dress with one hand, he used his hand to guide himself inside me. His eyes bored into mine in the mirror as he flexed his cock.

"Do you see that, baby? How hard I am for you? You feel how much I fill you up?"

I nodded and he growled, "Say 'Yes, sir.'"

"Yes, sir."

It really was a sight to behold. The bathroom's low lighting cast an ochre glow over us. My breasts and their stiffened nipples jolted. One veiny hand rested on my throat, and one forearm angled from my waist to my hip. Dylan's eyes traveled over my body in the mirror.

"See how fucking gorgeous you are when you take me? Why would I not want to look at you?"

His lips surrounded my earlobe, nibbling to my groan. My fingers drifted between my legs, circling my swollen clit.

"You are fucking perfect for me, Jeannie. Don't you ever lie to yourself and say you're not."

"Yes, sir."

He squeezed the pooch below my belly button, cut with a horizontal scar. I whimpered his name, moving from my clit to cover his hand. It takes a very confident woman to be comfortable with that area being noticed during sex, and I was not fully that woman. I didn't believe in feeling shame over my body because what does that accomplish? Still, it's fair to say it wasn't my favorite part of my body.

Dylan didn't care.

"I love this part of you. You are this beautiful because you carried our babies. Own it. We made this part of you together, Jeanine. It's fucking sexy as hell."

Pleasure rushed from my toes, taking in my mostly clothed husband and my mostly naked self, his backward hat, his forever-stubbled face, his delicious scent, and those deep brown eyes that were my personal safe haven.

Everything we'd gone through in the past few months squealed its way into my brain on balding tires. Our eyes connected in the mirror, and I realized just how much I needed us to figure out our issues. I couldn't let nights like tonight get away. This was worth saving.

"Dylan, I want us to work. I need us to make it through this."

He nodded, his brow lowering and eyes going wide while he continued pumping into me. "We're going to make it, Jeannie. I'm not letting you go again. I love you too much to lose you."

"I love you, Dylan," I cried, bracing my hands on the counter for leverage and letting my shoulders fall back against his chest.

"That's it, baby. I've always got you." His fingers returned to my clit, his circles getting more furious. "Let go for me. Eyes on me, on us. Watch how much we're made for each other."

I pressed my shoulders forward, intensifying the angle of his penetration and how he stroked my clit.

"You have to come too," I choked out as his other hand met my shoulders, my hips bouncing back against him with every thrust.

He shook his head with a smirk. "Such a needy little cunt you've got."

I met his gaze in the mirror. "But it's yours."

"All fuckin' mine."

I begged, I pleaded, I shifted all my weight to one leg as my focus went to our shared pleasure, to hooking my other leg around his hip to hold him close and spread me wide.

Cusses, names, cries, blinding stares, and collapsing into each other. His lips were on my neck as we fell back against the bathroom door. He cupped my breasts, and we shared a lazy smile in the mirror.

"Just like old times," I said.

Dylan's hand came to my jaw, moving it up so our eyes would meet. "Better than old times. We're more now."

THIRTY-ONE
JEANINE
NOW | DECEMBER

"AND YOU JUST LEFT HIM standing there in the garage?" Rachel Beatty's eyes were wide as we sipped cocktails around a tiny table in the bar we used to love. We were reunited, and god, did it feel good. Obviously, I texted with her constantly, but having her in the same room was the best, easiest feeling.

I nodded solemnly.

"Oh, babe. You gave it to him good."

I tossed my head to the side. "I hate to think of it like that. And I hate that I had to leave to get him to pay attention. I just hit my wall."

She tossed back the bottom of her old fashioned, plucking

the cherry out of the drink and catching it between her teeth. "You didn't do anything wrong. It's better that you know when you're at your limit and leave than staying and making everyone else lose it too. And you knew his mom was coming to help. You didn't totally hang him out to dry."

I chomped on my lower lip to stave off more serious emotion. "I hope the kids are okay."

"The kids will be fine. And when they grow up, they'll understand, just like we understand our moms now."

I tossed an almond in my mouth from the table between us. "I guess I'm really stuck. It seems like everybody else just becomes a parent and their marriage is great and everything is fine. No one shows you how to be in love with the people you're with day in and day out. And right now, I'm not in love with how my life has turned out. I'm a terrible mom."

"Oh, stop that," Rachel snorted. "Babe. Get ready. Even the most well-adjusted people have times when they're not happy with their lives. People who look like they're doing amazing after having a kid have shredded pelvic floors. People who show how in love they are with their partner have the nastiest fights. People who look like they have it all together are covering up how dead they are inside. Comparing yourself to what you think someone else's situation is will not change anything for you. You have to look at your life and your circumstance and figure out what you want to do differently."

I picked at the cocktail napkin, softened from the dripping condensation on my glass. "Dylan said he's going to be different. The move's been hard on him too. And he's been so sweet since he came to get me. But what about when we get back home? He says he has this plan. But I'm scared that won't work, and then what?"

Rachel crunched an ice cube from her otherwise empty

glass, eyeing me. "I don't doubt that Dylan's gotten neglectful over time and that the move screwed you both up. You know I say this with so much love, but do you think you're depressed again?"

My eyes welled. "You're not the first person to bring that up."

She grabbed my hand on the table. "It's okay if you are."

I took a shaky breath. "If I am, it makes me afraid that I'm the problem and not him. That I just need to get with it and wake up and love my life. I feel guilty for not loving it."

She shrugged. "Why can't it be a little bit of all of it? A little bit of your brain, a little bit of your circumstance, and a little bit Dylan trying to toxic positivity his way through it? He won't let you express when you're upset. He made the decision for your family without asking you. That's enough to make anybody depressed."

I pulled the soggy cocktail napkin off the table and dabbed my eyes, grateful I was facing the back of the bar and only Rachel could see my face.

"Do you think meds would help you again?" she asked. Rachel had been around for my last bout of depression, and when I started the long process of weaning off the meds once my life stabilized. She weathered the irrational phone call when I dropped my dose too quickly, hid in a closet, and said Dylan hated me.

"I don't even know where to start with all that in Columbus. New doctors, new insurance, all of it. Dyl says he'll help me, but we probably also need to find a therapist for us as a couple. When is there going to be time for all this stuff? I'm running all over the place as it is."

She flattened her lips with soft eyes. "You need to let him help, honey. He can't help you if you don't let him try. I know he doesn't want you to feel this way, J. It's okay that you do, but it doesn't need to be this hard."

I sniffled. "I was so proud of myself for not needing the meds anymore, you know? I thought I'd figured it all out and defeated it somehow."

She shrugged again. "I'm going to be on my anti-depressant for the rest of my life. Do you think I'm weak?"

I sat back, affronted. "No! Of course not. Never."

"See? Then why be so hard on yourself?" She squeezed my hand again before letting it go. "I'll be interested to see what Dyl's got up his sleeve with this big plan," she said in a joking voice, then straightened, "but you've also got to meet him halfway."

I growled, giving her a goofy glare. "I hate when you're right."

She tossed her honey-colored locks over her shoulder. "I personally love it."

"Okay, great, stop gloating. I promise I'm going to get your rundown, but can I tell you about how my college summer fling tried to steal me from Dylan this week?"

Rachel's jaw dropped and she let out a gleeful, "WHAT?"

LATER, I sat at the game with my favorite of the L.A. Princes WAGs. Dyl surprised us with a suite, which he told me not to check our bank account to see how much that cost.

He said I was worth it, and I deserved time with my girls.

"So, you're here because Dylan screwed up and you did the pack a bag and go thing?" Jessie Miknevicius had her daughter Maddie slumped against her chest, falling asleep.

I nodded and winced. "I'm not too proud of it."

"Sometimes when things are really bad, you have to let

them know in a way they can hear it," she said, raising her eyebrows.

"I mean, there's a high chance I'm depressed and need meds again. That makes you way more likely to fight."

Jessie gave me a sympathetic grimace. "Ben and I had our share of troubles after Maddie was born. I had postpartum anxiety pretty bad. Add that to some PTSD that I never really addressed properly, and I was a hot mess."

"Aw, Jessie, I'm sorry. How are you doing now?" It was like looking at her in a new light. Jessie sometimes seemed insecure at the wives' gatherings, but she was also kind of a badass. I'd never have guessed she was going through a lot behind closed doors.

"Much better now that I'm medicated and back in therapy. I even got Ben to go!"

"Ooh! A modern miracle!" Kitty Gatto sidled over, Guy Stelle's wife, reaching for Maddie and cooing as Maddie snuggled into her.

"Best godmother ever," Jessie said. "She loves you so much, Kitty."

"She knows what's up," Kitty said, bouncing Maddie to lull her to sleep. "I only caught the end of that. How's Ohio treating ya?"

I frowned. "It's not the same. We miss you guys. The vibes aren't the same."

"I'm sure there are good wives there too, though," Kitty said. Her eyes lit up. "Mara's there, right? She's a million times better than Sydney."

Sydney, Jack Leroy's ex-wife, had been responsible for creating a rift in the WAGs group, bullying newer wives like Jessie and Kitty. Once she was out of the scene, harmony was restored.

"Oh, yeah. Mara's the one who got me stoned off my ass at

our Halloween party," I said, turning to side hug Annie Markham, looking pristine in her crisp office outfit. She was the Princes goalie Nick Oberbeck's fiancée and a sports agent. "Hi, pretty! You just come from work?"

"Ugh, yes," she said, stepping out of her high heels and flexing her feet. I'm a taller woman, but Annie's in a league of her own, probably reaching six feet in her heels. "But I couldn't miss this."

"We were just telling Jeanine to hang out with Mara," Kitty said.

"And what I was getting to, other than her getting me high, was that I really don't know her that well. My first couple of parties weren't too great with the Rusties wives."

Jessie nodded, squeezing me to her. "I was overwhelmed when I started coming to these things. I had trouble with girl friendships. Like I'd had some, but I've always struggled to find my people—"

"Until now," Kitty said. "Right? You love us, right?"

"That's what I was going to say, you goober," Jessie laughed. "You and Jeanine were the ones who made me feel welcome. I was mad Mikey didn't tell me you were cool sooner. I could have used you on my team."

"I was on your team!" I objected.

"Yeah, well, I guess I didn't feel like I fit until I gave it a good shot. Big groups of people are hard for me, but I do really well one on one. I just tried each person until I found my ones."

"Aw, am I your one?" Kitty asked, leaning her head on Jessie's shoulder.

I sighed. "It's true. Most of them are really nice. I overheard a couple talking shit about Jack and Dylan, and I don't know. It's weird to not fit after I had it so good with you all here."

"Give it a shot," Jessie urged me. "And give Dylan a shot too. The more you dig into life there, the better it'll feel."

Rachel had wandered over, listening to the last part of our conversation. "Oh, that's so interesting. Such good advice."

"You guys are ganging up on me!" I protested.

"Only because we love you," Rachel said, putting her arm around me.

THIRTY-TWO
JEANINE
NOW | DECEMBER

Made it home. Love you. Glad I got to
see you

RACHEL

Come back anytime. I guess I need to come
see you next so I can have an excuse to buy
a coat

AFTER PAYING a massive long-term parking bill at the airport, I pulled into the garage at home. The kids would already be in bed, as I had a delay during my layover in Chicago.

This meant I was facing Dylan's mom with no buffer.

She sat at the kitchen counter, drinking a glass of wine. "Finally," she said as I walked through the door.

"Hey, Carla," I said with a smile. "The kids do okay?"

She rolled her eyes. "Yes. And all the other days I had to parent your children."

I sucked a breath through my nose, doing my best to keep

up the smile as I set my bags down and looked through the mail at my desk. "Well, I really appreciate you coming to take care of them. Dylan and I needed that time."

Her nostrils flared. "Did my son need you to leave your post as mother of his children to go have some affair in wine country?"

Holding a fake smile was no longer an option. "I'm not going to dignify that with a response."

"That's pretty disrespectful," she snapped. "I've been here, slogging through it with your children who clearly need a heavier hand, and you've been out flitting in the California sun."

"Carla," I said, emptying my hands and planting them on the counter, "since it seems we're dropping pleasantries, I'm going to give it to you straight. Being nice has never gotten me anywhere with you. What's the saying? It's insanity to do the same thing the same way and expect different results? So I'm changing my methods.

"Dylan invited you here. Not me. He seems to have some misguided thought that you would change and see that I am not the diabolical demon you've made me out to be. I thought I'd make the best of the situation and take the break I so desperately needed. If I had stayed here and we tried to play nice, I don't know that it would have gone well. I'm tired of faking like you don't constantly try to cut me down and pit Dylan against me. What's your end game, Carla? You want him to divorce me? What is your real problem with me? Or would no one be good enough for your precious boy?"

She stiffened and held her head up. "I told him you were a head case from the beginning. Flighty. Not even fit to look after yourself, so you glommed onto him," she said. "He's been cleaning up after you since you two got married. He only asked you to marry him because you went and got knocked up. He should have gotten an annulment when I told him to."

Oh, the irony. The irony that the whole reason Dyl and I fell apart was because I was always cleaning up after him, that my life was solely dictated by his. And it was her fault that he was that way, letting her whole life revolve around him.

"First of all, there is nothing wrong with having mental health issues, just like there's nothing wrong with having any other disease. Second, if your son only married me because I was pregnant, then why did he stay when I wasn't? Why did he have three more kids with me?"

"You coerced him," she spat.

I shook my head. "I wish he could hear you now. Your son pursued me. Your son begged me to love him, because he probably never got it from you. You dangle the carrot in front of us, like *I'll love you when you do this*, but we never get the damn carrot. I've spent years trying to please you, Carla, to fit into some impossible mold you dreamed up. I've hit my wall. I can't continually take abuse from you and keep running back for more, hoping you'll wake up to the fact that despite your best efforts, I'm not going anywhere. Dylan and I have our issues, yes. But we're willing to work on them and not just sweep them under the rug."

"Abuse," she scoffed. "You kids are too sensitive."

Wow. She's good at determining the takeaways.

"Carla, would you like to leave my house now? I'll gladly pay for your hotel room to get out of my face. I've got a family to support, and if you're not going to contribute to that, you're welcome to leave."

"After all I've done for you—"

"Thank you," I said over her, "for taking care of our children while we had some much-needed time to focus on our relationship. Will you be staying here tonight, or shall I book you a hotel?"

"You abandoned your children. You abandoned my son. I would never abandon Dylan," she said.

"There's the door," I said, grabbing my bag and heading upstairs to unpack. "I'll have Dylan call you when he's home."

Can't wait to be home with you

JEANNIE

Waiting up for you

You don't have to

I want to

<3

"MISSED you more than ever this time," I said, tucking Jeanine into my body in the bed. We'd just had our late-night reunion sex after the team got home from the road trip.

"I missed you too, Dyl." We hummed, squeezing each other a little tighter. Her face went stony, chewing her lip and looking away from me.

"What is it, J?"

"You might want to call your mom."

I drew my head back. "What happened?"

"We may have fought when I got home. I threw her out."

I winced. "I was afraid of that. I really didn't want her to lay into you."

"Well, she did. She said I abandoned you. That I've conned you into staying with me."

"Jesus. You know none of that's true, right?" Jeanine nodded. I propped up on my elbow so I could look deeper into Jeanine's eyes. "I didn't want to break our bubble in California, but I see what you mean now about her being so harsh. I actually got into a fight with her the day she got here."

"You did?" Jeannie's fingers idly combed through my chest hair.

"I told her she had to choose whether to respect you or lose us both. All because she was griping about you not cleaning the refrigerator shelves. So what did she say to you?"

"Well?" Her voice was a high-pitch squeak. "She kinda came out guns blazing when I got home, so I decided to shoot straight. I told her she'd never been nice to me, and I asked what her end game was."

"And what did she say to that?"

Jeanine looked up into my eyes. "She said all I do is weigh you down. That I'm a head case who coerced you into having children with me. Essentially, that I trapped you so I could leach on you."

I flopped back on the pillow and Jeannie curled up on my chest. "Fuck."

"Yes, that."

"I don't know what else to do. I think I have to cut her off. I'm glad she could be here when we needed help, but that doesn't give her the right to abuse you. And who knows what she says to the kids."

"She said our kids clearly need a heavier hand," Jeannie said.

"Jesus, fuck."

Jeannie's eyes moved over me. "It's your decision. I'm not pushing you either way. She's your mom. But I do reserve the right to protect myself and our kids from her wrath."

"I at least need a break from her. I'm afraid if I fully cut her out, I'll lose Dad too. But I can't let her keep hurting you. I can't keep hurting you, letting her go at you like that. It hurts me that she has so much animosity toward you." I shook my head. "I need to think about it, but I need to do something."

"This means a lot to me, Dyl. I know this isn't easy for you."

I kissed her hairline and tightened my arm around her shoulder. She had a lot to gain from me cutting my mom out, but she didn't push me. That's how I knew mentally she was in a somewhat stable place. This is probably how Jeanine felt leaving me, like you don't know how to show them what they're missing unless you're gone. But was I really ready to take such a drastic step with Ma?

I was proud of her for sticking up for what she needed, even if it hurt me.

Because something our marriage couldn't endure anymore was hidden feelings.

IT WAS time for me to put The Plan into effect. I only had a few one-off away games before Christmas. I'd mostly be home, and able to help Jeannie more frequently.

Jeanine wasn't wrong to doubt whether or not I actually had a plan. Most of the time, I wouldn't. But I put some thought into this one. I had to work around school plays and art shows and games for me and the kids, but I put in three different occasions that were just for us.

I was also going to make every effort to show up to the kids' holiday events. I could help her with getting the kids ready for them.

Here was The Plan:

1. Cook Jeannie a special dinner for a date night in

2. Have a Christmas movie marathon with kids' movies and after they went to bed, grown-up movies

3. A spa day where I'd talked a few of the guys into sending their wives

4. Snow tubing with the kids

5. Dinner and her favorite Christmas musical, White Christmas, at the big theater in town

BONUS: Our first snow as a family?

Okay, I had no control over that last one, but we were far more likely to see snow in Columbus than we had been in Los Angeles.

I was bringing the magic back. Because somewhere between kids and hockey and the drumbeat of life, we'd lost it.

And hopefully, by the end of all this, Jeannie and I would feel like a team again. She'd fall back in love with me, with our life. And then, we could live happily ever after.

We were off to a good start with my "rescuing" her from her parents' winery, but Jeanine deserved much more than that.

I bought a stationery set with a Santa theme so I could leave her a note every time part of the plan was coming up.

Also, to settle her planner mind, I wrote "The Plan" on the calendar for every day where she needed to make sure she left the schedule open.

So on the first morning I was back, I set out a note.

We'll start the plan off close to home
Where I'll be cooking at the stove
I've got dinner covered, baby
The meat will fall right off the bone (?)

Okay, I was working on the poetry part. But it would make her laugh and that was important.

I didn't get to see her reaction, because she was already out taking the kids to school and then working a WAG volunteer event. I found the card carefully tucked back into its envelope on her desk space.

There was a part of me that needed validation from her. I wanted to know she was all in and liked my ideas. So I texted her, because you can't expect what you want without communicating what you want.

> Can't wait to spoil you rotten tonight

I didn't hear back from her until after I got out of practice.

JEANNIE

> Had to pick Bella up from school. Stuffy nose and threw up

I groaned. Of course, one of our kids would get sick when I was trying to thrill my wife to make her love me again.

> Oh no! A stomach bug and a cold?

JEANNIE

> Prob not. She always pukes when she gets a cold

Seriously?

Still, I went to the store to get all the supplies to wow Jeanine that night. I could just take over with the kids and feed Jeanine after bedtime. How hard could it be?

Can you get Grey and Al? There's no way I can put B in the car

On it babe

I GOT HOME to Jeanine holding Bella and walking her around the kitchen. Alice and Greyson thundered through the kitchen to head straight for the TV, something I'd promised them in the car while I assessed the situation with Bella. She had that bounce you use when kids are really tiny and you're just trying to get them to sleep. Jeanine's shirt had a damp spot on it, her hair was up in a lopsided ponytail, and she looked miserable.

"Aw, my girls," I said.

"Her ear hurts," Jeanine whispered.

I grimaced. "How are you?"

Bella woke from her nap on Jeannie's shoulder with a start, wailing out a "Mommy!"

Like she anticipated the flood, Jeanine speed-shuffled to the sink as Bella unleashed a tide of puke, a splatter as it hit J and the floor. Jeanine patted Bella's back. "It's okay, sweet pea. Let's try and get it in the sink," she said as she leaned over the sink.

I stifled a gag, coughing to try and stave it off. Jeanine shot me a death glare over Bella's head as she vomited into the sink.

"I'm sorry!" I said. "You know I don't do good with puke."

"No one does, Dylan," she grumbled. "Some of us just

have to."

That made me feel sicker, because she was right. "So she throws up when she gets a cold?"

Jeanine's jaw feathered. "Yes," she said tersely, then blinked hard. "She swallows snot, I think, and it upsets her stomach."

"Poor thing," I said. Bella seemed done throwing up for the moment, so I held out my hands. "I've got you, sweetie. Let's go get you cleaned up."

"I want Mommy!" Bella said, clinging to Jeanine.

"Mommy needs a break, baby. I've got you."

"Is Mommy leaving?" Bella wailed.

Jeanine's eyes filled with tears as I took Bella out of her arms. "No, baby. Mommy's not leaving," she said.

AFTER I GAVE Bella a bath and Jeanine got a shower, I left J to rock Bella. "I was planning to take over, but I need to get food on the table for the kids," I said.

"It's fine, I get it," Jeanine said, lifeless behind her eyes.

I kissed both of them on the top of the head. "I'll relieve you as soon as I'm done cooking."

I scrambled to cook a box of mac and cheese for the older two, popping the appetizers I'd gotten into the oven for Jeanine. Thank god I hadn't overestimated my culinary abilities and just got a frozen thing I needed to heat up. I poured her a glass of her favorite white wine. I left Alice and Greyson to start eating while I ran the wine and appetizer up to Jeanine.

I walked in to find them both asleep in Bella's rocking chair. I jogged into our bedroom to put the appetizers and wine on Jeanine's nightstand. Then I carefully pried Bella off Jeanine and put her down in her crib.

I scooped Jeanine up much the same way, carrying her to our bed.

"What are you doing?" Jeanine grumbled.

"Putting you in bed. You're exhausted."

She sighed. "I am. But I was promised something special tonight, meat on the bone, etcetera."

I frowned, studying her. "I don't want it to be an obligation, babe. The point is for it to be fun for us."

She threw up an exasperated hand. "When will we not have a sick kid? When will I not be tired?"

There was a crash downstairs, followed by a "Mommy!" Jeanine moved to get up, but I held her back.

"You stay here. I've got it." I put the plate and wine glass in her hands. "I'll go manage that, and when dinner's ready I'll come get you. But we're not eating until the kids are in bed. I don't want any interruptions."

Jeannie softened, her eyes rounding. "Thank you."

"Mom!" came the shout again. I kissed her quickly and left, shutting our bedroom door behind me.

THIRTY-FOUR
JEANINE
NOW | DECEMBER

RACHEL

(pic from school pageant)

Aw tell Greta I'm so proud of her. Love the costume

I WOKE up disoriented from my nap, an amazingly delicious smell floating on the air. The smell reminded me of California.

I took a sip of the wine Dylan put on the nightstand and tried one of the appetizer bites. Not bad.

I sauntered into the kitchen, finding him concentrating at the stove. "Smells good," I said.

He looked up with a grin. "You're up! How was your nap?"

"Needed," I said, kissing his cheek and holding him from behind. "Thank you."

He gave the pan's contents another toss, then turned to face me. "All you have to do is ask, and I'll help you out. Whatever you need, J."

And there came the dark feelings again.

"What?" He looked genuinely confused.

I rubbed my forehead. "I'm just frustrated."

"Tell me."

I sucked in a breath. "I'm tired of having to tell you what I need. I just want you to jump in and help. If you regularly helped, you'd know how to help. If you paid attention, you'd know that Bella swallows snot and pukes every time she gets a cold. I know you're trying to learn, and we need to talk to each other more about what we need, but it's also frustrating that I even have to teach you. It's another task."

He stared at his toes. "I feel like I do help when I'm home."

I closed my eyes. "You're right. You do. But sometimes I wish you'd just . . . want to spend time with me. I could clean later."

Dylan screwed up his face. "Which is it, Jeannie? You want me to help, or you want me to hang out with you?"

I clamped my jaw to keep from crying. "Forget it. You're right."

He put a gentle hand on my upper arm. "Help me understand," he said, lowering his face to meet my eyes. "I want things to be better. I can do a lot of things, but I can't guess what you want."

Those soft brown eyes with the pinched brows and the concern painted all over his face melted me. A tear slipped out of my eye. "I want it to not be so hard. I know what I'm saying doesn't make a lot of sense, and I wish I could make my brain work better."

He nodded. "Okay."

"Every day, everything feels like I'm running through Jell-O. It's like lead runs through my veins instead of blood. And raising the kids is harder here than I thought it would be. Then you add in our new city without my friends, and you being gone all the time, and my parents aren't a few hours away anymore, and—" I drew a choppy breath, "I just want to lay my head in your lap sometimes and have you cuddle me and remind me that I was once a human that existed outside all of this."

Dylan pulled me into his chest, locking his arms around me as I cried. He cupped the back of my head and kissed my hair, then my forehead. He pushed me back. "I'm here for whatever you need. Whatever I can do. And know that I'm willing to work on my part here."

I paused. "What do you mean?"

"I mean, if we need to go to therapy together, I'm down for that."

I sealed my arms tighter around him. "Really?"

"Yep. Whatever this takes." He sniffed the air as it got cloudier around us. "I will keep holding you, but first, I need to get out these fish tacos that I might be burning for you."

I laughed, stepping back to use a paper towel on my face. "You burned me some fish tacos?"

"I did," he said with a grin. "Not exactly meat falling off the bone, but I did my best."

He removed the fish from the oven, which was indeed a darker brown than it should have been. We sat to eat, where Dylan had some restaurant-style chips and salsa waiting.

I had to smile. "You did really good, Dyl."

He chuckled. "We haven't tasted it yet. It might be awful. I have to credit Royce. He put together the menu and told me what to get."

"Aw, that was nice of him." I grabbed Dylan's hand. "Even if it's awful, I love it."

He rolled his eyes. "I feel like one of the kids. Should I make you some macaroni art and you call it a Van Gogh?"

"Oh, stop," I said, waving him off.

"Jeannie, sometimes I think you lump me in with the kids."

My eyebrows shot up. "I'm sorry?"

"It's not meant to be an attack, J. That's probably something we need to work out."

I rolled my lips. "Well, there are times where it feels like I'm the only parent, because you're so playful with them, it's like I've got four kids."

Dylan glanced anywhere but at me. "Right."

I put my elbows on the table and massaged my temples. "I'm not trying to attack you, either. I want to be honest, not cruel."

"Feels like something we should work on," he said.

I reached for his hand. "I'm sorry. Maybe therapy together will help?"

"Hope so." He pursed his lips and chewed the bottom one.

"I still have this lingering fear that I'm the problem, Dyl. Like maybe you're actually doing everything right, and I'm just perceiving it wrong because of depression. I'm embarrassed that I ran away and your team knows about it and that Bella would even think I was leaving again. I should have never given her a reason to fear that."

"Jeannie," he said softly. "We both have a hand in this. I know I'm part of the problem, so I have to be part of the solution."

"Goddammit, Dyl. That's corny, but it's sexy."

He cracked a smile again, the smile I fell in love with. "I'll take anything that ends with me being sexy. Come here." He scooted his chair back and stood, where I gladly met him in a hug. "One thing at a time. Let's get the basics covered so you get some breathing room, and then we'll get you back to scrappy cocktail waitress Jeanine."

I cackled. "You just miss scrappy cocktail waitress Jeanine because she'd give you a blowjob anywhere."

"Huh. Did she? I seem to not remember that part of her. I

remember that she teased me about shit all the time and had me crawling everywhere after her like a sad little puppy."

I looked up at him and patted his cheek. "You were also on your knees a lot."

"And you were bent over stuff a lot," he added.

I grinned. "Maybe I'm feeling a little scrappy right now." My fingers curled into the collar of his shirt, ripping it to the side and replacing it with my lips. He pulled me up into a kiss, his tongue hot and seeking, his teeth scraping my lip. I snaked my hands under the hem of his t-shirt, scratching over his skin as I lifted his shirt over his head. Once off, I pulled out of our kiss to skim my lips over every inch of exposed skin.

He moaned my name and then I was tugging at his waistband, pushing it down until his firm erection sprang free. I worked him in my hand as I sank to my knees, keeping my eyes on his the whole time. I peppered up his shaft with little kisses, letting some of his precum smear on my face. I took Dylan's hand, dragging his thumb through the mess and sucking it into my mouth.

"Jeannie," he warned.

I took a teasing lick journey over the tender skin. "Hmm?"

"I didn't cook you dinner so you'd blow me."

I bobbed my mouth on his cock a few times to his groans. "Maybe this is what I want."

He sucked air through his teeth, looking to the ceiling and shaking his hands like he was trying to keep control. "You want to blow me?"

"I love giving you head, Dylan. You know that."

"You do?" he asked as I went harder, hollowing my cheeks and slurping. "Shit, J."

I popped off. "I love having this control over you. Of being able to just be the two of us, zoning into each other, being the one to make you lose it."

"Fuck, that's hot, Jeannie." He closed his eyes and let me work for a while. "I like eating you for the same reason."

I raised my eyebrows at him, willing him to talk while I was overwhelming him.

"You're this goddess when I eat you out. It's just us, me focusing on you. Making you let go of all the ways you've become so tightly wound." He whimpered, stroking a hand over the back of my head. "I might need it now."

I took a long lick up his shaft. "Been a long time since I finished you on my knees."

"Because I always want you to come too," he said, then with a wicked smirk, "and there's nothing quite like busting one in my wife's pussy."

My hands moved on him while we talked, one hand holding his balls and the other pumping his shaft. "Which do you want tonight?"

"This is your night, baby."

I shook my head. "It's ours. You've done a lot of taking care of me. I want to do something nice for you."

His thumb passed over my lips. "Edge me, then I'll eat you till you come, and then make you come again on my cock."

"Counteroffer," I said.

"Let's hear it."

"You eat me, then . . ."

"Yes," he asked, putting his hand over mine to slow me down. "Easy, now."

"Pearl necklace."

"Jeannie," Dylan whined, his head falling back on his shoulders.

"Then if you get it up again, you can fuck me."

"Sold. Off your knees, woman." He tugged me up by my arms and hauled me to the other end of our dining table. He pressed my tailbone against the edge of the table, leaning over me. He held the back of my neck and propped his other hand on the table, forcing my head back to look at him. He took my mouth in a depraved kiss, grinding himself against me where his pants were still open as I writhed under him. I was breathless when he pulled away, my breasts heaving. His gaze was voracious as his hands met the hem of my shirt, lifting it over my head and burying his face between my breasts. His hands unclasped my bra, then came up to cup my neck once again, his breath feathering over my upturned face.

"Dyl," I breathed.

His lids were hooded and his tongue peeked out between his lips as he watched my mouth. "What is it, baby?"

God, his voice was so low and full of want that I was already a puddle before he even got my leggings off. His palm flattened against my belly, fingertips sliding under the band of my underwear. I clutched his shoulders, panting as the pad of his finger grazed over my clit.

"Tell me, Jeanine." His finger traveled up and down my slit, my nipples hardening at his workings.

"I love when you eat me out. Like, a lot. And if you could do it longer or more often, that would . . ."

Another finger moved over my clit. Dylan was in this mode that I fucking adore, where he's in a sex-crazed daze, almost hypnotized. His nod was drowsy. "Guess I'll have to start doing it more often then, huh?"

"That would be nice," I said, in the understatement of the year.

He plunged a finger into my pussy and I cried out, clenching around him. His lips hooked upward on one side. "Still so tight, Jeanine. Let's get these pants off."

I pressed my heels into the edge of the table to lift my bottom as he withdrew his hand, tugging my pants and underwear down and off. His pants were still somewhat on, but he stood back, his warmth gone from me. The blast of cold air made me instinctually cover myself.

"No," he whispered. "I want to see my wife."

I dropped my hands back, holding myself up on my hands and letting my heels fall off the end of the table.

His eyes roved over my skin, giving his cock a firm grip. "So fucking beautiful, Jeanine."

He stepped forward, lifting my left foot and kissing the arch of it. My head fell back, the pleasure unexpected. Then he kissed the space below the inside of my ankle and I gasped. A lazy grin spread over his face. "You like that?"

I nodded, pressing forward shamelessly to beg for more. "It's not gross?"

He shook his head. "Something new," he said, running his tongue up the inside of my arch until he reached my toe. "How have we never done feet in all this time?"

I laughed. "I'm not sure. We've tried damn near everything else. You chase me, you fake kidnap me, you wear a mask, you tie me up, we do it in public . . ."

"You want me to taste these little toes?" This was how we broadened our horizons together: a sense of humor and curiosity. There were plenty of things we tried that just weren't worth the hassle. He raised his eyebrows at me to ask permission, and I'd never done foot shit a day in my life, used to having mangled dancer's feet for so many years. But this was, for whatever reason, a whole fresh level of hot.

I sighed out a "yes" and his mouth surrounded my toe, his tongue circling it. This was a new frontier: the view of his plump lips surrounding my toe, bobbing on it slowly, filling his mouth with my smaller toes, his eyes alternating between being closed reverently and peeking at me. It was the closest I'd gotten to coming without being touched in the more obvious places, maybe ever.

"Dylan, it's so good."

He smirked as he explored further, working his way back down my arch to my ankle again, nibbling up the inside of my calf. He thrust to pull my leg up his body at the end of the table, still propped on my elbows.

"Get on your back so I can eat."

I lie back, and he pulled the dining chair up to sit. His tongue peeked out to lick his upper lip as he examined me spread before him, his hands on the tops of my thighs and my center just below his face, my hamstrings against his chest and shoulders. "My favorite fucking meal."

His lips and warm breath traced the creases of my thighs, my mound, just over my labia.

"Dylan," I begged.

"Got you good and wet, didn't I?" he cooed. "Look at this."

A finger dragged through my wetness and I shuddered. I arched my hips up, pleading for him to relieve me.

"You must want it pretty bad, huh, baby?"

"Yes," I whimpered. "Please."

He didn't suspend me any longer, letting his tongue travel from bottom to top, my sigh loud and long.

Then he stopped teasing me. He slid two fingers into my pussy, watching my face as he did. My body bowed upward in response. "That's it, Jeanine."

From there, his tongue was sloppy, circling and exploring, his lips pulling heavy sucks. His fingers inside pulsed, strumming against me with precise abandon.

"Fuck, Dylan, this is it," I squeaked, my mouth dry from panting so hard. He continued, bringing me closer and closer as my hand reached for his head. His narrowed brown eyes met mine as he worked to get me there, his face lightly bouncing against the rolling of my hips. "Yes, baby, oh my god, shit—"

And then I was basically silent, a series of whimpers from

my vocal cords as I wriggled against his mouth, coming to his satisfied hum.

And his hand working in his lap.

He stood, helping me stand up and smashing his mouth against mine.

"Clean my face," he said. With a series of sucking kisses, I cleared my arousal from his skin, then he buried his face in my neck. "Goddammit, I love how you taste."

My hand circled his cock, pumping a couple times. "And maybe I like how you taste."

Dylan lifted me to drop me to my feet, him taking my place sitting on the end of the table. He shucked his pants and boxer briefs the rest of the way down and sat back. The table creaked under his weight and we made big eyes at each other.

"I don't give a fuck if it breaks," he said, gathering my hair in his hand and offering his cock to me with his other.

I sat in the chair between his spread legs, his cock right at eye level for me. I didn't waste much time with the build-up. I'd already done so much and I just needed to feel him, hot and hard in my mouth.

"Can I push?" he asked, and I hummed.

He tried thrusting up into my mouth, me continually gagging and getting more saliva on his cock.

"Knees," he said, and I shoved the chair back, the wood back of the chair thunking against the hardwood floor.

We shared a nervous laugh, hoping we wouldn't wake the kids. While I was smiling up at him, he grazed a thumb over my cheek. "You're so perfect, J."

I took his cock back into my hand and got back to work, until he held my head still. "Can I fuck your mouth?"

I nodded, lowering my chin and dropping my jaw open farther. He held the back of my head for leverage, his other hand clamping the back of the table.

"Fuck, Jeanine. You make me feel so fucking good."

His thrusts became more stuttered and the first pulse from him hit the back of my mouth. He pulled out, our hands working together to jerk him onto my collarbones and chest. I met his eyes and stuck my tongue out as he breathed out hard, letting him see the little bit he'd left in my mouth. He ran his thumb over my tongue and dragged a trail of it down the front of my throat.

"How do I look?" I asked.

His breaths were ragged, his eyes wild. "Like you're all fucking mine."

He bent forward to kiss me, then leaned his weight on the table's edge, breathing out a heavy whoosh of air.

That whoosh didn't let him hear the crack.

We had one of those tables that doesn't have legs on the outside, but rather a singular base in the middle that supports the whole thing. Fewer banged knees and all that. But a big oak table can only take so much when all the pressure is put on one spot.

It almost played out in slow motion, Dylan's eyes going big and his whole naked self tumbling to the floor along with our now-split dining table. Sadly the split wasn't a clean break, with jagged splinters poking out here and there. I immediately laughed, as one would when one's husband breaks the dining table while he's naked and one is still covered in his cum.

But his shriek of pain, followed by whisper screaming so we didn't wake the kids, made my laughter stop.

"Oh, baby, no, are you alright?"

"My ass!" he hissed out. "My fucking ass!"

"What can I do?" I asked, reaching over the splinters of half our table to get a fistful of napkins from the dispenser in what was once the middle of the table. I wiped his mess from my chest quickly and crouched to help Dylan, who was acting much like a laboring first-time mother. He rolled on one hip, squalling with most of an erection still maintained. Impressive!

"I think I broke my ass!" he squealed. "I'm gonna be in so much trouble, because of my ass! I'm not supposed to break stuff outside the rink!"

Since Greyson was Dylan's mini-me, I was reminded of how he would sulk as a toddler if he got a minor injury. That made me have to work even harder to stifle my laughter, knowing my very much adult husband would not appreciate it.

"Let's not worry about that now. Can I get you some ice and look at it?"

"Okay," he whined. I helped him stand and got him to lie on the couch. He limped like he'd injured a whole leg or two.

I held a hand over my mouth as I walked away, trying so hard not to laugh. It was one of the more ridiculous things I've seen in my life. But then he made it worse.

"Alexa, what's the strongest wood for a dining table?"

Then our little house robot took the liberty of answering his question. I full-on piggy snorted, folding in half over his ludicrous question.

"Jeannie, it's not funny!" he whined. "My ass hurts! I'm going to get in trouble at work! Our dining table is fucked!"

"You're right, you're right!" I said, suspending my face over the freezer to let the cold air cool my burning hot face from stuffing down my laughter. I got the ice pack and went over to check his injury.

"Let me see it," I said, and he shoved his butt up farther, giving out pathetic "OW" sounds all the way.

"It's in my actual butt crack," he moaned.

I pressed my finger into a spot at the top of his crack. "Like here?"

He let out another yelp that told me I'd found the spot. "Is the bruise huge?"

"There's no bruise, baby. It's just a little red. I'll ice it and get you a blanket. Want me to get anything else?"

Dyl looked foolishly hot, his muscled body naked and stretched out on his stomach, his hands making a pillow for his head. He gave me his best doe eyes. "Can I have some mac and cheese please?"

I chuckled. "And you tell me not to treat you like the kids."

We spent the rest of the evening with me feeding us bites of mac and cheese straight from the pot while we watched a show and giggled.

When we finally got up to bed an hour or so later, I bent over him to turn out his light.

"Was it worth breaking your butt?"

Dylan reached up to kiss me, tugging my face close to his. "It was worth my butt and the table, baby."

CHAPPY
U did what to ur ass

Busted it

On what?

Jeannie and I had been doing stuff and I sat back on the dining table and it broke

(dead emoji)

"WHAT'S'A'MATTER, PICKLES?" Colton teased. "Jeanine kick your ass?"

I just grumbled in response, sitting down gently and leaning to the left when I got to our team meeting.

Leroy leaned forward. "You get pegged? You gotta use a lot of lube, my guy."

A laugh rippled across the group. "How do you know that, Leroy?"

"It's just what I hear," he said, putting out his hands.

"How are things with her? You get your stuff worked out?" Lindberg asked.

I couldn't help but get a soft smile. "I think we're headed in the right direction."

Coach entered at that point. "Alright, let's get going—Sorrento, why are you sitting like you got a stick up your ass?"

A louder laugh broke out. "I think I bruised my tailbone."

"Jeanine really did kick your ass," Colton laughed.

"Guys, don't make fun of Pickles' kinks," Leroy chimed in. "This is a safe space."

Coach raised his eyebrows at me. "Bruised it doing what?"

My throat felt crackly. "I sat on something and it broke."

He crossed his arms. "What the hell did you sit on that it broke?"

"Is this important? Can I just go see PT?"

"I think the people want to know," Lindberg said so earnestly, like his request was innocent.

"You sat on something, it broke, and your big ass didn't pad your fall?" Leroy asked.

"Don't talk about Pickles' skinny pancake ass," Colton teased. "He's sensitive about it."

"I do not have a pancake ass. My ass is huge," I argued. "It was just an unfortunate circumstance."

Coach put out his hands. "What broke?"

"I'd rather talk about this in private," I said.

An objection broke out from the rest of my asshole teammates.

"Fine. It was my dining table."

A hush went over the room as everyone tried to figure that out.

"Did . . . Jeanine also get injured?" Colton asked.

"No." I stood, wincing as pain issued from the base of my

spine and my teammates erupted into laughter again. "Am I excused?"

Coach rolled his eyes. "Go ahead."

The physical therapist stood to follow me, and someone was following her. "We've got a student today, Dylan. Is that cool?"

I sighed. "What's one more person seeing my bruised ass?"

I ONLY ENDED up missing one game from my bruised butt, PT recommending massage and ice. They were professional enough to not even giggle once.

So it was a normal Sunday evening off when Plan #2 went into effect.

The note I left for J that morning read like this:

> We're looking for the magic
> Because losing it is tragic
> So let's all watch some movies
> And after bedtime for the little booties
> Mommy and Daddy will get un-sapphic?

Again, not a poet, but I did use a limerick rhyme scheme. Give me some credit.

Alice and Jeanine had caught Bella's cold while Bella was starting to get better, and this part of The Plan was conducive to having sick kids. I kept everyone out of the basement while I got everything set up.

"Okay, Daddy said he's ready!" Jeanine said, and I loved hearing the excitement in her voice. She'd been pushing through her cold, but her red nose, watery eyes, and drawn cheeks told me she didn't feel good. I'd done my best to step up my dad game while she was sick, taking over with the kids when I was scratched from Saturday's game.

I'd strung up white Christmas lights and bed sheets, and with a sheet down on the floor, I'd even sprinkled some fake snow. I had a tray with a hot chocolate bar and all the Christmas movie options up on the screen. I even made sure to have Jeannie's favorite Christmas tea ready since she's not much for hot chocolate.

The kids walked in with dropped jaws, with Jeanine behind them looking about the same. I couldn't tell if her watery eyes were from the surprise or being sick. The kids' gleeful shouts were thanks enough, rolling in the fake snow on the floor and throwing it at each other.

"Daddy, it's amazing!" Alice cried as she made a floor snow angel.

"Can we do this every Christmas?" Greyson asked.

"Hmm," I said, trying to drag out the suspense. "What do you think, Mommy?"

"I think if Daddy's willing to set it up, I'm in."

"Of course, I will," I said, launching all three kids into a scream.

"Let's put Mommy on her throne first," I said, leading her to an upright pillow against the couch, wedged into a nest of blankets, including her very favorite knit blanket. I offered her a hand to help her sit. "Feet out, Mommy."

Jeanine quirked a brow and her cheeks went pink, but she stuck her feet out of her blanket. I pulled a pair of fluffy socks out of my pocket. "Fluffy socks for everybody!"

"Wow, Daddy," she said with a grin and a sniffle, leaning for a box of tissues and honking her nose into one.

"Hold that thought," I said, rushing just outside the pillow fort to get her cup of tea. I placed it in her hands and kissed her forehead. "How's that?"

She held the mug under her face, then made a half heart with her hand. "Perfect, Dylan. You crushed it."

I leaned to kiss her for real and she drew back. "You'll get sick."

"Oh well," I said, pecking her anyway.

I got the kids settled in with their socks and hot chocolate, and we all snuggled up to Jeanine. As the kids got wrapped up in Frosty the Snowman, I looked around at my family. Jeannie's head was on my shoulder, we each had a girl on our laps, and Greyson's head rested on her leg.

It was perfect. I didn't take enough time to appreciate just how good I had it. I chose the woman next to me almost a decade before, and we built this beautiful family. A little faster than we originally anticipated, but that was fine. Greyson with all his curiosity and rambunctiousness. Alice with her independence and attention to justice. Bella with her sweetness juxtaposed with her mom's sassy attitude.

My heart was overflowing. This was what I did everything for. This was why I got slammed around on the ice. I put my body on the line so I could have moments like these. They're quiet, gentle, and oftentimes, average. I'd put in extra effort for this one, but it was a reminder to lean into the average times too. Average is underrated.

Everybody squirmed around plenty, and Jeannie eventually fell asleep with her head in my lap, my fingers combing through her hair. I had to move her when the pizza arrived at dinner time. But when I opened the door to bring the pizza in, I got a special surprise. I saw plenty of snow growing up in Pittsburgh, but I knew the kids had never seen it, and maybe even Jeanine.

"SNOW!"

"What?" Grey's voice was heard first. Then with some shouts of "come on" and "hurry," feet thundered up the stairs from the basement. A groggy yet confused Jeanine followed behind them.

I was outside in just my slippers. Alice and Greyson pulled on their shoes and ran out, almost tripping from the excitement. Bella ran out in her socks, Jeannie calling after her to put on her shoes. I scooped Bella up, looking back to the doorway and holding my hand out for Jeanine. She wrapped her cardigan tight around herself and stomped out in her boots.

The older kids were twirling around and looking up to the sky with their tongues out, the finest dusting of snow already settled on the grass. Bella tried to flop out of my arms, and I rushed to the doorway to slip on her shoes so she could run around.

As I set her down, I pulled Jeanine into my arms. "I made this happen, you know."

She laughed, the sound muffled by her congestion. "Oh, did you?"

"Yep. It was an asterisk on The Plan. Family's first snow."

With stars in her eyes, she looked up at me. "Well, thank you for putting in a good word for us. It's my first snow too."

"Aw, J." I kissed her cheek and she snuggled closer to me. She rested her head against my chest and we watched the kids frolicking in the snow.

"They're so happy," she whispered.

I kissed the top of her head. "Are you happy, baby?"

"I think I am."

We let them play for a few more minutes before going inside to enjoy our pizza dinner and Jeannie's favorite, *White Christmas*. And as Danny Kaye and Bing Crosby tap-danced into their half-nonsensical happily ever after, it was time for the kids to go to bed. They gave J big hugs and I love yous, then I took them to bed so Jeannie could rest.

(pic from basement with family piled into blankets)

Part of The Plan

RACHEL

Awww. Way to go, Dyl

DYLAN HAD a fresh-out-of-the-dryer pair of pajamas ready for me when he came back from putting the kids to bed.

He settled into the spot next to me, snuggling up. "You want to watch *The Holiday* or *Christmas Vacation?*"

"Let's do *The Holiday,*" I said, lifting my shirt over my head to put on the pajama top. "*Christmas Vacation* is a little too real given our Thanksgiving."

I swapped my yoga pants for the pajama bottoms and burrowed into the nest of blankets and pillows with a sniffle. My decongestant was at least working so I wasn't completely miserable, just tired. "You want to dim the lights?"

Dylan took so long to respond that I looked at him over my

shoulder. He looked like he was about to get sick. "Dyl? What's up?"

"Jeannie, I feel like we should talk about Thanksgiving."

That was not the response I expected. "Now?"

Dylan looked further deflated. "Yeah, now." I sat up and he took my hand, staring at it in his lap. The longer he lingered, the more my stomach turned.

"Go on, then. Tell me how immature it was of me to not just shut up and take it from your mom. Tell me how everything your mom said was true. Tell me how irresponsible it was for me to leave less than a week later because I couldn't take it anymore. Tell me how I'm irrational and a tyrant and a bad example for our kids and selfish and how I just need to be medicated so I can suck it up and deal with life—" I paused to draw a breath, and he cut in.

"That's not what I was going to say, if you'd give me a chance. I want to talk about this and come up with a solution together."

My chin popped back. "Wow. Okay."

"My mom is rough on you, and I hate that. But you've also been hostile to her since the beginning. I'm not saying she's right and you're wrong, but I think we need to give her a chance to get better."

The words themselves were so rational. Out of context, you'd think Dylan was the picture of maturity. But given the volume of hostile things she'd said to me over the years, including when I got back from California, it didn't seem fair.

"I see. And are you going to inform her that she's being given a second chance? Are you going to inform her that you were thinking of cutting her out?"

His tongue traced his upper teeth. "I haven't quite figured out how to do that yet."

My jaw quivered as I held my teeth together. I didn't expect such a surge of adrenaline over this. But then, his mom and thoughts of her set me on edge. Dylan was being very calm and rational, though, and I needed to do the same. "Do me a favor?"

"Yeah?"

"Figure it out. Soon. Because Dylan, this Christmas stuff, it's great. I don't want you to think I'm downplaying it, because I know you're putting in a lot of effort. But it doesn't fix the big stuff."

He tugged at his hair. "I can't fix it overnight, J."

"You also can't keep pretending we don't have problems. Just because we're not explosively at each other's throats doesn't mean nothing's wrong. And sometimes I just need you to see where we're struggling."

"I'm telling you right now that I see it," he argued. "What else do you want?"

"I want you to stop theorizing and fucking do something about it!"

"I defended you when she was being nasty about you before I left for California. You want me to call her up right now and cancel our nice night together and go yell at my mom for being a bitch?"

"You're so irrational, J," I said, mocking his voice. I knew I was being immature, but I was so tired of this kind of shit.

"That's not what I'm saying!"

"You sure about that, captain?" I asked. "Because that's sure what it sounds like."

"Stop," he barked. "What the hell is going on? We never do this, Jeanine."

My breaths were short, shallow, and shaky. "Yeah, well, maybe we should have started a long time ago when your mom said it was my fault we lost a baby. When I was your wife, and she said I was your slutty Hooters waitress girlfriend. When she said you could get your marriage annulled after I lost the baby."

Dylan's mouth popped open and he looked stunned. "You heard it all, then," he said.

"I should have stood up for myself because you sure as hell weren't going to stand up for me." I pressed my lips together to stop tears from forming. Dylan just sat there, stock still and silent. "Did you want to leave me, Dyl? When all that happened?"

My question snapped his attention back to me. "Jeanine, you almost *did* leave me then. Don't make this all about me." He shook his head, the tip of his nose going red like he was going to cry. "That time was really hard, Jeannie. You packed your bag, and then when you finally did go . . . he was there."

The air was knocked clean out of me. I cocked my head to the side. "You said that wasn't my fault, that he took advantage of me being in a vulnerable state."

"You're right. It wasn't your fault." Dylan rubbed at his eye. "I'm just . . . never going to trust that guy."

"Again, not my fault," I pointed out.

"No, it's not. But that time was terrible, J. You were hurting, and I was scared of what you might do. It was really hard on me, but I couldn't tell you. I just wanted you to love me and you were . . . unreachable."

I stretched to snag a tissue from the box. "So what, you wanted to leave? I didn't want to hurt you, Dylan. I didn't want to drag you down. You probably should have left. I'm a fucking head case and you could have found a cool chill girl to go along with whatever you wanted—"

"Jeannie, don't talk like that." Dylan scooted closer to me, taking both of my hands despite one of them having a very soggy tissue in it. "I didn't want to leave you then, and I don't want to leave you now."

"Don't want to," I said with a hiccup, "but are you going to do it anyway?"

Dylan got on his knees in front of me, both of us still sitting on the floor. "I'm not leaving you, baby. I don't want to. I've never once doubted the decision to be with you, even when it hurt and when it was hard. And I don't want you to leave, either."

"You see that you already did leave me, right, Dylan? You left me the second you chose hockey over my happiness. And then you abandoned me. You told me this was all fine, and you and I both know it's not fine."

"It's not that simple, J. It wasn't a matter of hockey or you. It's my job. My sport. The thing I love to do."

I planted him with a look. "The thing you love more than your wife?"

He blinked hard and hung his head, then looked up at me. "Jeanine, I want you to hear this with an open mind. You don't get to fight me on it until you've heard it all."

"Don't tell me—" I was winding up for another rant.

"Jeanine!" he snapped. "Please?"

I jumped, surprised he raised his voice. "Okay."

"Hockey is not flexible. Hockey isn't as strong as you are. I know you can recover from hard things, J. We've been through the worst kind of hell together, and I had confidence our relationship could weather this change." I rolled my lips between my teeth. "But I should have been better about saying that. You're right. I shouldn't have been so . . ."

"Obnoxiously optimistic?" I supplied.

He chuckled. "Sure. Yes, that." Then he pressed his lips together, seemingly thinking. "Jeannie, I was scared too. Furious. I felt betrayed. I didn't want to move here. And I was afraid if I didn't hold it together, we'd all come apart. I needed you too, but I didn't know how to ask for you. I still need you."

I reached for his hand and rubbed my thumb over the back of it. "I would have supported you in that, Dylan. Then both of us wouldn't feel so alone. You didn't communicate that you were sad or scared or furious or betrayed. You just left me alone."

"I know, and I'm sorry," he said.

"I'm sorry I didn't see you hurting," I said. "But you need to tell me what you need."

He gave a wry smile with a little snort. "Likewise. You could have told me more before you left. But that's all behind us. The best we can do is . . ."

"Keep going," I said.

Dylan nodded. "I want to keep going with you. All the way to the end. You and me, baby."

I cracked a smile. "You and me, against the world."

Dylan's hand cupped the side of my face as he pulled me to him, nuzzling me. Then he paused. "I love you so much, Jeanine, but can you please get a tissue?"

I gasped and pushed him away. "How dare you! Mr. I Don't Care How Sick You Are."

He cackled as I got a tissue, tugging my legs toward him and lowering my pajama bottoms. "Come here, you. I assume you're not sick down here."

I squealed and giggled as he lifted my pajama top, placing soft kisses on my stomach and the undersides of my breasts. "Nope, just sick in the head."

He sank his teeth into the side of my stomach. "Don't talk about my wife like that," he snarled, then punctuated his next statements with little nibbles. "My wife is beautiful, and strong, and smart, and," he reached my underwear and pulled them to my feet, "fucking delicious."

The movie played in the background as Dylan dropped to his stomach. I moaned and sighed when his tongue swept over the crease of my inner thighs, at his mercy.

"Tell me, baby. Were you going to run off with your high school hottie and leave your family behind?" His tongue licked a stripe up either side of my slit.

I lifted my head to look at him. "You're still hung up on that, huh? I haven't given it a second thought. He wanted me to bring the kids too, ya know."

He paused, staring up at me with his tongue still attached to my pussy. He drew it back in his mouth and his jaw fell open. "Wait, he did more than what I saw him do?"

"Ah, yeah. He may have tried to shoot his shot. He said I could take the kids and run off to be with him."

The betrayal was all over Dylan's face. "That fucker thought he was going to steal my entire life? Not just my wife, but also become stepdad of the year? Oh, I don't fucking think so."

His mouth latched onto me with such fervor that I had to peel him up by his forehead. "Hey," I said. "Give me a little credit. I have taste."

He raised his eyebrows at me. "You didn't when you were twenty."

"Slim pickings," I scoffed. I sat up, pushing Dylan back on his ass and shucking his shirt off, then gesturing for him to remove his pants. "You think I'd give up this rich, hot, ripped man and the best dick of my life for a little hometown hero and likely incel like Andy?"

Dyl pointed to the screen. "Happens in the movies all the time."

I laughed. "He said he'd waited for me since I broke up with him. He really tried his hardest. Pulled out all the stops."

"Nuh-uh. He waited for you that long? J, that's romantic! Give the guy a chance!"

I leveled him with a look. "It's weird and pathetic."

"Aw, poor guy. You're so mean, Jeanine!" He held a straight and indignant face until I sank down on his cock. "Fuuuck."

"I'll show you mean."

He spanked me and since I was feeling fresh, I smacked him in the face. I'd never once done that and Dylan got the best twinkle in his eye. "Jeannie! You're nasty!"

"Yeah, I can be real nasty. Try me."

Dyl thrust up into me, gripping my ass and spanking me again. I lifted my hips clear off him, standing over him. "Say you're sorry," I taunted.

"J, no, my dick is cold! You got it all wet and warm and you're—youre—" he sputtered.

"Oh, no! The little man's dick is cold!" I cackled.

"Oh, you're gonna get it now, brat."

"Oh, no! The little man is going to get me!" I put my hands on my cheeks like I was fake scared.

Dylan sat up and pulled behind my knees so I had to bend, then grabbed my waist and pinned me under him. We were both laughing so hard, never tired of our little wrestling matches. "How the tables have turned, brat."

I smirked, biting my lip and rocking my body underneath him. I dropped my voice. "What are you gonna do to mee—ah!" Dylan rammed into me, then did it a second time, harder. "Fuck yes."

"Who's a little man now?" Dylan sealed my wrists in one of his fists and pressed them over my head. "Am I a little man, or am I the guy who's ruined you for anyone else?"

"The latter," I gasped, my eyes fluttering shut as my legs circled his hips.

"That's what I fucking thought, wife."

Dylan's rhythm was steady, hard, and fast. His eyes grew wilder when he let go of my wrists. I sank my fingers into his shoulder blades, knowing he was probably close to coming. "Dylan, please don't stop. I need more."

"Jeannie," he cried out desperately before releasing into me. My eyes held his, something feral unleashed between us. He took a testing push of his hips, shuddering. "Too sensitive, fuck."

Dylan withdrew from me, staying propped over top of me. A curl of sweat-soaked hair fell over his forehead as he kissed me, sliding his hand down my stomach and letting out a low laugh when his fingers met the mess he left inside me. "I still need to give this cunt every last thing it deserves."

His fingers sank into me, but it didn't feel enough. "More, Dylan."

His eyebrows went up and he smirked. "That'll be four, baby."

I moaned at the fullness, the stretch, and the rhythm of his hand. "I want them all," I whispered.

"Fuck, J." Dylan took a moment to adjust his hand, grouping his fingers together and sliding his thumb into my opening with them. He stared, panting. "So fucking hot."

I dug my heels into the blanket below me, accentuating the rocking of his hand. I whimpered his name, and curses, and pleas, and then it was just my eyes on his, an intrigued smile on his face. His bicep flexed with each push, his tan skin and dark hair reminding me exactly how hot my husband is, his determination and tenacity why he was the one I chose over acting, and why I'd never miss the pain for the joy of moments like these. Connected, consumed, a bond forged by fire and blood and tears and the most tenacious kind of love.

Something unbreakable.

I shattered, and Dylan rose to my face, his lips taking mine before gazing into my eyes. "You are the fucking air I breathe, Jeanine Wendlock."

I was sweaty, and messy, and so was he, but the best kinds of messes were the ones we made together. I smiled and held his face, running my fingers through his damp hair.

"I think it's Jeanine Sorrento these days."

Dylan had the most gorgeous smile as his head hung over mine. "You know, I meant to go all slow and romantic," he laughed. "Roaring fire, gushy movie, blankets, soft lights."

I giggled. "You telling me you didn't like that?"

He hovered over top of me. "I loved that."

"Maybe let's make the post-sex snuggles soft and romantic."

Dylan dipped to kiss me. "Deal."

He cleaned me up with tissues and tucked our bodies together. We lay on our sides, sweat-dampened skin melding with a blanket over us. I was perfectly surrounded by the man I chose as we watched what was left of the movie.

"Oh, hey, you wanna know something crazy?" Dyl asked.

"Sure."

"I think Mara pegs Jack."

My mouth fell open and I turned to look directly at Dylan. "What?"

"He's brought it up more than once now. He said I should make pegging part of The Plan. And then when my ass hurt, he told me I needed to use more lube for pegging."

I laughed, flipping to my back to face the ceiling. "And here we thought we were the kinky ones."

"I mean, more power to 'em," Dylan said. "I'm happy he's happy."

"Oh, definitely. To each their own." I snapped to look at him again. "Wait, is this your way of telling me you want to get pegged? That might be the one thing left we haven't tried."

"No! No! I don't want it!"

"I don't know, buddy, sounds like you do." I weaseled my finger toward his butt and he squealed, jumping away from me.

"Bring it back over here!" I demanded, cackling but only chasing him as far as I could without coming out of the warm blanket.

Dylan and I were fighting for moments like these, and though the struggle was tough, the celebration made it all worthwhile.

RACHEL

Can't wait to hear The Plan for today

Don't do anything I wouldn't do

I love you Rach but I'm not sure you're the best person to say that

"READY TO GO, MOMMY?"

Dylan was prancing around the house like he had ants in his pants, buzzing with some mix of nerves and excitement. He told me not to eat breakfast and that he packed me a coffee. This was another day of The Plan, and I wasn't sure what was in store for me.

He was so keyed up he forgot to write me a poem for this one. He fumbled through an apology, but I really wasn't worried about it.

Things had been great since our movie night, even though we fought during it. We also made up in the best way, and the fight helped us sort out some old feelings. I truly was falling back in love with my husband.

And that made my life easier to fall in love with.

Dylan got me a short list of names for doctors to see about getting back on meds, and a list of therapists. I had an appointment on the books with a doctor for early January. Once I knew help was on the way, it helped lighten the load that much more.

So on this particular morning, I was pretty excited to see what Dylan had in store.

"I haven't had a chance to put makeup on," I said.

"You won't need it where we're going."

I narrowed my eyes. "Am I good to go in what I'm wearing?" I was in my standard school drop-off uniform: exercise tights, a tank, a sweatshirt over it, and a baseball cap.

"Yes. Yes. Let's go."

We dropped Alice and Grey off first at their school, then drove to Bella's. Texts were coming in rapid-fire from Dylan's teammates.

"Somebody's popular this morning."

"Just the group chat," he mumbled. "I need to silence it."

"You are so stressed right now, Dylly Bean! You're getting me nervous."

He steadied his hands on the steering wheel. "Don't be nervous. It's relaxing, I promise. Or, at least, I think it is."

I shook my head. "I really do not know what you have up your sleeve. Are we about to get matching tattoos? We should really eat if that's what we're doing."

Dylan finally laughed. "Not tattoos."

A few minutes later, we pulled into a popular brunch spot in the trendy neighborhood adjacent to ours. "Ooh, fancy breakfast?"

He took my hand as we walked in. "Sorrento?" he asked at the host stand.

"Right this way."

We entered a back area with a giant booth, which was

stuffed with Dylan's teammates and their wives. We were greeted by a big "HEY!" and applause. I jumped back, laughing. I did not expect a gaggle of people to be excited by our arrival.

"They're here!"

"Thanks for getting us a spa day, Jeanine!" Lacey shouted.

Dylan looked at Lacey with dagger eyes. "She doesn't know yet!"

"Eep! Forget I said anything. We're so glad you're here!"

I turned to Dyl. "I'm going on a spa day?"

"Surprise!" he said with a wince.

I saw what he meant about it being relaxing but also maybe not. I didn't know this group of women well, so that's the not-relaxing part. But Jessie's words rang in my head: "Just go one by one."

I liked Lacey. I liked Christine. I loved Mara. That's three of the five. That just left Greer, who was dating the goalie, Harlan Royce, and Erica Garner. They were two of the people talking shit about me at the Halloween party, but I was willing to forgive and forget in the name of group harmony.

Dylan squeezed my hand, and I realized I'd been semi-zoned out with a big smile plastered on my face. I turned to him and planted a kiss on him, getting more cheers from his friends. "Thank you. I love it."

He patted my butt and gave me another kiss. "I love *you*."

"You old flirt," I joked.

He guided me to a seat and everyone shifted so we could sit together. I slid in next to Mara.

"Hi! I'm so sorry I haven't called you. I feel bad," I said to her, tapping the table between us. "How have you been?"

She was just starting to wave me off when the server approached. "Do we have a bride and groom here?"

I glanced around the table and realized she meant Dylan and I were getting married.

"Who, me? Oh, no. Together eight years. Three kids. All that's behind us."

"I'd still marry her again, though," Dylan said.

I gave him a light shove. "You schmooze."

Breakfast was loud and boisterous, with the guys leading some jokes and their partners giving it back just as hard. Mara and I were both quieter, both of us the newest additions to the group. Just like they had at the Halloween party, Mara and Jack touched constantly. Jack's hand stayed on her: toying with her fingers under the table, putting his hand on her knee, putting his arm around her shoulder.

Instead of feeling sad like I had when I saw them touching on Halloween, I could look at how far Dylan and I had already come. His hand was on my knee under the table too, and I leaned into him so we were nestled together in the booth.

"Pickles is making us all look bad," Lindberg said. "He fucks up, and he launches a five-part groveling adventure."

"Yeah, where's my plan?" Christine asked.

"You told them about The Plan?" I asked.

"I did, but I didn't leak it to the wives," Dyl said, putting his hand up.

"I was just trying to point out, 'HA! Pickles fucked up!'" Lindberg whined. "And all Christine heard was, 'he's sweeping Jeanine off her feet.'"

"He's been doing good," I said, patting his shoulder. "It's penance for making me move to the Midwest."

"I didn't get penance," Mara said, smiling at Jack. He whispered something in her ear that made her cheeks go pink.

"Hey! The Midwest is best!" Greer cut in.

I grimaced. "Sorry. Forgot you're from here."

"I'm kidding. You'll have to take us all to your parents'

winery as part of The Plan. Ohio wine just isn't the same," Greer said. "Dyl can fly us all out there, right?"

"I'm in," Christine said, raising her hand, causing all the other female hands around the table to shoot up.

It felt good to laugh with a big group, and I was reminded that there are great people everywhere in the hockey community. Not everyone's a winner, but there are a lot of good eggs. It's still the same mix of transplants and people who have to start over far from home, taking whatever hand the league deals them. I'd been giving Dylan a hard time for picking hockey over my happiness, but seeing him so happy among his teammates reminded me that his happiness just as important. Hockey wouldn't be forever for him, so making the best of these dwindling years made sense.

And fundamentally, I loved him and wanted him to be happy.

After breakfast, all the guys drove us to the spa, a really cute place with a homey but minimalist design.

Our group got robed up and sat in the lounge area.

"Okay, so really. What did Dyl do?" Greer asked once a quiet settled over us.

I swallowed hard and drew in a half-breath. "Nothing specific. He's still a great guy."

"He didn't cheat?" Erica asked.

My stomach turned. "Not that I . . . know of?" I looked around at them. "Unless someone else has something to share?"

Lacey threw a hand. "Stop making Jeanine freak out. She doesn't have to tell us anything." She turned to me. "I've never heard of him being anything but obsessed with you and freaking out because you left."

A lump rose in my throat. "Yeah. I probably shouldn't have done that."

Mara leaned toward me, extending her hand with her soft smile. "You did what you had to do."

I ran my fingers along the bottom of my robe, the plush terrycloth soft and soothing to the touch. "It wasn't one thing. It's just the stuff that builds up over eight years of being together. His mom has always been awful to me and he just let it go. He acted like this move was no big deal when we were both actually really depressed about it. He always tells me I'll figure stuff out instead of just hearing me and being with me."

"He's not the only one with that," Christine grumbled.

"But none of those things make him a bad person or a bad husband," I said.

"No, of course not," Mara said. "It's the stuff that slips by when you're living life."

"Especially with little kids," Erica added.

I nodded. "But if everyone's dealing with the same problems, how are you all not losing your minds over it?"

"Maybe we are," Lacey said quietly to everyone's sigh. "This life's just hard. We need each other to get through it."

Tears heated my eyes. This moment was what I'd been missing in Ohio. I was so stuck in my own head that I couldn't accept that Ohio WAGs had the same issues as California WAGs, just with a different set of people.

"And the sun shines like way less here," Mara added to everyone's laugh. "Seasonal affective disorder and all that."

"Sitting in cold hockey rinks all the time, no sunshine, partners who are gone all the time," Greer said. "It's enough for anyone to lose their shit."

I wanted to say some words of gratitude, but I wasn't ready to cry in front of this group of women. Thankfully, my massage therapist came around the corner and called my name, giving me an excuse to go. But I was going with a much lighter heart than when I walked in.

I WENT BACK to my locker to grab a purse snack because spa water alone was not carrying me through the day. I quickly checked my phone, and I had a text from an unsaved number.

614-999-9999

Hi Jeanine! I just wanted to see if you or Dylan were coming to Bella's art show. We're going to wrap it up in about a half hour.

Holy shit. Oh shit. I checked my calendar. *I thought the art show was tomorrow?*

Either way, it didn't matter. I called Dylan in a panic.

He answered quickly. "Done already, baby?"

I jammed my legs in a pair of underwear, getting my foot stuck in the compression leggings. "No, shit, Dylan, Bella's art show is right now!"

I hopped around trying to get the leggings on my feet and fell over the bench behind me. I did my best not to yell even though my ass took a beating on the hard floor.

"I thought it was tomorrow?" Dylan asked.

"No, her teacher just texted me. There's only another half hour of it!"

"Shit. Oh god. She's probably crying."

"Come get me now, Dylan!"

"Slow down, slow down—" he tried.

"We have to go now! We're going to miss it!"

"J, I think only one of us can go. It'll take too long if I come get you."

At that point I was fully crying. All Bella wanted was for me to see the Christmas ladybug she made.

Dylan's keys jangled in the background. "It's okay, baby. I'll go now. Take an Uber. Pay whatever you need to. And they have my card on file at the spa. Just go."

I opened my ride-share app, and of course, it needed to update. I screamed, and a spa employee came by to check on me, AKA to shush me.

I left my favorite sports bra behind because it was one of those compression ones and was too hard to put over my head. Despite the odds, I was in a car headed to the preschool ten minutes later. I was like a coked-out guy at a strip club, pouring twenty-dollar bills into the passenger seat to get him to run red lights.

Irresponsible? Absolutely. But I would do anything for my children.

Even with my continued efforts to make it rain, I pulled up outside the school to find Dylan holding Bella on the sidewalk. Bella looked especially grumpy, with her face all tear-stained. I waved in the most upbeat way possible, and Dylan gave me a pained look. The whole scene shattered my heart. There went all the muscle relaxation from the massage and facial, not to mention the pedicure I'd never get to experience.

"Hi, ladybug!" I chirped as I ran across the street to her school. "Can I still see your Christmas ladybug?"

Bella scowled at me.

"Miss Cece just left," Dylan said, giving me sad eyes. "I'm sorry, Mommy."

I nodded quickly, trying not to cry because I let down my preschooler, who would also likely cry. "Bella, honey, I'm so sorry. I made a mistake on my days and that made me miss it. I really thought it was tomorrow."

"It's my fault," Dylan said. "I probably read the calendar wrong."

"No, it was in the email," I admitted. "I just read it wrong. I thought it would be on your last day of school. Did you and Daddy take any pictures of it?"

"I did just for you, Mommy," Dylan said, pulling out his phone. "Can Mommy hold you?"

Bella clung tighter to Dylan and I waved it off. "That's alright, honey. Oh, wow, would you look at that! Did you make that all by yourself, Bella?"

"Yeah," Bella said, starting to brighten.

"Is that his Santa hat?"

Dylan flinched when Bella barked at me. "Those are *her* Santa pajamas!"

"Oh, my mistake. Wow, she is really stylish, Bella. That is so amazing. I am so proud of you."

Bella beamed, and Dylan tickled her belly. "I told you Mommy would love it. Hey, I think this calls for some hot chocolate after we drop Mommy back off at the spa. What do you think?"

"Oh, no, I'm not missing hot chocolate time. Can I join you two?" I asked.

"You sure, Mommy?" Dylan's brow knit.

I nodded. "I enjoyed my time there, but I'd rather be with you two."

Dylan pocketed his phone and held up half a heart with his lip out, then leaned in for a kiss. "Hot chocolate for everybody," Dylan said, "even little girls with stinky toots."

"I'M SO SORRY ABOUT TODAY," Dylan said when we flopped down on the couch after putting the kids to bed. "I really wanted you to be able to relax. I can't believe I screwed up the days."

"It's my fault. I'm the calendar keeper. I'm bound to make a mistake every now and then."

Dylan frowned. "Yeah, but I should help you."

"That's sweet, but it's easier if one person does it all. And hey," I said, sitting up to ask for a kiss, "thanks for treating me today."

"You're welcome! I'm sorry you had to miss your pedicure."

I tossed my head from side to side. "I'll survive. It was good to get to know the girls a little better, and I'm glad I got to have hot chocolate time with you and Bells." I took a breath. "I treasure these kinds of moments the most, Dyl, when you and I get to sit and just unload. I love being Mommy and Daddy, but sometimes I don't care how messy the house is or whether the laundry's folded. I just want some time with you."

Dylan laced his fingers with mine over my knee. "I like this too. I always thought house cleaning came first."

"I mean, we can't have rats in here," I joked, "but the last couple weeks have made me reconsider what's important. It's not big grand gestures. It's just . . . living life with you? The little stuff? I know it sounds cheesy, but I think it's true."

He nodded. "I like the little stuff too." He took a long gaze into my eyes, and a soft smile curved his lips. "Hang on. I have an idea."

He jumped up from the couch and ran upstairs. He came back with a bottle of nail polish and a bottle of lotion. "Ta-da!"

I chuckled. "Do my toes look that bad that you're forcing me to paint them?"

"No, potato head. I'm painting them. But first, I'm rubbing your feet."

I squirmed down on the couch and put my feet in his lap. "By all means, pamper away."

THIRTY-EIGHT
DYLAN
THEN

"HEY, BABE. YOU PLAYED REALLY WELL." Jeanine raised up on her toes and laced her hands behind my neck, leaning in for a kiss.

"Thanks. You have fun with Rachel?"

"We always have fun," she said with a grin.

Seeing Jeanine without swollen eyes was a relief, her smile relaxed, and her gorgeous eyes sparkling. It had been so long since she was anything close to okay. We'd finally gotten her an urgent doctor visit, and they got her started on some depression meds about a week before. She was also still going to her miscarriage support group and had an appointment to see a therapist in a few weeks. Things were on the up and up, though we hadn't addressed the rockiness after her last Temecula visit.

"Do you want to go out with the team or go home?" I asked, locking my hands behind her lower back.

She pressed her lips to my ear. "Whichever, as long as I get to have you in the car right now."

My eyebrows went up. "Oh yeah?"

"I miss it," she said, rubbing her nose with mine.

I spun on my heel and took her hand, heading for the parking garage. "Let's go."

"YOU'RE sure you're ready for this? You want me to pull out?"

Jeanine's pants were around her knees with her feet on either side of my hips, her bare ass in my hands. Her hands were settled on my shoulders, and my pants also to my knees. She was rocking her pussy against my cock, admittedly not the clearest way to make a decision.

"I want you to come inside me," she rasped, then bit her lip.

My hands slipped to her hips. "Are you sure?"

"Yeah. Why wouldn't I be?"

I squeezed her hips to stop her rocking, trying to get some blood flow to my brain and away from my dick. "I need to know you want me, J. A couple of weeks ago you weren't sure about me."

Her brows knit. "Of course I do."

I cocked my head to the side, pleading with her to level with me, so she went on. "I want you, Dylan. I want to spend my life with you. And I want to try again for a baby with you. I think you'll be an amazing dad, and I think actually trying this time might be fun."

I pressed my lips together and she looked a few breaths away from crying.

"Do you want a baby with me, Dyl?"

I squeezed my eyes shut and sucked in a breath. "I do. But I don't want it to destroy us if it doesn't work out."

She shook her head. "It won't."

"It can't," I said. "I can't lose you, J."

"You won't."

Our gazes locked, and everything passed between us: all the pain, all the joy, all the ways we were mirror souls and twin flames, all the reasons why Jeanine was mine and I was hers.

"I can't, baby," I whispered.

"Can't what?"

I worked to fill my lungs, the pressure of the moment making it unduly difficult. "I really can't lose you, Jeanine. It would break me."

Her chest heaved, once, twice. "Then keep me."

I let those words wash over me. She was asking me to commit, and I needed the same from her. We'd just said our wedding vows a few months prior, but this moment had more weight. Right after we said "I do," our high-flying fantasy rug was pulled out from under us.

I thought I'd lose her. To Temecula. To Andy. To grief. To the darkness inside her.

But all I wanted was her. Her, staying with me, committing to me even when life hit us in the face with a ton of bricks.

"Stay with me, Jeanine. Don't give up on me. I'm not always going to do everything right, but I love you so fucking much. I want this more than anything, but I need to know you're not leaving. Please."

Her thumbs stroked over my ears. "I'm not leaving. I'm here."

"Forever?"

Her throat worked as she swallowed. "Forever."

I sealed my arms around her and kissed her harder than I ever had. Harder than our wedding day, harder than when she told me she'd marry me and have a baby with me, harder than when I was trying to reach her in the depths of her darkness.

And from that kiss, we made a choice. Our bodies chose a

future together. I chose to love Jeannie, no matter how hard it could be sometimes. She chose me, even though she didn't know what could lie ahead.

We chose each other in a commitment more solid than any wedding vow.

Update: spa day was really fun. I like the girls

RACHEL

Aw I'm so glad J

You're still not being replaced

I know. But there's room for more people to love you and I'm happy to share

I AWAKENED to the sound of . . . jingle bells? And Dylan's booming voice.

"Bundle up, family! We're heading for the hills!"

Greyson, forever an early riser, was already waiting at Dylan's side, joining in the shouting. After the couch stabbing incident, we converted Bella's crib to be open so she could get in and out. Better to let her get in and out safely than trap her and make her climb out. Bella sidled out looking a little grumpy with her stuffed rabbit under her arm and her thumb in her mouth.

"Bella, honey, don't suck your thumb," I reminded her. Too tired to argue yet, she just scowled at me.

"Where's Alice?" Dylan asked, spinning in a circle.

Bella laughed at him, forever as charmed by her dad as I was. "Daddy, she's not up yet."

He knelt down and tucked her under his arm. "Let's go get her."

He shuffled into Alice's room with Bella jingling the bells.

"Go away," Alice grumbled, pulling her sheets over her head.

Dylan knelt at her bedside and put on a soft voice. "But there's going to be snowwwwww."

Alice lowered the sheets slightly, letting just her eyes out. Grey and I laughed from the doorway.

"And we're making cinnamon rolls first. Don't tell Mom," he stage-whispered.

Having to play my sometimes-hardass role, I said, "I heard that."

Alice was up with a reluctant grin, and we all headed to the kitchen.

"You still haven't told us what we're doing, Dad," Greyson complained.

The kids all took their seats at the kitchen island, watching Dylan with rapt attention. He handed me a small envelope with a Santa on it, the same as my other poems. "Mommy, will you do the honors?"

"Oh sure," I said, prying the envelope open and clearing my throat as I read Dylan's poem aloud.

> Today is going to get a little chilly
> But it will be such fun if you're willing
> We're riding tubes across the snow

I can't wait to see your faces glow

I looked at him for further explanation, and he was beaming. "We're going snow tubing!"

"What's snow tubing?" Alice asked.

"It's like sledding in a floaty tube thing like you ride at the beach. Doesn't that sound fun?"

The kids cheered and Dylan came to stand beside me. "Sound good, Mommy? All of us having a day out together."

My protective hackles were up, but I tried to moderate my mama bear tendencies. "Is Bella old enough?"

The twinkle in his eyes dimmed the tiniest amount. "The website says it's at the discretion of the parents. I think it's okay."

"Can she hold on that long?" I asked.

"We'll give her a test run. Okay? Or I'll stand with her while everyone else goes down. We'll keep her filled up with hot chocolate."

I nodded. His comment about me treating him like one of the kids was a bit of a wakeup call. He was their parent too, and I needed to trust him to act in their best interest, even if activities like those made my stomach churn.

My agreement earned me an excited smile and a kiss. "It'll be so fun, I promise."

I pinched his tight sides, however much you can pinch a sheet of muscle. "Cinnamon rolls?"

He knew I'd outlawed them in our house because the kids' sugar crash was never worth the glee they brought.

"I'll deal with the fallout," he assured me.

He's not one of the kids. He can make decisions for the kids too.

It was great to look around and see the kids so excited, and I liked that parts of The Plan included them as well. As much as

I'd love to have five big activities dedicated to me, I'd feel guilty continually getting treated without them. I felt guilty enough about the spa day mixup. This would be a way to make it up to Bella.

And I was working on not being such a stick in the mud.

But I had to admit, Dylan went out of his way to make the day fun. He made a playlist for the car with all our favorite Christmas songs. He packed snacks, which is usually a big weakness of his. He'll take the kids somewhere without me, not pack snacks or water, and then wonder why they start whining. A professional athlete of all people should know the power of snacks.

But no, I'm the snack captain. I'm the one who makes sure no one gets hangry, Dylan included. Don't forget, I'm the one who set up his fancy bento boxes after games.

Though I couldn't complain this day, because he'd seen his own shortcomings and actually planned ahead. Perhaps he was learning something from implementing The Plan.

The ski resort that had tubing was an hour away from our house, though, and he forgot to factor in that Greyson gets carsick for any car ride over twenty-five minutes. Yes, it is that exact. Under twenty-five? No problem. I legitimately map out distances to see how many minutes we're in for and whether I need to pack extra bags for him to puke in.

So sure enough, on minute twenty-six, I'd lost track of time, and it hadn't even crossed Dylan's mind. We had bags in the car, but I couldn't get them fast enough. Guess who was holding out her hands for her eldest child to vomit in?

After a pit stop at a gas station where I requested multiple plastic bags and bought a ginger ale, we were back on the road. Thankfully, Dylan thought ahead and got us tubing reservations.

The air was fresh and cold on the ski mountain, and I'll

admit, I was pretty excited. Something fun and wintery to do with the kids that didn't involve hours at the rink? Sign me up.

Once we had the kids sufficiently bundled, they found the first open patch of snow, flopping on their backs and making snow angels. Dyl and I took a minute to watch them having fun.

"We got the best ones," he said.

I leaned my head onto his shoulder. "We really did."

"And I got the best wife." He turned to me with a smirk.

"Oh, you old flirt," I said, pinching his cheek through my glove. "I love you."

"I love you, Jeannie. So much." He bent for a short and sweet kiss.

They say some people are natural bucket fillers. They make everyone around them feel full and cherished and valued. This moment reminded me that Dylan is a bucket filler in his heart. He was such a good team captain in L.A., and his leadership and positivity was noticed in Ohio. And the way he looked at me right then filled my bucket right to the top. Those warm brown eyes always had a way of making me feel like I was someone special just because he thought so.

"When are we going tubing?" Alice cut in.

"I'm going, I'm going," Dylan said, shuffling off to the lodge to get our lift tickets.

We arrived just before 10 a.m., finding the park decently full but not overcrowded. We got our tubes, and the kids sat in theirs while we dragged them along, Dylan taking the older two and me handling Bella.

I'd never been snow tubing, and when I saw the hill, I grew a little leery.

"Dyl, that's . . . really steep. And a lot of bumps," I said.

"Their website said people rarely get hurt. People don't fall out," he said. "And I checked reviews that confirmed that."

That last part put me at ease. We got in line to ride the lift, where our tube handles clipped onto a rope and were pulled to the top. Bella thought this was a modern miracle, her mouth hanging open. We watched some groups go down the slopes with their handles held together and Alice called back to me, "Mom! I want to do that!"

To make me feel more secure, Dylan rode along with Bella for the first run to make sure she knew not to let go while I raced Alice and Grey.

I didn't expect it to be that fun. It's simple, really, just sledding on steroids. But I was exhilarated when I caught air off the first big bump. Plus, Dyl whirled me backward at the start of one of my runs, which for whatever reason had me hysterically laughing.

It was one of those family fun moments you hope the kids will remember forever.

We took a break for lunch, everybody chowing down on simultaneously mediocre and wonderful chicken tenders and fries. I got Dyl's attention while the kids were eating like a bunch of rabid foxes and made my hands into a heart. He winked and leaned in to kiss me.

"The best ones," he said. "I'm the luckiest."

We decided we'd go out for one more hour before calling it a day. Greyson and Dylan were dedicated to figuring out the tricks of the trade: which lanes were the fastest, what positions and techniques made them go farther. Greyson desperately wanted to go down on his stomach, but the guy working the lift yelled at him for trying. Dylan was able to sneak in a run on his stomach, giving a "shush" motion to Grey so he wouldn't tell. And Dylan's superman run was uneventful.

I remember exactly where I was standing, and how helpless I was watching it happen. I'd just gotten to the bottom of the slope, Alice and I waddling back to the lift. The lift worker wasn't looking at Grey, and he made a break for it. He ran at the fastest lane, prepared to go down on his stomach.

He got a little too much of his weight forward and after going off the biggest bump, he flipped forward, landing on his elbow. The tube slid down the rest of the way without him, leaving him halfway up the slope.

I felt the way my baby screamed in my soul.

They say moms can lift a car if their child is trapped under it. I don't know about that, but I ran up that hill in my bulky winter gear like my ass was on fire.

Greyson was both freakishly loud and disturbingly still. Something was very wrong. He alternated crying and yelling for me. *Mommy.* He hadn't called me that in probably a year or more, deeming himself big enough to call me "Mom."

"Mommy, my arm," he cried when I got to him, the tears going cold on his face. Dylan arrived next to us maybe a minute later. I already had all fifty-five pounds of my son scooped into my arms and was ready to run.

"I got him," Dylan rushed out, trying to take him from me. If I were a cat, I'd have hissed at him.

He was the reason Greyson was hurt. He encouraged bad behavior, and now my son was in agony.

"Get the girls and call 911," I bit out, already starting down the hill. I couldn't even look at Dylan, I was so mad. "We need to go to the E.R."

"Mommy, it hurts so bad. I'm scared," Greyson wailed.

"I know, sweet pea. We're going to get you some help," I panted, the adrenaline still carrying me through. I had a stray thought that maybe I should work on getting my strength back up because while the super-strength was convenient in the moment, it'd be nice to have all the time.

I waited by the road with Greyson on my lap. "It's alright,

buddy. We're going to take a ride in the ambulance. That'll be something new!"

Dylan and the girls trotted up beside us, sitting on the bench with us while Dylan was on the phone. "I'm here with them now," he said to the operator. "He's awake. Just looks like maybe a broken arm."

"A broken arm?" Greyson went into a further panic. "Mommy, I don't want a cast. That'll be so itchy."

"I'll sign it!" Alice chimed in.

"Not helpful, Al," I murmured. Silently, I prayed he didn't need surgery, and if he did, I didn't want him getting it at a rural hospital. The bulge under his coat sleeve was enormous, and I was terrified to take his coat off. I didn't even know if you were supposed to, or to leave it on to contain swelling.

"Hang in there, bud," Dylan said, kneeling in front of us. "I know this is scary, but you're being so brave."

"Dad, I just wanted to be cool like you," Grey said through sobs. "My hockey season is over now."

Dylan couldn't meet my gaze, but he had to feel the daggers I was staring into him.

"You are cool, Greyson. All on your own. And hockey will always be there. It's not going anywhere."

The ambulance pulled in and we had to decide who was going with Greyson and who would stay with the girls.

Before we could fight over it, Grey chose for us. "I want Mom."

Dylan kissed Greyson's forehead. "That's a good choice. Mom's really good with doctor stuff. Me and the girls will be down to see you as soon as we can, okay? I love you, buddy."

At that point, Grey was on a gurney and being loaded into the ambulance. They had a few things to check before we took off for the hospital. One of the EMTs was making Grey laugh while he cut his sleeve open.

Dylan's hand slid down my arm. "I'm so sorry, Jeannie."

I felt like the skin under my hat was boiling. "You should be apologizing to our son."

Dylan nodded. "I know. Keep me posted, okay?"

I looked back to make sure Greyson was distracted. "What if he needs surgery, Dylan? Did you think about that when you were showing our son how to be unsafe? You are the reason our son is potentially getting surgery in a rural fucking hospital."

Dylan chewed his lip with tears in his eyes, nodding. "I know." He wiped over his mouth. "I feel awful. This was supposed to be fun and I . . . I ruined it. I just . . . I love him so much."

He turned his face the other way and sniffed, and for a moment, I felt bad for him. I put my hand on his arm. I wanted to hug him, but I knew we were both trying to keep Grey from spinning out.

Dylan was trying to be a better husband and dad, and he got carried away.

But sometimes being the fun parent comes back to bite you. Or in this case, it bit our son.

FORTY

DYLAN

THEN

JEANINE GREETED me at the door when I got home from being away on the first round of playoff play. She basically leapt on me when I crossed the threshold.

"Well, this is nice," I hummed, crossing my arms behind her back to wrap her up as tight as I could. "You do okay while I was gone?"

"Uh-huh," she said. "I have a present for you."

"A present, huh?" I grinned into a kiss. "You don't have to get me anything, babe."

"Well, sometimes I do. Come on."

She dragged me in, and I dropped my bag by the door. We were still in my apartment, staying until the perfect house for us came on the market. She sat me down on the couch and handed me a small box, kind of the shape of a bracelet box.

"Thanks, babe. What is it?"

"Open it!" she cried. "You're killing me."

I peeled back the paper, looking at her for any clue as to what it might be. She held a smile, eyes wide and excited.

I got the paper off, hearing something rattling around inside. I gave it a gentle shake and she flapped her hands.

"Dyl!"

I laughed as I lifted the lid, then gasped. My face got warm as my eyes took in the sight: a pregnancy test with two lines on it.

"Jeannie," I whispered, leaning forward to smash her to me. Then I pushed her back. "Really? This is ours? It worked?"

"It's ours," she nodded, tears misting her eyes. "It worked."

My hand covered my mouth, breathing through the cracks in my fingers. I was elated and terrified all at once. Yes, we were trying, but you never really know how you feel about something until it's actually happening. Each month that went by, I didn't know what to do. She'd always tell me when she was on her period, but the days leading up to when her period would have started were tense. As I learned, so many period symptoms mimic early pregnancy symptoms. It's a high-stakes mental gamble, once a month.

But now it was here. I'd been out of town for a playoff game. It wasn't a deciding game, so Jeannie opted to stay home. I hadn't been there for the period suspense this time. "I don't know what to say, J."

Her face dropped. "You're happy, right?"

I nodded, pulling her close again. "So happy, baby," I said into her ear. "How are you feeling?"

"Happy. A little nauseated."

"That's a good thing, right?"

"I think so," she said, her smile dimming. "I'm kinda scared too. It's hard to get excited when you know how it can end. But then you feel bad not being excited, so you let yourself have hope—all with the possibility that it could fall apart. "

I rubbed her leg. "I get it. I'm scared too. But it's you and me."

"You and me against the world," she said. "And maybe this little peanut."

"BABE, I don't want to rush you, but I think we're going to have to start telling people soon."

We were sitting on the couch one afternoon, having just finished lunch and about to go to bed for my pre-game nap. It was the pre-season, and she hadn't been pregnant long before the last season ended. Before that, we had a tradition of fucking before my naps, but she was showing no desire to do that—or have any sex for that matter. At first, she said she wanted to wait twelve weeks since that's when statistically the pregnancy would be more in the clear. It was sixteen weeks that day, and she hadn't shown any inclination to want to pick sex back up. I was patient because the worst-case scenario would be us losing the pregnancy and her blaming it on sex.

And that might be the end of not only sex, not only us, but of Jeanine too. She was too fragile. I had to respect her need for space.

But I was sad. She didn't want me anymore, or maybe she did, but she was afraid. The doctor told us it was safe, but that seemed to not matter to Jeanine. She'd given me one hand job in the last few months. I'm not saying my wife should have been my sex servant, but I wanted her to want to play with me that way.

She just didn't.

"Chappy and Rachel know," she argued. "Does anyone else need to know? Is it their business?"

"Well, probably not. But I'm excited and I want to share it. People want to share our joy."

Jeannie put a protective hand over her stomach, which was

really starting to show at that point. It wasn't going to be a secret much longer. "Do we have to tell your parents?"

Silence cut through the room, and J stared at the floor. "I think they'd like to know they're having a grandbaby."

"What if we tell everybody and then we lose again?" she whispered.

I put my arm around her. "Then we'll have our friends and family to hold us up."

She sniffed and nodded, swiping her finger under her nose.

"It's sixteen weeks, baby. The doctor said everything looks healthy."

"I know," she said. "It's just not as joyful this way, when you know what can go wrong."

"You're right," I said, kissing her cheek. "It's not. But maybe we need to try to find the joy. This little baby deserves that. We need to celebrate the good stuff."

Jeanine turned to me, her face so close to mine. "My sunny boy," she said, rubbing our noses together. Her fingers grazed my cheek and her eyes dropped to my lips. Softly, slowly, her lips brushed mine. I let us draw apart slowly, then waited. Would she kiss me more?

Yes, she would. Jeanine laced her fingers behind my neck and crawled into my lap, straddling me and grinding against me. Right when I was about to ask if she missed me, she spoke.

"I missed this so much, Dylan."

"I missed you so bad, baby. You sure you're ready?"

She laughed a little. "I've been so fucking horny, but I've been afraid to do anything about it."

"God, that's fucking torture. For both of us."

Her face turned sour and she pushed back.

"Let me be clear: I know why you were afraid to, and that's totally fine. But we both want it now, right?"

She nodded.

I stood from the couch, taking her with me. "Then let's go get naked, baby. This is the longest I've ever been without you and I'm not wasting another second not being inside you."

GREYSON JOSEPH SORRENTO was born on January 2, to two very happy, very terrified, and very prepared and simultaneously unprepared parents. Watching Jeanine labor was a beautiful thing. Grey didn't make it easy on her, flipping sunny-side up while she was in labor and causing her a massive amount of extra pain. Her labor dragged into a second twenty-four hours. When she felt sure it was time to push, he just wasn't budging. She pushed for one hour, then two. The doctor offered to try a vacuum-assisted birth, which would make Jeannie need more anesthesia. There were also no guarantees that it would work, resulting in a C-section anyway.

"I don't know if I can go on," she sobbed into my face. "I want him so bad."

I held both of her sweaty hands in mine. "We'll get him, baby."

"I'm too tired," she cried. "I think I broke my asshole pushing."

Just then, the monitor started beeping fast, and the doctor went rigid. She mumbled something to one of the nurses, who jogged out of the room.

"What's wrong?" Jeannie asked.

"Jeanine, you either need to push now or I think we're going to have to do a C-section. Your baby's heart rate is changing, and that's usually a sign we need to intervene."

Jeanine nodded, her lip trembling. "Do it. I can't push anymore."

A nurse who had been with us most of the day stepped in while the doctor went to prepare for surgery. "Things are going to move fast, and we need you to help us out, okay? We're going to do your spinal block as soon as we get in the O.R. and as soon as it's in effect, we'll get your baby out."

"Okay," Jeanine said, then turned to me with tears in her eyes. "I don't want to lose him, Dyl."

"We won't," I said, but I really wasn't sure. I'd never been through this before and I was just as scared. Another nurse wanted me to leave with her and get on some scrubs.

"Dyl, don't leave me," she cried as I was almost at the door.

The nurse gave her a reassuring squeeze as she prepped her for surgery. "He'll be right back with you, sweetie. He'll be waiting in the O.R."

I rushed back to her bedside and bent to give her one last kiss. "You're going to do great, baby. I know it. We're going to meet our boy so soon, okay? I love you, J. I'll see you in a minute."

A cold sweat flashed over me, because I really am not great with gore. Blood? Sure, hockey's full of blood. Gore, though? I was about to see my wife's entrails? No thank you. My heart was already pounding from the rush of being in the room. Now it was getting heavier because I was afraid of what I would do when I saw the gore. I changed into the provided scrubs in the locker room, chanting under my breath. *Don't pass out. Don't pass out.*

We got in the operating room and the anesthesiologist was talking to Jeanine as they strapped her arms down. I could read the panic in her eyes, and I went into the zone. J needed me, and I was more than capable of being there.

Then I noticed the high, fast beep screaming in the room. The doctor and nurses all spoke in hushed but urgent tones.

This was still serious for our little baby, and I had no time to feel squeamish. Our boy and Jeannie were too important.

I kept my hand on her shoulder as the doctor worked below a drape at Jeannie's neck, but there was a mirror on the ceiling so she could see what was happening. My wife's body was just open with organs all over the place, and here she was, awake and watching it all go down. The wildest thing of all was how calm the doctor and nurses were. Just another day at the office for them, whereas for me, it was the craziest medical miracle I'd ever witnessed.

"Okay, Dad, here he comes!"

It all happened so much faster than I thought it could. The doctor scooped her fingers under the squirming mass that was our son, like something out of a sci-fi movie.

And I heard the best, most reassuring noise I'll ever hear in my life: his first wail on this earth. I looked down at Jeannie, both of us crying, relieved, elated, a painful chapter of our lives coming to a sudden and loud close.

In a well-rehearsed and second-nature move, a nurse dried him off and the other expertly wrapped him up in a blanket.

"He's here, J. He's perfect."

Greyson was placed in my arms and with the most careful steps I've ever taken, I walked him over to where J could see him. All the tears that we'd shed to that point were gone. We had him.

"We're going to have so much fun together, little guy."

A nurse nudged me. "She can hold him. It's good for him to be on her chest, Dad."

I shuffled forward and placed Greyson on Jeanine's chest.

"You're here, Grey," she said. "Welcome home."

We'd come so far. Just a year before, we were trying to figure out whether we were even qualified to have a baby at all. Now, Jeanine brought our son into the world.

All I could do was stare. We were a family now, my beautiful wife and my amazing son holding every piece of my heart from then on.

FORTY-ONE
DYLAN
NOW | DECEMBER

THE GIRLS and I walked into Greyson's hospital room in Columbus with a "get well soon" balloon, a bag of items he and Jeannie needed from home, and stuffies from each girl for Grey. Jeannie fought for a transfer to the children's hospital after it was determined that he'd need surgery. So there he was, two screws later, which he'd have to have changed out a few times as he grew.

I barely slept that night, a complete mess. Jeannie wouldn't call me, just sending texts. She sent my calls to voicemail. I knew she was furious. I was furious with myself.

But I still wanted to hear from her. I knew it wasn't alright, but I wanted to hear that it was.

Maybe she was right. Maybe I was one of the kids.

And that stirred up a whole new level of self-loathing.

Grey had a soft cast on his arm, but was sitting up playing a game with Jeanine. J was smiling at him, but she looked like hell. Bags ringed her eyes and for the first time in our marriage, she looked old. Not like I'm blaming her for aging or she wasn't beautiful, but she usually maintained a youthful glow. She looked dried out and tapped out. Haggard.

"Hi, buddy!" I said. "How are you feeling?"

"Good," Greyson said, then winced as he accidentally slapped his arm into the bed rail.

I lowered the offending bedrail and sat on the edge of his bed, kissing the top of his head and putting my arm around him. "They treating you okay in here?"

Jeanine's smile softened as she waited to hear his answer. "They're really nice," he said, his legs folded under him and picking at his ankle. "But I want to go home."

"I know," I said. "We want you to come home when they say you're good and ready, though."

Jeanine wouldn't meet my gaze. It was heartbreaking enough that my son was sitting in this hospital bed because of me. It just added insult to actual injury that Jeannie might never forgive me.

And who could blame her?

"Stuffie!" Bella sang, holding it over her head so Greyson could see.

"Aw, thanks, Bells," Greyson said, trying to smile for her. "A wolf too!"

My seven-year-old was trying to put on a brave face for his little sister, and that alone was enough to make me want to throw up.

"And I got you a cat so you'd think of me," Alice said. She was going through a big cat phase, obsessed with some cat show and constantly asking for one as a pet even though she was terribly allergic.

"You would," Greyson joked. He went to push her with his casted arm like he normally would, then stopped himself.

This was killing me. Tears filled my eyes, and I turned, pretending to stifle a sneeze. I couldn't let Greyson see me cry. I needed to be strong for him and not scare him.

This was up there with losing our first pregnancy. It was fucking awful.

Greyson was alive, but he was in pain because of me. I put fun ahead of his safety. Me, his dad, who was supposed to guide him and keep him safe.

I couldn't hold back anymore. A little sob leaked out.

"Daddy, what's wrong?" Alice asked.

I turned back to the bed, my ruse called out. "Girls, why don't you and Mommy go to the cafeteria and get a snack?"

"Come on, girls," Jeannie said quietly, standing to usher them out. When the door closed behind them, I sat in the chair Jeanine had occupied, propping my elbows on the bed.

"Greyson, I'm so sorry. I should have been more grown up when we went tubing."

Greyson's brows lowered. "You are a grown-up, Dad."

I nodded. "I am, but I didn't act like one. I love getting to be a kid and play around with you, but I got too into playing and forgot to be your dad."

"I like it when you play," Grey said. "Mom's always a grown-up. Sometimes she's mean."

That chilled me. The divide between our roles was so clear our kids had internalized it. I needed to rewrite that script. "Mommy can be a kid too, Grey. She's a lot of fun. She's been feeling less fun lately, but I know she's fun. It's one of the reasons I love her."

"She doesn't show it," he grumbled.

I gave a wry smile. "Part of that's my fault. I need to do a better job of being an unfun dad sometimes so she can show it." I patted his hair. "I'm glad she was here with you. She's a good mom."

"Me too. She's been really nice since I got hurt."

"I told you she was good at doctor stuff."

Someone knocked on the door and a nurse poked her face in. "Hey, Grey!" she chirped. "I need to come check you over."

She pushed through the door, wheeling a cart with a blood pressure cuff behind her. "Is this Dad?"

"I am."

She blushed, then narrowed her eyes. "Does Dad play hockey?"

"I do," I said. "Greyson does too."

"I thought you might from the last name," she said with a smirk, then blushed deeper and changed the subject. "Greyson, you're going to wow your friends with your new robot arm. Can you show me the arm?"

He giggled and held out his arm. "He started calling it that after the doctor told him he had metal in his arm. He's a funny one."

"Thanks for taking care of him," I said, but choked up on the last part.

She gave me a sympathetic smile. "We've been doing pretty good, haven't we, Grey?" She waited for his nod. "Okay, I'm going to look at your cut."

Greyson whimpered and retracted his arm. "No, no."

I put my hand on his leg. "You have to let her see, bud. She'll be gentle."

"Why don't you squeeze Dad's hand with your not-robot arm?" she offered.

His small, warm hand in mine reminded me just how little he still was. I always saw him as big, bigger every time I came home. Growing like a weed. But at the end of the day, he was still my little boy.

With a gloved finger, the nurse poked around the wound, then twisted her lips. "It's a little warmer than I'd like."

"Is that normal?" I asked.

"Some of it's the body's immune response to try and heal itself up," she said, continuing her prodding while Grey's hand tightened on mine. "Let me go get your doctor and have her take a look."

She peeled off her gloves and took a pump of hand sanitizer on her way out.

Grey had my eyes, turning that brown on me. "Is something wrong, Daddy?"

Another knife to the heart: Greyson calling me Daddy. He'd stopped calling Jeanine and me Mommy and Daddy a while before. It was another indicator of just how vulnerable he was feeling. He needed us.

"They're going to get you figured out," I said, not really sure myself. Did he have an infection? How the hell did my son get an infection in one of the best children's hospitals in the country?

The doctor breezed into the room with a broad smile, olive skin, and a ponytail of deep brown hair, planting her hands on her hips. "Where's the kid with the cool robot arm?"

Greyson was beaming. Healthcare workers who work with kids are genuinely saints. Another wave of emotion passed over me.

She offered me a hand, which I shook. "I'm Doctor Haddad. Are you Dad?"

My voice was still crackly, but I managed a "yep."

"Dad, he's done so good this whole time," she said, cleaning her hands after our handshake. "Kath tells me we need to take a look at this incision."

She silently examined the cut, mumbling numbers to the nurse, who typed them into the computer. After peeling off her gloves and tossing them aside, she stared at Grey's arm as if weighing her options.

"Kath, will you get me a swab?"

The requested swab was produced from a drawer and the doctor dabbed it over the injury.

"Alright, Greyson. We're going to send that Q-tip off to the lab to make sure your body's doing the right thing. While we're waiting, we're going to try a cream called an ointment on this to see if that helps at all. Is it itchy?"

"Itchy and hurts," Grey said.

"The cream should help with both, and we'll check it again in a few hours."

"When can I go home?" he asked, his voice so tiny.

I squeezed his hand a little tighter.

"When we're sure you're all patched up. Let's see what this cream does and what the lab says. Do you have any questions, Greyson? Dad?"

"Can I talk to you outside?" I asked.

The nurse said she'd hang out with Greyson while I talked to the doctor. I squared up to her in the hallway. "Does he have an infection?"

"We'll see what his labs say. If he does, we're catching it early. I don't want to sugarcoat it. It could be fine, or it could get bad. We'll keep a close eye on him. He's in the right place."

I stared at the floor between our feet, nodding and scraping my teeth over my bottom lip. I sniffed, trying to hold back the tears that kept surfacing for me.

"Will you be here for a while?" she asked.

I nodded. "As long as I can be."

"I'm going to send our social worker in to chat with you, and Jeanine if she's here too." It struck me that the doctor knew

Jeanine's name without even checking a chart. Jeanine had been so involved in his care that his surgeon knew her.

"Thank you. Thanks for taking care of him."

"Of course. Let Katherine know if you think of any questions for me." And with the swish of her lab coat, she took off down the hall.

Jeanine and the girls rounded the corner as I was trying to pull myself together. So many emotions crossed Jeanine's face when she saw me: concern, anger, outright fury, and the one that hurt the most, disappointment.

"What did the doctor say?" she asked as she got close. "What's wrong?"

"Girls, go talk to Grey, okay?" I said, opening the door to his room for them.

Then it was just me and Jeanine and all the rightful animosity she felt toward me.

"He, um . . ." I started.

"What?" she asked, her face paling. I slid my hand into hers and gave it a squeeze, but she didn't return it.

"He might have an infection. They took a sample off his wound, and they're starting with an ointment. It's early and they're being proactive. She said she didn't want to sugarcoat it —" Emotion choked my words.

Jeanine's face crumpled as she held my eyes, a tiny squeak coming out of her throat. A hot tear dripped down my cheek.

"This is all my fault, J," I whispered.

She didn't disagree with me, and that was the worst part. Even if it was true, I just wanted some signal that she wouldn't hate me forever.

"What are they doing next?" Her voice was graveled.

"They're putting ointment on it and checking it again after his labs come back."

Her jaw clenched and she swallowed. Her fist balled and unballed.

"Jeanine, I'm so sorry," I cried.

She didn't offer to hug me. "I'm mad at myself," she muttered.

"Why would you be mad at yourself?"

"None of this is nice," she said, looking at the narrow space between our feet.

"That's okay. I deserve it."

She raised her eyes to mine, striking a tear from her cheek. Her words came out in bursts, shaky breaths escaping through her nose between phrases. "I'm mad that I knew what you did was stupid and I didn't stop you. I decided to stop being your mom, and that was the moment when you really could have used it. If I hadn't let my guard down, we wouldn't be here right now. Greyson would have enjoyed his first day of winter break this morning instead of into post-op." Her whole body shook. "You don't want me to treat you like the kids? Act like their parent."

She wiped her tears on her shirt sleeve, stood in front of the door to Greyson's room, drew a deep breath, straightened her smile, and went in.

Everything she said was true. I had to change.

A COUPLE HOURS and a few cartoons later, a social worker knocked on the door. A Black woman with waist-length braids and stylish glasses, she immediately put Grey at ease. "Hey Greyson, I'm Jasmine. I heard you're into Spiderman. Which one's your favorite movie?"

"*Across the Spider-Verse*," Grey answered quickly.

"That's my favorite one too! I know you can probably walk,

but just in case, let's put you in this chair and we'll go down to the playroom."

Alice and Bella got a kick out of helping wheel Greyson to the room, which had a vestibule where we could still see them but talk privately with the social worker, decorated with festive window clings. Jeanine sat in the single chair probably meant for the social worker and not on the couch next to me.

The social worker didn't miss a beat, sweeping her braids over one shoulder, straightening her glasses, and handing us each her card. "Like I said, I'm Jasmine and I'm a social worker for the hospital. I'm here for anything you might need to get through Greyson's surgery and recovery. I understand he's here because of a tubing accident."

"Yes," Jeanine bit out while I nodded.

"A lot of accidents are just one-off, but do you have any concerns for Greyson's safety at home?"

Jeanine's eyes were cast to the floor as we both said, "No."

Jasmine nodded, jotting a note on her clipboard before putting it aside, folding her hands in her lap, and giving us her full attention.

"And how are you two doing with all this?" Jasmine's voice was soothing but professional.

Jeanine sat back, crossing one leg over the other and folding her arms across her chest.

"It's my fault," I started, seeing that J wasn't going to talk. "I encouraged him to go down the slope in a way that wasn't safe, and he got hurt."

Jasmine hummed and nodded. "So, Dylan, would you say you're feeling responsible for Greyson getting hurt?"

I swallowed a lump in my throat, my next speech a little garbled. "That about sums it up."

"What else does that stir up for you?"

I clicked and unclicked the pen in my hand multiple times. "That I'm a bad dad."

"What about you, Jeanine? Dylan's feeling like the accident is his fault and that reflects on him as a father. How do you feel?"

"I wish my husband would act more like a father and less like a friend."

Jasmine shot me the quickest side-eye, seemingly assessing me anew with Jeanine's perspective.

"Alright. Now we're getting somewhere," Jasmine said. "It's normal for things like this to bring up a lot of other emotions. Sometimes these cracks expose bigger problems in the relationship."

"Aren't we here for Grey?" I asked. I wasn't ready to unpack every problem Jeanine and I'd been cycling through with a stranger we'd never see again.

"You are, but I'm here for the whole family unit," Jasmine said. "My goal is to bring all of you out of this stronger and wiser. Because in the end, that helps Greyson too. Seeing your child sick or hurt is a big stressor on a family."

Jeanine scoffed and Jasmine smiled, a patient kind of look. "Jeanine, what did that bring up for you?"

J picked at her nails. "I'm just really mad at Dylan."

"I don't know what I can do other than be sorry, Jeannie," I argued, trying to get her to talk directly to me.

"Jeanine has a right to her feelings," Jasmine said. "Jeanine, Dylan seems like he wants to be with you and comfort you. If I had to guess, I'd say you need each other."

"Yes," I agreed, bobbing my head.

"Jeanine, do you want Dylan's affection right now, or is that not what you need?"

She folded in on herself, looking at her knees. "I don't know." Little gasps leaked from her as she let go, fully crying. I knelt in front of her and pulled her close. Her head landed on my shoulder, and I kissed her cheek. "I hate seeing him like this, Dylan. I'm scared."

"I know, baby. Me too."

Jasmine made some notes on her paper, then said, "I'll give you two a moment," and left to talk to the kids.

"What if it's really bad, Dyl?" she sobbed.

"I don't know. I wish I knew. All we can do is wait."

She nodded.

"I love you, Jeannie. We'll get through this."

She sobered and sat back, smearing her nose on the back of her finger. I reached to grab her a tissue from the table next to her and handed it to her. "What if Grey doesn't? What if it's MRSA and he goes septic or something?"

I wasn't even sure what that meant, but it sounded pretty bad. "Let's just go one step at a time, okay? They'll check it again here soon."

She sniffed and pressed the heels of her hands to her cheeks. "Okay. Yeah."

"He's a healthy boy. We've got that on our side."

She nodded again. "I'm sorry I can't stop being mad at you. I don't want to be. I'm tired of fighting."

"No, you're right to be mad. I'm mad at me too."

She coughed a sad little laugh. "But are you mad enough at yourself if I'm not mad at you?"

I had to laugh at that. "No. I need you to also guilt me to keep me in line."

"Good. I will."

"It's something else for you to do," I shrugged.

"I need something," she chuckled.

I ran my thumb across her cheek. "One thing at a time, baby. You and me."

"You and me, against this infection," she said with one side of her mouth curling upward.

We're home now

RACHEL
Give Grey a big hug for me

I RETURNED UPSTAIRS after doing the minor cleanup needed to get ready for the next day. The Rusties wives sent over enough food to get us through Christmas while Grey was in the hospital, both restaurant stuff and meals they made. The gesture made my stomach twist because it wasn't just the girls who went to the spa. Even Dylan's team nemesis, Dotsenko, had his wife send something for us. I don't know if it was a matter of guilt or Dylan getting along better with his team-mates, but we had much bigger concerns for me to waste time questioning it.

Dylan stood in Greyson's doorway, staring into the dark-ened room. His fingers gripped the doorframe so hard his nails went white. His head dropped forward and his other hand came up to his face. A loud sniff and a shudder sounded.

We'd just gotten home from the hospital that evening. The

Rusties were out of town, but Dyl had stayed back to be with Grey. No one wants to play the week of Christmas, and especially if your son is in the hospital.

Grey's white blood cell counts were a little elevated, so they opted for a course of IV antibiotics to be on the safe side. By the time they sent him home, they were confident everything was healing properly.

So in theory, all was settled. Grey was finally home, and we didn't have to see a doctor again until the following week.

I'd just gotten out of the shower, having not had one since before the accident Sunday. The emotions of it had hit me at various times over the prior two days, and Dyl was struggling too.

I couldn't just stand by and watch the man I loved fall apart without feeling anything. I approached him and put my hand on his shoulder, which made him cry harder. He gripped my hand and I rose on my toes to kiss his fingers. Dylan whimpered and I pulled him away from Grey's doorway.

"You'll wake him," I whispered. I ushered him into our room, shutting the door behind us. Then I fell into my husband's arms and we squeezed each other so damn tight we could pop a lung.

"I love him so much," he cried. "Everything's my fault."

"He's okay now," I said, loosely clawing over his ribs.

"I know, but," Dylan gasped, "I hurt my son. He was in so much pain."

"Accidents happen, baby." I couldn't believe I was saying it after all the hostility I'd harbored for him.

"I never want to hurt him," he said. "I never want to hurt the girls. I never want to hurt you, Jeannie."

I pressed my lips into the divot of his collarbone. "We hurt the ones we love the most."

He chuckled. "I guess that's it."

"Come on, let's lie down."

We faced each other in the bed, just my bedside light on. "I'm going to be better, J. I need to help you with all the stuff that adds up, and I need to be more of a dad."

I shrugged. "I think it's good that you're playful with them. They love that."

"But I need to leave room for you to be the same way."

I thought for a moment. "I need to get back to a playful place. Sucks when I feel like my brain's working against me."

Dylan nodded. "We'll get you back."

"I don't know if it's a matter of coming back, because every time something like this happens, I grow and change through the process of living it. I'll never be who I was when you met me."

"No," he said. "But I love who you've become even more. We've gotten to grow together, and I think that's something to celebrate."

I laughed as heat pinched my eyes. "God, I am sick of crying."

"These are good tears, though, yeah?"

"Yeah."

We fell asleep like that, snuggled up together, not as the same people we were when we met, but as two people who had weathered life as a team.

FORTY-THREE
DYLAN
NOW | DECEMBER

> Tell your wife thanks for making my wife look so hot

MIKEY

Wait, what? How?

Did they do one of those boodwah photo shoots or something

It's boudoir

Ducking talk to text!

FUCK. FUCKING.

WHAT DID I MISS WHY ARE JESSIE AND JEANINE HOT

Nothing, dickhead. Jessie picked out dress options for J

(pic)

Oh right. She told me that

HI JEANINE YOU LOOK PRETTY

Watch it

Relax, my wife's tits are bigger than yours

Did you just talk about my wife's tits?

No I was talking about your tits

Keep up

"WOW, J."

She sat on the pouf in the middle of our outrageous walk-in closet, bending to fasten the strap on some very expensive heels. The dress was also of note, showing off Jeannie's va-va-voom curves without being too revealing. My eyes traveled over her, especially enjoying how her cleavage poured out the top of the dress when she bent to buckle her shoes.

"You weren't supposed to see me yet," Jeanine said, looking at me from under her lashes.

I leaned on the door frame. "Maybe I like watching you put the shoes on. Are those the kind with the red bottoms?"

Jeanine stood with a giggle, kicking up a heel. "Mmhmm. How do I look?"

I reached for her, clutching her waist and pulling her close. "It's gonna be everything I can do not to fuck you before we're back home." My lips skimmed her throat, her nipples visibly hardening. I could see all the way down her dress from my vantage point, and good god, did she look amazing.

"You could do it now," she hummed.

My stomach dropped and my cheeks heated. "With the babysitter downstairs?"

She patted my cheek. "Ooh, does that stir you up?"

"It just feels so . . . uncivilized." I nuzzled her nose.

"You like uncivilized," she cooed.

"I do. But I need to build the suspense on this one," I said. "It's like having Christmas without Christmas Eve otherwise."

She stepped back and looked me up and down. "You look amazing too, babe. Not your usual suit."

I popped my thumbs under the lapels, the ornately decorated blue silk shining in our closet light.

Her face fell. "I'm still worried about leaving Grey."

I rubbed her arm. "I know. Meghan's good with them, though, and his meds are keeping him comfortable. I already gave him his night dose and locked up the rest."

Jeanine nodded. "Thank you. It's just weird to leave him and go do something fancy after all that."

"I know. But I think we owe it to ourselves."

"Are you going to tell me where we're going?"

"Nope. Still a surprise. But the outfits will definitely work with it."

Jeannie laughed, the berry color of her lipstick catching my eye. "This is Columbus. I bet people will be there in jeans."

I snuck up behind her and whispered in her ear, swatting her butt. "Then you can stun them with how gorgeous you are. Come on, we'll be late."

"Mommy! You look so pretty!" Alice shouted when we came down the steps.

"Do we get to eat ice cream?" Greyson whined, asking the truly important question.

Jeannie grinned. "Whatever Miss Meghan says is fine with me." She turned to the babysitter. "Alice's EpiPen is on the side kitchen coun—"

"I already told her, babe," I said, putting a reassuring hand on her waist.

"And about the alarm system?" She cocked an eyebrow.

"Everything, honey."

"Go have fun," Meghan grinned. "I'll call you if anything comes up."

"Call me," I said. "Jeanine needs a break."

The look Jeannie gave me right then was worth the expensive shoes, the dress rental, and every bit of coordination this night took.

I MANAGED to get a reservation at a hard-to-get-into Italian restaurant. We nestled into a semi-circular booth facing the bar, the décor like a dark Tuscan grotto. We ordered a selection of small plates and shared dry gin martinis.

"I know things haven't been perfect lately," I said, taking her hand. "But I want to make it through with you."

Jeannie's lips twisted, looking down at our joined hands. "Even though this time sucks, it's probably good we're talking about stuff now."

"Oh, that reminds me," I said. "Not to bring up administrative shit on a date, but we just need to pick a time with the couples therapist. I have a few options."

J's eyes sparkled. "You already made arrangements?"

I nodded.

"Thank you," she whispered, her eyes going glassy.

"Happy to do it, baby." My eyes started to mist too. "This has been hard, but I'm happy with where we're headed. I think we're going to be better than ever."

"I think so too," she said through a trembling voice. "I love you so much, Dylan."

"I love you too. There's no one else I'd rather fight it out with."

She laughed. "Even when I'm furious with you?"

I grinned. "Even when you're mean and scary."

She slapped my arm. "Dick. You know what dumbass shit Rachel sent me from the internet? Someone tweeted that you look like you're a good listener."

I dropped my mouth open. "What do you mean, Jeannie? I'm a great listener!"

She pursed her lips and I cackled. "To what you want to hear."

"To everything!" I objected, knowing I was yanking her chain and pissing her off.

"Lies, lies, lies. Are you going to tell our therapist you're a pathological liar, or are you going to make them figure it out for themselves?"

"Figure it out," I said, taking a smug sip of my martini. "Are you going to tell them you're a brat who thinks California's better than everywhere else?"

"Well, California is better," she said in her best valley girl accent. "And you like it when I'm bratty so you can call me your bratty little hole."

The waiter had somehow approached our table with the stealth of a cat burglar, our first round of small plates in hand. I struggled not to spit out my drink. The waiter's face went bright red. "Anything else I can bring you right now?"

"No, that'll be hole," I said, then froze. "I mean all! I mean all! That'll be all!"

The waiter turned tail and practically sprinted away from our table as we fell out laughing.

"Dylan, I swear to god. Now our sex life is going to be on the internet too."

I wiggled my eyebrows. "And everybody'll be jealous of that good, bratty hole I'm getting."

She narrowed her eyes. "If this drink weren't so good, I'd throw it on you, asshole."

I lifted an oyster shell and encouraged her to do the same.

We cheersed them, and I added, "Don't forget. You're the hole, not me." Then I winked and sucked back my oyster.

RACHEL

So what's the date?

I still don't know after dinner, but he brought me out somewhere nice. Got me all hopped up on gin martinis

Have fun, bestie. You deserve it

I'm worried about Grey

He's fine. Enjoy the break

THE NEXT PHASE was something I somewhat predicted, but not the full extent of it. Dylan had gotten us seats to the traveling Broadway production of *White Christmas*, but I didn't know how good our seats would be.

"Good evening, Mr. Sorrento, Mrs. Sorrento," said the man who checked our tickets. "Right this way."

I was on Dylan's arm and turned into him. "What did you do?"

Dyl just smirked. "It's all part of The Plan."

"That the usher knows our names?"

"Jeannie, for once in your life, just go with it, you sassy cocktail waitress," he teased.

I growled at him and he laughed.

"Everyone's looking at us," I whispered. "We're over-dressed."

He paused, making sure I met his eyes. "They're staring because you're fucking hot and your tits look like a classic artist sculpted them."

"They're staring because you're a medium famous and acting rich," I hissed as we kept walking.

"Nope. Definitely the boobs." Then he leaned into my ear. "I'm going to stuff my face in them later."

The usher turned back to us at that moment, and Dylan put on an overzealous smile, like he was the picture of a gentleman.

The door opened to a box a few back from stage left. "Enjoy the show," the man said before leaving us to it.

"Oh, you spoiled me bad," I gasped. "Dylan."

"You like?" he grinned. "They couldn't get Danny Kaye tonight, but it'll have to do."

"How much—"

"Nope. That's my business. Not yours. The Plan is on my own budget."

"Dyl—"

"Jeanine," he said slowly, wrapping his arms around my waist from behind. "I don't play hockey so I can hoard all my money all the time. I do it so sometimes," he kissed under my ear, making my nipples go stiff, "I can treat my beautiful wife."

I melted back into him. "Fine. Treat me."

His chuckle was low and dark. "I plan to."

I was surprised the seats in the box weren't fixed to the ground like other theater seats, instead being nicer armchairs you can move. He pulled one out for me and I sat. "Well, thank you. This is really nice. I feel like I need those theater glasses on a stick."

His eyes danced. "You're welcome, baby."

He held my hand in his lap and I got to feel one of my favorite . . . textures? The feeling of his thick, muscular thighs under suit fabric enraptured me from the beginning. I remember all the times he had me in his car after games, the sinew under a fine blend of materials rising to my hands. And I'm pretty sure he knew that made me nuts.

As the lights went down for the first act and the orchestral overture started, he scooted his chair to be right next to mine. My dress had a slit in it, and he slowly worked his fingers to touch my bare skin, gently tickling the inside of my knee. By the time Bob and Betty were counting their blessings instead of sheep, my breasts were heaving from his teasing.

And he hadn't even gotten anywhere close to my pussy. Just soft caresses, the pads of his fingers on my skin. During some dialogue before the final song in Act I, Dylan leaned into my ear.

"During this intermission, you're going to go in the ladies' room and take off your panties. When you come out of the bathroom, I want you to slide them in my pocket."

My eyes bugged out at him in the low light, and he pretended to be watching the show. He casually turned to me and lifted one of those very sexy dark brows. "Yeah?"

"Yeah," I sighed.

"Good girl," he mouthed with a squeeze to my knee.

Holy Christ. I had butterflies in my stomach, goosebumps up my arms, and hair standing up on the back of my neck. How could he still do this to me? We'd been together eight years, and I was still getting completely hot and bothered by my husband. We must have been doing something right.

So when the curtain dropped, Dylan stood and held out a hand to help me stand. Wobbling on my tall heels, I lifted my skirt so I didn't step on it.

"Wait," he said before I slipped my hand into the crook of his arm. "Show me the heels again."

"Dylan Sorrento, if you don't watch yourself, I'm going to think you're a foot guy." With a smirk, I extended my leg from the slit of the dress.

Dylan bit his bottom lip as his gaze combed over me. "I'm the luckiest asshole on the planet."

"So you admit, you are an asshole," I hummed, walking ahead of him. As I reached the door of the box, he palmed my ass.

"You bet I am."

Dylan escorted me to the ladies' room, and on the way, a group of women stopped us. "Dylan Sorrento?"

He put on his for-the-fans grin. "Yep!"

"Do you mind if we get a picture?"

He ogled me with drowsy eyes. "Only if you get my amazing wife in it."

"Dylan," I chided him. "I'll take the picture."

"No, no, J. You belong in it," he said, turning to the women. "Have you seen this gorgeous dress?"

"Dylan—" I hissed.

"What? I just want to show you off," he said, leaning closer to me as the women asked a passer-by to take the picture.

So those women got a photo of themselves, my husband, and me with my husband's hand suspiciously close to my breast.

"Enjoy the show," he said as we left them.

"You are such a fucking schmooze," I said as we reached the place where we had to part to go in the bathroom.

"No," he said, pulling me close. "I'm just obsessed with you, and I want everyone to know you're mine."

Butterflies, goosebumps, raised hairs. Again.

Dammit, Dylan.

I smiled to myself as I went in a bathroom stall, obeying his request to remove my panties. I stuffed them into my tiny purse, hoping nothing hung out.

I found him waiting for me outside the bathroom, looking ridiculously dashing. Moments like those are when it hits me just how hot Dylan is. His suit was a deep midnight blue, close but not completely matching my dress. It fit like a glove, giving hint to the carved marble of his muscles below it. And I was the person who got to know that he has the most scrumptious dusting of dark hair on those muscles. I'd probably had my mouth on every inch of his body in eight years, and his on mine.

Because he was mine.

When I made it over to him, he greeted me with a kiss. He stayed close, handing me a glass of champagne. "Do you have something you need to give me?"

"Where shall I deposit it? Perhaps your pocket?" I hummed. "You'll have to hold this glass."

He did, and watched as I tucked my purse by my breasts, opening it to extract the panties. "These?" I asked, raising my brows.

I didn't miss the catch in his breath when he said, "Mmhmm."

I wadded them up in my hand and slipped it down to his pocket, tucking them inside.

"Very good," he said, so low I could feel the rumble between my legs.

A man walked through the lobby ringing chimes to tell everyone to get back to their seats.

"Let's go," he said, giving my champagne flute back. "Wouldn't want to miss the show."

As we reentered our box, I headed for my seat, but Dylan caught my wrist and pulled me back. The theater lights dimmed as he took my glass and set it on the side table. In one quick motion, he spun me around and pinned me against the back wall of the box.

"Dylan," I said, pretending to be upset when I was not upset in the least. "They'll see us."

His eyes heated, his head dipping to my collarbone. He nibbled, nipping me with his teeth, causing my hips to jerk into his. He held me so tenderly, but there was no doubt what he wanted. His face journeyed farther south, into my cleavage, drawing his tongue along the exaggerated sweetheart neckline.

"Yes?" he asked as his hand slipped into the slit of my skirt. His fingers caressed my hip, dragging slow circles into the sensitive skin.

"Yes."

We met in a kiss as the music started. I wrapped my leg around his hips, finding him thick and hard for me. My Dyl, who thrilled me, filled my cup, made me whole. My Dyl, who reminded me of my wildness, and worked to bring me out of my hole. My Dyl, who created a special occasion just for us to enjoy some time together.

His hips found a rhythm with mine and I had a vague concern that my dress would have a streak on it by the time we were done. He kissed everywhere: my neck, my shoulders, the tops of my breasts. I pushed his jacket off his shoulders, loosening his tie and unbuttoning his shirt one, two times, raking my fingers through his exposed chest hair.

"We should sit," he said. "Your favorite song's coming up."

When I was about to protest, he dragged a chair behind the

curtain at the edge of our box. He sat and patted his thighs. "Sit."

Any fight had left me. I couldn't fully understand what he wanted, but whatever it was, I knew I wanted it too.

I sat on his lap facing the stage. We were mostly hidden from view, but I could still see the stage. He probably couldn't, but from the way he was licking up the exposed skin of my spine, he had other concerns.

"I got us these nice seats because you've been such a good girl," he whispered in my ear. "Now pull up the skirt on this gorgeous dress and let me reward you."

His fingers bunched the fabric, inching it up bit by bit, and I shifted so he could slide it back. The skirt covered enough in the front, just in case someone above us on the other side of the theater could see us somehow. My legs now bare, he hooked his feet on the insides of mine, spreading my legs wide. He was holding me open, leaving me at his mercy, my skirt still draping over the scandalous parts.

"That's it. Now don't be rude. Watch the show."

His fingertips traced up the inside of my thigh from my knee. When he reached my wetness, which had smeared on my legs, he swirled his fingers through it and placed a gentle kiss on my shoulder blade. "Did you make a mess, Jeanine?"

I nodded, afraid to talk and draw attention to us. He was good at keeping his voice low, but I sucked at it. This fact had been proven by our Halloween tryst when Alice thought I was hurt.

With one soft finger, he drew over my clit and down to the source of my wetness, dipping a finger inside. He held his finger to my lips. "You'd better clean up your mess, Jeannie."

I sucked his finger into my mouth, tasting a mix of his salty skin and my own tangy arousal.

"You really are such a good girl," he cooed. "I think I should do something really sweet for you."

His hand returned to my pussy, obscured by my skirt that was bunched in the front. He drew my labia together and rubbed up and down slowly. My head dropped back as I tried to close my legs, but he held them open. "Watch the show, Jeannie. Let me take over."

So I did. I leaned to the left and back against his chest, and he to our right, gazing at each other. If I looked too long, he flicked his chin toward the stage.

He bunched three of his fingers and worked circles around my clit. My hands gripped his wrists, one where his hand was holding me steady at my stomach and the other draped across my thigh, doing mind-melting work.

"Yeah, that's good," he rasped in my ear. "Just hold onto me."

My eyes closed as my mouth dropped open, struggling not to outwardly pant as he switched to a single finger working the most delicate circles over my swollen clit. My legs buckled against his and I heard his laughing exhale: smug, satisfied, thrilled with himself.

"That feel good, baby? I don't even have a finger inside yet." His ring finger dipped, the one that held our wedding band. It pressed up into me, his other hand leaving my stomach so he could finger fuck me and rub my clit at the same time.

I shuddered, trying to lean forward as a method of closing my legs, but he hooked his chin around my arm to hold me in place.

"Are you close, baby?"

I nodded, stuttered breaths coming out of my nose. People in the adjacent box had to hear my loud-ass breathing.

"Do you want me inside you?"

Again, a nod. His hands left me. "Stay there."

"Dyl," I whimpered.

He shifted behind me, presumably pushing his own pants down. The soft skin of his heavy cock pressed into my lower back. "Here's what's going to happen, Jeannie. You're going to sit on this cock, and I'll push up into you. My hand doesn't stop until you come. But you cannot move, and you cannot make a sound. You got it?"

I looked back and met his eyes. This was insane. We were fucking in a box at a theater because we couldn't wait until we got home.

"Now sit."

I raised up like I was looking for a dropped coin and he lined himself up. I settled back into him until I was fully seated. The fullness, the stretch, the position wearing out my inner thighs from where he was holding me open, it was all getting so intense. He shifted to be more under me and held my bare hip. As promised, his other hand rubbed me so perfectly while he bucked up into me. I struggled to not show how much he was bouncing me, and he seemed focused on keeping smooth, even strokes.

I wanted to grab my breasts, to touch somewhere other than lacing my fingers with his on my hips. He dragged our right hands down my thigh.

"So good, Jeannie," he whispered from farther behind me, working to stretch the position. I reached between my legs down to his balls, cupping them in my hand. A loud moan escaped him, thankfully drowned out by the music. My thighs pressed in on his, trembling as my edge drew nearer.

"There you go, baby." He inched his legs a little more together, a relief for the delicious pain of my screaming inner thighs and lower abs.

I suppressed a guttural moan as I came. "Fuck, Jeannie, I feel you, fuck, fuck," Dylan said as his thrusts got more violent, followed by the sweet relief of him pulsing along with me.

I collapsed back against his chest, and his arms wrapped tight around me as our legs folded together. I leaned into his ear. "You better not have stained the dress. I can't ship the rental back with a big white streak."

Dylan wheezed a laugh, kissing me over my shoulder. "I'll pay the damages on the dress. We're keeping it."

"We are?"

A soft puff of air left his nose, brushing my skin. "This thing's going in the Sorrento Hall of Fame."

MA

Merry Christmas. Hope you have a great day.
Love you.

(pic)

Kids are happy so I'm happy

You look it

PRESENTS WERE STACKED all around us, and wrapping paper littered the floor.

"You did it, J," I said. "Another great Christmas."

"We did it," Jeanine said, catching my eye. "Thanks for all you did this time. It really does help. Means a lot."

Her gaze stayed on me, softening. "And thank you for The Plan."

"Except for the part where I got our son hospitalized," I said.

She laughed. "I wasn't going to bring that up, but yeah, except that part."

"The Plan's not over."

She raised her eyebrows. "It's not?"

"Now it's time for the bigger plan."

"Which is?"

I reached for her hand. "We do the hard part. We keep working on this. On us. We keep fighting for each other, against each other. Fighting for us."

She snorted. "No one else I'd rather go through the swamps of hell with, Dylan."

I leaned in to beg for a kiss. "I hope you think it's worth it."

She nodded. "It's worth it. I want you, Dylan." Her eyes misted. "I always want you."

"Come here," I said, pulling her so she could straddle my lap. We were both in our stinky all-day PJs, unshowered and blissfully dirty. "I'll always want you too."

"You don't know that," she sighed, sticking out her bottom lip and draping her arms over my shoulders.

"I do know."

"What if my skin gets prune-y and my vagina dries up and my boobs are saggy?"

My hands scraped down her back, resting on her waist. "I'll still want you."

"What if I lose my memory and think you're the devil and the only choice you have is to be my mean nurse?"

"I'll still be there, wanting you." I paused, a vague memory coming to me. "Wait, isn't that the plot of one of your movies?"

"Shut up, it could happen," she laughed, then tipped her head like she was thinking. "When I'm a corpse in a casket?"

The thought alone was enough to knock the air from my lungs. "That's when I'd want you the most, Jeannie. I don't want to think about saying goodbye to you. I hope I go first so I don't have to live without you."

She frowned, rounding her eyes at me. "I was just going to

make a dead person fucking joke, but you had to go make it the saddest thing in the world."

I rubbed my nose to hers. "What I'm saying is, no matter what happens, I'll still want you. It'll always be you for me, Jeannie. You and me against the world."

She leaned forward to kiss me. "You and me."

JEANNIE FELL asleep while we were snuggling on the couch, some Christmas movie droning in the background. J was curled up with her head on my chest, drooling away on me.

I held my phone in my hand, staring at the messages from my mom. Something about them wasn't sitting right.

She didn't ask to video chat with the kids. She said *hope you have a great day*, nothing about the kids or Jeannie. Let's face it: Christmas is most fun for kids. We, as their parents, get to enjoy the magic through them. And like I said, they were happy, so I was happy.

And though I'd been that kid for Ma at one point, I wasn't a kid anymore. I thought maybe she'd want to see what the kids were enjoying about Christmas.

But as I scrolled up in the chain, I noticed that attitude was nothing new from her.

I'd sent her plenty of pictures. I sent updates on how Greyson was doing over the last week.

She sent me stuff about old teachers or coaches of mine she ran into, what was new at the Catholic church I grew up in. But it was always me initiating conversations about anything related to the kids or Jeanine. What kind of grandmother didn't check in about their grandson in the hospital? Jeanine talked to her parents every day, sometimes multiple times a day, while Grey was in the hospital.

I sent a picture of Jeannie and I from our *White Christmas* date, and her response was *you look nice*. Not *look at the two of you!* or *wow, you two are gorgeous*. It could be read to be only directed at me.

When Jeannie and I fought about Mom's behavior last, I don't think I saw just how serious it was.

Ma didn't care about the kids, or Jeanine. Just me.

But that's the thing: the moment I married Jeanine, or even brought her into my life, I wanted Ma to appreciate her too. She was part of my life, and thus part of me. I chose Jeanine to be my wife, my family.

Ma never accepted Jeanine.

So much so that she didn't really accept our children either. She was happy for me when I told her Greyson was on the way, though she was mad at how long it took me to tell her.

But when Jeannie got pregnant with Alice and I called to tell Ma the good news, she didn't respond so warmly. "Did you want more than one, honey?"

I hated that it took me this long to see what Jeannie had seen for years: Ma loved me. Just me. Not Jeanine. Not Greyson, Alice, or Bella.

My mother didn't respect my family.

But I am my family. I chose them without reservation.

If my mother didn't love my wife and kids, I couldn't waste time with her anymore.

It made my stomach turn, but I knew what I needed to do.

Have I told you I love you today?

JEANNIE
Not yet

I love you J. Miss you so much baby

Love you too. Miss you

"YOUR SON DOING OKAY?"

Colton Jones and I waited for our drinks at the small coffee shop across the street from our hotel, one of those ultracool places where I find it hard to blend in.

"Yeah, he's a lot better, thanks. And thanks for sending food. We got to bring him home before Christmas."

"Poor lil dude," he said. "That probably sucked."

I got unexpectedly emotional reflecting back on all of it. "Pretty rough. Did I miss anything while I was out?"

"Same old shit, different day," he sighed, stepping to the counter as his name was called out. Colton smiled with a "thank you" when he picked it up, and the man behind the counter did not seem immune to Colt's charms, doing a double take and cooing out a "you're welcome."

Colt was an interesting guy. He had a contagious smile that, even as a straight dude I could admit, was very handsome. While he could be very jovial, he also had a serious side. All his jokes and kidding around aside, he took his role as captain seriously.

My name was called and while I smiled at the same barista, I clearly didn't have the game I once did. "What the hell? You got a smile, a second look, and a sweet little 'you're welcome!'"

"You trying to pick up dudes in Buffalo?" Colton asked. "I didn't peg you for a cheater, Pickles."

"I'm not! I just like to know I've still got it. The world has moved on from me. Sucks."

"Hard getting old, bud," Colt said, patting my back as we headed for the door.

"I'm only four years older than you!" I objected. "When does the silver fox thing kick in?"

He grimaced, glancing at my hair. "When you stop being in denial and dyeing your hair shoe polish black to cover your grays."

"Fuck off! I do not!" I argued, giving him a shove. "Alright, let's talk captain shit. What's going on?"

Colt groaned. "I don't know how to whip everybody out of this funk. It's like before we take the ice, we're resigned to the other team being better than us, even if they're not."

"Do you want my advice, or are you going to tell me to fuck off?"

"No, I'm all ears. I feel like I'm fucking up the whole thing."

I pushed the button at the walk light to cross the street. "You're too fucking nice."

"What do you mean?" he scoffed. "I did fine being semi-nice as college captain."

"This ain't Harvard—"

"Alden," he corrected me. "But go on."

"Don't immediately start making excuses. Fire 'em up a little. If we suck, tell us we suck! If we're fucking around, call it out. If you don't do it, everyone takes it upon themselves to do it. That's how you get everybody picking and falling apart. And —" I said, taking a sip of my iced coffee, "tell everybody to have fun. It's a fucking game. We can win it if we act like it's our game and they're just playing it."

He walked in step with me in silence, mulling it over.

"Right?" I barked.

"Right," he responded, jumping to the side with a little fear in his eyes.

"Fuckin' right?" I yelled louder, a pigeon taking flight at my voice.

"Fuckin' right!" he yelled back.

"Let's fuckin' go!"

"Let's! Fuckin'! Go!" Colt said, holding his throat from straining his voice.

"There ya go, bud," I patted his back and rubbed his shoulders while we walked through the hotel's sliding doors. "Let's go work for it."

WITH SHAKING HANDS, I dialed the second contact on my favorites list. I put this off, not wanting to ruin the holidays with a big change. I also wanted a little time to myself on the road to make sure this was what I wanted. Since I made my decision on Christmas night, I'd been sleeping poorly.

But that gave me my answer. I was making the right decision. I had to pull the plug.

"Hey, Ma."

"Dylan, what a surprise!" Mom said through the phone. "I wasn't expecting to hear from you this week."

I sat in a hotel room in Buffalo, getting up from my pre-game nap. I tossed and turned until my alarm went off, too anxious about this conversation.

"I had a minute, and um, I wanted to talk to you."

"Well, your mother's always happy to hear from you. Did you have a nice Christmas? I got your picture."

My stomach twisted. Not only did she not ask if the family or the kids had a nice Christmas, but the "happy to hear from you" comment had an extra sting to it with what I was about to say.

"Um, yeah. Kids were happy. It was a real chill day. Grey's doing better."

"Oh, right. Good."

How could my mom have forgotten that a week ago, my son was hospitalized?

I sucked in a breath. "Mom, I need a break from our relationship."

The line went dead. Or at least, it sounded like it did. "What?"

I cocked my head and shook it, stretching my eyebrows. "I've asked you repeatedly to respect Jeanine, and to respect my choices as an adult. Every time, I'm hopeful you can be an adult and see me as one too. But you've proven that you're not capable of that, and I need to spend some time apart from you."

All I heard was frantic breathing on the other end. "Ma?"

"Did she put you up to this?" she bit.

"If you mean Jeanine, no. She's not even here, Ma. I'm in Buffalo. She's home with the kids."

"And you're telling me she had nothing to do with deciding to cut me from your life?" she blubbered. The theatrics had begun.

I expected some blowback. I had to remain calm and firm or this wouldn't end. "This is my decision, Mom."

"She's never liked me—" She was preparing to launch into a rant about being the victim, which was a response I anticipated.

"Even if that's true, there's no excuse for you treating my wife like she doesn't deserve me. There's no excuse for you not caring about my children because they're partially hers—"

"That's outrageous!"

"But it's true, isn't it? Greyson was in the hospital last week, and the first thing you ask about is *my* Christmas?"

"Well, I care about *your* happiness," she snapped. "Is that so wrong?"

"My happiness," I said, willing my heart to stop thumping so hard, "is intertwined with the health and happiness of the family I chose. I'm not a single guy, Mom. I chose to marry Jeanine because I love her. We chose to have kids together because we wanted that joy. When they struggle, I struggle—"

"And what about me? The one who gave you *everything*, Dylan. You're just going to kick me to the curb when I'm the reason you even get to live this life?"

I clamped my jaw shut. This was one of her more insane arguments. "I am your child, yes. But I am not *a* child. There's a difference. You don't get to decide how I live my life as an adult. And you don't get to take credit for my success when I'm the one doing the work every day."

"You give *her* credit—"

"Ma, why do you hate Jeanine so much? What is this thing you hold against her? Why do you need to control me, my life, so badly?"

"She has everything, Dylan. Everything." Mom was fully shouting. "She got the three kids. She got the house. And she didn't have to work for a single bit of it. She just had to glom onto you—"

"You have used that phrase before, and I am asking you right now to never use it again. Do you understand?"

The line went silent.

"Let me get this straight: you hate Jeanine because she has what you wanted?"

And then the call dropped.

Mom had always told me she only wanted me. She raved about how I was the only child she ever needed or wanted, that she didn't need any more kids because I was perfect.

Was there more to that story? I couldn't know, because she hung up before I could ask. That's the kind of call where you don't just dial again.

I was going to tell her I'd check in with her over the summer, after we'd gotten through this season. I was going to tell her I was happy to re-evaluate our relationship after a break.

But my mom hung up, so I wasn't going to be evaluating shit for a long time.

Hey! I'll be late but I'll at least have drinks for everybody

MARA LEROY

We're late too. Diaper explosion

CHRISTINE LINDBERG

We'll get it warmed up for you

"AN OAT MILK matcha latte for you," I said, passing a cup off to Mara, "and a skim vanilla latte for you."

"Thanks, J!" Christine said, putting Clark down while Mara put her youngest, Hazel next to him. They looked at each other for a moment, then promptly disregarded each other. Clark headed for the toddler section of the playground. "I wish he liked to play with other kids."

I tossed a hand. "Eh, they're at the parallel play age. It'll come when they're older. Neither of them are preschool age yet."

"Everybody have a good Christmas?" Mara asked.

"Seb prefers Hanukkah, but he's a good sport," Christine

said. "He grew up with both, but he calls Hanukkah the underdog. He wants Clark to have the same experience. We did a menorah earlier in the month with eight nights of activities."

"It's not even the biggest Jewish holiday, right?" I asked.

"Not at all, but Seb's competitive. He likes how Hanukkah's not the commercial nightmare that Christmas is. And it's not like Clark cared either way. He likes the lights and making food and all the songs and stuff," Christine laughed, pulling her phone out of her coat pocket. "Oh, I think Lacey's going to stop by soon."

"Oh, great! I haven't seen her since the last volunteer day," I said.

"Speak of the devil!" Mara said, greeting Lacey as she strolled across the playground.

"I'd have gotten you a coffee if I knew you were coming!" I called as she got closer.

She sighed. "That's alright. I already had too much. How are all the babies?" Lacey looked over the playground for our kids.

"Not fighting at the moment, so we're good," Mara said, doing a quick headcount of the four kids under her purview. In addition to her two biological kids, she had Leroy's kids as her stepchildren. "But none of that matters! Jeanine, tell us about the rest of Dylan's big plan! I heard about Greyson's arm. That's so scary."

"Oh, well, ha," I started. "Yeah, you were all there for Plan #3, and then Plan #4 was when Grey broke his arm. Thank you all, by the way, for sending over food. That was so thoughtful. We were struggling for sure."

The three of them nodded at me, giving me sad eyes. "We want to help you, Jeanine. Any way we can," Lacey said. Her earnest response, combined with thinking about everything with Greyson, had me tearing up.

"I appreciate it. So much. I was afraid of . . . a lot of things with you guys, if I'm honest. I felt like I wasn't fitting. But you've been so kind, and yeah," I gave a watery laugh and dabbed under my eyes. "Anyway. For Plan #5, he took me out to a really fancy dinner and my favorite musical, *White Christmas*. And now we're in the next phase, which is actually working on our issues."

"Do you think it's going to work?" Christine asked quietly.

My smile was wry. "We both want it to work. We want to be together. As long as we keep that in mind, I think we'll be okay. He even made a big step, telling his mom we're taking a break from her. She's made my life hell since we got together and I honestly never thought he'd do it."

"Oh, wow. That's huge," Mara said. "How is he feeling?"

I tossed my head from side to side. "Sad, but it was necessary. Now I just hope things get better at work for him."

Lacey rolled her eyes. "I told Gavin to stop letting Dottie be a dick to Dylan."

"Oh no!" I gasped. "Now he'll think I'm the parent tattling to the principal."

"Somebody's gotta keep him in check," Lacey sighed. "He can be pretty rotten."

"I just hope they win a little more," Mara said to everyone's laughter. "Even I'm running out of nice things to say to Jackie when he gets home."

"Don't we all!" Christine added.

"Oh, it's alright, Mara. You can just peg your way back to happiness," Lacey said with a smirk.

"Lace!" Christine chided her.

Mara jolted so hard that she almost spilled her matcha latte. "I'm sorry, what?"

Christine, Lacey, and I looked at each other before eyeing Mara.

"Maybe tell your husband to stop running his mouth," I said, grimacing. "I think he's rather open about your . . . adventures. Which is fine! We all have things we like! And he must be really happy about it."

"No, oh no, this, nope. Uh uh. I'm going home. This is some bullshit. That little asshole's gonna be in so much trouble," Mara said, moving to get her cane and stand.

"You gonna punish him?" I asked to everyone's giggles.

"Yeah, take him down a peg," Lacey added.

Mara covered her mouth, convulsing with laughter.

"Kids! Let's go!" She turned back to us. "Anybody want to help me bury a body later?"

FORTY-EIGHT
DYLAN
NOW | JANUARY

> Come down to the tunnel so I can say hi to the kids during warmies

JEANNIE

> They're excited. See you soon

"SAY HI TO DADDY!"

Jeannie held Bella on the other side of the glass while Alice and Greyson stood beside them.

Jeannie brought the whole family to this Sunday game. I pressed my forearm against the glass and Greyson returned it with his soft-casted arm. He only had a week to go before he was totally done with it.

"Hey, it's the robot arm guy!" Leroy said, skating up next to me. "How's it feel, bud?"

Grey's mouth curled up a little. "It's good."

"You're tough as nails," Leroy said. "You'll be out here playing with us in no time."

"You'll be retired before he makes it, Jack," I joked.

"Well, if he's lucky, I'll be his coach." He skated off to take a few more practice shots.

"Daddy, I wanna see Russ T.," Alice whined. "Mommy told me you'd find him for me."

I coughed a laugh. She was referring to the team's mascot, a rusty nail that walked around the arena. Its name was, who could guess it, Russ T. Nail. "I'll put in a good word. What section are you in, Mommy?"

"127," she said with a grin, those turquoise eyes made brighter by the ice under me.

"How are you doing, Mommy?"

"Glad to be here." She widened her eyes at me. "You look good, Daddy."

I wiggled my eyebrows. "After bedtime?"

Just then a puck clipped the glass next to me and Bella shrieked.

"Get back to work, ya bum. Go make us proud," Jeanine said with a wink.

"Love yinz. See you after the game."

"CUE IT UP, JONESY!"

Colton shook out his hands, cracking his neck and holding up a small piece of paper. "I got the read tonight, boys. Let's get out there and show 'em how we do it."

I cringed a little at his pump-up attempts, but they'd been getting progressively better the more he practiced. I didn't want to shoot him down, and I'd told Leroy to pretend it was good until it was. Fake it till you make it, I guess.

"Fuckin' go!" Leroy shouted at him.

"We've got Korowski."

The team responded, as we always did, with a clap.

"We've got Pickles."

clap

"We've got Leroy."

clap

"We've got Crabs."

Sebastian Lindberg, but Mr. Crabs was his most frequent nickname.

clap

"We've got me."

clap

"And in the net, we've got our baby boy prince, Royce."

clap

"Let's hold the fuckin' line, let's fill the fuckin' corners, and let's bring this one home," Colt finished.

And with a chorus of "let's fuckin' go," we headed out into the hallway.

SPEED WAS something I'd been working on in my training. I'd done more box jumps and knee-ups than I cared to remember, trying to increase the explosive power of my legs. Jeannie had even commented how my pants were tighter around my thighs now.

In this game, it was going to pay off. We were against the team with the fastest player in the show. Aging as I might have been, I was determined to keep up with the young pups who could skate at absurd speeds.

We were down 3-1 in the second, and my line with Leroy was going in. Beaudry, the stupid fast guy, was at center ice and headed for our zone. I tore after him, trying to swat the puck away from him. I was on him like a mosquito, buzzing around him and getting in his way.

But dammit, this kid was good. Still, I managed to get my stick between his and the puck. We were flying, the speed carrying me too fast for me to get control in time.

I did keep him from scoring right then. But what I also did was slam my left foot into the net, forcing me to fall flat with my foot caught behind me.

I'm a flexible guy, but no amount of flexibility can prevent a knee from going farther than it should.

The pop and the pain were instantaneous. I fell back, my body coming to a full stop against the wall as the goal ripped off its posts.

Fuck. Fuck. Fuck. This is it: the career-ending injury. I'll never skate again.

I was panting from the exertion, and coughing from the pain because I didn't know what else to do. My compression pants felt like they were going to split from the swelling, the pressure extending to my shin pads.

Whatever was happening, I was fucked.

Play stopped immediately, if for no other reason than the goal was off its posts.

Jack was the first by my side. "You good?"

"No. I think this is it, Jackie. My knee. It's swelling fast."

"Medical's coming, brother. Just hang on."

All I could think about was Jeanine. Greyson. Alice. Bella. All there, watching me, with Jeanine probably losing her mind. Hell, I was losing my mind.

Medical was able to get me up and help me skate off the ice without using my left knee. After they got me down the tunnel, I tried putting weight on that leg. It felt like the whole thing was going to give way.

"Don't do that just yet," the therapist said. "Let's go check you out."

They got me up on a table in the PT room, and that's when

I started to lose it. Taking off my skate and the rest of my gear was agony. I'm not too much of a crier, but the pain itself made my eyes water. "Can somebody get my phone? I need to talk to J."

The PT intern rushed out of the room, but when she came back, she had Jeannie with her.

"J."

One side of the table cleared out as Jeannie stepped in, wrapping me up in a hug.

"I think this is it, J." My breath caught. "It's over."

"You don't know that," she hummed, rubbing her hand over my back. "Let's find out what's going on."

She held both sides of my face and kissed me. I was sweaty, and snotty, and just generally hockey gross, but she wasn't deterred. "Let's find out what's going on, and I'm right with you. Okay? Whatever you want to do, I'll back you up. You and me."

"I don't want it to be over," I said, hardly recognizing my choked voice.

She pursed her lips, eyes scanning over my face. "It might not be, baby. You want me to stay with you?"

I nodded, letting out the kind of whimper only she ever heard from me. "I love you, Jeannie."

Jeannie held my hand and stepped close to my head on the table, glancing at our trainer and the PT to let them step back in. "I love you too. We've got this. You and me, okay?"

"You and me," I said, coughing from the pain.

Jeannie kissed my temple, and my grip tightened on her fingers as my leg was gently lifted. She shifted so my arm was folded at my chest, her holding my hand at my opposite shoulder. Someone brought her a chair so she wasn't hunched over me. I responded to the people working on me, letting them know which ways hurt and where I could feel nothing. But my eyes stayed fixed on Jeanine. She was my peace and solace, her gentle hands smoothing my sweaty hair back. She whispered quiet things to me while the medical staff chatted. She told me she was there, that it would be okay, that she had me.

And for all those months when we struggled, that had been what I needed from her. I was hurting, maybe not like she was. I initially thought of it as if I was on land and she was underwater, but looking back, I can see that we were both floundering in dark water. I might have been closer to the surface than she was, but we were both submerged all the same.

"We're going to have to send you home to get the swelling down and do some imaging in the morning. Any test is going to be too unclear right now."

I glanced up at Jeanine. "The kids?"

"They're with our friends."

Our friends. I hoped Jeannie saw the significance of that small phrase. We had friends again. It was still early, and they weren't Rachel and Chappy, but we had friends.

"Do you want me to get them or just go home?"

"I need to go home. I need you."

Soooo this is Dyl's knee right now

(pic)

RACHEL

EW OMG

I mean

Yikes. I'm so sorry.

For both of you

"LET ME GET YOUR DOOR."

Christine still had our kids from the night before when Dylan got injured. It had been a long day of outpatient appointments, one after the other. The team doctor, an orthopedic consult, imaging, a follow-up, and an initial consult between all the members of his care team. The privilege of being a professional athlete is having a care team that can meet like that.

He'd torn his MCL, which of all the ligaments, apparently that one was the least troublesome. He didn't need surgery, but it was going to be a full-time job to rehab it. Dylan pivoted once his left foot was on the ground and winced, sucking air through his teeth.

"No twisting, no twisting," I reminded him. "Rely on the brace. Take the crutches."

"I'm so pissed," he grumbled.

"I know, baby. Let's get you back on the couch."

I sat on the floor next to the couch where I got Dylan settled with an ice pack and a pillow for his leg.

"Thank you," he said.

"It's just six to eight weeks," I said. "You'll be back before you know it."

He sighed. "Realistically, probably not until April."

"Well, that's still this season."

He rested his head back on the arm of the couch, pinching the bridge of his nose and squeezing his eyes shut. "What if this is the sign that it's time to quit? This is going to be so much work."

I laced my fingers with his. "Do you want to quit?"

"If I quit, we can go back to California."

I stuck my lip out. "Sure. But what do you want?"

"I want you to be happy. And I screwed up in coming here."

I shook my head. "I used to think that, but I don't really think that anymore."

He peeked an eye open to glance at me. "You don't?"

I shook my head. "I think maybe we needed this. It's not pleasant, but we needed the shakeup. We've got work ahead of us, but I think we're going to make it."

"I think so too."

I rubbed my lips together and ran my fingers through his hair, just like I did when he first got injured. At least his hair was clean now. When we got home from the game, I gave him the strangest and most pathetic bath, the swelling in his knee truly alarming. "What do you want to do if you quit?"

"What do you mean?"

"You never want to talk about it, but surely you've thought about what you want to do if you retire. Where do you want to go?"

He scoffed. "I used to think I'd go home to Pittsburgh and coach or something, but that's . . . complicated now."

I nodded. "So what does that leave?"

"Honestly, Jeannie? Wherever you're happy. As long as I've got you, I don't care where we are. As long as we're okay."

"Right, but what do you want to do? Coach? Teach? Twiddle your thumbs?"

"See, that's the thing. Jack knows he wants to coach. It's not that clear for me. I keep hoping when the time comes, I'll just know."

"Buy a red Ferrari?" I teased. "Mid-life crisis?"

"Only if you'll ride shotgun," he said.

"Please. We both know a red Ferrari is for picking up chicks . . . or other middle-aged dudes."

"You're the only chick I want."

"But I am not the middle-aged dude you're looking for."

"No, you're not." Dylan's eyes softened and he tugged on my hand. "Come give me a kiss, woman."

I raised up on my knees and leaned over his upper body. He yanked me over him to have all my weight on his chest. "Dyl! Your knee!"

"Well, just don't kick it. I need to really kiss you."

Our sweet, soft kisses were some of my favorites. I held my face over his as we pulled apart. "What do you want to do, baby? You ready to hang it up or do you still want to play?"

His fingers threaded into the hair falling in my face. "I still want to play."

I puckered for a kiss, which he met with a goofy suction noise. "Then we'll get you in playing shape, hockey boy."

Dylan wrapped his arms as tight as they could go around my back, crushing me to him. "Thank you." He paused. "What are we going to do for you, though?"

I nestled into his neck. "You've been taking care of me a lot lately. You're fully entitled to some time where I take care of you."

"No, but beyond medical care," he laughed. "When are you going to sing and dance again, J?"

I wormed my way into the crack of the couch. "It's so hard to decide if that's what I want. I kind of like that time frozen in the past. I need to figure out what makes grown-up me happy. It might be theater, but it might be something totally different."

"Well, think about it. Any hobby. I don't know. I want you to do something that lights you up. You're helping me get back to my thing. I need to help you get back to yours."

"Figure skating? Ice dancing?" I asked. "I'm at the rink half my life anyway. May as well make use of the time."

"Ooh, you in one of those skimpy little fake skin tone outfits with the sparkles?" He drew his fingers down my neck, making me giggle. My bucket filler was back at it.

"You would just care about the outfit."

He smirked. "I like you dressed up. But I really like you happy. I haven't seen performance Jeannie in so long. I want that glow back on you."

"Thank you. I'll think about it." I kissed him again as his fingers tucked my hair behind my ears. "Whaddya want for dinner?"

Dylan's expression went dazed. "You."

I laughed. "I mean with calories. And you shouldn't bend your knee yet."

"Um, one, you can sit on my face right here and you probably have calories or something, and two, that lemon chicken thing you make."

I blinked hard and shook my head. "Wow, that was two very different answers."

"Well, I need to eat you more, and also I tried to make that chicken while you were gone and I fucking ruined it."

"How did you ruin it?"

"The rice? And the chicken? I don't know. It doesn't make sense, J. I don't know how it got messed up. But, who cares about that? Pants off, before the kids come home."

I didn't move, then squealed as he plunged his hand straight into my pants.

"You think I'm messing around just because I can't chase you? Get your ass up here."

Why the hell is PT a full time job

CHAPPY

Right?

"JEANNIE, CAN I HELP AT ALL?"

My darling wife had been a flurry of activity since she got the kids from school and came to pick me up from my training session. I was in my first full week of Operation: Knee Recovery. I still couldn't drive, but I had PT sessions that lasted about the same as the kids' school. Looking back, she probably hadn't sat since she got me up for physical therapy that morning. I sat at our kitchen island with my leg stretched over the next two stools, the air filled with the pot roast she threw in the crockpot in the morning.

She had her headphones in, flipping through the kids' school folders.

"J!" I shouted, clapping my hands.

"Hah?" She ripped one earbud out.

"Can I fill anything out? That's one thing I can do."

"Well, I need to look up a new doctor for the kids, and there's a spot here where I have to fill in the doctor's name. Grey and Alice both have field trips next week."

"Can't I do that?" I asked. "That's desk work, right?"

She hesitated for a second, grabbing her water cup and taking a drag. "Uh, yeah, I guess so. You'll have to check the insurance, though. We don't have the new cards yet for the year, so you'll have to look up our number."

I nodded. "Alright. I got it."

She sighed. "Yeah?"

"Yeah. Anything else I can do?"

"Maybe start with that. It'll keep you busy for a while." Jeannie peeked over the counter on her tiptoes. "How's your swelling? You need a new ice pack?"

I poked around my knee, wincing. "Probably need a fresh one."

She checked the clock over the stove. "Almost time for your next meds too."

She returned to my side with an ice pack and counted out two pills. After she packed my knee, I put my hands in their designated spots on her waist. "Hey," I said, pulling her close. "I see you doing all this running."

She just flicked her eyebrows up, looking amused. "I've been trying to tell ya, ya dingus."

"Whatcha listening to?"

"A book," she said, gasping as my lips trailed up her neck to her ear.

"A smutty little book?" I whispered, capturing her earlobe between my teeth.

"No," she said, but I felt the heat blast off her face.

"Liar," I said, snapping her phone out of her back pocket and checking the screen. A shirtless man looked back at me with a hockey stick over his shoulders. "Who the fuck is this?"

Jeanine covered her face, giggling. "No one! It's just a cover! I didn't pick the cover!"

"J, he has like no body hair! Is this who you're cheating on me with? You want me to shave to look like that?"

"Only insecure men think it's cheating. Where do you think I get all my good ideas from?"

My jaw fell open. "Since when?"

She tried to snatch her phone from me, but I held it out of her reach. "When I went for my medication evaluation, my doctor suggested I inject more joy into my life. She told me to read books I actually enjoy and stop trying to read self-help garbage—"

I lit up her home screen, taking in the roided-up man looking back at me. "Jeanine, you know that guy has never played hockey a day in his life. Look at his muscles! He's too big to be a hockey player. We're not that jacked."

She smirked, pulling up the cover photo again. She sighed, dropping her cheek into her hand like he was such a dreamboat. "Looks pretty good, right?"

"Jeannie!"

She cackled. "What? I'm injecting joy into my life. How do you think we got started doing primal play?"

My eyes widened and my jaw dropped. "I thought it was a game of tag gone out of control!"

She simpered and scrunched her nose, like she was about to tell me Santa wasn't real. "That's what I made you think."

"You're telling me you've been reading this kinky ass shit for years, Jeannie?"

She tossed her hand. "On and off. I usually stop when I'm going through a hard time, but my doctor recommended I focus even more on joy then."

I sighed. "I mean, it's good advice. I get it. I want you to have joy in your life." I flipped her screen on again. "But this guy, Jeannie?"

"How many times do I have to tell you that I don't pick the covers? Sometimes even the authors don't! And besides, Rachel said this was a good one."

"Rachel reads them too? Does Chappy know?" I leaned to get my phone out of my pocket to text him.

"We're going to buddy-read our next one," she said.

"You guys share porn links?"

"Ugh, it's not porn. You wouldn't get it. And anyway, not like you've never seen something stimulating." She lifted her brows at me and tipped her head.

I huffed because she was right, but I still felt defeated. She leveled me with a look. "Are you seriously mad, Dylan? Jealous?"

"No!" I objected, sobering. "No. No, I'm not mad. Or jealous. No. I just, I had no idea. Here I am thinking you're listening to cute little mysteries and you're over there having the time of your life."

"It was medical advice for me to have the time of my life," she sniffed. "We only get this one journey on this rock circling the sun. I've gotta live it up."

I snuck a kiss into her neck again and traced her curves from her breasts to her ass. "That mean we're having the time of our life tonight?"

"If you're good and get those forms filled out, big guy." With that, Jeanine raised an eyebrow, stuffed her earbud back in, and sauntered to the back door, sticking her head out. "You kids want a snack?"

"Hey, wait," I said, calling her back over and waving my hand to make sure I got her attention.

She pulled the headphone case out of her pocket and put them away, looking at me in question.

"Why don't you go play with them after this?" I offered. "I'll take anything I can off your plate."

Jeanine glanced back at me from where she got cut veggies and a container of hummus out of the fridge. "Yeah, that'd be nice."

"I could . . . find some help for you?"

Her hands were busy spooning hummus onto four plates, one heaped extra high for me. "No weirdos?"

"Absolutely no weirdos will enter our home," I said. "You really think I'd let anyone near you and the kids I didn't trust?"

She tossed her head from side to side. "That's true. You have one hell of a protective streak. Speaking of, what time is Colton coming over? And did you ever figure out if he's bringing someone with him?"

"6 o'clock, and I don't think he's seeing anyone seriously. I don't want to rub it in."

J grimaced. "Noted. I will not bring up girlfriends."

The kids piled in from outside, all lined up in a row at the kitchen island while they had their snacks. Jeannie stole veggies from my plate and teased the kids about which one of them was the best singer. She made each of them perform and we rated them. Alice took home extra bonus points because she added a dance element.

But the best moment of all was when she finished up and shouted, "Last one to the climbing tree's a rotten egg!"

The kids tore after her and I could hear their laughter from the yard while I worked on Jeanine's doctor-finding project.

A FEW HOURS LATER, Colton pushed back from our dining table, replaced since the infamous butt bruising incident. "Jeanine, I've got a chef and this dinner was fucking—"

"Watch it," I cut in with a wink to J. "This isn't the rink."

Jeanine gave me a quick eye roll but she was smirking.

"Sorry, my bad," Colt said, turning to the kids. "I have a potty mouth."

A chorus of "eww" came from the other end of the table.

"Can I show you my dance?" Alice asked.

"I want to play beauty shop," Bella demanded.

Jeannie gave them a good-natured smile. "Girls, I'm sure Colton wants to talk to Daddy. He's Daddy's special guest."

"No, no, I'd love to see the dance, and I'm definitely in for beauty shop," Colton said, his whole face lit up. "As long as you don't mind me talking to your dad while you give me a makeover."

"What about me?" Greyson asked.

"You've got homework, bud," Jeanine said. "Finish that and we'll see if Colton's still down to play."

"I'll stick around," Colton said, leaning toward Greyson. "I'll wait for ya."

The girls rushed away from the table. "Plates away, girls!" I called after them, but Jeannie just tossed a hand.

"They're too excited for all that," she said, rising and gathering all the plates. Colton tried to help her, but she waved him off. We stood and moved into the living room. Colton sat on the floor, anticipating the girls descending upon him with their beauty shop frenzy.

"So, looks like things have been good in my absence?" I probed. "It's almost like I was the problem."

It was true: the Rusties had been on a winning streak, picking up three of the last four games.

"Nah. We're just getting in the groove," Colton shrugged while Bella plopped her makeover kit in front of him.

"Pink or red?" Bella asked.

"Hmm. What's your favorite?" he asked her.

"Pink."

"Good choice," he said.

"Do this," she said, leaning into his face with her lips puckered.

Colt put on his best pucker, but flinched when Bella's poor aim decorated the whole area around his mouth. Alice stood behind him, pinning bits of his hair into bows. He grinned at me when they were done.

"Looks great, bud," I said. "I knew you'd find your stride. You feeling more comfortable?"

"Yes and no—" he started, cut off by Alice.

"Can I paint your nails?"

He looked to me for help. It was fun watching him fall prey to my daughters. "She asked you a question, Jonesy. You'd better answer."

Colt drew a shallow breath. "Um, how about my toes?" He peeled off his socks and stuck out his feet. Alice knelt at his feet and pulled out a blue sparkly polish.

"Perfect choice, Al," I said. "So you're not comfortable?"

"I'm just afraid after all this, we won't get anywhere. We'll start next year just as shot as we started this year."

"Nah, they'll remember. You got it."

"I don't know, man," he sighed, peering over his knees at Alice's work on his toes. "I've been here a long time and I'm just afraid . . ."

"Afraid of what?"

"It feels like I'm waiting on my life to start. But like, this is it. I'm captain in the top league. And I don't have," he gestured to the girls, "this."

"Do you want this? Just because a lot of guys have families doesn't mean you have to."

"I don't know. I don't know if what I need is here or not."

Fuck. He was really opening up. I hadn't had anyone do

that since I stopped being captain in L.A. "Do you feel like you want to leave?"

He forced a smile. "Nah. Just kinda going through it."

I bent and put a hand on his shoulder. "If there's anything I can do to help you, just say the word, man."

JEANINE DRAMATICALLY PUT her arms out and flopped down on the couch at my feet. Before that, she'd cleaned up dinner while Colt and I talked, helped with homework, started laundry, moved laundry over, vacuumed a mess off the floor from who knows what, and made sure my leg was comfortable.

"Jeannie, I need to ask you something."

"No more questions," she moaned. "I'm tagging out."

"No, I'm asking this one. Are you a witch?"

She flopped her head to look at me. "Hah?" she asked, just like she had when she couldn't hear me over her smutty book.

"How do you do all this shit all the time?" I asked.

She shrugged, puffing out a laugh. "I just do it."

"I bet you're exhausted," I said.

She shook her head. "All day. Every day."

I sat up and leaned toward her. "I am so sorry that I'm just seeing it now. I really don't give you enough credit for everything you do."

"Thank you."

"I should be thanking you," I said, reaching to lace our fingers together. "And I'm serious. Since I'm just doing my PT, if you want me to hire you some help, just say the word. I'll interview the people for you. I want you to be able to focus on your health. And to do something fun for you."

Jeanine nodded. "I appreciate that. I'll think about it."

"And Jeannie . . ." I popped my jaw forward, my face getting hot.

"Yeah?"

"Thank you. For taking care of me. For helping me get back to the game. You could have chosen to go home, but the fact that you're willing to stay after everything . . ." I sucked a breath through my nose, wiping under my eye. "Jeannie, I just love you so much."

"Aw, Dyl," she said, sticking her lower lip out. "You're going to make *me* cry."

"Can you come hug me, please?"

She beamed, carefully arranging herself until she rested on top of me.

"Thanks for not leaving me," I whispered, sniffling. "I don't deserve you, baby."

She snorted, kissing under my jaw. "You absolutely do. Promise. I'm lucky to have you."

I squeezed her so hard, overwhelmed by how much Jeanine did for me, for our family every day—but especially now that I was injured.

I kissed her neck, murmuring into her skin. "Did you sign up for your ice dancing stuff yet?"

"Not yet," she said.

"Go do it now!" I urged her, giving her butt a playful slap.

"Let me rest, for fuck's sake!" she snapped, only half-mad. "I run all day for you and now you're like 'Do this, do that.' *You* fucking do it, Dylan!"

I chuckled. I loved being able to fire her up. "Don't tell me that! I fucking will!"

"You won't," she dared.

"Don't threaten me with a good time," I said. "I'll have all your outfits ordered by morning and have your instructor waiting at 8 a.m. Monday."

"I'll believe it when I see it."

FIFTY-ONE
JEANINE
NOW | FEBRUARY

"IT'S JUST FUCKING BULLSHIT. I'm doing everything I'm supposed to be doing and for some fucked up reason, it's not healing right."

A storm cloud named Dylan sat in the front seat of our SUV, his arms crossed over his chest and a fresh ice pack around his knee. We'd just come from the orthopedist's office, who said his latest MRI didn't look quite like she wanted it to. Count this as another of the times he looked like an overgrown version of Greyson throwing a tantrum.

"If I remember from my dancing days, bodies aren't always obedient to what they're supposed to do," I said.

He glared at me.

"Get it all out now and then lose the 'tude, captain," I warned. "We're about to pick up the loudest ones of all."

"I just need to fucking be alone. I don't need advice, or condolences, or to vent."

"Thank you for telling me what you need," I said very robotically because I was trying not to laugh. He was usually so level-headed and goofy at home, so to see his hockey temper was almost funny. Especially because he was doing exactly what he said he didn't want to do: venting.

"I've eaten the anti-inflammatory foods, and it's not like I ate bad before that. I sleep. I do what they tell me and don't do what I'm not supposed to, and it's still like this. It's just—god-fucking-dammit!" He slammed his hand on the dashboard, then winced because it obviously hurt. I just folded my lips between my teeth and serenely turned into the car line at Alice and Grey's school. "I mean, what the fuck, Jeanine?"

I looked at him. "Sorry, baby."

"That's it?! That's all you've got?"

"Well, it's not fair."

"I need to get back to work!"

I nodded as I waved to the teacher working the carline. "I know, baby."

"Are you patronizing me?" Dylan demanded.

I finally caved to an eye roll. "Dylan, do me a favor and go use a punching bag or something when we get home. I know you're upset. You have a right to be. The best you can do is keep doing what they tell you to do."

"I want a second opinion," he harrumphed.

I sighed. "If that's what you want, we can get you one."

He held up a hand, stopping himself. "No. That's alright. I know I'm not being fair."

"It's just one extra week, Dylan. I know you want to get back out there. We'll get you back out there, even if it takes until next fall."

He put his eyebrows up. "If they think I'm not going back till next fall, oh, they've got a new thing coming."

I bit my tongue to keep from saying the obvious.

He snapped to look at me. "What?"

"I don't think it's up to you, or them. You need to heal so you can play again and not just injure it again right away."

He groaned. "Stop being right! It's annoying as fuck!"

"Ope! Here they come!" Alice and Grey ran out of the school building for our car, letting themselves in. And with their burst of energy and Mom-guess-whats, Dylan's woes had to take a backseat.

FIFTY-TWO

DYLAN

NOW | MARCH

"READY?" My physical therapist stood on the ice, holding out a hand for me to try skating.

Jeanine stood on the other side of the glass. She'd just finished her skating workout, looking extra hot in some cutesy purple outfit that I'd picked out. She initially told me she'd only wear what she picked, but I think she wanted to show her support today by wearing one of the Dylan picks. She gave me a thumbs up, and I made a sign of the cross over myself to show how nervous I was. I could read her lips: *you got it, baby.*

My knee was doing so much better, but this was a big step forward. Skating engaged every muscle and tendon that I'd injured. Even a simple push might snap it all over again, and drop me right back to square one. But it was either try now and have some hope of returning next month, or lose all hope of returning this season.

With a deep breath, I stepped onto the ice on my non-injured leg. *So far, so good.* But now was the real test.

I put my weight on my left leg and pushed.

"Easy!" the PT warned. "Just glide. No hockey stops."

I took another step, then another. But in my bad leg, I felt no pain. Stiffness, sure, but it wasn't painful.

Jeannie stood in the corner of the first turn, hands covering her nose and mouth and her eyes watering. She raised her brows to ask how it was going. I grinned and she literally jumped for joy and cheered, blowing me a kiss.

It would still be a long road ahead—some time before I could practice with the team and even longer before I'd play in a real game. But in this moment, I realized that playing again was within reach. I could come back.

And I hadn't done it alone. That beautiful woman in the purple skating outfit had gotten me here. She left me alone when I needed to be frustrated alone. She listened to my bitching. She made sure I took my meds on time. She kept everything else at home running so I could focus on recovering. She drove my ass to appointment after appointment.

She did this just as much as I did.

In some ways, I felt like I owed her everything. But in another, I was starting to see how our marriage ebbed and flowed. Sometimes, she needed the attention and care. Sometimes, it was me.

We'd started couples therapy, and the biggest gap we'd identified was that we both struggled to advocate for ourselves. Twin flames strike again, I guess. We didn't like to be needy, and we wanted our needs to be anticipated rather than stated.

But that strategy landed us where we were. It might have worked for the brief period before we had kids, but once life got hectic, that wasn't a sustainable method. So slowly, over time, we each gave too much of ourselves and had nothing left of our own.

It was time for a new version of us. We were Dyl and J 2.0. We asked for what we needed, and we understood that sometimes, we couldn't expect our partner to fill those needs.

And that had to be enough.

We broke ourselves trying to be unbreakable, to pretend nothing was wrong because we didn't want it to be.

But the cracks were what made us stronger. Our ability to break and still come back to each other, time and again, was maybe the most beautiful thing about our love.

Because no matter how broken we felt, we both wanted to glue us back together.

MY DEWY eyes blurred the arena around me.

Ohio had just dominated in their last game of the season. Partially, it was because the visiting team put in their newest recruits, basically eighteen- and nineteen-year-old kids who were getting their first NHL play. For the visiting team, it was essentially a long scrimmage. For us, it was a chance to win at home.

And for the Sorrento household, it was Dylan's first game back from his injury.

He's usually all business on the ice, but I didn't miss his grin as he took his first pass of warm-up shots. He was back home on the ice, for as long as he wanted to stretch his career.

The Rusties finished just shy of a wild card spot for the playoffs. And while that was disappointing, they'd put in a lot of work to shape up and improve their cohesion. Dylan kept working with Colton to boost his captain abilities, and it showed.

Dylan talked all the time about how improvement was on the horizon. They had some new players coming up who held promise for the next season, and there was a predicted management reshuffle over the summer.

What blew me away about this final game was the rabid excitement from the fans. You'd think they'd have won the Stanley Cup for how loud the crowd cheered. They'd lost their last three games, but winning this final home game was apparently enough for almost all the fans to stay in their seats, cheering their heads off.

The team skated to center ice, putting their sticks up to salute the crowd. Dylan found me and blew me a kiss, then waved to Greyson. The girls were home with a sitter, but we decided Grey was old enough to choose if he wanted to go to the game.

"Ooh! You got a kiss!" Christine said next to me.

"I can't believe people are this happy," I said. "We aren't headed for a Cup run."

She nodded and smiled. "Yeah. They're pretty awesome here. You should come to the next foundation gala."

"Aw, I like to let the guys just do their thing there. People don't want to meet us," I laughed.

"You'd be surprised how excited people are to meet us! The fans here are so supportive. Even when we've been the worst, they cheer like this."

"That Midwest kindness?"

Christine shrugged. "Maybe?"

I started this season feeling like a fish out of water, even in my closest relationships. I was ending it feeling like a part of a community. And more than one community at that. Not only was I progressing pretty well at my ice dancing pursuits, but I auditioned for a local musical and got picked. I didn't go out for a big role, but I was having a blast. Our first show was scheduled for May and Dylan was begging me to sing the songs and perform for him. I hated doing that. Truly no one wants to do a musical performance for one. It's just awkward. But didn't hadn't overlapped with my stage career for long, and he wanted to support me getting back to something I loved.

Dylan and I were thriving in couples therapy, though sometimes we walked out of there feeling like we got beat up. Apparently, our twin flame toxic trait is giving up too much of ourselves trying to make other people happy, also known as codependency. Sometimes our car rides home from therapy were silent, tentatively touching each other to test the waters.

But even on the worst days when we hauled out our foulest drama, it was worth it. Dylan and I had so much love for each other and the family we built. Even when I left in December, I wasn't really entertaining leaving him. I was asking him to wake up and step up.

And he did.

But that meant I had to as well.

I was on a new medication and feeling a lot better. After one trash therapist, I found one who fit what I needed. Dylan hired a sweet grandma to look after our kids and help out around the house, and she treated our kids like they were her own.

We were headed for a good place, but I knew there would always be another difficult season waiting for us somewhere. That's just how life works.

There's always going to be something in your life that determines the melody. You can't always control that. Sometimes you get to sing the melody, but more often, it's about finding harmony: blending with the sound, meeting people where they are, and complementing each other.

The thing about marriage is if you're lucky, it's the longest of long hauls. Seasons will always change, and new challenges will arise. The important part isn't what has been, though that shapes you. It's what's there now that counts. It's accepting what you must and adjusting to what you can. It's asking each other what we need, both for ourselves and for our relationship —and asking often.

We're told love is about the happily ever after, but that doesn't just show up in the mail. Happily ever after can't be added to a bridal registry, or bought as a couch when you move in together. Some days, happily ever after is incredibly easy. On other days, it feels like getting raked over hot coals.

Sometimes you need the hot coals to bring back a little fire.

Every day I wake up with Dylan on the other side of the bed is a day worth a song and dance.

Grey and I waited for Dylan in the wives' room after the game. Dylan came out with a bunch of flowers wrapped in brown paper and a smile, minus one tooth. He'd lost one to a puck at practice a few days before, and we hadn't gotten him to the dentist for his fake tooth yet. I was still getting used to my slightly different Dyl.

It didn't stop him from grinning big. He handed me the flowers and knelt to hug Greyson first.

"Thanks for coming to the game, buddy. Love you so much."

I bit back tears watching my two boys hugging. When I married him, I knew he'd be a good dad, and it's such a treat to soak in those moments when it's so apparent.

Dylan stood and gave me the biggest hug, lifting my feet off the ground and making me drape the flowers over his shoulder.

"Thank you for this season, baby," he whispered in my ear before kissing my cheek. "Thank you for pushing me to be better."

I swallowed hard, trying not to cry. "Thank you for working on it with me. For trying. For being patient with me. It means everything, Dyl."

He pulled back and kissed me, slow, soft, and sweet like he

does, until Greyson objected with an "EW! Dad!" garnering some chuckles from the families around us.

Dylan rubbed his nose with mine. "I'm always going to love you, Jeanine. It's you and me against the world, baby."

"You and me. Always."

WANT MORE JEANINE AND DYLAN?

Sign up for my email newsletter and receive a story from their early days as parents at

www.danigalliaro.com/unbreakable-bonus

CONTENT WARNINGS

Your mental health as a reader comes first.

Unbreakable is intended for audiences 18+ and contains the following:

- Accidental pregnancy with pro-choice discussion
- Pregnancy loss
- Depression, fear of suicidality (no plan or action taken)
- C-section birth scene
- Legal marijuana and alcohol use
- Injury (non-fatal)
- Child injury (non-fatal) with hospitalization
- Difficult mother-in-law
- Explicit sex scenes including
  - Praise and degradation
  - Light bondage
  - Primal play
  - Mask play
  - Squirting

- Face sitting
- Brief foot play
- Fisting
- Cum play
- Public sex
- Impact play (spanking)

ACKNOWLEDGMENTS

Well, shoot. This one took it out of me. Married people are officially the hardest flavor I've written to date. Man, do we come up with some stuff to fight about, and all of it's valid.

As always, books aren't made in a vacuum, so I have plenty of lovely people to thank. So thank you to Roxana for your editing prowess.

To my Cincinnati author coven and all my author besties for holding my ass up (and helping me sort out which exact order of words is the hottest in a primal scene).

To my ARC readers for reading and promoting Unbreakable.

To my street team for having the utmost faith in me even though I'm just a stack of ferrets in a trench coat. I'm so grateful for all you do to spread the word about my work.

To Jamie, Jela, and Florence at Happily Booked PR for always making me look more aesthetic than I am, and putting up with my neurotic edits of posts.

To Amanda at It's Just Peachy Pages for taking my prompt of "rust, ice, and flowers" and making such a gorgeous cover. Then you spoil me with logos and stickers and things and I truly don't deserve you.

To my beta readers, some of you who read it TWICE or THRICE: Janney, Brooke, Suzanne, Meghan/Skeeeemp, Melly, Amy, Tristan, Ashley, Amanda, Jenn, and Monica. You're saints and angels, and I'm honored to have your input. I hold our deeper conversations about the challenges of marriage and families close to my heart.

To Melly, thank you so much for weathering my texts, voice memos, and hemming and hawing about how to make Dylan suck but not so badly that we hated him. Tell Andrew thanks for all the hockey checks and that I'm sorry I used his name as the annoying ex. It's not personal.

To Shelby, for the ceaseless hype and the ability to make me cry at the drop of a hat with one text. I don't deserve you and I sure am glad we're friends.

To my besties who send and receive knife emoji texts.

To my parents for their undying support.

To my kids, for puking at exactly 26 minutes into a car trip, for saying things like "nist" and "yeyyow," and for being the bright little rays of sunshine you are. Don't read this until you're at least like fifteen, but preferably older because marital books are probably beyond your comprehension at that age. You know what? Maybe read somebody else's romance. It's probably weird to see your mom write this. But I hope seeing me tippy-tapping away at my computer encourages you to go for your dreams too.

And finally, to Mr. Galliaro for trusting me that I wouldn't just spill every fight we'd ever had into this book (I didn't, that would be bad writing anyway). We've been together double the time Jeanine and Dylan have, and you're still my favorite.

ALSO BY DANI GALLIARO

Unintentional Puck Bunny Series

Puck Funny

A brother's best friend, high school to pro hockey romcom

Puck Honey

A fake dating roommates to lovers romcom

Puck Money

A goalie x agent friends-with-benefits hockey romcom

Nature of Love novella series

Total Eclipse of the Heart

A small-town barista x astrophysicist romance

It's Raining Men

An MMMF storm chaser why choose

Glittery: A Christmas Novella

ABOUT THE AUTHOR

Dani Galliaro is a stack of ferrets in a trench coat, hunched over a keyboard, pecking out stories about fake people with real problems. A proud West Virginian and Appalachian, Dani spends her spare time yelling at hockey, reading, musing on how the 70s were the best decade for music, and wollering on her family.

You can follow her tomfoolery on TikTok, or see her more professional, curated feed on Instagram.